Anne Allen lives i
has three children
children live nearb
number of moves,
for fourteen years a..... .....g in love with the island
and the people. She contrived to leave one son
behind to ensure a valid reason for frequent returns.
By profession a psychotherapist, Anne has now
written two novels, the first being *Dangerous Waters*.
Visit her website at www.anneallen.co.uk

Praise for Finding Mother

'A sensitive, heart-felt novel about family relationships, identity, adoption, second chances at love...
With romance, weddings, boat trips, lovely gardens
and more, Finding Mother is a dazzle of a book, a
perfect holiday read.' *Lindsay Townsend, author of
The Snow Bride*

Praise for Dangerous Waters

'The island of Guernsey is so vividly evoked one feels
as if one is walking its byways. An atmospheric and
tantalising read.' *Elizabeth Bailey, author of The
Gilded Shroud*

'I loved Anne's flow of writing, her romantic storyline and well-presented characters'. *Bex 'N' Books*

'A wonderfully crafted story with a perfect balance
of intrigue and romance.' *The Wishing Shelf
Awards, 22 July 2013 – Dangerous Waters*

Also by Anne Allen

Dangerous Waters

finding mother

Anne Allen

Sarnia Press
London

Sarnia Press
Unit 1, 1 Sans Walk
London EC1R 0LT

A CIP catalogue record for this book is available
From the British Library
ISBN 978 0 9927112 0 7
Typeset in 11pt Aldine401 BT Roman by Sarnia Press

Printed and bound in the UK by
LightningSource, Milton Keynes

To my children, Louise, Craig and Grant, with love

"Oh, what a tangled web we weave, when first we practise to deceive."
Sir Walter Scott, Marmion, Canto vi Stanza 17

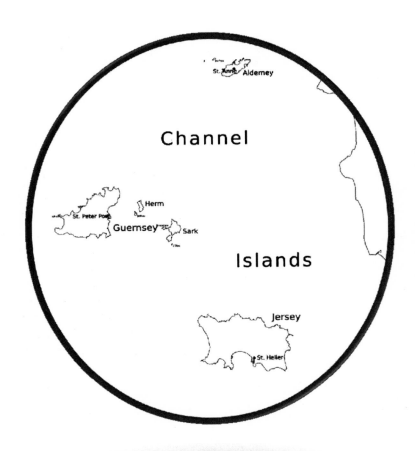

chapter 1

'I want a divorce!'

Nicole's cry hung in the air as she slammed out of the house. She flung herself into the driver's seat of her car, an Audi TT parked adjacent to its twin. After substantial and unnecessary, but therapeutic revving, the car shot out onto the road as Tom appeared at the front door, shouting something Nicole couldn't and didn't want to hear.

Half a mile along the road towards Bath, she pulled into a layby and, leaning her head on the steering wheel, sobbed.

A few minutes of unrestrained tears later, Nicole reached for a tissue from her handbag and, using the vanity mirror for guidance, wiped the black streaks of mascara from her face and blew her reddened nose. A few deep breaths helped restore her breathing, but her head continued thumping from the release of emotion.

I thought crying was supposed to be good for you, but I've never felt so awful. Well, not since I broke my leg skiing when I was twelve. In a rare moment of clarity she wondered which was worse – a broken leg or an unfaithful husband. It was a close call. Reclining the car seat, Nicole stretched out her tall, slim frame, allowing her clenched muscles to finally relax. What a mess!

It had all started when she wanted to order a food delivery from Sainsbury's and couldn't find her credit card. After calling out to Tom if it was okay to use his – being a joint card – Nicole took the answering grunt from upstairs to mean a yes. As she opened his wallet a bill fell out.

Picking it up, the heading caught her eye; 'The Stratford Manor Hotel, Warwick Road, Stratford-upon-Avon'. *Odd, when did Tom stay there?* Opening it out Nicole saw it was a receipted bill for two nights in the name of 'Mr and Mrs Oxford' dated for the previous weekend. Nicole held onto the chair as the realisation hit – he was still being unfaithful. Tom had assured her he'd got it out of his system and was now a devoted husband. Except it appeared he wasn't.

Nicole's feet felt as if encased in lead boots as she went upstairs to the bedroom. As she flung open the door to the designer decorated room which, at least for her, had represented love and harmony, Tom was shrugging into his jeans. He was freshly showered after his run and his light brown hair stood up glistening and spiky.

Moving slowly into the room she threw the bill onto the cream velvet bed-throw. Tom stiffened and looked up, the turned down mouth and contracted eyebrows offering the mournful look of a penitent.

'Please, darling, it's not what you think…'

'Oh, what is it then? Entertaining a new writer, perhaps?' Nicole's voice sounded harsh, even to her own ears. As a television producer Tom often met with programme writers. But meetings were not usually conducted in a hotel bed, or so she assumed.

Tom opened his mouth but nothing came out. Unheard of for him.

'Didn't you tell me you were attending a conference in Birmingham last weekend? At a city centre hotel?'

'Yes, but I. . .I wanted to get away from everyone. That's why I moved to Stratford.' He must have seen the disbelief on Nicole's face as he went on, 'It wasn't anything important, really it wasn't, darling. It's you I love, you know that, don't you?'

He reached out to Nicole but she stepped back from him, a coldness clutching at her heart. The thought of being touched by those adulterous hands made her feel sick. Anger at his betrayal triggered off a flow of adrenaline, propelling her through the bedroom door and down the stairs, giving herself time to grab her bag and car keys before slamming out of the house.

Thinking now of her parting shot at Tom, Nicole asked herself if she really did want a divorce. They appeared to have everything. Both successful in their media careers – she being an investigative journalist for the same television channel – beautiful, renovated farmhouse near Bath; exotic holidays when they found the time; and no children to restrict them.

She fell madly in love with Tom twelve years ago, when they'd met at the radio station where they then worked. He seemed equally smitten and proposed two years later with a huge diamond solitaire.

Nicole sighed as she thought back to those early days when the world was at their feet. Both dynamic and ambitious, they progressed into television to further their careers. And there Tom met temptation.

Another deep sigh escaped her lips as she lay back with her eyes closed. Her marriage mirrored her life generally – glamour and glitter on the surface but no real substance.

It was too depressing for words and Nicole knew that something needed to change if she was to love and respect herself again. It was clear Tom had *not* changed and, at thirty-seven, it wasn't likely to happen. At least not until he lost his looks or his power. Or both. Nicole wasn't proud that she'd been seduced by great sex, an expensive lifestyle and the kudos of being not only a "name" in her own right, but also of being married to an even bigger one in media. Everything came too easily for her, beginning with the very comfortable and spoiled upbringing of an only child in Jersey. The only thing to have marred the idyll had been her adoption. She'd known forever and, as a child, it hadn't bothered her. But the problems building up in her marriage had led to feelings of discontent and unease. Unease in herself – who on earth was she really? Nicole knew she wasn't like her parents, which was natural. She wanted to know who she was, who she *really* took after. That might help her to change the person she'd become and didn't actually much like.

Okay, pay-back time. Nicole squared her shoulders as she sat up and started the engine before swinging the car round to face the house from which she'd driven so furiously what felt a lifetime ago.

'We need to talk,' she said, coming into the kitchen and finding Tom slumped in a chair.

'Darling! Thank God you're back! Please, please let's start again. I swear I'll never so much as look at another woman if only you say you forgive me and will stay.'

He certainly looked miserable. She took in his tousled, uncombed hair, the pulled-down corners of his mouth and the blue eyes missing their usual sparkle.

Tom rose to meet her but she shook her head and motioned for him to stay seated. His gaze was wary as Nicole sat opposite him at the scrubbed pine table at which they hardly ever ate together, so busy were their respective schedules.

Nicole took a deep breath, willing herself to stay calm and not let emotion sabotage her hastily rehearsed speech.

'I *do* want a divorce, Tom…'

'No, you can't, darling! Let me…'

'Please let me finish! Then you can have your say. What's happened is merely a symptom of what's wrong with our marriage. And, I now realise, has been for some time. I really believe we've stayed together for the wrong reasons and it's time to think of the future.'

She cleared her throat. 'We... didn't really talk about having a family but it could be that I'll want children one day.'

Nicole leant on the table as if it would give her the strength she needed to continue.

'But I'd want a stable, happy home for my child and that's not guaranteed with you. I'm not sure I can trust you. Not now,' her voice fell to little more than a whisper as she plunged the knife into their ailing marriage.

Tom's eyes widened and his mouth opened wide in panic as he sought to save the relationship which had been his rock for so long. He reached out to grab Nicole's hands but she pulled them out of his way, letting them twist together under the table.

'Please, darling. I know I've behaved badly and have been an absolute idiot. I have no excuse. You've been a brilliant wife and we've enjoyed such a great time together. Remember that trip to Paris? And that time in Venice? Surely you don't mean to throw away everything we've shared!' He flung out his arms.

Nicole couldn't bear to look at him and kept her gaze focussed on a spot half-way down his navy T-shirt.

'We've achieved so much together – our careers, this house; doesn't this mean anything to you? We're the Golden Couple of television! A team – and a damn good one!'

She knew that in some ways Tom was right. They *were* a well-respected team at work. Admired and envied by those clambering up the ladder behind them. And she knew that if they were no longer a couple then she'd have to start again somewhere else. It would be impossible to stay at Bristol. A miserable thought. But her reputation would be enough to open doors elsewhere. At the moment she was tired, tired of the cheating and lying at home and tired of the pressure at work to strive forever upwards.

She raised her eyes slowly, finally letting them rest on his, steeling herself against the look of pain she saw there.

'It's no good, Tom. Maybe this was meant to happen. For my part, I need to discover what I *really* want from my life. Yes, we've had good times, wonderful times. But that's going back years. When was the last time we took a romantic break together? When did we last laugh together?'

Tom looked stricken. Even she didn't remember so he certainly wasn't likely to.

She ran a hand through her expertly cut bob and went on, 'We're not having any fun *now*, Tom. And material possessions aren't making either of us happy, are they?'

Nicole waved her hand around the Smallbone kitchen which once represented her idea of happiness. She remembered the line in the company's advertisement which had attracted her – "A Kitchen for Life". *Hmm, pity they couldn't offer a marriage for life!*

'Please, Nicole, let's not rush into anything. I can understand that you're hurt and angry but that's not the time to make major decisions. How about a trial separation? To give you time to see what you really want? I *know* I don't want to lose you but I'm happy to give you space, if that's what you want.' Tom's eyes pleaded with her from the other side of the table.

Nicole thought for a moment. Perhaps they both needed time to think. 'Okay, I'll agree to a separation, let's say six months.' She noticed the hope flicker in his eyes. 'But I'm not promising there'll be no divorce. I still feel that's the way to go. But I can't leave my job at a moment's notice, either. So I'll carry on for the two months left in my contract and then go. Might take a sabbatical to keep my options open. And I want you to move out. You could get a flat in the city.'

Tom took a deep breath which was part groan.

'Yes, if that's what you want. Do you want me to leave today?'

She heard the despair in his voice and anger hardened her resolve.

'Yes! It's going to be bad enough bumping into you at work so I need to be here on my own. You can move back once I go away.'

His eyes widened. 'Where will you go?'

'To Spain, to see my parents. They'll be back from their cruise by then and I can have a little time with them at the villa.'

'Only a little time? So will you come back here afterwards?' he asked, brightening.

Nicole shook her head. 'No, probably to Jersey. I'm going to ask Mum for help in tracing my mother. My *real* mother,' she said, her eyes unfocused.

chapter 2

The sun beat down on the concrete and tarmac of Alicante airport, and a heat haze shimmered over the roof of the car park. The smell of diesel and hot metal hung in the air. Nicole's scalp prickled with the heat as she walked behind her father wheeling her suitcase in the direction of his Mercedes. At her arrival through the double doors marked "Salida", they had shared a perfunctory embrace, the norm from the man who had problems showing affection.

'Nicole! Bienvenidos a Espãna! Your mother's at the villa preparing a paella in your honour and sends her love. Now, let me take your case, there's a good girl,' was all he'd said.

She now looked at him with affection as he marched ahead of her. He had been a kind, if undemonstrative, father. She understood that her mother had had problems conceiving and they had adopted as a last resort. Her father should have had a son, she thought, trying to keep pace with him through the labyrinth of the car park. He retired as an advocate in Jersey a year ago and she was sure he'd have been pleased to have passed the baton to a son. Not that Nicole couldn't have followed him into the law if she'd wished, but she had wanted something less dry and more glamorous for a career.

This was her first visit to her parents since they had moved to their retirement villa in Javea, an hour up the coast. Both golf addicts, they chose the town because of the high standard of the golf courses as well as the ever increasing British ex-pat community. They retained a *pied à terre* in St Helier, telling Nicole she was welcome to use it whenever she wanted.

As they settled into the comfortable leather seats, her father switched on the air conditioning. By the time they'd driven through the exit barrier, the car felt so cool that Nicole was regretting putting her sweater in the boot with her case. There was little conversation while her father concentrated on the tricky manoeuvre of steering the car onto the busy road leading to the Autovia A7 heading north.

Nicole was amazed at the volume – and speed – of the traffic whizzing past on their left and was grateful that she didn't have to drive. She had had little experience of driving in Europe but had complete confidence in her father's ability to cope. He and her mother had been regular visitors by car to France and Spain over the years and Ian was a careful driver even though he loved powerful cars. The current model, a LHD car looked brand new and Nicole smiled at the thought that he was still enjoying his "boys' toys".

After about ten minutes they were away from the intensity of the traffic encircling Alicante and Nicole sensed her father relaxing as he settled at a steady 100kph.

'You and Mum settled in now?' she asked, glancing at his tanned profile.

'Yes, we are. Of course, it was an advantage already knowing the area well and we'd made several friends at the golf club over the years.' He pulled out to overtake an open lorry piled with old tyres before continuing, 'Your mother's a member of the local bridge club and recently joined the amateur dramatic society helping with the costumes. So we keep busy. I'm thinking of joining the mountain rambling group as another way of keeping fit.'

'Hope you're not overdoing it, Dad. You need to be careful in this heat.'

He glanced at her and smiled. 'Don't worry, I don't go mad when it's hot. And my doctor says I'm in very good order for my age. In fact the old blood pressure has gone down since we moved here.'

'That's great. It's time you took it a bit easier. You always worked so hard that when I was little there were times I wondered who you were, this strange man appearing at odd hours,' she chuckled.

He frowned. 'I hadn't realised that you'd felt like that. But you know I was working hard to provide for you and your mother. You deserved the best.'

'I know, Dad. And I'm very grateful, really I am. I just want you to look after yourself now.'

Her father cleared his throat and concentrated on his driving, leaving Nicole to take in what was, for her, an unvisited part of Spain. She had partied in Majorca and Ibiza as a clubbing student and visited Barcelona with Tom several years ago, enjoying a resonance with the Spanish lifestyle. The memory of their trip flashed into her mind, bringing with it the pain of the separation, her stomach clenching in response. *Oh, God, how am I going to cope when we reach the villa? Mum and Dad didn't say much when I told them what had happened, but then they never do. And when I tell them what I want to do...*

Nicole's mood was matched by the dry, arid looking landscape of the hinterland and the built up areas bordering the coast. A far cry from the remembered images of the Balearics. But as the car sped along she began to notice a subtle change in the vista that gave her hope that better was to come.

What had been low brown hills now gave way to higher and greener hills, almost small mountains, flecked with trees and shrubs. Once they had passed the skyscrapers of the ubiquitous Benidorm the coastline settled lower to the eye and the sight of sparkling deep blue sea lifted her spirits. By the time they by-passed Altea Nicole caught glimpses of an older Spain, with majestic ancient churches rising above the red tiled roofs of traditional village houses. Bordering the sea, woody headlands sheltered extravagant villas and a marina harbouring an array of classy-looking yachts and what appeared to be a small, new waterside village. The hills of Altea rose to the left and were almost overgrown with white villas looking depressingly similar in style and size.

The sight of Calpe served to lower her spirits once more as it was a miniature version of Benidorm with tower blocks bordering the beach. But then the horrors receded as they drove towards Benissa and the land of the citrus groves and almond trees. The old homes of growers and farmers shared this more fertile region with the occasional new villa favoured by up and coming Spaniards or those ex-pats happier to live inland than cheek by jowl with their countrymen on the coast. Splashes of colour erupted from tumbling purple bougainvillea covering walls and terraces and the pink and white oleander growing by the roadside. The beautiful colours served to cheer her, giving her hope that she could cope with what lay ahead.

'Won't be long now,' said her father. 'I'm going to leave the motorway soon and take the road through Gata so you can see more of the area. What do you think so far?'

'Well, this part is as I'd expected. Didn't think much of the area around Alicante, I'm afraid.'

He chuckled, 'I'm not surprised, it's rather arid around there and even worse as you go further south. But, as you can see, it's now more fertile and as you go towards Valencia all you see for miles are citrus groves, mainly oranges, as you would expect. Your mother takes great pleasure in providing freshly squeezed orange juice for breakfast and, when we're feeling extravagant, the occasional Bucks Fizz. And if you prefer a gin and tonic we have our own lemon and lime trees in the garden.'

'Sounds good, Dad. That might be just what I fancy before dinner. And where are we now?'

They had turned right off the Autovia, virtually driving back on themselves round a steep bend before coming out onto a dual carriageway.

'Just north of Benissa and heading towards Gata, which I think you'll find amusing,' he smiled.

A few minutes later the open countryside, dotted with an occasional villa or trading unit, gave way to the steep enclosing grey hills of a working quarry. Heavily laden lorries joined the main road and it was bleak even under the shimmering sun and clear blue sky. But after the Merc had negotiated a few hairy bends they were greeted again by green hills, glossy orchards and on the far horizon to the east, a brief glimpse of the sea.

'Do you see that rather odd-shaped mountain ahead? A bit like an elephant? That's the Montgo, where we live,' Ian said, pointing ahead.

Nicole followed his finger and agreed that the mountain, which was more of a large hill, did appear a bit elephantine. She could see a small town ahead and a sign proclaimed that they were entering Gata. At first there was nothing unusual to see but as they drove through the main street Nicole noticed that virtually every shop was selling cane and wicker ware. Displays of baskets, chairs, loungers and small tables spilled out onto the pavements and she broke into a grin.

'I see what you mean. Is all this stuff made here?'

'No, not now. Very little, apparently. But it used to be the cottage industry of the town and it's known around here as the Wicker Capital of Spain. Most of it's now imported from China, which we discovered when we bought a picnic basket here a few months ago. Still, it boosts the local economy, which is a good thing.'

He turned right at some traffic lights and then added, 'Right, should be home soon.'

The Montgo was now looming ever larger and Nicole could see lines of mainly white, but some coloured villas, massed on its flanks. They finished at a level about two-thirds of the way up the mountain, the rest green and yellow scrub. Small roads criss-crossed up from the main road running along the base.

Her father indicated left and turned into a two-way road snaking up the mountain with the two lanes divided by oleander bushes. A few hundred yards along he turned right into a tarmacked road which dog-legged round until it reached a dead end. Along the way individual gated villas faced the road with sightless, shuttered windows. The car slowed by the last villa on the right and her father pressed a control on the dashboard, prompting the tall, wrought-iron gates to open inwards onto a steep drive.

Stopping at the top of the drive Ian said, 'You get out here and I'll put the car away.'

As Nicole thankfully uncurled herself from the seat her mother opened the ornately carved oak door, her arms open ready for a hug. Nicole's heart beat faster as she realised it was crunch time. Time to face her mother and open the can of worms, safely lidded for so long.

'Darling! It's so lovely to have you here at last. Do come in out of the heat.'

'Hi, Mum. You look well,' Nicole said as she took in her mother's appearance. She was a few inches shorter than Nicole, with a trim figure and coiffed light-brown hair, coloured to hide the ever increasing grey. Nicole noticed a few more lines on the beautifully made-up face and thought, not for the first time, that it was a pity that her mother couldn't be more relaxed about herself. She had always needed to look immaculate and had never, to Nicole's knowledge, ventured out of the house without full make-up and carefully styled hair.

By now they were standing in a cool, marble floored hall off which were several rooms guarded by smaller versions of the imposing front door. Mary led the way down a corridor and flung open a door.

'Here's the room we've set aside for you, darling. We have another two bedrooms for guests so I decorated it especially for you. Do you approve?'

'Mum, it's lovely! Of course I approve!' Nicole gazed around the predominantly cream room. Scattered on the pale marble floor lay the colourful Persian rugs from her old bedroom in Jersey. As she looked further Nicole also recognised the bedside lamps and tables. On one of the walls she felt touched to see a collage of photos of herself as a child and teenager. A large, float-y mosquito net hung from the ceiling, draped around the half-tester bed, creating an ethereal, albeit practical, effect.

Tears pricked at her eyes as she realised how much thought her mother had put into making her feel at home. And she about to play Judas!

Nicole threw her arms around her mother, saying, 'Thanks, Mum. You've created a little haven of peace in here. Just what I need!'

Her mother was looking pleased and slightly embarrassed when her father knocked on the door and brought in her case.

'Would you like to unpack and freshen up before we show you around? And a G and T will be ready when you are!' he smiled.

'Thanks, Dad. I'd love a shower and a change of clothes. Travelling always makes me feel unclean, somehow.'

Her mother pointed out the en-suite, stocked with large, fluffy towels and toiletries and she was left on her own, being told there was no hurry.

The cool marble-tiled bathroom boasted a powerful walk-in shower and Nicole washed away the tensions and grime of her journey. She would have liked to wash away the pain of the past two months as easily but this wasn't possible. There was still an ache in her heart which never left her. Forcing aside her unhappy thoughts she dressed quickly, conscious that she might be about to cause hurt to two people who did not deserve it.

The sun was beginning its descent over the mountains on the other side of the valley as the little family sat around the pool, glasses in hand. Nicole had been given a thorough tour of the villa and its extensive grounds before they settled down with a drink. She loved what her parents had created here in what she recognised as an idyllic place to live. It was so peaceful and soporific relaxing by the turquoise pool, the only sound the rustling of cicadas moving in the breeze that carried the intense perfume of jasmine from a nearby bush.

The villa had been built to her parents' specifications; her father employing a local Spanish architect to design and oversee the works. The result was a modern villa enjoying the latest comfort-inducing conveniences of under-floor heating and hidden air conditioning, blended with the traditional Spanish features of stone-built fireplaces and arches and carved wooden doors.

'You've done a great job, you two. It's beautiful, and the views are to die for!' Nicole said, waving an arm at the distant mountains.

'It was the views that drew us here. That and the size of the plot. The original house was badly built, as they tended to be back in the '80's. So it was easier to knock it down and start again. We're certainly happy here, aren't we, Mary?'

She smiled at her father and Nicole thought that she'd never seen them so relaxed and "together". As an only child her she'd been particularly sensitive to the atmosphere between them and had noticed the occasional tensions. Her mother had been a stay at home wife and mother and although it was clear she loved creating a home, she was too intelligent not to be bored after hours spent alone with a small child. Her father had been not only a busy advocate but a member of various committees and clubs which had kept him from home. But it now looked as if they had worked through those old issues and were content in each other's company in their adopted country.

'So, who looks after this wonderful garden?'

'We both do our share but we employ a gardener for the heavy work and he also looks after the pool. So when we're too old and decrepit to do much the garden won't suffer,' her father replied.

Nicole was keen to keep the conversation away from her and Tom, and it looked like her parents felt the same. His name hadn't been mentioned and she guessed that they would wait for her to say something. Her stomach was churning quite nicely now but she wanted to wait until after dinner. Perhaps they'd all be more relaxed then.

She continued asking her parents questions about the villa and their new friends until Mary announced that she was just going to re-heat the paella and that dinner would soon be ready Nicole's offer of help was refused and she and her father sat in companionable silence before being called up to the terrace.

As the villa had been constructed on the hillside the main rooms were on the same floor but there was a large under-build on a level with the garden and the pool. Terraces led from the sitting-room and dining room. The local style of terrace, a *naya*, was built with a solid, beamed roof supported by pale stone arches and windows which could be glazed for year-round use. The villa possessed two open *nayas* and one enclosed and on one of the former stood a large wooden table spread with bowls of salad and the steaming paella served in the traditional iron pan. A bottle of cava nestled in an ice bucket and a bottle of Rioja was quietly breathing at the end of the table.

'Gosh, Mum, you must have been slaving away for hours. I feel like the proverbial Prodigal Son offered the fatted calf!' Nicole grinned at her parents who, though they hadn't said much about how they felt, had gone overboard with the meal. Something she was used to.

Her mother laughed. 'I suppose it might appear like that, particularly as we haven't seen you for ages. But really, we do eat well here and I'm teaching myself to cook our favourite Spanish dishes. Golf and swimming ensure we always have good appetites! Ian, please serve the wine and Nicole, dear, do help yourself to the food.'

Nicole, after two helpings of the fragrant seafood paella, was relieved that dessert turned out to be a selection of fresh fruit. Now nearly eight o'clock, it was still light but the temperature had dropped to a comfortable level. Picking up her glass of wine, Nicole took a deep breath.

'Um, I spoke to Tom last week and he's moving back to the house tomorrow. He wanted us to meet up for a "review of the separation" as he put it, but I wasn't keen. I didn't see what it could achieve,' she said, swirling the Rioja in her glass.

Her father coughed, a habit borne of old from his days at the Bar prior to expressing an opinion or beginning an interrogation of a witness. Her mother shifted in her chair, looking uncomfortable.

'You don't think you'll get back together, is that what you're saying?' he asked, frowning.

Nicole sighed. 'I do still love him, Dad, but he's hurt me too much. I can't trust him anymore and that's not good if our marriage is to work. You and Mum brought me up to believe trust was as important as love in a relationship. And even though I've missed him like hell these past two months, in some odd way I've actually felt a relief, a sense of being free.'

'Perhaps that's partly to do with having a break from your job, darling. From what you've said you'd been working very long hours for months,' her mother commented.

'Could be. I'm certainly looking forward to my sabbatical! What do *you* think I should do about Tom?'

Nicole looked from one to the other, aware she'd put them on the spot. 'Sorry, perhaps that's not a fair question.'

'It's perfectly fair. It always helps to ask other people's opinions when you have a major decision to make,' Ian replied. 'They are only opinions and you're the one who has to make the final decision. For what it's worth, I've always liked Tom and I knew he could provide well for you. But I do not condone his...his behaviour and if it hurts you and makes you unhappy then it might be better if you do part.'

Nicole felt touched. Her father had never expressed his thoughts on either Tom or her marriage before and yet he was still taking her side.

Her mother chipped in, 'I agree with your father, darling. Neither of us want you to be unhappy and if Tom can't behave himself then he's not going to be the right husband for you.'

'Thank you both. It means a lot to me to know you're here, rooting for me. But there's still a few months left before I have to make the final decision so I've got time to sort out my feelings and what I really want.'

'You said you'd like to stay here for a week or so. Which is fine, of course, and we'd be happy for you to stay longer. But you haven't said what you plan to do or where you're going after you leave here,' her mother observed.

'Ah, no, I didn't.' Nicole looked from her mother to her father and, seeing the same look of concern on their faces, felt like the Judas she was.

'Please do *not* take this as any reflection on you both as I think you've been great parents,' she paused as her parents exchanged wary glances. 'But this business with Tom has brought home to me something that's been bugging me for years. I'm not sure who I am any more. I don't take after either of you, which is natural. It's important to me to try and understand myself better as, to be honest, I don't like myself much these days. What I've become. The answer, I feel, is to trace my roots, understand my genetic history, if you like.'

She took a deep breath and went on, gazing earnestly at her silent parents, 'I want to find my natural mother, the woman who gave birth to me and then...and then...gave me away.'

chapter 3

Mary had been dreading this.

Ever since 1996 when the law in Jersey changed to allow adopted adults sight of their original birth certificates. Until then she had felt safe – safe from the usurpation of her title and role of mother by a complete stranger. At that time Nicole was busy and happy with her job and Tom in England and the danger seemed remote.

But not now.

Nicole had uttered the words Mary had hoped never to hear. Now she was afraid that she would lose the girl she had loved unreservedly since the moment she had first set eyes on her, a little bundle tightly wrapped in a hospital blanket. A mop of dark hair topped a perfectly shaped head and a pair of bright, dark eyes stared straight at her. Mary had known then that there *was* such a thing as love at first sight. The baby – not yet bearing a name – was three days old and unaware that her mother had left the hospital to return home without the child she had nourished in her womb for nine months. Mary had been unable to understand how a mother could give up her child in that way, but as she was allowed to hold Nicole for the first time was, at the same time, fervently grateful that she had.

Mary married Ian when she was twenty-five and he twenty-eight and had assumed that she would be a mother within a year or two. Ian insisted that she give up work when they married so that she could devote her time to looking after him and their new house. This was fine by her with the prospect of motherhood just around the corner but when, month after month, the dreaded periods arrived exactly on time, Mary became more unhappy with being just a housewife.

After three years of marriage Mary was desperate and took herself off to her doctor.

There followed a round of invasive and, for both of them, embarrassing tests. Mary recalled that awful meeting with the consultant. She had continued to hope that the tests would show that something could be done – a "miracle cure" – and she would instantly become pregnant. She sat with Ian in the consultant's office, hands tightly clasped, her stomach clenched with anxiety and on hearing his words, 'I'm...so...sorry...insufficient...eggs...low...sperm... count...chances of conceiving...' she had felt as if she'd been punched in the stomach and crumpled up in a tearful heap. Ian, his jaw set tight, showed no emotion as he tried to calm her and she remembered thinking that it was all *his* fault.

As they drove home Mary experienced the varying emotions of sadness, depression and anger. She was angry with her body, with Ian, the doctors and even the proud mothers she saw pushing their prams down the street. She barely left the house for days, dreading bumping into anyone with a baby or small child in tow. Ian was kind and initially treated her with patience as if she was ill, but as the weeks passed his patience grew thin. It was at this point that Mary decided that adoption was the answer after all and rallied enough to pressurise Ian into agreeing with her.

They had been on the adoption waiting list for a year when they heard that they were now top of the list and that a baby was to be offered up for adoption within the next few weeks. Mary read the letter from the Children's Service twice before she accepted that it was true and phoned Ian at work, something she did rarely, bursting out with excitement, 'We're going to have a baby!' Ian's pleasure had been more restrained but sufficiently real for him to arrive home earlier than usual, bearing a bunch of deep-red roses, a gesture normally reserved for her birthday.

The next few weeks dragged by for Mary, consumed by the anxiety that something would go wrong; that the pregnant mother would change her mind or the child, heaven forbid, be stillborn. They prepared the room that was to be the nursery but bought little in the way of clothes, furniture or equipment, not wanting to tempt fate.

Then it happened.

The phone call came one Saturday morning as Mary was preparing to leave for her grocery shop.

'Mrs Le Clerq? Good morning, John Knight from the Children's Service. I'm happy to tell you that the expectant mother gave birth to a healthy baby girl yesterday. We hope that you and your husband could collect her on Monday. Does that fit in with you? I know it's short notice but...'

'That would be perfect, Mr Knight. I've got to buy a few things first which I can do today. Oh, thank you so much! The. . .mother's still agreeing to adoption?' Mary's heart was beating so fast she thought she'd burst.

'Yes, she signed the preliminary forms today and will be leaving the hospital tomorrow. But you know nothing's final for the next five months and we go to court for the adoption order.'

Mary arranged to be at the hospital with Ian on Monday morning. As she put the phone down he came into the hall and Mary threw her arms around him, saying, 'We have a little girl and we've got to go out and buy everything she'll need, now!'

★★★

'Mum, are you all right? I'm sorry if I've given you a shock, the last thing I want is to upset you.' Nicole chewed her lip as she gazed at her mother's strained face.

Mary seemed to come back from wherever she'd been and smiled at Nicole.

'I'm fine, darling. I was just remembering the first time I saw you. It was in the hospital and you were like a china doll. I was afraid you'd break if I dropped you. I'd never held such a small baby before and you just stared up at me with your big eyes as if to say "And who are you, then?" Didn't she, Ian?' Her mother turned to him and he nodded, reaching out for her hand.

Nicole was close to choking on the lump in her throat and gulped some wine. She'd never given any thought to how it must have been for her parents to be handed a tiny scrap and told it was theirs to take home and care for.

'I guess it would have felt quite weird suddenly becoming parents without the usual nine months preparation.'

'It was certainly scary! My mother offered me all sorts of advice, but as I was born just after the war things had changed rather a lot and, of course I was breast fed, no bottle feeding in those days! But I did have my trusty Dr Spock to guide me and my health visitor was wonderful. So we all survived.'

Nicole found it difficult to say anything, it being clear from her mother's tight expression that she was trying hard to be brave. She took another sip of wine before continuing.

'If I do find my...natural mother, it's not going to stop me loving you both. After all, you're the ones who raised me, educated me and gave me such a good start in life. You *chose* to be my parents and that's something no-one else can take from you. I only want to find out how I became *me* and that'll be easier if I can meet with the woman who...who gave birth to me. Then I'll have the whole picture and not just the half of my upbringing.' Nicole blew her nose as tears started in her eyes.

Her parents looked at each other before her mother patted Nicole's arm.

'It's all right, Nicole. We do understand, it's only natural that you want to trace your...your birth mother. Have you made any enquiries yet?'

Nicole shook her head.

'No, I wanted to tell you both first. I know I can obtain a copy of my original birth certificate and I was planning to request it when I arrive in Jersey. Thought I'd go there after spending some time here with you.' She twirled her wine glass, feeling reluctant to ask the all-important question. 'Do...do you know anything about her, Mum?'

Her mother darted a look at her father, who nodded.

'Not very much. As the islands have an inter-island adoption policy we knew the mother would be from Guernsey. We were told that she was an unmarried teacher who'd spent time in Jersey before giving birth.'

Nicole sat motionless, except for her hand swirling the wine around in her glass.

'So, I'm actually a donkey and not a crapaud!' She grinned at the islanders' names for each other, trying to relieve the palpable tension.

'Would that matter, darling?'

'No, I guess not. Just means my search will take me to Guernsey as well as Jersey. At least I'm less likely to have already bumped into her. But it's not as if she's at the other side of the world. Though I guess she might have emigrated like so many islanders.' She frowned. Oh no, it would be awful if she had to trek around the world in search of her mother. Please God, let her still be in Guernsey, she prayed.

'So, that's all you know?'

'Yes, darling. I'm sorry, but I'm sure you'll learn more in Jersey.'

Nicole nodded, disappointed.

Ian cleared his throat, saying briskly, 'Well, we wish you all the best with your search, Nicole. Now, what would you like to do while you're here? There's a very good tennis club your mother has joined.' It was clear her father wanted to draw the focus away from a subject he found painful.

'Tennis sounds good, Dad. But only when it's not too hot!'

'How about early tomorrow morning? I can book a court and then we can show you around the town,' her mother suggested, her face clearing, as if she too was happy to leave behind the spectre of Nicole's search.

Her mother went off to book the tennis court and they spent the rest of the evening discussing the cruise. Nicole admired the many photos they'd taken, giving all her attention to her parents. She was touched by their solicitude, keen to make her as comfortable and welcome as possible. She caught herself wondering if it was their fear of losing her that had triggered off the unusual warmth now emanating from them. Or maybe soaking up the sun in this lovely country had allowed them to finally relax. She sighed. Whatever had wrought the change she was happy to accept it, looking forward to their time together. Something she'd been ambivalent about until now. As long as no-one mentioned Tom or her search for her mother, all would be well.

chapter 4

Nicole enjoyed exploring Javea over the next few days, appreciating her parents' love of the town. It wasn't just the climate that was welcoming. The arenal offered not just a great beach but a fantastic choice of restaurants, shops and cafés to sample during the daily and evening promenades. At night the arenal pulsed with life, attracting both tourists and ex-pats from various countries, while whole Spanish families, from *ninos* to a*buelos,* arrived late in the restaurants, laughing and chatting volubly.

The old Town and port held their own fascination and ambience and Nicole became seduced. Sitting in a café on the arenal one morning with her parents, she realised how much she missed living by the sea, enjoying the special effect it had on everyone. The young Spanish workers looked animated and relaxed as they sat outside the cafés drinking and gesticulating, but always well behaved. Nicole thought back to nights out in Bristol which invariably entailed being the unwilling spectator not only to fights but young revellers vomiting into the gutter. Not a pretty sight. She grimaced at the memory. It was also obvious to her how much the Spanish respected their elders, always giving them pride of place in family outings. Something her parents' generation lacked in the UK and would be much appreciated. She wasn't too proud of her own record in this regard, acknowledging that she'd almost ignored her parents once she became involved in her new life in England.

As she gazed at them now, it struck her how much less stuffy they were. Her father, always so formal in his manner and dress, was now transformed in linen slacks and short sleeved shirt. His tan, against the deep blue shirt, made him look ten years younger. Her mother, in a strappy floral sundress and straw hat, glowed in a way unnoticed by Nicole until now. At that moment a couple of fellow Brits came up and spoke to her mother who smiled at them.

'Ian, Nicole, let me introduce you to Sandy and Yvonne, fellow members of my drama group. Shall we squeeze up and make room for them?'

The newcomers settled into their seats, more coffees were ordered, with the talk soon focussing on the latest play being produced. Nicole watched with wonder as her mother emerged from her father's shadow and took centre stage for once. *Well, well, well, things are looking good. Mum's come out of that shell of hers at last. Good, and about time too!*

While Nicole was a child her mother had not seemed keen on socialising; she remembered times when her father suggested her mother accompany him to a particular function and she would demur, pleading tiredness or lack of a babysitter.

Holidays had been infrequent and not entirely happy occasions, at least not for Nicole. There were no foreign beach holidays as, after all, they lived on an island contoured with golden sands. Instead they'd skied each winter in the French Alps, sharing a chalet with childless friends of her father's. In the summer they went driving through France, sometimes as far as northern Spain. The trips tended to be more cultural than fun for a child. Nicole felt alone, missing the companionship of children her own age, always glad to return home to meet up with her friends.

Chewing her lips, she thought back to her childhood. It was a shock to realise she'd been happiest when with her school friends, like Susie, than with her parents. Life at home had been subdued, more talk than play. Her mother had done her best to play games with her, but she'd been awkward, as if unsure how to relax and be childlike. And her father! Well, he hadn't even tried, just patted her on the head in passing. They'd been generous with money but not with their time; she'd felt alone in their adult world. It struck Nicole that she may have quashed her innate extrovert nature in order to fit into the family "mould". Her real personality only surfaced when she went to university and learnt to let her hair down. So, perhaps her real mother or father were more like her? It would be good to find out!

As she looked at her mother now, Nicole saw that she had at last found her rightful place in the world. No longer the "Advocate's Wife", but another ex-pat keen to embrace a new life, choosing her own persona. Nicole frowned. Perhaps she needed to be some place new where she was free to choose a new identity, sloughing off her old skin like that of a snake. Time to let go of the old. It wasn't that she didn't enjoy the trappings of success, she did. But she also wanted to dig beneath the surface, just as she'd done when she'd first become a reporter at the radio station. She knew there was something vital missing in her life but didn't know what it was. Sighing, she wondered if she'd find it if, and when, she found her birth mother. Nicole didn't want to be like Mary, not finding out what made her happy until she retired. No, she wanted to find out *now!*

It had not been difficult for her parents to persuade Nicole to stay two weeks with them, the slower pace of life and the user-friendly climate were sufficiently enticing. She couldn't remember when she'd last been so relaxed and felt sad on her last evening. They were going out for a meal in their favourite restaurant in the port in celebration.

As she was standing in front of the mirror in her bedroom, brushing her short bob into place, her mother appeared in the doorway.

'All right to come in, Nicole?' Her mother hovered, as if uncertain of her reception.

'Of course.' Nicole swung round, giving her a warm smile.

'Just wanted to say how much we've enjoyed having you to stay, darling. It's been ages since we've spent so long together, just the three of us.'

'Well, I've enjoyed being here and I'm very envious of your new life, Mum. And it certainly seems to suit you both.'

'Yes, it does. And I've made more friends here than in Jersey. But family's much more important so I hope it won't be long before you come back.' Her mother's smile looked strained.

Nicole threw down her brush and hugged her.

'Course I'll be back, as soon as I can. What girl could resist a free holiday in the sun, with all mod cons included?' She grinned at her mother who kissed her lightly on the cheek.

'If it's only cupboard love that'll bring you back...!'

They both smiled but Nicole noticed that the smile didn't quite reach Mary's eyes.

The next morning her parents drove Nicole to Alicante airport and as they said goodbye before security, she received a warm hug from her father.

'Take care of yourself, now,' his voice gruff as he released her.

'Will do, Dad. See you soon,' she smiled. *Mm, the old boy's softening up a bit.*

After another hug from her mother Nicole joined the queue, offering a quick final wave to her parents. She sensed the thinly disguised concern behind the smiles and waves and felt sad that her quest, although natural, was the cause of pain to her parents. She knew no matter what transpired in her search for her birth mother, that she would still love them and acknowledge their hard work in her upbringing. But even as she was settling into her seat ready for take-off, Nicole pictured her mother's tearful face as they had said goodbye. She wondered if her mother was not so much upset with her leaving as with the possibility that she might find another mother to love more…

By late that afternoon a somewhat tired and travel stained Nicole was on another plane coming into land in Jersey. From her vantage point in a window seat she could make out the familiar outline of what had been, for many years, her home. The sight evoked mixed feelings. The leap in her stomach was the feeling she associated with safety – coming home. Although now, strictly speaking, it wasn't her home any more, she still had a sense of belonging, of self. Nicole realised with a jolt that this was the first time she'd returned to Jersey when her parents were absent. *Mm, this was going to be odd.* Fear and trepidation lurked beneath the surface.

She took a deep breath as the plane taxied to a stop. Nicole knew that not so far away, in an office in St Helier, lay a file that held her secret. Within the next few days or weeks she might be granted access to that file and for the first time since she had embarked on this journey she was afraid. Afraid of what she might learn – not only concerning her real mother, but about herself.

chapter 5

Prior to leaving Spain Nicole arranged an appointment with the children's service in Jersey for the day after her return. As she woke that morning it was all she could think about. It wasn't as if she'd learn anything that day; the helpful lady on the phone had warned her it might take a few weeks. But it was the first, fateful step.

She picked up the phone.

'Susie! Hi, it's me.'

'Hiya! Are you here?'

'Yep, got in yesterday evening and was so bushed had an early night. Are you free for a coffee this morning? *Sans enfants?*'

Susie giggled. 'Yes, I've got some "me" time today, thank goodness. Paul's at school till three and Bettany's at nursery today. Shall we say ten thirty, usual place?'

'Great. Can't wait. Bye.'

By ten Nicole was out of the door, striding towards the main shopping area of St Helier, a short walk from the apartment. Its central position was a deciding factor when her parents sought their *pied à terre*. The bright and airy apartment also possessed two bedrooms, giving Nicole her own space. She had been touched when her mother had said, 'We want you to know that you can come and stay whenever you want. Even if we're not here.'

At the time she was still with Tom and rarely visited Jersey, but now she envisaged coming over more often. A great chance to catch up with friends like Susie.

Nicole was the first to arrive at their favourite café near the Victorian indoor market. That part of town, minutes away from King Street and the big stores, boasted the small boutiques that became a big draw for the girls in their teens. Nicole looked forward to a trawl through the shops with Susie, whose forthright opinions made shopping a fun experience.

Susie breezed in and threw her arms around Nicole in the manner of a long lost sister. In a way that was what she was to Nicole who, laughing, begged Susie to let go so that she could breathe.

'I had to make sure you were real and not a figment of my imagination. It's been so long...'

'I know, I know. And it's my fault, should've been over ages ago. Forgive me?'

Susie, head tilted to one side, looked serious for a moment before a smile lifted the corners of her wide mouth and she laughed.

'Of course! But boy, have we some catching up to do!'

Nicole grinned and after they had ordered their large *café au lait* studied her childhood friend for a moment. She hadn't aged a bit, her round face was as smooth as ever and her blonde curly hair still spiralled out of control. Susie caught her eye and grinned.

'I know what you're thinking, I'm fatter than ever! The curse of having children!' She shook her head. 'And you're still so slim. It's not fair!'

'You're not really jealous. Your curves always got you more attention from the boys and helped you land that dishy husband of yours!'

'True. Craig's always said he liked having plenty to grab hold of. Still, wouldn't mind losing a few pounds...' She sighed and then, reaching out for Nicole's hand murmured, 'Has it been very bad?'

'Well, it's been better!' Nicole pulled a face. 'But in some ways it's been a relief. I think, subconsciously, I *knew* Tom was still unfaithful but didn't want to acknowledge it. 'Cos then I'd need to deal with it and that would affect my job, my lifestyle. Pathetic, isn't it? I let the bastard carry on cheating on me rather than face the truth and get on with my life.'

'It's not pathetic. You just needed to feel strong enough to break free and now you have. And that's great! You never deserved to be treated like that and you know I never felt Tom was good enough for you.'

Nicole grinned. 'Yes, you made that clear when you poured a glass of beer over him at Bettany's christening! Just because he'd criticised that mini dress you'd talked me into buying.'

'Well, he deserved it. Pompous ass! Fancy saying it made you look like a tart! Hope you've still got it?'

'Oh, yes. And I might wear it for our girls night out at the weekend. See what effect it has on Jersey manhood!'

They laughed.

After a sip of her coffee Susie's expression was more serious as she looked across at Nicole.

'So, you want to trace your birth mother?'

'Yes, it's become a real quest for me. Something I simply *have* to do. I feel as if there's a few pieces missing from the jigsaw of my life and without those pieces I can't make the right decisions about the future. What I should be doing, who I was *meant* to be. Even though I'm aware there's a risk...'

Susie nodded.

'She could be an old hag you wouldn't give the time of day to. Or she might be someone you'd be very proud to call mother. Knowing you as I do, I think it's more likely to be the latter, don't you?'

Nicole frowned.

'But why should it? I know the argument about nature versus nurture and that bad blood will out etc. So who's to say that my real mother isn't a horrible person?'

'Hmm, if she was that horrible why did she go through with the pregnancy? She could've skipped over to England

33

for an abortion. Would've been a lot easier for her. Instead, she must've put her own life on hold for quite a while to give you a chance of life and a good home. That's got to be in her favour, hasn't it?'

Nicole's face softened.

'True, put like that I guess she did make it hard for herself. And I've always been grateful for my life – in spite of wayward husbands!'

'There you are then! Anyway, I've got good vibes about it all. I could wish your mother lived in Jersey as it might encourage you to spend more time here. So we can relive our yoof!' Susie chuckled.

'Hey! We're not that old! And whatever happens, Susie, I've decided that I must spend more time here and, with my parents now living in Spain, I can let my hair down!'

'That's my girl! Craig's going to be doing a lot of babysitting while you're here. Poor sod! Still, it's about time. He has his nights out with the boys and I've not been out for what feels like forever.'

'Believe it or not, but my social life has been pretty sporadic lately. Anyway, tell me how my gorgeous goddaughter is. And her handsome big brother, who must be, what – five?'

'Yes, he is. Full time school now, doesn't seem possible, does it? And Bettany's three in a couple of months and I admit, in all modesty, is as beautiful as her mother,' Susie replied with a simpering look, before dissolving into giggles.

By the time Susie had regaled Nicole with all the latest news re her offspring it was approaching midday. They dashed out for a quick shopping spree before grabbing a sandwich to eat outside, happy to enjoy the warm and sunny June weather. The brief spree had resulted in purchases for them both. Nicole, so much less tense than she'd been on waking, was shocked to realise the time.

'Oh, my God! I need to get moving. My appointment's in half an hour. Just as well La Chasse isn't far.'

Grabbing her bags she kissed Susie goodbye, promising to phone later.

She made it to the children's service with five minutes to spare and only a tad out of breath. The receptionist directed her to the office of Mrs Evelyn Lewis, just along the corridor.

A warm, motherly looking woman reached out to shake her hand.

'Good afternoon, Nicole, please sit down. I gather that you've come back to Jersey specifically to pursue your search. Are your parents no longer on the island?'

'They've a flat here but they live mostly in Spain now that Dad's retired.'

'Lucky things! A wise move after the summers we've just had.' She frowned. 'Do they know that you want to trace your birth mother?'

'Oh, yes. In fact I've just been to see them and although I guess they're a bit worried about the outcome, they're very supportive. As they've always been. They told me I was adopted when I was five and it's never been a problem. Until now.'

Mrs Lewis nodded. 'I'm glad that you have their approval. It can be very hard on parents in this situation, particularly the mother. Do they have any natural children?'

'No, they couldn't have any.'

'I see. Now, you said it hadn't been a problem until now. What's changed?'

Nicole cleared her throat, wishing she didn't have to admit the truth to this stranger. 'I…split up from my husband recently and it's brought home to me that I need a sense of identity, of belonging. How I've become "me", I guess. I've thought about it over the years, particularly since my, er, marriage started going pear-shaped. Perhaps if I found and met my natural mother, I'd be able to understand myself better. If that makes sense?'

'Yes, it does. But I'm sorry to hear about your marriage. No chance of a reconciliation?'

'Well, it's only a trial separation but there are…problems.' Nicole pulled a face, feeling her shoulders tightening.

'I see. Don't worry, it doesn't affect our decision with regard to your receiving information about your birth mother. We do like to understand *why* someone wants to trace their natural parents in case there are issues involved. For example, what are your feelings towards your birth mother?'

Nicole pursed her lips. 'To be honest, I'm not really sure. I feel upset that she felt able to give me away, but on the other hand my adoptive parents made me feel loved and took great care of me. In some ways I was spoilt, certainly materially.' She leaned forward and went on, 'I want to know *why* she gave me away. What happened in her life to make her do such a terrible thing. Terrible for her, I mean, not me,' she added, seeing Mrs Lewis's raised eyebrows. 'My parents always stressed how special I was, that they had chosen me.'

'Good. It sounds like your parents handled the adoption well. As did you. But have you thought about the impact on your birth mother if you now turn up?'

'Yes, a bit. I realise she may be married with children and not want them to learn about me. I wouldn't just barge in! She might not want to meet me and that would hurt, I admit. But I need to *try*, don't I?' Nicole, feeling her shoulders rise even higher, appealed to Mrs Lewis, who smiled encouragingly.

'Well, it's certainly your right to try and meet her. I see no reason to refuse your request for information, based on what you've told me. Now, what, if anything, do you know about your adoption?'

'I understand that my mother was from Guernsey and a teacher at the time I was born.'

'I see. Well, the file should hold more information but we are restricted in what we can tell you. If, for example, your mother specifically asked not to be contacted by you then we have to honour her wishes. But this does not mean that you cannot be given a copy of your birth certificate, showing her name etc. In England adoptees have more rights than here, I'm afraid.' Seeing Nicole's face drop, she quickly added, 'Don't worry, we'll help you as much as we can. Now, let's sort out the paperwork shall we? Have you brought your ID?'

With the formalities completed, Mrs Lewis arranged that she would contact Nicole as soon as the birth certificate was available. In the meantime she would also request access to her adoption file.

'This should all be through within a couple of weeks. I look forward to seeing you again soon.'

Mrs Lewis smiled warmly as they shook hands.

Once she was outside in the street, Nicole took a deep breath, finally letting her shoulders relax. *Mm, not sure if that was good or bad. Seems a lot depends on whether or not my mother is dead against meeting me.* As she set off towards the nearest café, she felt haunted by the fear of rejection. Again.

chapter 6

The mad and enjoyable night out with the girls was just what Nicole needed. The sexy mini-dress was indeed much appreciated by the Jersey men hovering around the group in Liquid Envy and Nicole was never short of a dance partner. But, in spite of her avowed intention to test the waters, man-wise, she was not serious. Much as she enjoyed flirting and being flirted with, in her heart she was still hurting. As she remarked to Susie, 'I'm not ready to trust any man as far as I can throw him. A spin round the dance floor is the most they'll get from me!'

Nicole and Susie made the most of the summer days and headed to the beach to make sandcastles with Bettany while Paul was at school. As Nicole helped the little girl to search for shells to decorate their castle she felt a rush of warmth flow through her. *Oh, my God! I can't be getting all maternal, can I?* Always so focussed on her upwardly-mobile career, she had given little thought to having a family. And Tom made no secret of his wish to delay fatherhood as long as possible. So why now, she mused, gazing at the cherubic face framed by blonde curls. Bettany was adorable, she acknowledged, very easy to love with her spontaneous hugs and kisses. But would she really want a child of her own –now? Not exactly great timing when she was as good as single. She sighed, shaking her head.

'Anything the matter?' Susie asked from her supine position on the beach towel.

Nicole gave a short laugh. 'Only that I seem to have discovered my latent maternal feelings!'

Susie sat up, her mouth open.

'Well, what a turn up for the book! Thought you didn't want kids?'

'No, I didn't, or at least not till later on. But I'm thirty-five now – '

'And the clock's ticking louder than ever! But what's brought this on so suddenly?'

Before Nicole could answer, Bettany called her.

'Look, Aunty Nickle, aren't they pretty?' She held out a variety of pearlescent tiny shells.

As Susie watched the two heads bent together she let out a throaty laugh.

Nicole looked up and as their eyes connected she knew her friend had sussed her out.

'You're in love! With my daughter! You've finally felt that little arrow in your heart, haven't you?'

'Okay, okay, I admit it. I can now see how fulfilling having a child might be. Especially if she's as cute as this little scamp here,' she laughed, grabbing Bettany for a mock fight.

The child squealed as Nicole tickled her and Susie joined in, so that soon they were all rolling around, laughing, on the sand.

Later, as they were driving back, Bettany fast asleep in her car seat, Susie looked across at Nicole and said, 'Don't you think it's somehow significant that you've discovered your maternal feelings just as you might be meeting your real mother?'

Nicole, lost in thought, turned towards her friend.

'It has occurred to me. But at the moment I don't know if I *will* be meeting my mother. And, without a man, my chances of motherhood are, to put it mildly, non-existent!' She frowned.

'Hey, don't be so negative! I'm sure your mother will want to meet you and you've got plenty of time to meet Mr Right, or, at least, Mr Nearly Right. Didn't take you long to hitch up with Tom did it?'

Nicole thought back to those heady days when she and Tom were so much in love that they lit up any room they entered. Oh, what happened? What went wrong? Was it her or was Tom just incapable of being faithful? Maudlin tears pricked at her eyes and she brushed them away, hoping Susie hadn't seen them. But she had.

'Oh, Nicole! Do you still love him?'

'I...I don't know. Guess so. I'm so angry with him and hate what he's done but...'

'I understand. It's hard to stop loving someone just 'cos they're a bastard! Not that Craig's a bastard – but I have loved one or two in the past,' she added hastily, seeing Nicole's shock.

'Would you consider going back to Tom?'

'I don't *think* so, but I'm not as sure now as I was.'

'You wouldn't go back just to have a baby, surely?' Susie cried.

Nicole shook her head. 'Of course not. I'm not that desperate for a child! But I am confused.' Her sigh was so heartfelt that Susie reached over and touched her arm.

'It's okay. You've got loads to think about just now. It will sort itself out in the end. Auntie Susie says so!'

Nicole smiled at her friend, wanting to believe her. But knowing it wasn't that simple.

'Nicole, good to see you again,' Mrs Lewis greeted her as she returned to the office two weeks later. 'Been enjoying the fine weather?'

'Yes, thanks. I'd almost forgotten what great beaches Jersey has.'

Mrs Lewis nodded her agreement as she opened her file. 'Good. Now, here's your birth certificate as promised.'

As Nicole picked up the crisp, new copy with trembling hands, she saw her mother's name for the first time – an odd experience for a thirty-five year old. Hélène Ferbrache. Very Guernsey. The birth had been registered by hospital staff and there were no further details. Her heart sank.

She looked up to see that Mrs Lewis was smiling.

'You're in luck. Your mother wrote to us in 1997 to say that if you were to try and trace her she'd be happy for you to make contact – '

'Oh, that's brilliant! I...I can't believe that I'm hearing this. Can I see the letter?'

Mrs Lewis pushed it across the desk and Nicole scanned it quickly. Headed with a St Peter Port address, and written in beautifully neat handwriting, it went on... 'I wish to make it known that if my daughter now wishes to make contact then I am happy for her to do so. If I am no longer at the above address then a letter can be sent to me, marked Private & Confidential, c/o my parents Mr & Mrs R Ferbrache...'

Her mind raced. Not only did her mother want to meet her, there was a good chance she was still in Guernsey. So she hadn't emigrated! And she had grandparents, or at least she had ten years ago. She examined the letter more closely, wondering if the handwriting would tell her more about this "Hélène Ferbrache", her mother. But she couldn't decipher anything other than that her writing was as neat as it should be for a teacher.

Looking up she caught Mrs Lewis gazing at her in obvious delight.

'It looks like I've just made your day!'

'You sure have, thanks. Right, I'd better get a letter off asap. May I keep this letter?'

'I'll copy it as we need the original on file. Data Protection and all that.'

Nicole waited impatiently as Mrs Lewis went off to use the photocopier and after she had returned, shook hands before dashing off to meet Susie for lunch.

A couple of hours later Nicole and Susie bid farewell to each other outside "Blue Fish" after a convivial lunch; Susie to pick up her children and Nicole to compose a Very Important Letter under the influence of a couple of glasses of wine. *To my mother! Wow! This feels so weird.* As she walked back to the apartment she was struck by the irony of the situation. She was going to write to the woman who'd given birth to her in the home owned by the two people who'd raised her as their own!

After a strong coffee she made a start. But how to address her? Dear Mother? Oh, no, not that. Dear Mrs Ferbrache? Too formal. In the end she settled for Dear Hélène. Right, what next? Nicole made rough drafts, struggling to find the right words. What *did* you say to the mother you hadn't seen since birth? Several attempts later she settled on the final version –

Dear Hélène,

My name is Nicole Oxford and I was given your name and address by the Jersey Social Services. I'm the baby you gave up for adoption in 1972 and, if you were in agreement, I'd like to meet you. Although I moved to England some years ago, I'm in Jersey at the moment and would be happy to come over to Guernsey if that's easier for you.

You can write to me at the above address or phone me on 01534 180260.

I look forward to hearing from you,

Best wishes

Nicole.

After posting the letter she took a deep breath before phoning Spain.

A few days later she received a letter from Guernsey. But she knew something was wrong as it was from the Guernsey Post Office and inside the envelope was her letter, marked "Return to sender, no longer at this address."

chapter 7

Nicole swallowed her disappointment and sent the letter on to the address of Hélène's parents in Torteval. Not really a religious person, having been bored rigid in church as a child, she now decided to hedge her bets and pray. Couldn't do any harm, she reasoned, praying that Hélène was still in Guernsey and would somehow, soon, get her letter.

Whether or not there had indeed been divine intervention, a few days later she had a phone call.

'Hello.'

'Is that Nicole Oxford?' a woman's voice she didn't recognise. Neither young nor old but somehow diffident.

'Yes. Who's calling?'

'I'm Hélène Ferbrache. You wrote to me.'

Oh, my God, it's her! Nicole gasped and her hand holding the phone trembled.

'Mm, hello. Thanks for phoning. How...how are you?' Nicole, usually the most articulate of people, felt suddenly lost for words.

'I'm fine, thanks. I...was so pleased to hear from you. I wasn't sure if I ever would, had convinced myself that, after all this time, I wouldn't.' Nicole heard the woman draw a deep breath. 'That you hadn't given me a thought. Were happy in your own life.'

There followed a long pause.

'Well, to be honest I hadn't always planned to get in touch. I had such a busy life in England but I think, deep down, I'd always wanted to know more about you. Now...now feels like the right time.' Nicole's mind whirled. What to say? 'Mm, I was so happy to learn that you wanted me to contact you, but then found you'd moved.'

A deep sigh echoed down the line.

'Yes, I had to…move in with my mother about three years ago. My father died several years ago and now Mother can't manage on her own.'

Nicole heard the edge of bitterness in her voice.

'Oh, I see. You didn't…marry?' Nicole felt as if someone else was asking the questions, as if she wasn't actually part of this conversation. Hélène sounded strained, too.

'No. The opportunity never, er, presented itself. You're my only child.' Again the edge of bitterness could be heard.

'Right, well my parents didn't have any more children either. And all my grandparents are dead.' Nicole had a thought. 'Except your mother. So I do have a grandmother.'

'Yes, and I'm sure she'd love to meet you sometime.' Another pause and Nicole heard Hélène take a sip of something. Dutch courage, perhaps? She wished she had a drink to hand herself. Her head was all over the place and her hands felt clammy.

Hélène continued. 'Of course, we'd have to meet first and see how we get on. If… you still want to, that is…' Her voice tailed off.

Nicole's emotions were mixed. On the one hand she had set this in motion and had convinced herself it was necessary to meet her mother; on the other she felt as scared as Hélène sounded. Taking a deep breath she replied, 'Oh, yes. I'd really like to come over and meet you and then we could see…'

'Good.' Hélène's voice sounded brighter. 'The school holidays start next week so I'll be at home. Would you come over for the day?'

'Yes, sounds good. How about Monday?'

'Fine with me. I'll pick you up from the airport and we can go somewhere to talk and…get to know each other.'

After taking down Hélène's phone number Nicole said goodbye and sat for a while, lost in thought. She had rehearsed what she'd planned to say when they first spoke to each other but somehow it had all gone out of her head. Her mother was now a *real* person, not just a name in a file, on a piece of paper. And in a few days she'd actually see, and be able to touch, this woman who had nurtured her in her body for nine months, given birth to her but then let another woman take her. Right, she thought, got a lot of phone calls to make…

It was years since Nicole had been over to Guernsey and she didn't know it very well. So much smaller than Jersey, it looked from the plane to consist of more densely populated areas and fewer open fields than her home island. The tiny plane, sporting a red nose and called Joey, was one of the island hoppers connecting the two largest Channel Islands. It performed a slightly bumpy landing before taxiing up to the terminal. She was through to the main hall in moments and looked around for Hélène, who had told her she'd be wearing a red linen skirt and white top and had medium length, light brown hair.

There she was! Standing apart from the huddle of people ready to welcome other passengers, a hesitant smile on her face. Nicole thought she looked familiar, the hazel eyes…She moved closer.

'Nicole? I'm Hélène. It's so good to see you at last!'

They faced each other, both uncertain of the right move. After a moment's hesitation, Hélène reached out and gave Nicole a hug.

Nicole pulled back gently so that she could take a look at this stranger who was not a stranger. Her hair, although touched with grey, was a similar shade to her own. They had the same eyes but not the mouth. Hélène's mouth was smaller, thinner and etched with lines matching those around the eyes, making her look older than her years. *She doesn't look happy.* Nicole felt a spurt of sympathy.

'Well, we can't stand here all day or people will talk!' Hélène broke into the silence hanging over them. She led the way to her car and as she unlocked it said, 'I thought we could go to a place nearby on the cliffs. We can sit outside and have a coffee or something.'

'Fine by me.' Nicole felt her palms moistening and wiped them on her jeans.

They drove in silence down winding lanes leading from the airport, finally coming to rest in an area signposted Le Gouffre, where Helen parked outside a bright, cheery café with views out to sea.

'It's a Greek restaurant and if we want to stay for lunch I can recommend the food,' Hélène said. They chose a table set away from the others, offering a clear view over the valley.

'What a lovely spot!'

'Yes, isn't it? I come here when I need to get out of the house. I go for a long walk on the cliff path before recovering here with a coffee.' Hélène smoothed down her skirt before adding, 'How about a glass of wine instead of coffee? Might help us both relax a bit.'

'Yep, great. Feels like a blind date but somehow scarier,' she smiled at Hélène.

The older woman nodded in agreement and they ordered wine.

It helped.

'Nicole, as you're the one who's set this in motion, it's only fair that you ask the questions. I'm happy to tell you anything you want to know.'

'Thanks. Could you start by telling me a bit more about yourself and your family?'

Hélène took a deep breath.

'I was born here just after the war. My parents, Eve and Reg, were growers in Torteval and my mother and I still live in the old family home. I'm an only child, my mother miscarried after me and that was it.' She took a sip of wine. 'My father was quite a bit older than my mother and he retired in 1980. He…died of a heart attack in 2000.' For a moment she was quiet, biting her lips.

'I'm sorry.'

After a muttered thanks, Hélène continued.

'I…I was very close to Dad. It was a shock as he'd always been so strong. I was living in my house in Town and for a while Mother managed on her own. But her health started to deteriorate three years ago so I moved back to help her.'

'That must have been a big sacrifice.'

She gave a short laugh. 'It was. She's very independent and resents my being there but neither of us has much choice. It's either that or she'd have to go into care. Not really an option. As I don't have my own family to take care of, it would be frowned on if I put her in a home.'

'Mm, sounds like you don't get on with your mother,' Nicole looked at her, sensing a bitter woman. *Could this really be my mother? She's not at all what I imagined.*

'Well, I admit I was a lot closer to Dad. And Mother and I used to get on fairly well when he was alive. It's just a bit…difficult living together. Two women, no man around to act as ballast.'

Nicole nodded. 'Yes, I can understand that. You'd rather be in your own home.'

'For sure! But that's the way it is so we both have to get on with it. And as her health is only going to get worse not better I know it's not forever,' Hélène sighed. 'She's eighty-five but physically seems much older.'

'I'm sorry to hear that.' Her stomach clenched as she asked the vital question. 'Mm, Hélène, could you tell me something about my father, please?'

chapter 8

Hélène twisted a turquoise ring on her right hand as she considered the question.

'His name's Adrian and he was another teacher at the school so we were thrown together quite a lot and became...friends. We spent hours just chatting in the staff room when we had free periods, finding we had so much in common.' Hélène seemed to drift off somewhere before gathering herself and taking a sip of wine.

'I fell in love with him. And Adrian said he loved me but...' She faced her daughter.

'He was married, you see. He'd married young, only twenty-four, but his...his wife was pregnant with their daughter and he had to marry her. She was a Catholic and although Adrian wasn't, that's what you did if you were "caught".' Her face tightened, the frown lines etched even deeper into her forehead.

Nicole watched the emotions chase across Hélène's face. Hurt, anger...love? She felt a pang of pity for her until she remembered her own situation. Tom had cheated on her and could have fathered a child by another woman. The thought triggered the familiar ache in her solar plexus and she wanted to lash out.

'My husband's been cheating on me and it's been bloody painful! I've felt totally betrayed. It's not a nice thing to do, sleep with another woman's husband.' Her voice was icy cold.

Hélène gasped, moving back in her seat as if to ward off a blow.

'I'm so sorry about your husband. You're right, it's not a nice thing to do, to be the "other woman". I never set out to have an affair with a married man, I can assure you. I tried hard not to fall in love with Adrian. But we got on so well and it was common knowledge that his marriage wasn't happy. His wife hardly ever went anywhere with him and on the odd occasion I met them together she seemed a cold sort of woman who put him down.'

Nicole felt her anger subside a little. But she needed to know more.

'So, what happened between you and Adrian?' Her tone only slightly warmer.

Hélène breathed a deep sigh.

'We became close but had to meet in secret, at my place. Guernsey's too small and we were too well known to risk going out in public. I know it was wrong of me, us, but we *needed* to be together, if only for snatched moments. But it wasn't much fun knowing I couldn't see him for birthdays and Christmas or go away on holiday together. It was like living a half-life.' She stopped to take another sip of wine and asked, 'Look, would you mind if we had something to eat? I was too nervous to have any breakfast.'

'So was I!'

They ordered a selection of *mezethes* together with more wine and a jug of water.

For a few moments they ate in silence, both deep in thought. Nicole's mind was filled with images of Hélène and this faceless man, Adrian, her father, drawn together but not together.

'Is my...father still alive?'

Hélène looked surprised. 'Yes, of course he is. Why wouldn't he be?'

'Oh, I just wondered. Only he seemed to be in your past, not your present.' Nicole felt relief surge through her. If he was alive then she might meet him too!

'I see. We stopped being lovers after I found I was

pregnant with you. I'd hoped he would leave his wife and marry me but he wouldn't, couldn't. She would never have agreed to a divorce and Adrian didn't feel he could continue teaching here if we were living in sin.' She gave a hollow laugh. 'He was very ambitious, wanted to become a headmaster, which he did some years later. But he had to avoid scandal at all costs. Or so he said.'

She looked Nicole squarely in the eye.

'You have to understand that Guernsey was a very judgmental society. Still is, a bit. Hypocritical too, as lots of people have found to their cost. For us to be together, with you, would have meant leaving the island. And he wouldn't do that. It would've meant not seeing his children.' She gulped some wine

'Children? How many did he have?' Nicole's heart thumped. *She* was also his child!

'Two, a boy and a girl. After the boy was born, Adrian told me that they never… slept together again. His wife didn't want more children and as a Catholic…'

'Mm. Does my father know what happened to…to me?'

Hélène reached out to hold her hand.

'Yes, of course. At least he knew I was going to have my baby adopted. He wasn't a bad man, Nicole. He just wasn't brave enough to lose everything he'd achieved. I gave in my notice at school and went over to Jersey before I began to show. I stayed with a distant cousin until the birth and then returned here and got a job in another school. A girl's school with no young male teachers!'

'You…you never considered keeping me?' Nicole stammered. She was surprised by her feelings of rejection – odd, after all these years.

Hélène's face went white.

'I…I didn't feel I had much choice. It would have meant giving up being a teacher here, making it difficult for me to support us both. And I couldn't leave Guernsey as it meant deserting my parents.' She looked down at her hands and again twisted her ring. As she lifted her head, Nicole saw the tears in her eyes and had to force herself not to soften.

'I can see now that I was just as much a coward as Adrian. But I'd never considered myself as maternal. Teaching other people's unruly children can be off-putting.' Her mouth twisted. 'But when I first saw you, held you in my arms, I felt such a rush of love for you I was overwhelmed. I'd never experienced anything like it! It was so powerful that I nearly changed my mind about letting you go.' Tears were now streaming down her face and she wiped at her face to stop them.

'What...what stopped you?'

'I realised that I'd still have to face the challenge of what to do, where to go. And I knew there was a young couple desperate for a child, waiting for you. Waiting and willing to give you all that I couldn't. The love and care of a mother *and* a father.'

chapter 9

The two women sat in silence for a while, lost in thought, while Hélène dabbed at her eyes.

Nicole tried to imagine what it would have been like being brought up by a single mother struggling to cope on her own in England. Very different from her own comfortable upbringing in Jersey. And she had the advantage of Hélène as she'd been loved. Loved not only by her adoptive parents but by Tom, in spite of his transgressions. Whereas Hélène had lost not only her lover but her daughter. She began to feel less angry about Hélène's rejection of her.

'Hélène? Are you all right?' Nicole touched her arm.

She had started crying again and retrieved a tissue from her bag.

'Sorry. I...I was miles away.' She looked pale.

'I understand. It must be very painful for you to go over it all again. May I ask what happened with...Adrian?'

'Of course. When I told him about my pregnancy he...he made it clear he couldn't be with me, which is what I'd half expected, so I...we agreed not to see each other again. Not easy as we still worked together! But it was only for a term, before I left for Jersey. We lost touch after that.'

Nicole heard the pain in her voice.

'So he doesn't know I'm here? That we're meeting?' Nicole wasn't sure whether to be relieved that he was still alive or sad that he didn't know she was on the island.

Hélène shook her head.

'No. I haven't spoken to him for years. Did you...want to meet him?'

'Well, I guess so. But I don't want to cause any problems, for you or him, or his, er, wife.' Nicole saw the fear in Hélène's eyes. She obviously didn't want to see Adrian again.

'It won't be a problem for his wife. She died three years ago. Cancer.' Her mouth became a tight thin line.

Mmm, so that's why she's bitter. Why hadn't Adrian contacted her? Bastard! Perhaps I shouldn't bother meeting him after all. She could feel her own anger beginning to rise as it occurred to her that he might not want to meet *her* either!

Hélène looked around.

'Would it be better if we left here? I think we've been attracting some attention with all these tears. Do you feel up to meeting my mother?'

Nicole wasn't sure if she did. But how could she say no?

'Oh…okay. Then *she* knows I'm here?'

Hélène looked sheepish.

'I told her about you after our first telephone call.' She hesitated, her hands twisting her handkerchief. 'I'd never told her I'd had a child.'

'Oh, my God! That must have been quite a shock. Why didn't you tell her when you were pregnant?'

'I don't really know. Shame, partly. And I thought that the fewer who knew, the better. I could then pretend it had never happened.' They had stood up to leave and Hélène must have seen the hurt on Nicole's face, as she enveloped her in a warm hug, whispering, 'But now I'm very glad it did happen. I have a beautiful daughter!'

They drove in silence as Hélène negotiated the winding road to the family home in Torteval, one of the remotest parts of the island. Nicole's thoughts were jumbled as she noted the open fields and dotted granite houses, so reminiscent of Jersey. She could quite happily have hopped on the next plane home, but part of her was intrigued to see

54

the family home and meet her grandmother. They drove along the winding Route de Pleinmont before Hélène turned left onto a narrow lane leading apparently nowhere.

'The house *is* a bit remote but it has a lot of land which my parents wanted for their business. You can still see where the old greenhouses stood.'

Sure enough Nicole noticed small brick walls forming the outlines of what had been quite large buildings but there was no sign of the glass frameworks.

'Why has no-one used the greenhouses?'

'The bottom's fallen out of the growing business. In my father's day they had a big export trade in tomatoes. But they couldn't compete with other countries with lower overheads. So we switched to flowers which was great for some years until we were overtaken by Holland. There's only a few growers left now.'

As they turned a corner a large grey granite house emerged

Nicole gasped. 'Why, it looks like a castle!'

'The towers do give that impression, don't they?' Hélène grinned. 'It was built as a rich man's folly in the nineteenth century. Apparently he built it here for the views, which to my mind are its only saving grace. I always thought the house ugly, but it was a magical place to grow up in. Now our money's running out, it's cold and shabby. And I do miss my own little house.' She sighed.

'I can see it would be fun for children.' Nicole surveyed the house with its round towers at either end joined by parapets decorated with gargoyles. Stone mullioned windows and a huge old oak door complete with portico completed the gothic effect.

Just as they were about to enter the house, Hélène turned to Nicole, saying 'My mother spends most of her time in a wheelchair as she can't walk at the moment. Being more or less house-bound has made her a bit... difficult. She can be a bit sharp,' she pulled a face.

'Okay, thanks for warning me!'

They entered a gloomy, large stone flagged hall, lit by a window on the landing. A heavily carved oak staircase wound its way up in the middle. Panelled oak walls were enlivened with seascapes in ornate gilded frames. Doors led off in all directions.

Hélène led the way to a door on the far left-hand side, calling out 'Mother, it's me. And I've brought someone to meet you!'

chapter 10

Nicole stepped forward, feeling as nervous as when she'd first seen Hélène at the airport.

'Hello, Mrs Ferbrache. I'm Nicole.'

The old lady looked up from her wheelchair, positioned by the window.

Nicole found herself staring at a birdlike face framed by thin white hair, cut unflatteringly short. The hazel eyes appeared to look straight through her, the mouth a small splash of red lipstick surrounded by pale, wrinkled skin.

'So, you're my granddaughter, are you? I suppose it's about time that we met.' The slash of red opened up into a smile and a stick thin arm came out towards her.

Nicole grasped the proffered hand. It felt dry and cold but the grip was firm.

Hélène moved forward and bent down to place a light kiss on her mother's head before saying, 'Would you like some tea, Mother?'

Mrs Ferbrache looked between the two women standing over her.

'That would be nice. Although I think champagne would be more appropriate to the occasion, eh?'

Nicole saw the glint of mischief in the old lady's eyes. Glancing towards Hélène she noticed that her mother looked flustered.

'Champagne? I'm not sure if...'

'Don't worry. Tea will be fine. Is there any cake?' Mrs Ferbrache turned towards Nicole. 'I do like cake. Don't you?'

'Yes. If you have some...'

Hélène became brisk.

'Of course we have cake, Mother. I never let us run out, as you well know. I'll go and make the tea.' She hurried out of the room, catching Nicole's eye in passing. Her raised eyebrows and pursed lips said it all. Nicole turned her attention to the old lady. Her grandmother.

'Well, girl, you'd better sit down. Towering over me like that.' The old lady watched as Nicole settled herself in a nearby armchair. Two pairs of hazel eyes appraised each other. *My grandmother's probably shocked, and perhaps angry, that Hélène hadn't told her about me. I wonder if that's why she's sharp with her?*

Nicole felt awkward. She'd only just met her natural mother for the first time and now she was presented with a grandmother! And one who clearly liked to stir things with her daughter. She was beginning to wish that she had not agreed to come here when the old lady spoke.

'Cat got your tongue? I don't bite, you know.' Eve thrust her head forward.

'Maybe not but you were a bit hard on Hélène just now, weren't you? Do you enjoy teasing her?' Nicole was surprised at her own temerity. But she could sympathise with Hélène who had given up her independence for this small, sharp woman.

Eve looked taken aback, speechless. Then she let out a chuckle.

'Ah, so who's the sharp one now, eh? Good. I like people who can stand up for themselves. Or others. Hélène...well, she seems to have lost that.'

'Are you surprised? She's had to give up a lot to care for you. And I don't think she's been happy for many years.'

Eve looked shaken, as if what she'd said struck home.

'So, young lady, you think you know us already, do you?' Eve's compressed lips seemed to Nicole to express the old lady's anger at her forwardness. She was beginning to regret her remark when Hélène pushed open the door, wheeling an old-fashioned trolley laden with the *accoutrements* of afternoon tea.

'Here we are, Mother. I've got your favourites, chocolate cake and Victoria sponge. Have you two been getting to know each other?' Hélène looked warily at the two women facing each other.

'I-' Nicole began.

'You could say that we're beginning to understand each other,' Eve cut in.

'Oh, well. That's good.' Hélène searched Nicole's face for a hint of what had passed between them, but Nicole just shrugged. It was clear that Hélène's nerves were strung tight by the way the cups rattled on the saucers as she poured the tea. Nicole was beginning to feel as if she was at a Mad Hatter's Tea Party, half expecting a rabbit – or was it a dormouse? - to pop out of the tea pot. It was surreal.

Hélène gazed at her with a look suspiciously like that of a mother proud of something her child has accomplished. Just as Mary had done. Such as when she'd got good exam results or wore her first ball gown. It felt weird.

Eve began what sounded like an inquisition. Nicole, hoping it wouldn't last long, responded with a potted history of her life, ending with the admission that she had recently split from her husband.

Until that moment Eve had been nodding approvingly at Nicole's story but now she looked up sharply.

'Why have you left him? Have you met someone else?' Her tone was cold.

'No, *I* haven't, but Tom…well, he's been unfaithful and it's happened too many times.' Nicole's voice caught on a sob.

'Humph. In that case you're better off without him. I've no time for married men who can't keep it in their trousers.' Eve looked pointedly at Hélène who flushed.

Nicole understood what had happened and replied, 'I know that my father was married. Hélène's told me her story. I think we'd all agree that he wasn't honourable. Like my own husband.'

Eve's sharp gaze settled on Nicole.

'Well, young lady, I can see that you and I are going to get along just fine,' she said, a smile hovering on the wrinkled face.

Nicole smiled back, beginning to warm to her.

Hélène, looking drained, reminded Nicole that they needed to leave for the airport.

Nicole stood up and leant towards Eve, not sure whether to offer her hand or attempt a hug. Eve made the decision for her by offering her own hand and when Nicole shook it she clasped her other hand on top.

'I look forward to seeing you again. Soon, I hope.'

Nicole caught the twinkle in her eyes and smiled back.

'Well, I'll have to see…'

Hélène led the way out to the car but before switching on the ignition, she turned to Nicole and asked if she really wanted to return.

Nicole took in the strain on Hélène's face and reassured her that it was what she wanted.

'I've only just met you both and it's been…a lot to take in. But it would be good if we could all be…friends. It's just a question of time. Time to get to know each other. My mother and my grandmother!'

chapter 11

The short plane ride home – less than fifteen minutes - didn't give Nicole much time for reflection. But it was enough for her to try and get a take on what had happened that day.

It had been pretty momentous. How often does any grown woman get to meet, for the first time, both her mother and grandmother in one afternoon? And she couldn't help but compare them to the women she had known all her life. Mary's parents had died when Nicole was a baby but her paternal grandmother had lived until a few years ago, outliving her husband by ten years. Mary, the stay at home mother who had lived in her husband's shadow for many years and Hélène, the unmarried teacher. Then Gran, the woman who had seemed very old to her from childhood, and Eve, who she suspected had once been a very lively woman. Gran had given birth to her father, an only child, late in life. Nicole had never found her very loving.

'Nicole! Sit up straight, girl. And hold your knife and fork like *this.*'

She could picture herself, about five years old, having Sunday dinner with her grandparents, something she dreaded. It was *so* formal - they even had a maid to serve the food! – while they all sat round the huge mahogany table, perched on uncomfortable tall chairs. Nicole struggled to hold the heavy silver cutlery that her grandmother insisted she used, even though at home her mother allowed her to use a child-size set. Gran, stern, straight backed and grey haired maintained that children, even an only grandchild, should be seen and not heard. And only seen under close supervision for Sunday dinners. Nicole, with the benefit of maturity and hindsight, could now see why her father had been so stiff and formal himself. Poor Dad! He'd found it so hard to be at ease with her when she was small, only reaching out more when they could hold a proper conversation.

Eve and her gran were like chalk and cheese, she thought, idly looking down at the outline of Jersey slowly filling the horizon. Eve was mentally young for her years, still displaying a spark of mischief, unthinkable in her "other" grandmother. And Hélène was *so* different to Mary. Although her unhappiness was worn like a tight coat, stifling her, Nicole was certain that she'd been a bright, loving woman who had just had the misfortune to fall in love with the wrong man. Her father! She gulped and bit her lip hard at the thought but couldn't dwell on it further as the little plane bounced gently on the tarmac. Home again – for the moment.

Later that evening, after a quick supper and a large glass of courage-inducing wine, Nicole rang her parents.

'Hi, Mum, it's me. How are you?'

'Nicole, lovely to hear from you. I'm fine, thanks. Have you…have you been to Guernsey today?' Mary's throat felt dry and her heart thumped as she waited to hear about The Meeting. She nodded to Ian who came over and squeezed her gently.

'Yes, it's been quite a day! Not only did I meet Hélène but also her mother Eve. We seemed to hit it off…' Nicole described the day's events, her voice sounding neutral, almost as if it had been an average day out.

'We left it that I'd get in touch if and when I wanted to see them again. I…I might want to, if you didn't mind, Mum?'

Mary heard the hesitation in her daughter's voice and took a deep breath. Nicole had met her mother *and* grandmother and the world hadn't ended. She made it sound like a normal meeting of long-lost relatives which, of course, it was. Except that these were *very* close long-lost relations.

'Of course I don't mind, darling. This is what you hoped for and I can understand that you want to know these...ladies better. Fancy! A new grandmother as well! But you said she's frail?' Mary still felt her heart beating faster than usual.

'Yes, she's in a wheelchair but her mind's very sharp. I think Hélène finds her difficult to handle as she winds her up. I guess it's difficult for them as they're both independent.'

'Did...did Hélène say anything about your father?' Mary felt Ian squeeze her harder.

Nicole told her what little she knew about Adrian.

'I see. Will you try and meet up with him too?'

'I don't know. It's obviously a sore point with Hélène that he hasn't been in touch with her since his wife died and I don't want to do anything to make matters worse. He doesn't sound like a very nice man so perhaps it's better if I don't.'

Mary began to relax as they chatted for a few minutes before she handed the phone over to Ian. She walked outside onto the *naya* where they'd been having a drink after supper and picked up her glass. Taking a sip she realised that the first irrevocable step had been taken and all she could do now was wait. Wait and see if Nicole would still continue to love her and Ian as her parents and not prefer this...this other woman, Hélène. She felt tears prick at her eyes and gulped some wine. Surely Nicole wouldn't stop loving them...?

chapter 12

Nicole arranged to meet Susie for coffee to "spill the beans" as Susie put it so eloquently. 'I shall want to hear every detail, my friend. Every detail!'

Nicole laughed, 'Don't worry, you shall.'

As they now sat in the café, cappuccinos steaming in front of them, Nicole described her meeting with Hélène and then Eve at "the house like a castle."

Susie interjected at timely intervals.

'Do tell me again what Hélène looks like.' 'Had the house *really* got towers?' 'Tell me more about Eve.'

When Susie was satisfied she knew everything there was to learn, she looked at Nicole and asked, 'So, are you glad you've met them?'

'Oh, yes. Obviously, it's too soon to have learnt much about them and I can't tell if I take after either of them. I now know we share the same eyes which isn't much to go on!' She grinned. 'I'd really like to find out how much I share genetically with them, you know, personality, intelligence. That sort of thing.' *Or if I'm more like my father Adrian. Hope not, he was such a rat to Hélène. But do I want to take after her? She let herself be used by Adrian and looks so bitter and unhappy...*She pulled a face, adding, 'Then I could see what I'd like when I'm older.'

'That's a bit scary! I look at my mum, bless her, and hope I don't turn out like her!' Susie laughed. 'I love her dearly, but you know what I mean.'

Nicole nodded. 'Sure, no-one wants to become exactly like their mother. But we won't. There's always *some* differences, even if it's just the hairstyle.'

They both giggled as they pictured what to them were their mothers' unflattering, older woman hairstyles.

'Seriously, Susie, you know that you take after your mum when it comes to cooking as you're both brilliant cooks, but you share your dad's sense of humour.'

Susie laughed. 'So there's hope for me yet! I see it's important for you to spend more time with Hélène and Eve but that's not the whole story is it? You'd need to meet your father too.' She reached out for Nicole's hand before asking, 'You're not sure about that, are you?'

'No, I'm not. But that's a long way off and I might never meet him. Might not want to. In the meantime I have to decide when to go back to Guernsey and whether or not to stay *chez* Hélène.'

Susie's eyes opened wide.

'She asked you to stay?'

'Yes, when she dropped me off at the airport. I said I'd think about it. It's the best way to get to know them better, but it could be disastrous if we don't get on. I could just stay in a B&B. What do you think?'

Susie thought for a moment.

'It's a bit like meeting the in-laws, isn't it? If they've got a big enough house – and they certainly have – then it might look odd for you to stay in a B&B. As if you don't really like them. And if it doesn't work out you can always hop on the next plane.'

'You're right. I think Hélène would be hurt if I didn't stay there. I could hire a car and go exploring so it doesn't get too claustrophobic. I'd like to get to know Guernsey better as I've not been there for yonks. Not since we went over for your hen weekend and I can't remember us doing much exploring then,' she laughed.

'Only the nightclubs,' Susie grinned. 'Oh, those were the days! Single and care-free.'

'Hardly single! You were about to walk down the aisle and I'd already been there and bought the bloody T-shirt.' Nicole frowned as her mind drifted back to her own wedding day and the hopes and dreams that now lay shattered like broken glass beneath her feet.

'Hey! Don't get maudlin, girl. If it wasn't meant to be…Which reminds me, have you heard from *Him* lately?'

Nicole played with her teaspoon.

'No. I've been half-expecting him to ring 'cos it's been a few weeks since we last spoke.' She put the spoon down and looked up.

'He doesn't want to accept that it's over between us and is trying to woo me back with protestations of undying love and fidelity. He almost makes me believe him, but – '

'You know you can't trust him, girl! He's got a silver tongue all right, but promise me you're not weakening.' Susie grabbed Nicole's hand.

Nicole shook her head. 'No, I'm not, but it's hard not to remember the good times we had. And I do get lonely,' she sighed.

Susie's face softened.

'I know, I know. But just hang on in there, my girl, and everything will work out fine. Auntie Susie says so.'

Nicole smiled. 'Well, if Auntie Susie says so, who am I to disagree?'

Later that day, just as Nicole was wondering what to make for supper, the phone rang. Thinking it was Susie for another chat she picked it up, laughing, 'Miss me already do you?'

'Yes, you know I do, darling,' answered Tom.

'Oh!' Gripping the phone she sat down heavily on the nearest chair. 'Hello, Tom. What do you want?'

'Well, that's not very welcoming is it? And who were you expecting it to be, a new boyfriend?' His tone hardened.

'I thought it was Susie, not that it's any of your business. We agreed minimal contact so that I could make a decision without any pressure. You're just making it harder – '

'Nicole, please listen! I just wanted to know if you've found your mother.'

'Mm, yes I have. I've just been over to see her in Guernsey. And her mother, my...grandmother.'

'Wow! That's great. I'm so pleased for you. Really I am. It's what you set out to do when we had that... row.' He cleared his throat. 'Does that mean that you might be willing for us to meet up? I know we agreed not to meet unless you wanted, but I really need you to know how much I've changed –'

'Perhaps you have and perhaps you haven't. I'm not going to take your word for that.' Nicole began to feel angry. 'Look, I've got a lot of stuff to deal with and we're only half-way through the agreed six months' separation –'

'But –'

'No, Tom. Please leave me in peace while I sort my head out. Bye.' Nicole's heart was beating fast as she switched off the phone. Susie's words had been echoing in her mind throughout the call – 'Everything will work out fine.' She had to believe her friend was right, but it hurt, it really hurt. The tears seeped through her lashes, leaving trails of mascara down her cheeks. Damn the man! She reached for a tissue and a glass of wine. *Does he really think that just 'cos I've found my mother that all can be hunky-dory again? It doesn't change anything between us. And even if he has changed, do I want to go back to him?* She couldn't trust herself to answer that. Not yet.

chapter 13

Nicole thought long and hard about whether to return to Guernsey. Part of her felt she was stirring up feelings that she didn't want to acknowledge. Like, did she really want to be associated with these people who were little more than strangers and had such a different background to herself? At least she knew where she was with Mary and Ian, she'd known them all her life, had shared history. Understood each other. And were definitely becoming warmer in their old age, she thought wryly. Perhaps she should just walk away from the Ferbraches, put it down to experience, she'd been there and *not* bought the T-shirt. It would be easier, she wouldn't have to look at herself, see herself reflected in these other women. Then another part of her kicked in. The journalist part, *wanting* to know more, get the full picture. Even if it was unpalatable. She sat curled up on the sofa nursing a glass of wine, feeling as if the outcome was inevitable. The enquiring journalist always won in the end. With a sigh, she picked up the phone.

'Hi Hélène, it's me, Nicole. About my visit...'

A few days later she collected a hire car at Guernsey airport. They'd agreed to an open-ended stay, giving her the option to leave whenever she chose. That didn't make it much easier, she thought, throwing her case into the boot. Still feels like entering the dragon's den. Nicole reminded herself that she was a successful media journalist who had interviewed big name celebrities so why was it so hard to

68

get to know her own mother and grandmother? She smiled at the idea. *C'mon girl, go for it! They won't bite.*

Feeling better, she swung the car out onto Rue des Landes before turning left into New Road and the winding road to Torteval. It didn't seem long before she turned off the main road and along the lane to La Folie. The gothic structure, perched loftily on the cliff, was aptly named. A rich man's folly indeed! She still couldn't quite believe that the imposing granite building really belonged to her grandmother and longed to learn how it had come into the family.

Perhaps it was the crunching on the gravel as Nicole drew the car to a halt, but something must have alerted Hélène, for she opened the door before Nicole had switched off the engine.

'Nicole! I'm so glad to see you again. I do hope you'll enjoy your stay with us.' Hélène's smile looked uncertain, as if she wasn't sure how this visit would turn out.

'I hope so too. We've got so much to talk about; a lot of catching up.'

They hugged awkwardly before Hélène grabbed Nicole's case, insisting on taking it in for her.

'I'll take you straight up to your room so you can settle in. Mother's having her nap so I thought we could meet up for tea later. Till then you might like to explore the garden or go for a walk.'

They were ascending the ornate staircase and through the landing window Nicole caught a glimpse of the garden and beyond the sea sparkled in the distance.

'I'd love to. Is there a cliff path?'

'Yes, it follows right round towards St Peter Port to the left and Portelet Harbour to the right. It takes several hours to follow it all. Personally, I enjoy walking towards Portelet where it's more woody.'

Good, I'll be able to go for a long walk if I need to escape!

They were now faced with numerous panelled oak doors leading off the landing in different directions. The green painted walls were adorned with what appeared to be local landscapes. Faded Indian runners stretched along the wooden floor, softening their footsteps.

'I could get lost here,' Nicole remarked.

'As a little girl I was always getting lost,' Hélène chuckled. 'In the end my mother tied a little bell around my wrist so that she could find me. Like a miniature cow-bell.'

Nicole grinned. 'Sounds fun! Have you still got it in case I need it?'

Hélène laughed.

'I'm sure you have a better sense of direction than I had at four! Not many of the rooms are in use now, with just the two of us. We have a lady who comes in a couple of times a week to "do". Otherwise it's down to me.' Hélène pulled a face and Nicole nodded in sympathy.

'So, here we are. This is the room we've kept in reasonable order for guests, though to be honest I can't remember the last time we had anyone stay. Hope you find it comfortable.'

Hélène opened a door at the end of a corridor and Nicole stepped into a pretty, though somewhat shabby, room big enough for a family of four. The centrepiece was a half-tester mahogany bed, adorned with a floral bedspread and valance. The walls were covered in matching wallpaper and the two bay windows were hung with velvet curtains which had definitely seen better days. A pale Chinese rug lay spread at the foot of the bed.

'Oh, this is lovely, thank you. And it's so *big!*' She spread her arms out and spun round.

Hélène smiled, looking pleased.

Nicole stepped across to a window and gasped.

'Hey, this view is awesome! I can see why someone wanted to build a house here. Although something smaller would have been just as good,' she turned and grinned at

Hélène, before adding, 'I think I could just sit here and look at the view all day.'

They stood together, gazing at the lovely garden surrounded by a low height hedge to avoid blocking out the view. A gate at the far end led onto the cliff path. Beyond this the sea stretched out as far as the eye could see; Nicole made out the outline of an island on the horizon.

'That must be Jersey,' she turned towards Hélène.

'Yes, it is. Whenever I visited my parents I used to go for a walk on the cliff and look out to sea and think of you growing up there.' Hélène sounded wistful and Nicole touched her arm.

'And now here I am. In your home, sharing that amazing view.'

'Yes, strange isn't it? I never gave up hope but- '

'I know. If Tom hadn't...hadn't betrayed me, I might never have tried to find you.'

They remained silent, lost in their own thoughts.

Hélène was first to break the reverie. Clearing her throat, she said 'I'll leave you to unpack and freshen up. Fortunately, while my parents still had a thriving business, they added several en-suite bathrooms. Yours is through here,' pointing to a door. 'If you'd like to go for a walk the door to the garden's at the rear of the hall. I'll be in the kitchen, on the right before the back door. Shall we have tea in an hour?'

Nicole nodded and watched Hélène leave. It felt good to have some space for herself and she quickly unpacked. A brief look at the bathroom allayed her fears about ancient plumbing. Although it bore the hallmarks of the dreaded 70s taste - avocado suite and psychedelic tiles - it did boast a modern shower over the bath.

She found her way to the back door and stepped out into the warm summer's day. The garden really was lovely, she thought, admiring rose bushes heavy with their scented blooms, hollyhocks, alliums with giant heads, oriental

71

poppies and bright sunflowers. Sheltered by the hedges stood fruit trees, their out-spread branches bearing, as yet, little fruit. Probably plums and apples she guessed. An air of neglect hung over the garden, as if no-one had been out to dead-head flowers or weed the beds for some time. Its beauty still shone through and Nicole admired the granite paved terrace on which rested old wrought iron furniture. *Mm, nice place to sit in the evenings with a glass of chilled white wine!*

Wandering down towards the gate, she turned round to look at the house and gasped. The rear façade was nothing like the gothic front. Although she could see the round towers at each end – you could hardly miss them! – the rear of the house was traditional early Victorian, with large bow windows on each floor and French windows leading onto the terrace. The massive granite walls were almost hidden behind what looked to be a wisteria, although the flowers had now died away. Nicole could imagine it looked stunning in spring. The back of the house was definitely a big improvement on the front, she thought. In her mind, the small front windows created a forbidding aspect. Perhaps it had been intentional, to put off visitors. The idea amused her.

She turned round and headed for the cliff path. A slight breeze caught her hair as she struck out to the right. After a few yards she came across a bunker and old gun emplacement. A relic of the German Occupation in the 1940s, according to a nearby sign. Nicole had grown up with the stories of the Occupation and the impact it had had on the islanders. Jersey also bore the imprint of the Jack Boot in the form of bunkers, gun emplacements and underground tunnels to match those of Guernsey. She decided to ask Eve what she remembered from those traumatic times, if the opportunity arose.

Glancing at her watch she saw it was time to turn back but before doing so, took a last long look along the cliff, her eyes following the contours encircling small bays and outcrops of rock. Another quick glance towards Jersey, hazy on the horizon, and she began retracing her steps towards La Folie. Her grandmother would be ready to meet her and she mentally squared her shoulders in readiness.

As Nicole entered the kitchen Hélène was setting out plates of cake, cups and saucers on the old trolley. She turned round and smiled.

'Good timing. Mother's in her sitting-room and I'm just making the tea. Would you like to go in and join her while I finish up here? It's the room opposite, if you remember.'

Nicole nodded but, before she left, glanced quickly around the enormous kitchen. It looked as if designed for the use of several domestic staff, with old-fashioned units around the walls, a deep butler's sink under the window and a blackened range on which the kettle whistled its completion of duty. Two heavily marked pine tables sat in the middle of the room, accompanied by a number of pine chairs with rush seats. Nicole stepped across the hall to the room she'd entered what seemed a lifetime ago, but was in fact only two weeks.

Eve sat wrapped up in blankets in her wheelchair by what Nicole now recognised as one of the French windows into the garden. The curtains had been closed on her last visit. The old lady must feel the cold even on a warm day, she thought, moving towards her. Unsure whether to venture a kiss or shake her hand she was hesitating when Eve spoke.

'You can give me a kiss on the cheek. As you're family.' Her voice was weaker than last time and as Nicole bent to obey she noticed that her skin looked grey and the hazel eyes had lost their brightness.

'How are you, Mrs Ferbrache? Have you been unwell?' It felt like kissing tissue paper.

'Just a bit of a cold. Nothing to bother about.' A fit of coughing belied her words, leaving her struggling to breathe.

'Would you like some water?' Nicole asked, concerned.

With an effort Eve replied, 'No, I'm all right now, thank you. And do you think you could stop calling me "Mrs Ferbrache"? Sounds so formal from my only grandchild!' Eve peered at Nicole hovering over her.

Nicole felt surprised but realised Eve was right.

'Would you like me to call you Grandmother? I could as both my...other grandmothers are dead. Won't be upsetting anyone!' She smiled at Eve.

'Thank you. I'd never expected to be called that, not knowing –'

'Tea's ready, Mother. Sorry I took so long.' Hélène pushed open the door with the trolley. Nicole went to help.

'I thought I heard you coughing, Mother, so I've brought your cough mixture.'

'Thank you, just a spoonful.'

Nicole said, 'I'll pour it for you, Grandmother,' before taking the medicine and spoon to Eve.

Hélène looked shocked.

Eve must have seen her daughter's expression and explained how it had come about.

'Yes, of course. After all, it's what you are.' She poured the tea.

As Nicole sipped her drink she felt as if they'd all reached a new stage in their relationship. Eve had now laid claim to her as her granddaughter. It had felt odd saying "grandmother" again. The last time was when she'd visited her paternal grandmother and she'd never expected to say it again. It felt oddly unsettling.

The conversation over tea kept to the safe topics of the weather and current affairs. Nicole sensed that there was a truce between Hélène and Eve, who appeared subdued.

The grey tinge of her face was slightly improved by tea and chocolate cake.

Hélène broke into her thoughts.

'The doctor's due shortly. He usually likes a cup of tea first and then you and I will have to leave while he examines Mother. I'll go and make a fresh pot.' She hesitated and said, 'I don't know how to introduce you, Nicole. I wouldn't want to embarrass you by saying you're my daughter if you'd rather I didn't.'

'No problem. You can say that.'

Hélène nodded and left.

Nicole leant toward Eve, her forehead creased with concern.

'What's really the matter, Grandmother? Doctors don't call round for a cold.'

'No, you're quite right. I *do* have a cold but it's my heart that everyone makes a fuss about. I keep telling them that at eighty five my heart's bound to have its off days.' For a moment her eyes had a bit of a twinkle as she added, 'But I think the doctor comes round for the chocolate cake, not me!'

Nicole smiled at Eve, patting her hand.

'Is your heart the reason you're in a wheelchair?'

'That and my arthritis. On a good day I can still get about downstairs with my frame. But the good days have been less frequent of late.' She sighed before attempting a smile.

Before Nicole could reply the door opened and Hélène entered, followed by a tall, slim man in his late thirties, carrying the ubiquitous medical bag. As he glanced in her direction their eyes met. *He's gorgeous!* Nicole held his gaze while she felt the breath stop in her lungs and her heart race against her ribs. What on earth...!

chapter 14

'Here we are, Doctor. I'd like you to meet my...daughter, Nicole.

Looking surprised, the gorgeous man strode across to Nicole, reaching out his hand. As their fingers touched, Nicole felt something akin to an electric charge run through her body and she couldn't let go. Finally, after what seemed minutes but was only seconds, he released her hand.

'Hi, Ben Tostevin. I've the honour of looking after this lovely lady.' He smiled at Eve.

'Hi, Doctor. Nice to meet you.' She still felt dazed by what had happened. The only time she'd felt anything remotely similar was when she'd first met Tom. But that had been nothing compared to...

'Please call me Ben. After all, you're not my patient.' He smiled warmly and Nicole wondered if he could have felt the same reaction. Had it been the proverbial *coup de foudre* for both of them?

Ben, meanwhile, went across to sit on the other side of Eve, asking her how she was.

'I'm not too bad, Doctor. Just a bit of a cold.'

'Mm, well I'll take a good look at you after I've had some tea.' His eyes crinkled up as he smiled at Eve.

Hélène poured more tea and passed around the chocolate cake. There was a momentary silence as tea was sipped and thoughts gathered. Nicole tried not to stare at Ben, drinking in his grey eyes, strong jaw and short brown hair as she peeped over her tea cup. She felt a crazy desire to kiss his firm mouth.

Hélène put down her cup and faced Ben. 'I…I had Nicole after a relationship ended so offered her up for adoption. It seemed the best choice at the time.' Smiling at Nicole she continued, 'Fortunately for me, she tracked me down and she's staying for a few days while we get to know each other better.'

Ben looked at the three women before replying. 'Well, I'm pleased for you, Hélène. And, of course, for you too Mrs Ferbrache.'

'Yes, it was quite a surprise, Doctor. But a nice one,' Eve replied, looking at Nicole, who squirmed in her chair, feeling uncomfortable with three pairs of eyes on her.

Hélène suggested that she and Nicole should leave and Nicole was only too pleased to agree, helping to load up the trolley. While piling up the plates by the sink – no such thing as a dishwasher installed here – she said, as casually as she could, 'The doctor seems nice. Has he been treating Grandmother long?'

Hélène, pulling on rubber gloves, replied, 'Yes, he is. I think all his patients adore him. And he's been very good with Mother over the past five years, taking over when the old one retired. He was the first doctor to spot that Mother's heart wasn't too good.'

Nicole was drying a tea cup and put it down carefully on the side before saying, 'I guess being a GP keeps him pretty busy. I don't suppose his family would see much of him.'

'Actually, I don't think he's married. Probably too busy to meet someone,' she said lightly.

Nicole murmured a neutral 'I see,' while continuing to dry a plate within an inch of its life.

★★★

Meanwhile, Ben was finishing his examination of Eve. He looked serious as he packed away his stethoscope.

'Your heart is worse than when I last saw you, Mrs Ferbrache. I do wish you'd reconsider having that operation I recommended. It could give you a new lease of life.'

Eve, buttoning up her cardigan, looked up at him, seeing the genuine concern in his eyes. She sighed. 'I'm sorry, I know you must think I'm a foolish old woman, and you're probably right. But I don't want my body cut open and plastic bits inserted into my heart. You told me that as long as I avoided infections and exerting myself then I could be good for a few more years yet. I'll take my chance.'

'All right. But what about this granddaughter of yours? Isn't she a good enough reason to want to be more active? To live longer?'

That hurt. But Eve smiled to hide what she really felt. 'Well, she might be, but today is only the second time I've met her. She might decide she doesn't much like us and return to England. I didn't even know of her existence until two weeks ago.'

Ben's eyebrows shot up. 'What! You mean Hélène never told you she'd had a child?'

'No, she's good at keeping secrets.' *And she's not the only one*, Eve fidgeted in her chair. *Am I going to have to come clean now as well?* She sighed inwardly. 'She only told me after Nicole traced her through the Adoption Agency in Jersey.'

Ben continued re-packing his bag, looking thoughtful.

'It seems odd that Nicole has only just wanted to find her mother. She must be in her thirties.'

'She's thirty-five. Apparently she's recently separated from her husband and decided to try and find her natural mother. Wanted to trace her roots. That's what she told Hélène.'

Ben seemed to be absorbing this.

'Well, Doctor, are you going to give me another prescription or aren't you?'

He'd unwittingly packed away his prescription pad and hastily recovered it.

'Sorry. Here you are,' he handed Eve a scribbled prescription. 'That should help but I'd still like you to think about that operation. At this stage, drugs can only do so much.' He fixed her with an almost fierce stare.

Eve thanked him and said she'd think about it.

★★★

Hélène came out of the kitchen and, seeing Ben accompanied him to the front door.

'How's my mother, Doctor? And I want the truth, please.'

'She's very poorly. Even this infection is weakening her heart but she still refuses to have the op. Perhaps you can talk some sense into her.'

'I'll try, but if she still refuses to consider it, how... long before...?'

Ben frowned. 'A year at the most and could be a lot less. I don't understand why she's being so stubborn. It's as if she's afraid of going into hospital.'

'She *is* afraid. Her husband – my father - went in for what should have been a routine op and never came out.' Hélène choked back a tear at the awful memory. She and her mother had arrived at the Princess Elizabeth Hospital a few hours after her father's operation, bearing his favourite flowers from the garden. On arrival they had been ushered into a small room and told that Reg had suffered a cardiac arrest only moments before. Eve had gone white with shock and Hélène had burst into tears.

Even though it had happened seven years ago, Hélène was still affected by what had happened. She took a calming breath and was opening the front door when Nicole came into the hall. She was on her way to join them when Ben said goodbye to Hélène, gave Nicole a nod, and left.

chapter 15

Nicole felt puzzled by Ben. She had sensed a strong connection between them, the intensity of his gaze and the warmth of his protracted hand shake had said so much. She'd been convinced that he would at least have said goodbye properly. Oh, well, she must have got her wires crossed, she thought, returning to Eve's sitting room. Seeing her grandmother looking so small and frail put things into proportion and she pushed Ben to the back of her mind.

Eve looked up from staring at her hands and smiled.

'Can I get you anything, Grandmother?'

'No, thank you. I think I'll just have a little nap.' The door opened. 'Ah, there you are. I was telling Nicole I'd like a rest. Have you got time to get my prescription before they close?'

'Yes, of course,' Hélène picked up the prescription and asked Nicole if she'd be happy to stay in the house while she popped out, adding, 'Please feel free to explore the house and don't get lost!' she laughed.

Nicole was only too happy to agree and started her tour downstairs. She found room after room bearing the look of neglect and lack of use, the furniture covered in dust sheets.

One room appeared to have been a library with walls covered in what looked like custom-made book shelves, now staring blankly at her. How sad, she thought, walking round, her fingers leaving trails in the dust. The all-pervading air of mustiness seemed to seep into her skin and she gave an involuntary shake.

In another passage Nicole discovered what must have once been a very grand drawing room, complete with an impressive crystal chandelier, marble fireplace and French doors set into the bay window. Scattered scruffy modern sofas and chairs tried, and failed, to create a more homely look. A television stood in an alcove facing a couple of well-used, saggy armchairs. Books and magazines littered coffee tables.

Near the kitchen she found an elegant dining room replete with a ten-seat dining table covered in dust and tarnished silverware. Nicole sighed. All these rooms and only two women living here! And after Eve had been widowed she would have been alone until Hélène had moved in. As she gazed around Nicole could see that the house had a kind of beauty but she didn't sense that there had been laughter and joy in it for a very long time. *It's as if the house is in a coma, just waiting to be brought back to life. It needs people – children.* A thought struck her – it must cost the earth to heat! Frowning, she wondered how Eve and Hélène were managing financially. No wonder Hélène looks so worried...

The sound of the front door opening and closing took Nicole back to the front hall.

'This place is so big for the two of you. I now see what you mean about the cleaning! And I guess the utility bills must be ginormous.'

Hélène rolled her eyes. 'They certainly are. I've tried to persuade Mother to move into a care home but she'll have none of it. Wants to die here, she said.' She looked sad for a moment, as if trying not to think about the inevitable. 'We can only manage the bills thanks to my salary and the rent from my house. If – when – Mother is no longer with us, I'll return to my own home.'

'Do you miss your house?'

'Yes, I do. It's a lot easier to look after for a start. And the small garden is a great sun-trap. And being in Town

81

there's less need to drive, another bonus.' Hélène sighed then, gazing at Nicole she continued, 'It's what us women do, though. Look after our mothers when they're old. Will you look after yours, if she becomes unable to cope?'

Nicole hesitated. 'To be honest, I haven't thought about it. With Mum and Dad looking so fit and well in Spain… I guess I'll have to see how things go. But I have *two* mothers to consider, haven't I?' she grinned.

Hélène waved her hand dismissively.

'Oh, you don't have to consider *me!* You owe me nothing, Nicole. If I ever become incapable of caring for myself I'll be checking into a care home – or the Castel Mental Hospital if more appropriate!'

Becoming brisk, Hélène said that she needed to start preparing dinner and accepted Nicole's offer of help.

When the dinner was ready Hélène went to fetch Eve, wheeling her back into the kitchen.

Nicole thought that Eve looked a little better after her nap but, although she joined in the conversation, she ate little.

The talk was general; it was if they had all mutually agreed to stay away from "personal" topics. For this Nicole was glad. It had been quite a full-on day as the new girl in this little family and she needed to regain her sense of self. After finishing her meal she asked, 'What do people do in the evenings around here? I'd like to go out for an hour or two.'

'Well, the cinema's not far, at The Mallard complex on the way to the airport. The Guernsey Press will tell us what's on,' Hélène got up and fetched the newspaper from a pile on a stool.

Nicole flicked through and saw that one of the options was a rom-com with good reviews.

'I think I'll go and see "Waitress", it doesn't start for forty five minutes so I've got time to help you with the dishes before I go – '

'No, that's all right. You get off. I'll give you a key so that you can come and go as you wish.'

After a quick freshen up, Nicole collected a key and said her goodnights before driving to The Mallard. She would have preferred company but had no real choice considering she had no friends in Guernsey. Yet. And she felt in need of some fun after such an intense day.

The film proved to be only a qualified success. Nicole had laughed but the storyline brought up a few personal issues with similarities to her own story. An unhappy marriage – unwanted pregnancy – thoughts of adoption – gorgeous doctor lover.

It felt like an epiphany for Nicole. The thought of Hélène, in love with a married man, getting pregnant and giving up that baby, just as the girl in the film had once thought of doing, made her determined that *she* would get it right. Love a man who was free to love her and happy to have babies with her. And remain faithful. Not too much to ask then! Her other decision concerned Adrian. Much as she had doubts about him, she realised she needed to try to meet him or she'd always have a nagging regret. She'd ask Hélène tomorrow.

The next morning Hélène and Nicole had breakfast together while Eve had hers in bed. Hélène was worried and it showed. She could feel her forehead crease as she considered what Nicole had asked of her. *I know it's perfectly natural that she should want to meet her father but that means I'll have to contact him and I vowed never to do that...*her thoughts skittered about as she sought to find a way around the problem. *I suppose I could give Nicole his address and let her write to him.* For a moment this seemed the ideal solution until she realised that this was the coward's way out and that poor Nicole would be left waiting to see if Adrian replied and wanted to see her. Her heart sank as she accepted that it had to come from her. She had to prepare Adrian that his – their – daughter was in Guernsey and staying with her at La Folie…

Nicole broke into her thoughts.

'Look, I do realise that this can't be easy for you. If you really are dead against our meeting – '

'No, no!' Hélène shook her head and reached out for Nicole. 'It's not for me to stop you contacting Adrian, he's your father after all. You have a right to meet him if…if you both want to. He knows you were adopted in Jersey so he must know that your turning up was always a possibility.' She took a deep breath and faced Nicole squarely. 'I'll tell him about you and that you're here. Then it's up to him. I just don't want you getting hurt.' She clenched her hands together as she thought about what she would do to him if Adrian refused to see Nicole. He'd been a coward all those years ago, had he changed?

'Thanks. I know it's a risk and I may end up disliking or hating him whatever happens. But I need to try, for my own peace of mind.' Nicole sighed.

Hélène felt her heart tug at the sight of her daughter. Her maternal feelings were slowly re-establishing themselves and she felt lucky to have this second chance at motherhood.

Nicole said she wanted to go out for a walk and enjoy the sunshine and Hélène felt relieved. If talking to Adrian was going to be upsetting, she didn't want Nicole around.

After checking that Eve was all right, Hélène went off to her room to make the phone call that, until a few weeks ago, she had never expected to make.

chapter 16

'Adrian Bourgaize speaking.'

'It's me, Hélène.'

For a moment Adrian thought he must have misheard. Hélène? After all these years? Surely not! She'd been adamant she never wanted to speak to him again. And she hadn't – until now.

'Adrian? Are you there?'

'Yes, yes I am. I was just surprised to hear your voice after…How are you?' He pulled himself together.

'Fine, thanks. I'm living with Mother now. She's very frail and I felt I had to…'

'Of course. I'm sorry. It must be difficult for you. I read about your father, perhaps I should have written –'

'No, I didn't expect you to. And…and I'm sorry about Carol. Must have been hard for you.' He heard the tightness in her voice.

'Yes, it was. But the…children and our friends rallied round. And being Head kept me pretty well occupied.' He had to take a deep breath. 'You know I've just retired?'

'I'd heard. I'm still working as I have to support us both, with Mother having no real income. I'll have to carry on until she…'

Adrian heard the bitterness in her voice and his feelings of guilt rushed up from the deep place he'd buried them for so long.

'Oh, Hélène, I'm so sorry. If there's anything I can do to help?'

'There is, actually. *Our* daughter is here and wants to meet you.' The words were spat out.

'Our daughter! Oh my God!' Adrian gripped the phone tighter to stop it sliding out of his hand. 'How…how long have you known her?'

'She only contacted me a few weeks ago. It was a bit of a shock as you can imagine. But I'd always hoped that she'd try. '

'I can understand that. I didn't even know you'd had a girl.' He had another daughter! He did a quick calculation – she must be thirty-five – could be a mother, like Karen.

'What's her name? Is she married?'

'Nicole, and she recently separated from her husband. Apparently that's why she set out to find me. To…to understand herself better.'

'I see. And she wants to meet me too.' He wasn't sure how he felt about that. Nicole had every right to feel badly about him but surely she wouldn't want to meet him just to say that? Was this a chance to redeem himself in her eyes? And even Hélène's? He thought quickly.

'I would like to meet her. How long's she staying with you?'

'I don't know. But I'm sure she'd prefer to meet sooner rather than later.'

'Yes, of course. Could you please ring me with a time that suits Nicole? I have few commitments these days.' Adrian visualised his near-empty calendar and sighed.

'Will do. Bye Adrian.' The phone went dead.

Adrian wondered if the proverbial can of worms was now about to be opened. And if he would survive.

★★★

Nicole was glad to be out of the house with the chance to stretch her legs. The coastal path zig-zagged around the imposing cliffs and she had to watch her step. Striking out westwards again, she enjoyed the sensation as her skin met the gentle, crisp warm breeze. Heather and gorse provided a colourful contrast to the grass and she found herself relaxing. So much had happened in the past twenty-four hours that she felt emotionally drained. And confused. It felt as if she'd stepped into someone else's skin and was living their life, not hers. Like that girl in the film, she thought, she was only acting, but it *seemed* real. Her own life appeared to have vanished into another dimension since she'd started this journey to find her mother – and herself. Nicole decided to call it PM, Post Mother and AM, Ante Mother as she sucked on a blade of grass. Giggling, she felt better than she had since her arrival.

Okay, girl, you started this and you've got to see it through. You've torpedoed other people's lives now. Got to give them a chance to recover. Particularly Hélène. The thought brought her up sharp. She was beginning to feel fond of her "mother", feeling she'd been badly treated by life. Nicole couldn't begin to imagine what it must have been like to give up both the man you loved and a new-born baby. *Perhaps I can make it up to her?* The thought that Hélène was, on Nicole's behalf, having to speak to the man she'd loved so many years ago prompted her to check her watch and decide that she'd better go back. She wasn't sure who would need consoling the most – herself or Hélène

★★★

Hélène was in the kitchen, chopping up vegetables as if her life depended on it.

'Hi. Did you get through to…Adrian?'

Hélène looked up and forced a smile.

'Yes, I did. And he's agreed to meet you. He's suggested I phone him with a suitable time. When would you like to go? He's free anytime.'

'Tomorrow morning would be great, thanks. How…how was it for you? Talking to him?'

'A bit difficult. After more than thirty-five years, it was bound to be.' She put down the knife and rubbed her temples. Her head had ached since the phone call and she wondered if she should take a painkiller. Gazing at Nicole's concerned face she added, 'But we ...we've broken the ice now. And you two can meet without my being involved. I'm glad he wants to see you. Should help you...move on.' Her voice caught on a sob and Nicole stepped round the table and hugged her. They clung together while Hélène sought to calm herself. 'Isn't it supposed to be the mother comforting the child?' she asked, shakily.

'Not always. It depends. What about you and Grandmother?'

Hélène released herself gently and looking at her daughter, replied, 'We've never been good at hugging. I don't think she was hugged much as a child, not from what I saw of her mother, who wasn't at all maternal. My father was much more loving, always happy to cuddle me.' She bit her lips before straightening up, telling herself not to burden Nicole with her own grief. She went off to make the phone call and was back moments later to say she'd arranged for them to meet for coffee in St Peter Port the next morning.

'I'll lend you my Perry's guide, absolutely essential to finding your way around.' She rooted around in a drawer and passed it to Nicole.

'Right, lunch is ready. I'll go and fetch Mother if you could lay the table, please.'

Moments later she wheeled in a very pale Eve who managed a small smile as she nodded to Nicole. After the usual pleasantries were exchanged the three women sat in silence as they ate. Hélène kept glancing at Eve, feeling worried about her, but when she suggested that Eve might prefer to go back to bed, Eve snapped back that she was fine and not to fuss.

'Grandmother, would you like me to come and read to you after lunch? Or just chat? I'd love to know what it was like here during the Occupation if you felt up to talking.'

'I'm happy to talk for a little while, but I wasn't here during the Occupation. I was evacuated with my younger sister to England.'

'Oh, I see. Well, I'm sure you've still got some interesting stories to tell.'

Hélène looked on in amazement. Her mother had never offered to talk to *her* about the war! But, thinking back, perhaps she'd never asked. She'd always felt that her mother hadn't wanted to talk about it. She had to agree with Nicole, Eve probably had a few old tales stored away. She set to washing the dishes as Nicole wheeled Eve back to her room. Hélène felt a slight pang of jealousy at the thought that Eve seemed more at ease with Nicole than with herself. Perhaps it was just a generational thing, she consoled herself.

★★★

Nicole settled Eve by the window, but then asked her if she'd rather sit outside as it was a beautiful hot day.

'Perhaps I could try for just a little while. I seem to feel cold all the time – '

'I'll bring you straight back, don't worry. The fresh air might perk you up.' She pushed open the French windows and Eve sniffed the air in approval. The wheelchair rolled out easily onto the terrace and Nicole made sure she was not facing the bright sun.

'Comfortable? I can get you more rugs, cushions

'No, I'm fine, thank you.' Eve inhaled deeply as she looked around her beloved garden. 'It needs a lot of work, doesn't it? I haven't been able to garden for a couple of years. And we can't afford professional help.' She sighed. She knew she was being pig-headed by insisting she wouldn't move to a care home, but she so loved her garden, the view of the sea and the little independence left to her. *Not that I've seen the best of the view for a while now. Perhaps I should give in to Hélène and let her sell...*

Nicole broke into her thoughts. 'Would you like me to pick some roses for you? Some are overblown and won't last much longer, anyway. You can enjoy their perfume.'

'That would be lovely, thank you. You'll find some secateurs on the table in my room.'

She watched Nicole pick three beautiful, big pink roses and bring them to her. Eve held them carefully as she breathed in their intoxicating scent.

'Oh, thank you, my dear. Just what I needed.' As Nicole sat down on a chair, Eve continued, 'Now, you'd like to know a bit about what happened during the war?'

'Only if it doesn't tire or upset you.'

Eve shook her head. 'It wasn't as bad for me as it was for those who stayed here. At least I didn't have to live under the thumb of German soldiers like so many of my friends and family.' Sadness tugged at her heart as the memories surfaced. 'My brother was killed fighting for Britain like so many of the young Guernsey lads. My parents never really got over his death.' She looked up at Nicole, adding, 'He was supposed to carry on with their farm and produce heirs, and look after them in their old age.' Eve laughed bitterly. 'When my little sister and I returned after the war my parents barely spoke to us. Lottie, who was seventeen by then, couldn't stand it and went back to England. She later married a man she met there and never returned. Even when I married Reg and had Hélène my parents virtually ignored me.'

Eve looked out over her garden and smiled. 'They were the losers, though. Reg and I bought this house and land at a rock-bottom price and became very successful growers. Made more money than my parents ever made on the farm. I don't think they ever forgave us for that.'

Eve found herself retreating into thoughts of the past, to a time of much laughter…and tears.

chapter 17

Finding her way into St Peter Port had been easy; it was so well sign-posted that Nicole had not needed to refer to Perrys. However, having passed so many lanes and roads branching off the main road to St Martins she could see how useful it would be. Assuming she was to stay awhile.

Approaching St Peter Port down the steep Le Val de Terres, Nicole only partly registered the view over the harbour and out towards the neighbouring islands of Herm and Sark. Her mind was filled with so many conflicting thoughts about the meeting with Adrian, that she even contemplated chickening out. So sure she would hate him on sight it didn't seem worth the bother. Only the reminder that he was her father, holding the final piece of the jigsaw that was her DNA, persuaded her to see it through.

Years ago she had sailed with friends from Jersey and remembered the car park at the Albert Pier, bordering the visitor's marina. From there it was a short walk to the Dix Neuf Brasserie where she was due to meet Adrian. She vaguely recalled it was one of the watering holes on Susie's hen weekend.

As she walked past the Town church her heart was beating fast and she felt hot and sticky. After stopping for a moment to calm her breathing, she headed for the entrance. Hélène had told her to look out for a tall man, with thick greying hair, brown eyes and wearing a blue short-sleeved shirt.

As her gaze swept over the room a man who could only be Adrian stood up and advanced towards her.

'Nicole?'

'Yes. Hello, er, Adrian.' Her heart was still beating too fast for comfort but, as Adrian shook her hand, she guessed, from his own clammy hand, that he was just as nervous. He smiled tentatively before ushering her towards his table and pulling out a chair.

She had a moment to study him before a waitress came to take their order for two café lattes. *He looks younger than I'd expected. And his face looks a bit familiar...*

'You've got your mother's eyes. I would have known you even without Hélène's description.' One of Adrian's eyes twitched and Nicole found herself gazing at it. *He's not finding this any easier than I am. Good!* He continued. 'It was quite a shock talking to Hélène yesterday. After all this time...'

'It's been strange for me too. I only met Hélène and her mother a couple of weeks ago and now...now you. I'm not sure where we start.'

The waitress arrived with their coffees and as she left Adrian said, 'I owe you both an apology and an explanation, Nicole. As I do your mother.' The twitch speeded up.

Nicole sipped her coffee as she waited for him to continue. She didn't see why she should make it easy for him.

'I realise how selfish and cowardly I was when...when Hélène told me she was pregnant. I could only think about myself and my career.' He gazed at his coffee, as if unable to look at her. Slowly he raised his eyes and she saw the genuine sorrow reflected there. Mm, good.

'I couldn't face the resulting scandal if I'd left my wife and lived with Hélène. If I could have got a divorce it would've been different, I assure you.'

His eyes locked onto Nicole's, and she wondered if he saw the challenge within them. Her challenge to be honest at last.

'I loved your mother with all my heart. Carol and I...had grown apart even before I met Hélène and I no longer loved her.' He sighed. 'She said she still loved me but behaved as if she didn't. She...she did find out about Hélène, but not about you.'

'Your...your wife must have realised that you didn't love her anymore. Didn't she want to separate? To start a new life for herself?'

He shook his head.

'No, she wouldn't consider it. When I brought up the idea of living apart she became very angry; hating to be seen as a failure. And, to be honest, so did I. But I would have gladly separated if she'd consented. She threatened to make it difficult for me if I left her and I knew she could.' He sipped his coffee. 'Her father was a Deputy involved with the Education Department and could have made it impossible for me to work here as a teacher.'

He looked down at his hands cradling the coffee before lifting his eyes to face her. She kept her gaze impassive, but her emotions churned away inside. He was still making excuses...

'I've made a mess of things and I can only say how sorry I am. I'd understand if you wanted nothing more to do with me.'

Nicole wasn't sure what she felt. On the one hand, she thought that to his credit, Adrian had owned up to his failings but on the other he'd caused heartbreak to Hélène who'd lost both him and her only child. Although she'd expected to hate him, it hadn't worked out that way. He was an ordinary guy who had behaved badly, but he was no monster. Didn't stop her feeling angry with him though...

'I don't think I can spend time with you, getting to know each other better, unless you make some sort of amends to Hélène.' Keeping her eyes locked onto his – one still twitching – she asked, 'Do you still love her?'

His eyebrows rose in surprise.

'I...I don't know. Perhaps. It's been so long, we'll both have changed... But I have thought about her a lot and wished that we could be...friends again.'

'So, how about you ask her to meet up with you and take it from there? Apologise properly.' *Huh, here's me acting like a Relate counsellor and I can't even sort out my own marriage problems.* Ironic, she knew, but she really wanted to help Hélène, if she could. She was amazed at her temerity. But it seemed to have the right effect as Adrian agreed.

He gave her a hesitant smile.

'If I make my peace with your mother, will you let me see you again?'

'Possibly. I'll think about it. And you can't take too long to kiss and make up as I might decide to head back to England. Or wherever.'

They stood up, shook hands and said their goodbyes. Nicole genuinely wasn't sure if she wanted to see Adrian again and as she walked back to her car she wondered if Hélène would want to. *Mm, wonder if I've gone too far?*

★★★

Hélène was making a cup of tea as Nicole entered the kitchen. She looked up, searching for clues in Nicole's face. But she was giving nothing away.

'How did it go?'

'Okay, I guess. We didn't talk for long but I did give him a chance to...well, make amends. But it does involve you so – '

'Me? Why should your getting to know Adrian involve me?' Hélène gripped the mug tightly as Nicole repeated what she had said to Adrian. Anger started to burn slowly through her and her face must have registered her feelings as Nicole continued, 'Look, I'm sorry if I've been out of line here. If you don't want to see Adrian then please just say no. I was just trying to help.'

Hélène fought hard to keep her temper, she knew Nicole thought she was helping but...

'I don't want you interfering between us. I found it hard enough to talk to the man and have no intention of seeing him. None at all.'

Nicole looked shocked. 'Oh, I'm sorry, the last thing I wanted was to upset you. Let's forget it. It means I can't see him again as I made it conditional on his apologising to you, but...' She shrugged and left the kitchen, letting the door slam shut.

Hélène was left feeling drained and slumped down on her chair. *Nicole shouldn't have made that deal with Adrian without checking with me first. And now she's upset with me and she's only just arrived!* She held her head in her hands wondering if they could work it out or if Nicole would be booking a flight home. What a mess!

★★★

Nicole, feeling upset by Hélène's reaction, and not trusting herself to add further flames to the fire, dashed upstairs to grab her bikini and a towel before driving off. The beach beckoned.

She steered the car west until she hit the coast road and followed it around, eventually spotting a stretch of golden sand encircling a large bay. According to her Perrys it was Vazon Bay and looked wonderful. Nicole pulled onto the stony parking area, grabbed her bag and negotiated the steps almost hidden in the granite sea wall. Massed bodies stretched out on the fine sand made it hard to see a free spot, but after walking along the beach she discovered a small patch sheltered by the wall.

As she stretched out she replayed what had happened between her and Hélène. The sun's warmth and the sound of softly lapping waves on the shore helped her to calm down and be more objective. *Mm, Hélène does have a point, I guess. I presumed she'd want to see Adrian even though she'd made it clear she was still angry with him. I should have checked with her first. Oh, I'm an idiot! I've scuppered my chance of seeing Adrian again even though I'm not that bothered at the moment. But if they were to make up then maybe I'd want to get to know him.* The unsettling thoughts continued to tumble around in her head until, at last, the heat and sea air lulled her into a welcome doze.

Languidly stretching her limbs as consciousness returned, she realised she was hungry and walked up to the kiosk for a sandwich and coffee. Refreshed, she decided on a quick swim and ran down to the sea. Being low tide it was quite a dash to the water's edge, where she found laughing groups of children and adults either paddling or splashing about. The water struck particularly cold after lying in the sun and she had to force herself to go in deeper before breaking into a strong crawl. After an invigorating swim she emerged feeling ready to move on. Sidestepping children building sandcastles and the recumbent bodies slowly turning red in the sun, Nicole made her way up the beach to change.

Back in the car she considered what to do. Her mind was still full of the events of the past two days and she didn't want to return to La Folie. Getting out the map she decided to circumnavigate the coast before going home. *That should give me time to sort myself out!* As she drove north the bays and beaches she passed reminded her of those in Jersey, a bittersweet reflection, making her feel homesick. Vazon Bay itself she'd thought very like Jersey's St Ouens.

As a daughter of both islands Nicole felt torn with her loyalty. Added to which she had spent all her adult life in England. She smiled at the thought of her mixed- up background while noting the similarities as well as the differences between the islands. Jersey was the larger, at nine miles by five, with Guernsey a modest seven miles by five. The crapauds of Jersey naturally considered it to be the more bustling and sophisticated of the two. But Nicole conceded that, from what she'd seen, Guernsey was beautiful, with its own unique charm. Spying another sandy bay she pulled in briefly to admire it from her car. Checking her map she saw it was Cobo Bay and reminded her of Jersey's Anne Port, the sandy beach strewn with extensive rocks near the sea-shore.

As her gaze swept around the beach and back towards the car park, she thought she saw Ben sitting in a car further along. While she debated whether or not to approach him, the engine was started and the car driven past her. It was Ben. Her stomach flipped at the memory of their first – and only – meeting. She could recall the tingling sensation as their hands touched as if it had just happened. Had it been her own too-vivid imagination or had something special occurred between them? Feeling she must be losing the plot, she started the car and continued north.

Her drive continued at the sedate speed limit of 35mph enabling her to drink in the stunning views as she mulled over what she'd say to Hélène on her return. By the time she hit the road leading from the bustling St Sampson's Harbour into St Peter Port, she had decided that she had to apologise. Then it would be up to Hélène.

Driving slowly as the traffic built up, Nicole could see the islands of Herm and Sark basking in the sun. They seemed to be beckoning her as she sat in a line of barely moving vehicles. She'd been to Sark as a girl and had loved cycling the dusty lanes of the car-free island. But she'd never visited the even tinier island of Herm and vowed to go before leaving Guernsey. Which might be soon if she and Hélène didn't make up.

Driving past St Peter Port's main marina, the QEII, Nicole took in the racy yachts and gin palaces bobbing gently at their moorings. The hands on the nearby clock tower pointed to five o'clock as she negotiated the lanes of traffic towards the Le Val de Terres.

Half an hour later Nicole pulled up at La Folie. *Right, abject apology coming up.* Heading off to the kitchen, she found it empty so put the kettle on to make a much needed cup of tea. She had just taken her first sip when Hélène walked in, looking red-eyed.

'Thought I heard your car. Look, Nicole I – '

'I was completely in the wrong. You had every right to be annoyed with me for assuming you'd be happy to see Adrian. I should have checked with you first. I am so, so sorry.' Nicole bit her lips as she waited for her mother's reaction.

Hélène's face brightened. 'Why, thank you. That's what I felt and why I was upset. I didn't want you making such a big decision for me. Shall we call a truce?' She reached out for a hug and Nicole moved into her arms.

Her mother then made herself a cup of tea and sat down at the table.

'So, where does this leave us with regard to Adrian? Do you still mean not to see him again if he and I don't meet?'

Nicole frowned. It was an impasse.

'I honestly don't know. I've been thinking about it while driving around and can't see an easy solution. I respect your feelings and don't want to upset you further, which could happen if I formed a relationship with him. But at the moment I'm not sure if I actually want that. He hasn't behaved very well has he?' She looked across at Hélène, who was staring into her tea as if it held the answer.

'The thing is, I still feel Adrian owes you big time, and I got the impression that he still has feelings for you. He admitted that he's often thought about you over the years and seems to regret what happened.' Nicole took a sip of tea before adding, 'I think he's been unhappy for years.' Nicole wondered if she'd blown it.

98

Hélène looked up, smiling half-heartedly.

'You don't give up, do you? I think you've inherited the family stubbornness!' She drank her tea before adding, 'Well, perhaps I could meet him. Just the once, mind. So that he can show me how truly sorry he really is. Would that satisfy you?'

Nicole nodded. 'Thanks. Let's see how it goes and I might then reconsider seeing him again myself.'

Chapter 18

Eve joined them for supper that evening and Nicole asked her if she was well enough for a chat afterwards.

'I'd like that. You're a good listener and my cough's much better,' she smiled.

Hélène chipped in, 'I'll clear away. You take Mother to her room while I make a...a phone call.' She looked pointedly at Nicole who grinned. Eve wondered what was going on but thought it better no to ask.

In her sitting room Eve was settled in her usual place by the French window. One door stood open, allowing the warm evening breeze to flow in from the garden, enriched by the scent of roses and honeysuckle. *Oh, what I'd give to walk around my garden again!* She sighed inwardly as Nicole made her comfortable, tucking a rug around her thin frame.

'When we last had a chat you mentioned being evacuated,' Nicole prompted. 'Would you mind telling me more, please?'

Eve's mind was dragged back to that fateful day in June 1940 when she, aged seventeen, and her sister, Lottie, twelve, arrived at the harbour. They lined up with thousands of children and their accompanying school teachers at White Rock, ferried there by buses. She could still hear Lottie's cries, mingling with those of the other young children waiting to board the SS Viking. It had been painful to see them wrenched from their mothers, only the women with babies being allowed to leave. Space and time were at a premium; the Germans were on their way. Eve had not been upset, seeing it as an adventure, a chance to get away from the parents who had never had much time for her. It was agreed that she would work as a volunteer Land Girl, while keeping a close eye on Lottie.

As the memories flooded in, Eve could smell the smoke belching out of the coal-burning ship, mingling with the stench of vomit from the sea-sick passengers. The cries of the children tug at even her love-starved heart. She hugged Lottie close, reassuring her that all would be well.

'I'm sure we'll be back before you know it, Lottie. Our boys will drive that bully Hitler back to where he belongs, you'll see.'

'I want Mummy and Blackie!' Lottie cried, hanging onto Eve in the overcrowded cabin they shared with a dozen others. Eve frowned, knowing that Blackie, Lottie's pet rabbit, was about to become stew. She shushed Lottie with endearments as she rocked her to sleep.

For the island children, accustomed to peace and quiet, the noise and mayhem on board aggravated their fear after being virtually dragged from their mothers' arms.

As Eve reminisced she thought how much worse it would have been if they'd all known that it was to be five years before they could return.

'Are you all right?' Nicole's voice cut across her thoughts.

'Yes, I was just remembering the evacuation. It's all coming back to me...'

She told Nicole about the ship with its precious cargo of more than two thousand children and adults and how it had been a long, difficult crossing to Weymouth.

'We knew we were an easy target for enemy planes with the funnels smoking so much so the Captain zig-zagged about to avoid them. This made the journey a lot longer than normal. When we eventually arrived, hungry and tired, crowds were lined up on the quayside at Weymouth. Most of the little ones were starving, having eaten the meals packed by their mothers soon after we left Guernsey.

'At Weymouth we were put on trains for different parts of the country. Most of the children went to Scotland and the north, considered to be safer. The teachers were meant to set up local schools where needed. I was joining up as a Land Girl and allocated to a farm in Devon. Lottie was to go to a neighbouring family and attend the local school. Our train journey wasn't too long but it was dark when we arrived at Exeter station.'

Oh, how well she remembered that night! As she and Lottie stumbled onto the platform, carrying their small cases and gas masks, a tall, fair-haired young man in an air force uniform strode up to them.

'Are you the Misses Eve and Lottie from Guernsey?'

Eve had stood rooted to the spot. Not only was this young god smiling at her with a smile that went from ear to ear, but he knew who they were!

'Yes that's us. I mean, I'm Eve and this is Lottie. But…but how…?'

The god laughed. 'I was asked to look out for two young ladies carrying cases and gas masks and I believe that's a Guernsey flag on your case, Miss Lottie?'

Lottie nodded. Their father had painted the little flag on her case to "remind her of Guernsey", he'd said.

'Oh, right. And you are…? '

'Sorry, should have introduced myself. I'm Flight Lieutenant Philip Andrews, at your service, ladies.' His execution of a smart salute had the girls dissolving into giggles, with Philip joining in.

Eve regained her composure enough to reply, 'Pleased to meet you Flight Lieutenant. But why are you looking out for *us*?'

'I understand that you, Miss Eve, are joining us as a Land Girl and that Miss Lottie is to stay with one of our tenant farmers. My father owns an estate north of here,' the god waved his arm in what she assumed was a northerly

102

direction. 'I've just arrived home on leave, so it fell to me to escort you. The car's waiting outside.'

Philip smiled broadly and offered an arm to Eve and a hand to Lottie and they marched, that was the only word for it, thought Eve, out of the station. Spotting the gleaming limousine resembling the Governor's car back home, she turned to Philip and asked, 'Is it a big estate then? Your father's?'

'Pretty big. It's been in the family forever. But don't worry, you'll be based on our Home Farm which is quite small, really. And I'll look after you when I'm around.' Eve blushed at his intent gaze and studied her feet.

As the chauffeur went to open the front passenger door for Philip he said he'd rather sit in the back with "the ladies from Guernsey". Which he did. By the time they arrived at their destination Eve had lost her heart.

'Grandmother? Are you tired? If you'd rather I left – '

'Oh, no I'm fine, Nicole. I was just remembering.' She cleared her throat and told Nicole how they were taken to their new homes that night. She didn't mention Philip.

'I was joining three other land girls on the Home Farm and Lottie went to live with Mr and Mrs Jones who leased an adjoining farm. It was hard saying goodbye to each other but I promised I'd get over to see her as often as I could. And I managed to do that on my days off.' Eve paused, remembering the well-trodden path across the fields to the Jones's farm. Lottie had been so pleased to see her at first but, over the months had settled in and made friends with both the Jones's daughter and the children at school. She began to prefer to spend time with them rather than her sister.

At first Eve had felt hurt but gradually accepted that they were growing apart now that she, Eve, was virtually an adult. And there were compensations, she thought, smiling. The few boys her own age who were not conscripted seemed more worldly than the Guernsey lads. And how they liked to flirt! And then there was Philip…

Nicole got up to close the door; the evening air was cooling. The sound brought Eve back to the present.

'What was it like as a Land Girl?' Nicole asked as she sat down again.

'It was hard work, but I was used to that. We had to look after the animals; cows, pigs and chickens, which wasn't too bad. I'd helped with the milking at home after my brother left to join the army, so I ended up being in charge of that. The other girls were town bred, finding it a bit of a struggle and only too pleased to let me take over. We also planted the fruit and vegetables for the family and helped with the harvest.'

'What was the family like?'

'Oh, we didn't see much of them. Sir Michael and Lady Andrews they were, and they had a big house in the middle of the estate. There were several tenant farmers on the estate and Sir Michael employed a manager for Home Farm. He was away in London a lot. A member of the War Cabinet, he was. Lady Andrews often joined him, staying in their town house.' Eve coughed and took a few sips of water. *Oh, that magical night in London! If only…*

Nicole looked astonished. 'Surely two people didn't need a whole farm to provide for them!'

Eve smiled. 'No, of course not. The main part of the house had been commandeered as a convalescent home for wounded soldiers. Sir Michael and Lady Andrews had to move into a wing with the boys.'

'They had sons?'

'Yes, Philip and Richard. Richard was eighteen when I arrived and away on officer training in the army. Philip, well he…was twenty-one and in the Royal Air Force.'

Eve closed her eyes and for a moment had such a vivid feeling of being seventeen and meeting Philip for the first time that she could hardly breathe.

'Grandmother! Are you okay?' Nicole touched Eve's arm and she was brought back with a start.

'Oh, Nicole. Sorry, I...I drifted off. I think I'd like to rest now, if you don't mind.'

'Of course. I'll say good night then.'

Eve settled back in the chair and gave herself over to those bittersweet memories of a time which would be forever burnt into her brain. And heart.

chapter 19

'Well, did you phone him?' Nicole asked Hélène, returning to the kitchen.

'Mm, yes. He wants to meet for lunch tomorrow.' Hélène was reading the Guernsey Press, a glass of wine by her side. She offered Nicole a glass and after accepting, she joined her at the table.

'That's great! I'll be keeping my fingers crossed.' She looked at Hélène, who seemed a little pink in the face.

'Does...does your mother know who my father is?'

Hélène looked sheepish.

'No, I don't think so. Though she guessed he was married.'

'Will you tell her after you've met? Otherwise I don't know what to say if she asks *me*.'

Hélène's mouth twisted.

'I'll have to, then. Whatever happens tomorrow, although you heard what she thinks about married men...'

'Yes, but he isn't married now, is he? I think she'll be more forgiving of him now. That is, if you two were to –'

'Nicole! We haven't even met yet! I'm still hurt and angry over the way he behaved. And the way I feel at the moment there's absolutely no chance of us becoming friends, let alone anything else.' She took a gulp of wine, looking annoyed. 'You're trying to match-make us, aren't you?'

'Not exactly,' Nicole replied, crossing her fingers under the table. 'I'd feel happier if you two could be friends. So I don't feel like the piggy in the middle, that's all.' That bit at least was true, she thought.

Hélène studied her for a minute before saying, gently, 'And what about you? Do you want to be "friends" again with Tom? Or possibly more?'

Nicole sipped her wine as she searched her heart for an answer.

'My instinct is to say yes, I'd like us to be friends but no, I don't think I want to be married to him anymore. We had some great times – brilliant even – but the hurt...' She found herself unable to stop the tears and this time it was Hélène who came round and hugged her.

'It's all right, my dear. Just let it out.'

Nicole allowed the tears to flow. It felt good to be hugged by this woman who had also suffered. *Men, bloody men! Why do we bother with them?* She let herself be wrapped in her mother's arms. Unbidden, Ben's image popped into her head, making her feel even worse.

***

The next morning dawned bright and sunny and Hélène made a special effort with her appearance. Firstly, the clothes had to be right, she thought, searching through her limited wardrobe. She decided on a short-sleeved, pale green silk blouse partnered with a knee length skirt in swirling shades of blues and greens. Slipping on a slim dark green belt, she admired the result in the mirror. *Mm, not bad, these colours always suited me.* She'd washed and blow-dried her hair into a different style, framing her carefully made-up face. Examining her wrinkles and lines, she wished she'd paid more attention to skin care over the years. She would have liked to look more youthful but it was too late. Trying not to think why it suddenly seemed to matter, Hélène slipped on her sandals and ran down to the kitchen.

***

'Wow! You look nice! What a lovely outfit and you've done something with your hair. Suits you.' Nicole smiled.

'Thank you. I thought I'd better make an effort. I've always believed if you look your best you can deal with any situation.'

Nicole nodded, getting up from the table to make Hélène a cup of tea. 'Too right. I always made a particular effort when I was nervous. Especially if I was interviewing a celebrity with an inflated ego,' she laughed.

Hélène sipped her tea and gazed at Nicole. 'I can't imagine you ever being nervous about anyone or anything. You seem so confident and self-assured.'

'Most of the time I am, but I've had to work at it. It was the only way to survive in the media environment.' Nicole thought back to the early days as a journalist and how often she'd nearly ended up in tears after being ignored or criticised. It had taught her that she needed to seem as good as anyone else even if she didn't always feel it. Pulling herself back, she asked, 'So, where are you going for lunch?'

'The Auberge at Jerbourg in St Martins. It's perched on the cliff with fantastic views over the islands. Haven't been there for ages but I believe it's very popular.'

'Well, I'm sure you'll enjoy it. What do you want me to do while you're out?'

'All you need to do is check on Mother after I've left and then get her up for lunch when she's ready. There's plenty of salad ingredients in the fridge. I shouldn't be too long. We're meeting at 12.30 and I expect to be back by 2.30 at the latest. Or even earlier if it goes badly – '

'Hey, I'm sure it'll be fine. And don't worry about rushing back, I've no plans and can happily look after Grandmother for a few hours.'

Hélène nodded and went off to get Eve ready leaving Nicole to clear away. She had time for a quick walk before Hélène left so she went through the garden to the cliff path. This time she turned left towards St Peter Port although she knew she wouldn't get far that morning. Her mind was pre-occupied with thoughts of the coming meeting of her parents and how it would pan out. Acknowledging it was odd that she cared more about her parents becoming close again than she did about her own relationship problems, she pulled absent-mindedly at the heather. Now it wasn't just Tom she had to ponder over but also Ben. Even the thought of him made her heart beat faster and Nicole again wondered what had really happened between them. It had seemed so electric, so mutual…Would she ever understand men? The thought prompted a kick against some loose stones, sending them over the cliff.

Eve was lying on her day bed and stirred as the door opened.

'Hello, Grandmother, hope I didn't wake you?'

Eve pulled herself up. 'No, you didn't. Can you help me into that darned wheelchair please? If you take me through to my sitting room, perhaps we could have lunch on the terrace when it's ready.'

Once she was settled in her usual spot by the window, Nicole went off to prepare lunch. Eve gazed out of the open window breathing in the welcome fresh air. She wondered where her daughter had gone; it was unlike her to go out for lunch. Hélène didn't seem to have many friends but perhaps now, with Nicole here, she felt she could go out. Eve was aware that her insistence on staying in the house had restricted Hélène's life enormously. During term-time the cleaner came in every morning while Hélène was at work, but that was their only support. Eve hadn't wanted nurses or carers popping in at regular intervals, she valued her privacy too much. *Perhaps I've been too selfish. I'll have to talk with Hélène and see what can be changed. She looked so pretty today, as if she were meeting someone special. I wonder if it's anything to do with Nicole's father? Oh, no-one tells me anything!*

For a moment she felt annoyed about not being kept informed but she was brought up short by the knowledge that she'd withheld much more important information from her daughter. And her granddaughter. She was considering this when Nicole came in to wheel her outside for lunch.

★★★

Hélène parked her car at The Auberge, deliberately arriving ten minutes late. Usually a very punctual person, she didn't want to look too keen and be the first one there. She glanced briefly at the view, noting how clear the islands of Herm and Sark were today. It all looked so serene and she wished she felt the same. As she turned and walked towards the terrace she spotted Adrian, standing up and waving. Taking a deep, calming breath she joined him at the table laid for two.

'Hélène! I was worried you weren't coming, that you'd changed your mind. I'm so glad to see you. And you haven't changed a bit!' He smiled tentatively, leaning forward to brush her cheek.

Sitting down, she studied him. His face showed signs of tension, his eyes wary and his lips tightly compressed. But physically he looked in good shape. 'You look well, Adrian. Grey hair suits you, makes you look distinguished.' She meant it. But she still wished she didn't have to be here with him.

'Thank you. Would…would you like a drink before we order? How about a bottle of Pinot Grigio, that was your favourite, wasn't it?'

Mm, he'd remembered… 'Yes, thank you.'

As they waited for the wine they made a point of studying their menus. Hélène saw him shifting in his chair.

The waitress brought the chilled wine and Adrian asked Hélène to taste it.

'Santé!' Adrian raised his glass.

'Santé!

110

They touched glasses before sipping the golden wine. As it coursed through her, Hélène felt the knots in her stomach easing. Peering at Adrian over the rim of her glass, she noted that his mouth had softened a little. With a slight shock she realised she hadn't eaten out with a man for years; not since that pompous and boring accountant who droned on about how successful he was. And now here she was, being wined and dined by Adrian, a luxury denied her during their relationship as they had to be circumspect. Her mouth twisted at the memory of those furtive, illicit meetings and the pain they'd brought...

Dragging herself back she focused once more on the menu. The choice looked wonderful and in the end she chose scallops to start, followed by monkfish. *Might as well enjoy the food at least.*

'I've chosen. How about you?'

'Mm, think I'll start with the crab cake and then have the plaice.'

Adrian gave the hovering waitress the order before facing her. She saw his eye twitch. *Mm, he's not as sure of himself as he used to be, is he? And he a headmaster!*

'Hélène, you can't know how pleased I am to see you again. I realise it's all my fault, should have been in touch years ago. I...I took the coward's way out. But I want you to know how much I've regretted what I did.'

She noticed the genuine sadness in his eyes but steeled herself to remain quiet.

'Meeting Nicole, that lovely young woman we created, has made me realise not only what a fool I've been but what you must have gone through over the years.' He paused, taking a sip of wine before asking, 'Do you think you could ever forgive me?'

Hélène sipped her wine while she let his words sink in. *At last! He's said he's sorry.* She met his gaze, saw the pleading in his eyes and was just about to reply when the waitress bustled up with their starters.

Once she'd left, Adrian's question still hung heavy in the air between them.

'I...I don't know. Your...selfishness cost me my...my baby. My only child. You don't recover from such a loss over a plate of scallops!' She was surprised at her own vehemence and saw Adrian wince and pull back. Tears pricked behind her eyes and she reached for a tissue, determined not to break down in front of him. Not easy.

Adrian, his face contorted with what looked to her like guilt, said, 'You're right. Absolutely right. I can't expect you to forgive me. Not after what I put you through. I've no excuse, no redeeming reason for not sticking by you. I was a bloody idiot and I could only wish I could turn the clock back. But I can't.' He ran a hand through his hair. 'I can only say sorry for the pain I've caused you.'

Hélène toyed with a scallop.

'So why didn't you get in touch after...after Carol died?'

'Because you said you never wanted to see me again when you told me about the baby. I thought you'd move on, meet someone and...and marry.' He took a gulp of wine. 'I'd convinced myself that you were happy with another man and that the last person you'd want to hear from was me.'

'You could have tried to find out if you were right!' She felt the anger welling up again and fought hard to push it down. No way did she want to be the focus of a scene in full glare of the other diners. Coming here was a mistake...She started to stand but Adrian reached over and grabbed her arm.

'Please, Hélène, don't go! After all this time apart, can't we try and salvage what we had? That wonderful love we shared that made us laugh till we cried. The times when we lost track of time as we talked and talked. And made love.' His voice dropped to a croaked whisper; he still clung onto her arm.

She felt as if her heart and mind had been hijacked. Images of the treasured past filled her head and she too wished that the clock could be turned back. If only...

'Just...just give me a minute to go to the Ladies. I'll come back, I promise.'

She left him looking as if he didn't believe her, but she wouldn't walk away. Not yet.

Re-emerging a few minutes later, her make-up repaired, she walked briskly to their table and sat down.

He looked at her with such sorrow and guilt in his eyes that Hélène felt her heart soften. Just a little. In spite of all the pain this man had caused her, she felt the stirrings of that old love flicker into life within her being. The love that had given her a beautiful daughter, who she was determined not to lose again.

'I...I'll try to forgive you, Adrian. I can't promise anything, but I don't want us to be enemies, for Nicole's sake. She deserves better of us than that.'

His eyes lit up and he reached across and clasped her hand.

'Thank you, I know how difficult this must be for you and I'm truly grateful.' He shifted in his chair. 'If...if you were happy to, sometime in the future maybe, I'd be honoured to be your friend. To go out for a drink or a walk perhaps.'

She had to think. Did she want them to be friends again? Could she consider spending time with him, trust him not to hurt her again?

'I...I'll see. Give me time, Adrian. It's been – '

'I understand. Of course, take as long as you like. I can wait.' He smiled at her, somewhat tentative still, she thought. *He's not sure what I want yet and nor am I. It takes time to heal the pain of thirty-five years of loneliness.*

chapter 20

Eve sat with Nicole on the terrace finishing their lunch, as for some unfathomable reason, her mind insisted on replaying a long-ago memory which even now caused her pain. And guilt. She noticed that Nicole also looked distracted.

After Nicole had cleared away their plates she asked, 'Grandmother, are you up to telling me more of your time as a Land Girl? It sounds such a great story.'

'Yes, of course, dear.' Sighing inwardly, she replaced the memory in the sealed envelope deep inside her. 'Looking back, it was one of the happiest times of my life. I'd led a sheltered existence in Guernsey before the war and never expected to even visit England let alone live there for five years.' She paused, taking a sip of water. 'In spite of the hard work we had fun. Local dances took place in the village hall and the more mobile wounded soldiers used to join us, so we had plenty of partners. We were well chaperoned, but it didn't stop several of the girls from finding boyfriends. There were quite a few of us working on the local farms and we enjoyed the chance to put on our dresses and be swirled around the dance floor by dashing young men in uniform.' It was especially enjoyable if you happened to be in love with one, Eve mused, remembering the precious times when Philip was on leave and turned up unexpectedly. He always made a bee-line for her and they would spend the evening together, dancing every dance. Even after more than sixty years, she could feel the strength of Philip's arms around her and hear his infectious laugh. Together, they hadn't a care in the world. No war waged in the skies above them or on the land across the Channel. It was just them. In their own protected bubble…

'Did *you* have a special young man, Grandmother?'

'I…I really liked one of them, yes. He wasn't a convalescent, but lived…nearby and came home on leave. We loved dancing together.'

'Could it have been that young airman you mentioned, Philip Andrews?'

Eve took a deep breath. *This girl's smart! But I'm not yet ready to tell her everything.* She smiled at Nicole before replying, 'Yes, it was. How did you guess?'

'The way you spoke about him last time we chatted. You had a dreamy look. Remember, I'm a professional interviewer, trained to weed out secrets!' She laughed.

'Well, you're good, my dear. Are you returning to your work when you've sorted things out with that husband of yours?'

Nicole appeared thoughtful.

'I don't know. I can't see myself going back to work in Bristol, even though my job's being kept open for me. I could always look at other TV stations. With my background it shouldn't be too difficult to get a job. But I've still got three months to think about it.'

'I don't wish to sound impertinent, Nicole, but how are you managing without an income?'

'Oh, I've got savings and I inherited money from my grandmother. My expenses are few these days.' She looked stricken. 'Which reminds me, I should be paying for my keep while I'm here – '

'Nonsense, child! You're family, we wouldn't dream of taking your money. We can manage. We may not have much but it's enough for one extra mouth. Unless you are planning to stay for good?' Eve's eyes sparkled with mischief.

Nicole laughed. 'No, I'm not, don't worry. Not that I'm unhappy – '

'Only teasing. As I'm sure you're aware.'

★★★

The sound of the doorbell echoed down the hall and Nicole got up to answer it.

Surprised to find Ben standing on the step, she took a moment to find her voice.

'Ben! Umm, was Grandmother expecting you? She never said.' Nicole's heart pitter- pattered as she faced him.

Ben also appeared taken aback. Although Nicole couldn't help noticing how he seemed to be admiring her hot-weather outfit of shorts and T-shirt.

'No, I've been to see another patient nearby and decided to pop in on Mrs Ferbrache. If it's not convenient – '

'It's fine. Grandmother and I have finished lunch and Hélène's out. We're on the terrace. Please come in.'

'Doctor! What a pleasant surprise. A bit early for tea and cake but I'm sure Nicole would be happy to get you some.'

Eve smiled warmly at them both and Nicole waved away Ben's protest, only too happy to escape for a few minutes. Her reaction on seeing him had unsettled her.

'I dropped in as I was already nearby. How are you?'

'Not too bad, Doctor. I still feel tired a lot, but having young Nicole around is giving me a new lease of life.'

'Good. A new face is often a tonic. Is she staying long?'

Eve had caught Nicole's flushed face when she'd brought Ben outside and now studied him keenly. *Hmm, he's good- looking and has a nice smile. Wonder if he'd be interested in my granddaughter? A new boyfriend might keep her on the island!*

'We don't know. Nicole's on a sabbatical from her job, so she can do what she wants. She's a high-profile television journalist, you know, and told me she's not sure about returning to the station in Bristol. Her husband,' Eve sniffed, 'also works there so it might be awkward for her, poor girl.'

'Why "poor girl"?'

'I shouldn't really tell you this, but her husband's a philanderer. Got too much for her. And she's such a lovely young woman, too. Doesn't deserve to be treated like that.' Eve smiled to herself, hoping she'd sown a few seeds.

Before Ben could comment Nicole arrived bearing a tray. He leaped up to help her, setting it on the table.

'I've made a pot for us all and I even managed to find some chocolate cake.'

They sat with their tea and cake and chatted for a few moments. Eve, relishing the idea of pushing the young people together, spoke glowingly about Ben and how well he'd looked after her. Eve saw him shift uncomfortably on his chair, looking as if something troubled him.

'Your grandmother's been telling me you're a television journalist. Which sounds exciting. What kind of things do you investigate?'

Nicole seemed happy enough to talk about her work although she lacked her usual sparkle, Eve thought. In an odd way, she saw them as the re-incarnation of herself and Philip and wanted them to find happiness together. But for all her wishes, she had to admit that there seemed to be some tension between them. Definitely not at ease with each other.

★★★

By four o'clock Nicole was wondering where on earth Hélène was. Could it have gone horribly wrong and Hélène had gone off to be alone, licking her wounds? On balance it seemed unlikely, and she carried on weeding the flower beds to keep busy. She missed her own garden in England with its pond, shaded terraces and gazebo. She didn't garden herself, having someone in to do that. There hadn't been time to do it herself and Tom, well...The thought of Tom caused her to be extra ferocious towards an innocent flower she mistook for a weed, and dug it out. Fortunately for the other innocents nearby, she heard a car crunching on the gravel and, throwing down the trowel, ran to the front door.

Hélène looked surprised as the door swung open and Nicole rushed out, calling, 'Are you all right? How was lunch?'

'It was all right, thanks. After lunch I went for a walk at Jerbourg to give me time to think. I'm sorry I'm so late, I hadn't realised the time –'

'No problem. So, how did you leave it?' She couldn't help noticing that Hélène looked drained.

'Oh, we left it that if I wanted to get in touch I could. Adrian...would like us to be friends but I'm not sure.'

Nicole felt guilty. She'd railroaded Hélène into this.

'I see. Look, I'm really sorry if it was a bad idea...'

'It's okay, don't worry. We had to ...clear the air. And he did say how sorry he was, which made it worthwhile.' Hélène smiled and patted Nicole's arm.

As they walked into the house Nicole told her about Ben's visit and mentioned that Eve was now resting.

'Grandmother seemed a bit brighter this afternoon. Do you think the medication's helping?'

Hélène frowned. 'I don't know. I'd like to think so but...Did the doctor say anything?'

Nicole turned away, ostensibly to stack the tea- things in the sink but really to hide the flush creeping up her own cheeks.

'No, he didn't. Except he'll call again tomorrow as usual.' When she'd shown him out Ben had gazed at her intently before saying goodbye. But that had been it. No repetition of the long, drawn out handshake or big smile. She sighed, wondering what on earth was going on.

chapter 21

The next morning clouds scudded across the sky, propelled by a strong westerly wind. The temperature had dropped and Nicole felt it was a day for exploring the towers. Hélène hunted out the keys, explaining that 'the stairs are a bit iffy so do take care.'

As she entered the right hand tower the cool, musty air enveloped her in darkness. Hastening to find the light switch, she was rewarded by a pale glow from the single bulb lighting the stairs. The wooden steps creaked as she made her way gingerly up to the next floor. A door opened onto a large and empty room. Disappointed, Nicole stepped over to the nearest window and wiped away the grime with the threadbare curtain. She caught her breath at the view towards Pleinmont, able to make out a patchwork of fields, the gun emplacement she'd recently found and what looked like a tall TV receiver station. Beyond lay a concrete tower and the sea. The clouds hid the horizon, the sea and sky seeming to blend into a grey mass. The next window offered a bird's-eye view of the west coast and the hinterland dotted with cottages, churches and what looked like pubs or hotels. The last window overlooked the garden and the area beyond. Without the sun the colours of the plants and flowers appeared bleached.

Nicole crossed the landing to the other tower. Arriving in a room identical to the first, she was pleased to see stacks of boxes, old trunks and the usual ephemera associated with attics. The windows yielded similar views on two sides to the sister tower and the third showed the area towards the airport and St Martins.

Looking around at the dust-covered objects, Nicole felt a strong desire to start searching through them. But for what? She didn't know, just wanted to see what emerged from the family's stored treasures. Photo albums? Children's toys? Old letters? She sighed, knowing she had no right to pry without their approval.

Downstairs again, Nicole found Hélène in the kitchen, drinking coffee and flicking through a magazine.

'What do you think of our towers? Any Rapunzels waiting to be rescued?' Hélène chuckled.

Laughing, Nicole replied, 'No, that would be too much to expect. The views aren't bad, though. Better on a sunny day, I guess. I wondered if there'd be any photo albums up there I could see?'

'I've no idea. Haven't been up there for years. I don't remember seeing any since I was a child. I'll ask Mother. You want to see what we looked like in our youth? To see if there's any resemblance? I might have some photos in my room. I only brought a few of my belongings with me when I moved in. The rest is in the attic of my own house. Not knowing how long...'

Nicole made herself a coffee and sat down.

'Do you think Grandmother would let me browse through the stuff in the tower?'

Hélène frowned. 'I'm not sure. I once asked her if she'd like me to sort through it and throw away any rubbish and she became agitated and said no. I wasn't sorry as it may have raked up old memories. It'll need doing some day,' she sighed.

For a moment they were both lost in thought, aware of the significance of "some day".

'Forgive me, but there are times when you seem, well, not so close to your mother. And then other times...'

Hélène shrugged. 'I know. She drives me crazy with her stubbornness and she was never a very *loving* mother, but, deep down, I do love her.'

'I'm sure she loves you too,' Nicole replied, reaching out for her hand.

Hélène sniffed and dug out a tissue from her pocket, blowing her nose.

'Mother's not too good today. Said she'd stay in bed. The doctor's round later so we'll see what he thinks. I really wish she'd have that operation.'

'What operation?'

Hélène explained about the valve replacement surgery that Ben had recommended and Eve had refused.

'She's frightened that if she goes into hospital, she won't come out. Like my father.' The tears flowed more quickly now and Nicole felt helpless, giving Hélène's arm a quick squeeze. Hélène blew her nose again and straightened her shoulders. 'Sorry, Nicole. I don't know what came over me. I'm not usually that emotional. I think I'm on a roller-coaster these days. What with meeting you and…then Adrian.'

Nicole frowned. 'Yes, what…are you going to do about him? Are you still angry with him?'

'I don't know. Seeing him did bring up a lot of stuff for me, but he did seem very sincere. He…he does seem to care about me.' Hélène chewed her lip, seeming to drift off some-place else.

'I'm sure he does. But he'll find it difficult to say much if he thinks you're still angry with him.'

'I suppose so. By the way, are you seeing him again?'

'Yes. He's fulfilled his side of the bargain by apologising to you.' She sipped her drink. 'Even if you two can't be close again I'd like to get to know him.'

'Good.' Hélène stood up and rinsed her mug in the sink before asking Nicole what her plans were for the day.

'I thought I'd pop into Town this morning. Browse the shops and have some lunch. I'll be back by mid-afternoon.' No way was she going to miss Ben's visit to Eve.

'Okay, I'll look out some photos for you. Enjoy yourself.'

Nicole loved browsing the local shops and boutiques in St Peter Port but couldn't help comparing the choice with that found in St Helier. Being a bigger town, St Helier boasted several department stores as well as the local shops, but she liked the compact, if hilly, nature of St Peter Port, or Town as the locals called it. After an enjoyable lunch of Moules Mariniere, one of her favourite dishes, Nicole popped into the tourist information office for brochures and maps. It felt odd to be acting the tourist when her family were real "Guerns", but she wanted to learn more about her origins. Although the islands shared a similar history, from Neolithic man to the German Occupation and beyond, leaving dolmens and Occupation museums scattered on both islands, she assumed there'd be some differences.

Nicole was telling Hélène how she'd spent her time in Town when the doorbell rang.

'I'll go,' she cried, getting up from the kitchen table before her mother could reply.

'Hi, Ben.'

'Hi.' They stood smiling at each other for a moment, Ben remaining on the doorstep. Nicole finally ushered him in, saying that Eve was in bed.

He frowned. 'Sorry to hear that. I'd better go straight through.'

Hélène appeared and spoke quietly to Ben a moment before escorting him to Eve's bedroom. Nicole returned to the kitchen to prepare the tea. Hélène followed her and picking up a box from the worktop, said, 'I found a few photos. They're mainly ones I took after I'd left home. I think all the older ones must be in the tower.'

She sorted the photos into chronological order and spread them out on the table.

'That's us at my graduation in Southampton. A very happy day,' she smiled. 'And would you believe it, but it was the first time my father had travelled to England! Not unusual in those days but seems odd now.'

Nicole studied the photo. 'I can see the resemblance between you and Eve.' She peered at the man proudly linking arms with Hélène and Eve. Her grandfather. Dark hair, cut short, atop a weathered, but friendly looking face. Twinkly blue eyes smiled back at her. 'Mm, I can't see anything of your father in you.' She added, glancing between the photo and her mother.

'No, it was always agreed that I favoured Mother. As you can see, she was still very attractive in her forties. Must have been a bit of a stunner as a young woman!' She smiled.

'But you were lovely too, Hélène. And that mini-dress shows off your great legs!'

Hélène laughed. 'My parents were horrified that I could wear such a short dress to my graduation, but most of the girls were dressed like that. It was the fashion. But Mum and Dad were behind the times in rural Guernsey.'

'I can see how alike we are too,' Nicole said, looking hard at the smiling young woman in the purple mini-dress.

'Yes, but you have your father's mouth and chin.'

Hélène started explaining when and where the other photos were taken and they were so absorbed that they didn't hear Ben's entry.

'Family photos, eh?'

They turned round. Nicole felt the heat rise in her face as Ben came to stand by her, picking up some photos.

'Yes, Hélène's dug them out so we can look for family resemblances.'

He nodded, continuing to gaze at the pictures.

'How's my mother?'

Ben looked up. 'No worse. Just tired. I think she'll be well enough to get up tomorrow, but until she shakes off that infection she'll continue to get bad days like this.' He grinned. 'She's now sitting up in bed and asking for tea and cake.'

Hélène made up a tray for herself and Eve, leaving the others in the kitchen.

'I'll be mother, shall I?' Nicole said, reaching for the teapot.

'Thanks. Mm, Nicole, I hope I'm not being out of line, but would you like to go for a drink sometime? I understand that you and your husband are – '

'Separated, yes. And probably getting divorced,' she answered, looking down at her cup. *Is this a date? Or what? I know I fancy him but he's been a bit cool. So what's he want…?* Conflicting emotions raced through her and Ben must have mis-read her hesitation as he said, 'Look, if you don't want to – '

'No. It's…it's fine. I'd love to go out for a drink. I was just taken by surprise.'

'Yeh, well I don't usually ask girls out for a drink when I've just met them,' he grinned. 'But I thought you might be glad of a break from your…family.'

'Oh, that's kind of you. Thanks.' Feeling a bit deflated that he was only giving her "a break from her family" she managed a small smile. *It's a chance to spend time with him. Get to know him better. And let's face it, I am still married so…*

'I believe you don't know how long you're staying?'

'No, long enough to get to know everyone better, I guess. I'm growing quite fond of Hélène and Eve. And I'd like to get to know my father too.' And you, she thought, gazing into the grey eyes framed by eyelashes too thick for a man. And that smile!

'Your father? He's here?'

Nicole explained about Adrian without revealing his full name. Too soon to let all the skeletons out of the cupboard!

Ben placed his hand lightly on her arm. 'You're having quite an adventure of discovery, aren't you?'

Nicole nodded. 'Yep, sure am. So, where and when?'

'How about tomorrow night? I could pick you up about 7.30 and we'll drive to the west coast. A great place to catch the sunset later.'

'Sounds good. I…look forward to it.'

Just then Hélène returned and Nicole explained that Ben was taking her out for a drink.

'That's nice. Nicole needs to meet people her own age. She spends too much time cooped up with us oldies.' She smiled at them both as she took her tray to the sink.

Ben rose. 'Right, I'd better be off. More patients to see. Thanks for the tea, Nicole.' Turning to Hélène he added, 'I'll pop in tomorrow just to make sure that Mrs Ferbrache's better.'

Nicole escorted him to the door and as they said goodbye, he leaned forward and kissed her lightly on the cheek. A friend's kiss. But it felt good and her eyes followed the departing Ben as he drove out of sight. As she finally shut the door her mobile beeped, signalling a new message. She opened it and her heart, so buoyant a moment ago, sank. Tom.

"As am not allowed to ring, can I please write? Too important to send an email. Not know your current address so please text me. Thanks Tomx"

Nicole groaned. He doesn't give up, does he? As she replied with La Folie's address she wondered what on earth could be so important. Consoling herself that at least a letter was less invasive than a phone call, she headed back to the kitchen.

chapter 22

The next morning Hélène said she needed to pop out to the Post Office at St Peters but that the cleaner was due shortly and would look out for Eve if Nicole was going out. She looked out at the deep blue sky through the kitchen window, and nodded. The beach beckoned again.

A little later she was stretched out on the sand at Vazon. The beach was less crowded today and Nicole staked out her territory with a newly bought mat and a towel from the house. After a liberal application of sun-cream she rolled on to her stomach, covering her vulnerable back with her T-shirt, before picking up her phone.

'Hi, Susie, it's me. You'll never guess what's been happening here…'

A relaxed and golden-toned Nicole arrived home at lunchtime to find a decidedly frazzled looking Hélène in the kitchen.

'What's happened? It's not Grandmother…?'

Hélène shook her head.

'No, don't worry, she's a bit better today.' She took a deep breath. 'I…had a burst tyre just after I'd left the post office and hit a wall on the Route du Longfrie – '

'Are you hurt?' Nicole cried.

'No, I'm…fine. Thanks. It wasn't much of a bump.' She sipped some water. 'I was a bit shaken, the tyre made such a bang I thought I'd hit something else first. Anyway, I got out of my car to take a look and…and Adrian turned up.'

She refilled her glass before adding, 'He lives in St Peters, you see, and was walking to the shops when he saw what happened.'

'That was lucky! Did he change the tyre for you?' Nicole couldn't help thinking that this accident might have a silver lining.

'Yes, he's always been very handy with cars. Didn't take him long.' She looked down at her glass. 'Anyway, I was still a bit shaky so he suggested I went back to his place for a drink. Well, I could hardly refuse, could I? We had a coffee and then…then I came home.'

'I see. And are you sure you're all right? Only you look a bit flustered.'

'I'm absolutely fine. It was a shock, that's all. I'd never had a burst tyre before. But thanks to Adrian, it was soon sorted.'

'Good. Mm, how was it between you two? After all, you weren't sure if you wanted to see him again.'

'It was all right. We sat in the garden, which is lovely by the way, and…talked while we had our coffee. It was a bit difficult initially, but it got easier.' Hélène swirled her glass of water, not looking at Nicole. 'He suggested that we might go for a walk sometime and I agreed.' When she looked up, Nicole saw the pink spots on her cheeks.

'That's great! I'm so pleased! It'll be easier for me when I see him again, knowing that at least you two are talking.'

'That reminds me, Adrian asked if you'd like to have lunch with him tomorrow. He suggested Fleur du Jardin in Kings Mills, if that's okay with you?'

'Fine by me. I'd meant to ring him so that's good.' Nicole smiled at Hélène, thinking that perhaps her parents might yet be on course for patching up their relationship. Which just left her to sort out her own.

★★★

Hélène carried out a fresh crab salad to the terrace where Eve and Nicole were already seated. Eve, looking from daughter to granddaughter, sensed a change in the two women. After chewing thoughtfully for a few minutes, she placed her cutlery on her plate and looked directly at Hélène.

'Something's happened hasn't it?' Turning to Nicole she added, 'And you look pleased with yourself, miss.'

Hélène, glancing at Nicole who gave a nod, put down her knife and fork before replying. 'Yes, there's something I need to tell you, Mother…'

Eve listened in silence as Hélène told her about Adrian and how he'd met Nicole and then herself. And that they were trying to patch up their "friendship", as she called it. Eve felt a lightening of her damaged heart. She could see that her daughter looked different, the lines around her eyes and mouth appeared less pronounced. Less tense.

'Well, my dear, I'm glad you told me. I had a feeling something was going on. And it's only right that that man of yours finally took responsibility for his actions.' She paused, looking from one to another. 'You say he's widowed now?'

Hélène nodded.

'Do you think he'll make an honest woman of you?' Eve's chin jutted towards her daughter.

Hélène flushed. 'It's too soon to talk about that! We're barely friends…'

Eve pursed her lips. 'And you, Nicole, what's making you so bright-eyed?'

Nicole chuckled. 'Nothing gets past you, does it? I'm having a drink with Ben tonight. As *friends.*' She looked pointedly at Eve.

Eve smiled to herself. Her plan seemed to have worked. Good!

'That's nice. He's a good man and I should think he'll take your mind off your, er, problems.' Eve turned to Hélène. 'I've got some news, too.'

'Oh, Mother! Have you decided to go ahead with the operation?' She leant forward, stroking Eve's bony hand.

Eve shook her head. 'No, not that. You know how I feel about hospitals. But I've been thinking about the idea of carers and respite care.'

Hélène's sharp breath was audible.

'I realise how selfish I've been, forcing you to give up your home and stay with me most of the time.' Eve sighed. She hated admitting she was wrong, but… 'So, we'll arrange for carers from Social Services to come in as needed. And the doctor says he can arrange for respite care in a very nice home if you wanted to go away for a week or so.'

Eve saw the tears in Hélène's eyes.

'You're sure, Mother? You've always said – '

'I know, I know. But I've been a burden for too long and now that you've someone in your life –' Eve waved away Hélène's protest, 'Or may have shortly. Then it's time you had some fun.' Her eyes twinkled as she continued, 'If a place can be found soon enough, you might be able to go away during this school holiday. Go with a friend, perhaps.'

'Thank you, Mother, I'd love to go away for a few days. It's been so long…'

'What a wonderful offer, Grandmother! I think you're lovely,' Nicole said, reaching across to kiss Eve's cheek. Hélène also kissed her, a look of wonderment on her face.

Eve cleared her throat. 'Right, enough of the thanks and kisses, can I please finish my crab salad?'

They laughed and as they continued their meal Nicole chatted to Hélène about the proposed holiday. Eve, tiredness beginning to grip her, felt drained and in need of a lie-down. It was hard work pretending to feel better than you did.

***

At 7.30pm sharp Ben arrived at La Folie to collect Nicole. She had dithered for some time about what to wear.

Nothing too "obvious", she decided. Had to be low key as it was only a drink in a pub. No big deal.

The evening promised to remain warm so she settled on cropped jeans and a silky white top to set off her tan. Snatching up a sweater for later, Nicole ran down the stairs as Ben rang the bell.

'Hi! What a lovely evening,' she smiled at Ben, casual in jeans and T-shirt. As he bent to brush her cheek she caught a hint of his lime fragranced aftershave. Mm, nice.

'You're right, it *is* a lovely evening.' With his hand on her elbow he steered her towards his sleek, silver car and opened the passenger door with an exaggerated gesture.

'Your car awaits, Madame!'

Laughing, Nicole settled herself in the leather seat and a few moments later they were on the road to the west coast.

'Where are we headed?'

Ben glanced at her. 'Cobo. Have you been there?'

'I had a look the other day. There's a pub on the front isn't there?'

'Yep. It's where I often meet up with friends. Though not tonight,' he added, with a grin, 'They're busy so it'll just be the two of us. I thought we could have a walk on the beach first before heading to the pub.'

'Great.' *Well, at least I've got him to myself this evening and a walk on a beach is quite romantic, I guess.*

He pulled into the small beach car park where she'd seen him the other day. Reaching for her hand, he led the way down the steps. It was mid-tide and the sand glistened damply in the sunlight. As they strolled towards the shoreline the tangy smell of the seaweed clinging to the rocks became stronger.

Ben took a deep breath. 'Ahh! I always feel as if I've been let out of school when I come to the beach. The air's so invigorating after a day spent with sick people.' He turned to Nicole. 'Not that I mind being with my patients, you understand. Particularly your grandmother – '

She laughed. 'Don't worry, I know what you mean. Your work must be very stressful, especially if your patients are unlikely to recover. I couldn't do what you do.' She bent to pick up a delicate pink shell, turning it over in her hand. 'Did you always want to be a doctor?'

'Yes, since I was a boy. It runs in the family, you see. Both my father and grandfather were doctors. Dad only retired a few years ago and I took his place in the practice.' He caught her hand again as they headed for the rocks.

'We're unusual in being a family of doctors. Quite a few come over on licence from the UK. Is it the same in Jersey?'

Nicole nodded, enjoying the warmth of his hand in hers. A caring hand.

'You didn't want to be a surgeon or a specialist?'

Ben shook his head.

'Not a surgeon, no. For a while I did consider becoming a paediatrician as I love children. But there's so much more variety in a GP's work.'

Reaching the rocks, he guided her to the nearest pool. The sun's rays on the water made it sparkle like diamonds. As they bent down to watch the antics of tiny fish and shore crabs, their heads touched.

'Sorry...' Nicole began, but as their eyes locked he kissed her. For a moment they remained crouched on the rocks, locked in the kiss. Oh, that was nice!

'Look, *I'm* sorry, Nicole, I hadn't meant to...I mean I thought we could just be friends. You're married...'

'Separated. And I can't see us getting back together.' Her heart sank. *Friends! With that electricity...*

Ben frowned.

'That's as maybe but I don't want to risk falling for you in case you suddenly up sticks and go back to him.' He let go her hand and moved away slightly. Not looking at her. 'I...I had that happen to me before. She was English, here on a licence, and suddenly she went back to a boyfriend in London.'

As he glanced up she saw a flicker of sadness in his eyes.

'I'm so sorry, Ben. I can understand how you feel. It's horrible to be rejected isn't it? I felt like that when my...husband Tom was unfaithful. Several times.' She reached out and clasped his hand. 'Come on, shall we go and have that drink you promised me and have a proper talk?'

Ben nodded and helped her over the rocks.

A few minutes later Nicole found herself sitting at a small table facing the beach while Ben went inside to buy drinks. Unbidden, the memory of her first date with Tom popped into her head. It had been on a summer's evening at a riverside pub in Bristol, so shared uncomfortable similarities. Nicole shook her head as if it would erase the memory. She didn't want to go there. That was the past...

Ben returned and they sat for a moment watching the sun slowly sink towards the horizon. Hues of reds and golds spread across the sky, bathing everything with a golden tint.

'Do you feel like telling me a bit about yourself, Nicole? Your adopted family and your...husband?'

She described her parents and childhood in Jersey and told him, briefly, about Tom and how they became a couple. Ben seemed to listen intently, asking her the odd question.

'Right, enough about me. What about you, Ben? Your family?' Nicole grinned at him over the rim of her glass.

'Just one sister. My father's a retired GP and my mother was a nurse. A bit of a cliché, that,' he said, grinning. 'They've had a good marriage and spent their lives here. Something I'd like for myself.'

'How long's it been since the bolting girlfriend?'

'Three years. I got over her ages ago but I've been too busy doing up my house to socialise except with old friends. I...wasn't too keen on dating.'

'Mm. It's only been a few months since Tom and I split up and it's been hard. Although you can't just stop loving someone 'cos they behaved badly, it does make it difficult to think of going back. I'm sure he's psychologically wired to be unfaithful and I can't deal with that anymore.' She gazed down at her drink, lost in thought.

Ben reached for her hand.

'Perhaps it's time I ventured out into the water again. They do say there's plenty of fish in the sea!'

She looked up and saw his tentative smile.

'Maybe you should. After all, you're surrounded by it!' Giggling, she waved her hand towards the sea and he laughed.

'Okay, tell me more. You mentioned a house. Where is it and have you finished working on it?'

'In Town, not far from the surgery. It was badly in need of renovation and I've spent the past couple of years working on it and it's nowhere near finished. It's been a slow process as I'm trying to do as much as I can myself. Used to be good at woodwork when I was at school,' he grinned.

'Mm, just as well you're not a surgeon or you could ruin your hands. We had builders in to do ours as neither of us had the time or skills to have a go. But I do like choosing the finishing touches, making a place a home.' She felt a pang of sadness as she pictured the lovely farmhouse left behind. Mentally shaking herself, she smiled at Ben.

'So, apart from DIY, which to me sounds like hard work and not leisure, how do you relax?'

'I surf and join up with friends when they take their boats out. There's usually something going on, particularly in the summer. Barbecues, island hopping and meeting up for meals or drinks. And I do love travelling, though I'm not finding it as much fun on my own.' He twirled the lager in the glass before adding, 'When I was with Pauline we took several holidays together. But haven't been away much since,' he grinned ruefully. 'Most of my friends are married or in relationships so I travel solo.' Ben looked up, asking, 'What about you? Any hobbies or interests?'

'Like most islanders I've always been a water baby, but prefer the warmer seas of the Med or Pacific. I've travelled to lots of fantastic places around the world, but never on my own.' She sighed. 'I'm with you on that one, it's more fun to be with someone.' *Unless it's an adulterous husband,* she thought. Glancing across at Ben, Nicole imagined what it would be like to jet off with *him* to a faraway place. *Stop it!* She chided herself. *It's too soon to think like that. You've only just met and you're still married, for God's sake!* Clearing her throat, she continued, 'I've not had much time for hobbies but I do read a lot and enjoy going to the theatre and cinema. And walking. I aim to walk along the cliff paths while I'm here as the views are brilliant.'

Ben looked thoughtful, as if he was weighing something up.

'I'm going over to Herm with friends a week on Friday. They're renting a cottage for the week but I'm only staying until Sunday evening. If you'd like to come over for the day, you'd be welcome to join us. I'm sure you'd all get on.'

Nicole didn't hesitate. 'I'd love to, thanks. I was planning to pop over sometime as it's the only island I've not visited.'

'Great! We're going across in Nick's boat on the Friday evening. So, how about joining us on the Saturday? Bring your bathers as we'll be heading to a beach at some point. Nick's wife will be there so you won't be the only female, and there's another single guy. We'll have a lot of fun, I promise.'

'I look forward to it.'

As the sun melted into the horizon with a flash of gold, Nicole felt her heart lift. In a little over a week she was going to spend a whole day with the gorgeous doctor on a tiny island. Okay, there'd be other people around, but still…

chapter 23

'It's good to see you again, Nicole. What would you like to drink?'

Adrian sat opposite her in the garden of the old inn in Kings Mills, a large parasol protecting them from the sun.

'A spritzer, please.'

The waitress took their order and after she left Nicole said, 'It looks like you've made your peace with Hélène. I'm glad. Now it's up to us.'

Adrian took a deep breath. He knew he still had to win her over, encourage her to forgive him. Even Hélène was unsure, still playing it cool with him. But she'd agreed to go for a walk this afternoon. So there was hope.

'We're treading on egg shells a little and I wouldn't say I've yet "made my peace" but at least we're talking.'

'Did she tell you that Grandmother's agreed to go into respite care for a week?'

He nodded. 'Yes, Hélène's thrilled. She told me when I phoned this morning. I think she plans to go to France for a few days.'

'Yes. It's a pity you can't go together.' Nicole looked him in the eye.

He shifted in his chair. 'It's too soon to think of that. We...we don't have that kind of relationship. Yet.'

'Well, you could go as friends, having separate rooms. Just a thought.' Nicole sipped her wine, her face inscrutable.

'That would be up to Hélène!' He thought it a great idea but...Wanting to change the subject, he went on, 'Now, your mother's told me something about you, but I'd really like you to fill in the details.'

They ordered their food and Nicole talked about her childhood, university, work and meeting Tom. He frowned as she arrived at the current state of her marriage and felt his own guilt surface as she described her pain on finding out Tom was cheating on her. He also, paradoxically, found his hackles rise in her defence. It made for an odd sensation.

He encouraged her to talk about her work as a radio and TV reporter and she seemed to unbend, recounting amusing anecdotes.

As they were drinking their coffees, Adrian pushed his hand through his hair.

'I'm going to tell my children about you and Hélène. Won't be easy as Karen, in particular, was close to her mother.' He sighed. Karen's temper was as volatile as Carol's had been and their relationship was fraught at the best of times.

'Hélène said that Karen's married and has a child. So you're a grandfather.'

Adrian smiled. 'Yes, Luke's a great little chap, just turned two. Always laughing. Takes after his father, Dave, a high flying advocate with a dry sense of humour. My son, Michael, doesn't seem ready to settle down yet. Enjoys the social life too much to give it up.' He smiled fondly. 'I think he'll be a bit more accepting of you both. I'd like us all to meet up if my kids are agreeable. Unless you have a problem with that?'

'No, of course not. After all they're my only siblings.'

He walked Nicole to her car and gave her a hug and a peck on the cheek. She seemed to have mellowed a little towards him as she didn't push him away. But her eyes told him that he hadn't quite won her over. Not yet.

That evening Adrian handed out drinks to Karen and Michael before pouring himself a double Scotch. He needed it. They'd been surprised to be invited round for a drink, just the two of them, he'd said on the phone; he had something important to discuss. Dave was babysitting Luke.

As they looked at him expectantly, doubt set in. Then he remembered Hélène's face and his confidence returned.

'This is going to come as a shock and there's no easy way to say this, but I had an affair over thirty years ago and…and we had a daughter.'

'What! You cheated on my mother! How could you!' Karen's face reddened with anger. She jumped up from the chair, nearly spilling her wine, and paced around the coffee table before coming to rest inches from him. He stood up and glanced towards Michael, who although pale, remained quiet.

'If you'd let me explain – '

'Explain? What is there to explain? You were having it off with some trollop while – '

Adrian butted in 'While your mother was making my life hell! We weren't getting on and hadn't slept together since Michael was born. Although she professed to love me she certainly didn't behave as if she did. And…and I'd stopped loving her. I'm sorry, but it's true. And Hélène was no trollop!' He saw the angry tears falling down her face as she looked at him in disgust.

'Michael?'

His son stood up and walked towards him.

'I'd guessed that you were unhappy, Dad. In fact, it was pretty obvious.' He glanced towards his sister. 'You never went anywhere together and you spent most of your time in your study. Did…did Mum know about your affair?'

Adrian shook his head. 'Not to begin with. Not until I asked her for a divorce…' Karen gasped and spat out 'How could you?'

'I was in love with Hélène and wanted to be with her, but your mother wouldn't agree to either a divorce or separation. So I…I ended my relationship. Hélène had just told me she was pregnant and I...I knew I couldn't be with her.' He looked at his children, Michael still pale but calm and Karen, red-faced and tearful.

Michael spoke. 'So, what happened to the baby, our...our sister?'

'She was adopted. I didn't even know it had been a girl until recently.' He took a deep breath. Crunch time. 'She turned up in Guernsey a few weeks ago, after searching for her mother. And then...then we met.'

'You've met her? Your bastard?' Karen spat.

Adrian felt himself flush at the word. 'Yes, her name's Nicole and she was adopted by a Jersey couple. I found her to be a lovely young woman. I think you'd like her –'

'Huh! If you think I'm going to meet your –'

'Daughter, she's my daughter as much as you are, Karen.' He said gently, hoping to diffuse the situation. 'I want you to realise that I'm not blaming your mother for what happened between us. She was a good mother to you both and I wouldn't have wished her to get sick. But our marriage had been over for years and I hope that you'll give me credit for nursing her while she was ill.' Adrian felt drained. Karen was reacting as he'd known she would and he didn't know what more to say.

'Are you saying that you didn't stay in touch with this Hélène while Mum was alive?' asked Michael.

'No, after I ended it, she refused to have any contact with me. It's only since Nicole turned up that we've talked and met up. She's never married and we're...trying to be friends.' There, he'd said it now.

Michael reached out and gave his father a hug. 'I'd wondered why you looked happier these days, Dad. Go for it, that's what I say.' He grinned.

Adrian felt a weight lift. He turned towards Karen, who'd resumed her pacing.

'Karen? Don't you want me to be happy now?'

Karen glared at her father.

'Of course I want you to be happy. It's just I don't know how I could bear to see you with the woman who came between you and Mum.'

'But she didn't, Karen. Our marriage was over before I met Hélène. And because I couldn't be with her properly, she felt she had no choice but to give up her baby. You, as a mother yourself, must know how painful that must have been.'

Karen's eyes widened. 'Yes, I suppose so,' she said, biting her lip.

Adrian moved forward and reached out towards her. After a moment's hesitation she moved into his arms, resting her head on his shoulders. 'Sorry, Dad, it was such a shock...'

'I know. But I don't want us to fall out over it. I need to do what feels right for me now. And I want to make it up to Hélène and Nicole.' He stepped back and looked from Karen to Michael. 'I'd really like for everyone to meet sometime. You don't have to be friends if you don't want to. But it would mean a lot to me if you'd at least see them. Particularly Nicole as she has no other siblings.'

There was silence. Michael spoke first. 'It's okay with me, Dad. Whenever.' He smiled at Adrian.

'Karen?'

She looked up, her face still blotchy. Crying didn't suit her sallow skin. 'Okay. I'll meet them but I can't promise to like them.' Her tone still defiant.

Adrian smiled and reached out for a group hug.

'That's all I ask. I promise.'

chapter 24

The next few days meandered on their way. The only time Nicole saw Ben was when he dropped in to see Eve and joined them in the ritual of tea and cake. Eve's health seemed to slowly improve but Nicole sensed that no-one thought it would last unless she agreed to the operation.

From Nicole's point of view, a bright spot was the improving relationship between Hélène and Adrian. They went out for walks and met for coffee before, finally, Adrian had asked her if she'd have dinner with him. When Hélène told her about the invitation, Nicole saw how happy she was. It looked as though she'd begun to let go her anger and enjoy what she'd once lost.

The morning after the dinner date, Nicole found Hélène in the kitchen, nibbling toast.

'So, how did it go last night?'

'Very well, thanks. We went to a lovely Italian restaurant in Town. The food was really good and – '

'And the company?' Nicole grinned.

'Was good too!' She blushed, taking a bite of toast.

'Any chance that Adrian could go with you to France? It would give you time to get to know each other again.'

'Funny you should say that. We…we did discuss it last night. And he might come too.' The blush grew deeper.

'Brilliant! That would please Grandmother.'

'Do you think so? Why?' Hélène looked puzzled.

'You can see she wants you two to get together, wants Adrian to make "an honest woman of you", remember. And she did suggest you might go with a friend. I'm sure she meant Adrian.'

'Oh.'

Nicole left her to think about it while she got her beach gear together. She spent a lot of her time exploring the island and relaxing on the beach. When she wasn't needed to granny-sit, that is. As she stretched out at Vazon later, she found herself thinking about her family. She was becoming very fond of Eve and Hélène and tried to work out how much she took after them. Initially, she hadn't wanted to be like her mother, seeing her as a bitter, lonely woman. But now, as her romance blossomed, she was becoming the woman she must once have been. Warm and loving. And Nicole had admired her intelligence and sense of independence. Something she shared with Eve, who was perhaps *too* independent, Nicole thought, grinning. And then there was Adrian. Did she share any of his traits? Tricky call. He was more buttoned up, not so easy to get to know. But he had been ambitious. Something she did share. Her own ambition had not brought her joy, so perhaps she needed to rein it back. But being unemployed as she was, ambition didn't figure in her life at present. Her thoughts made her think about Mary and Ian and feelings of guilt prompted her to phone them. It had been a few days…

On Friday morning Nicole jumped out of bed, a broad smile on her face. Not only was the trip to Herm the next day, but Adrian had phoned last night to tell Hélène that his children had agreed to meet them for Sunday lunch. They were going to a west coast restaurant and Karen would be bringing Luke. Her sort-of nephew, Nicole thought, smiling to herself as she showered. As an only child she'd missed out on so much, but as part of this new family, Nicole hoped that she could at last experience the joys of siblings. Assuming they liked each other. Drying her hair, she couldn't help thinking that Karen might not be very keen on *her*, after what Adrian had said about her closeness to Carol. Ah, well time would tell…

★★★

Nicole looked surprised to find both women in the kitchen

'No breakfast in bed, Grandmother? You must be feeling better!'

Eve smiled. 'Yes, I am. Those pills that the doctor insists I take seem to be having an effect. Thought I'd see if I can manage with this today,' she tapped the Zimmer frame next to her chair. 'I need to get these old legs of mine working again before it's too late. Perhaps you'd see me into the garden after breakfast? Hélène's going out.'

When they had finished eating, Eve pulled herself up on her frame and took unsteady steps towards the back door. Nicole hovered by her side, looking anxious

With a sigh of relief, Eve lowered herself onto a chair on the patio.

'Oh dear me, I'm really out of condition, aren't I? Perhaps I need one of those treadmill things to get fit!' She gave Nicole a wan smile.

'I think you're doing great. We'll soon have you running up and down the hall,' Nicole grinned. 'Can I get you anything? Rug, cushions, water?'

'I'd love some water, please. Then I'd like you to sit with me for a while if you haven't anything better to do.'

'Of course I'll sit with you. Back in a mo.'

A few minutes later Nicole returned with a jug of water and two glasses.

'I thought you might like us to continue our chat about the past,' Eve said, after taking a sip.

'Great, as long as it doesn't tire you.'

Eve waved her hand. 'If I get tired I'll stop, don't worry. Now, where were we?'

'You were telling me about the dances.'

'Ah, yes. We always looked forward to them. But there were other ways to enjoy ourselves. We were entitled to a day off each week and quite often we'd catch a bus into Exeter for a bit of shopping. It wasn't easy to buy new clothes with the few Clothing Coupons allowed, so we'd buy material and one of the girls, Clare, sewed dresses and skirts for us. Sometimes the material was old curtaining which we bought from the market.' Eve paused for another sip. 'I still remember a lovely dark green velvet skirt that Clare made for me. I wore it to a Christmas dance in the village, matching it with a scarlet jumper and earrings like miniature Christmas trees I made from tinsel. Everyone remarked how Christmassy I looked.' She chuckled at the memory. They had walked arm in arm into the hall, the girls sparkly and shining in their bright clothes. 'We wove ivy and tinsel in our hair for extra colour.' Eve remembered Philip coming up, grabbing her hand and whirling her round the room. She'd felt intoxicated with excitement, and from then on Philip called her his "Christmas fairy".

Nicole seemed to notice her far-away look.

'So, was Philip there to admire your new outfit?' She grinned.

Eve sipped her water. 'Oh, yes he was there,' she replied, before telling Nicole what he had called her, provoking a giggle from her granddaughter.

Eve continued.

'We didn't just shop on our days off. Sometimes we'd go to a film matinee. I loved dramas starring my favourite actors, John Mills or Michael Redgrave, or comedies when I needed a laugh. After long, hard hours in the fields we were glad to sit in the cinema and forget there was a war on. I loved George Formby with his ukulele and cheeky songs.' Eve smiled to herself as she recalled sitting in the back of the cinema laughing at George Formby's antics one afternoon. Not with the girls, but with Philip. It had been one of their rare afternoons together and such fun. After the film he'd taken her to the nearby café for afternoon tea and they'd even had time to call into a pub for a glass of cider. She felt completely spoiled. And loved.

Eve became aware of Nicole's intense gaze and gave herself a mental shake.

'How long did you stay on the farm, Grandmother?'

'Until the end of the war. I couldn't return to Guernsey and there was nowhere else to go. As volunteers we were free to leave when we wished and two girls did go home after a couple of years. Conscripted girls arrived to replace them. Clare stayed on with me, having been orphaned in the Blitz and with no other family. We had friends in the village and became fond of our bosses, Mr and Mrs Coombe. They treated us like family. Their only son John was away fighting so we were his replacement. Both as workers and as "children." Eve sipped more water. 'When John finally returned, he announced that he wanted nothing more to do with farming and planned to go to university. It was the right decision for him but his parents took it hard. A lot of the young men who'd left farms wanted more from life after being away fighting so long. It's one of the reasons Land Girls were still needed after the war ended.'

'So you could have stayed on the farm?'

'Yes, I could. But I wanted...needed to get back to Guernsey. Although I hadn't exactly missed my parents,' Eve said, pulling a face, 'But I hadn't got any reason to stay in England.'

'What about Philip? Weren't you still friends?'

Eve felt her eyes water. She said softly, 'No. His...his plane was shot down on 20th April on the last bombing raid against Berlin. He...he didn't survive.'

★★★

Hélène returned later that morning, after visiting the care home offering respite care. Impressed by both the accommodation and the staff she was anxious to confirm her mother's stay.

Eve sat by the window in her sitting room, gazing out to the garden.

'How did you manage with the frame, Mother?'

'Quite well, thank you. I had a little walk in the garden with Nicole before coming in for a rest.' She peered at Hélène. 'Did you go to that home?'

'Yes, and it was lovely. I'm sure they'll look after you very well. They've got a vacancy in a couple of weeks but need to know today if we want it.' She took a deep breath, mentally crossing her fingers. 'Shall I book it, Mother? Are you happy – '

'Yes, yes, go ahead, dear. I haven't changed my mind. You deserve to have a holiday. Is that man of yours joining you?' Eve smiled at her bemused daughter.

'Mm, yes he is.' She gave Eve a hug, feeling enormous relief. Adrian could go ahead and book the ferry to St Malo and start looking for places to stay. Her stomach fluttered at the thought.

'I'll ring them now, Mother. Back in a minute.'

★★★

After her daughter left, Eve was alone again with her thoughts. It had been an eventful morning, what with using the frame again after weeks in that blessed wheelchair, nearly confessing all to Nicole and now agreeing to respite care. But it felt good and Eve was happy to see her daughter smile again. She would do all she could to encourage Hélène's relationship with Adrian. There was a lot of pleasure to be had in playing matchmaker, she thought, thinking also of Nicole and Ben. Closing her eyes she drifted off to sleep.

★★★

Nicole felt pleased with her efforts in the garden. The beds were beginning to look healthier with the flowers and shrubs finally outnumbering the weeds. It had been hot, sticky work but worth it as she wanted to do something for her grandmother. As they had walked slowly in the garden earlier, it had been apparent how much Eve loved it, hating to see it so unkempt. She had pointed out her favourite flowers, even remembering when they'd been planted.

'We planted that pink rose bush when your mother was born. We'd not long moved in and the garden was a mess. Hadn't been touched for years, so Reg set about digging the soil over ready for planting. He'd always had a fondness for roses so they took pride of place.' Pointing to a vivid display of purple and pink hollyhocks, Eve continued, 'But they're my favourites. So majestic against the hedges, aren't they? Although I have to say that the perfume of the roses is hard to beat.'

It wasn't long before Eve became tired and Nicole walked by her side back into her sitting-room, offering to cut some roses for her. She made up a vase of the pink ones and placed them next to Eve's chair, the heady scent soon filling the room. Nicole returned to the garden and the weeding.

As she worked Nicole recalled the pain in Eve's eyes as she mentioned Philip's death. He'd obviously meant a lot to her, she thought, tugging at a particularly intransigent specimen. No more had been said and a moment later Eve had suggested a walk in the garden. As Eve shuffled along Nicole asked about Reg and how they'd met.

'We'd known each other before the war as he owned a small neighbouring farm. He was older than me and, to be honest, I'd not paid him much attention. But he seemed to have a soft spot for me and would bring me flowers from his garden.' Eve paused and leant on her frame. She could picture Reg in his battered corduroys and patched-up Guernsey sweater, clutching a small posy of freesias as he hopped from foot to foot on the door step. His brown eyes used to crinkle up as he smiled and he was a kind, gentle man. Not cut out to be a farmer, but he'd inherited it from his parents and knew nothing else. Eve's parents had encouraged Reg to court Eve, seeing the possibilities from the joining of the two farms. Their son had made it clear he wasn't keen on marrying and it would have kept the farm in the family for the future.

They had reckoned without Eve, who wanted more from life than to be tied down to life as a farmer's wife. Particularly on Reg's small farm. And she hadn't been attracted to him. Not then.

'So, what happened after the war? Did you and Reg become an item?' Nicole grinned.

'I suppose so. He'd waited for me for five years, hadn't courted anyone else. Or so he said.' Eve pointed to the house. 'This place was up for sale. It had been taken over by the Germans and was in a terrible state. The real owner had left Guernsey before the war and couldn't be traced, so the States put it on the market at a rock-bottom price. Reg loved it, saw the potential for building greenhouses for growing, which is what he'd always wanted to do, and sold his farm. We ...we had some savings and got the builders in. The wedding took place at the same time.' Eve recalled those frantic weeks as she'd been pulled along by Reg's enthusiasm, not only for her as his wife, but for their new home and business. It hadn't been easy and there had been times when, alone, she had shed tears for what might have been. But over time Eve had come to accept her new life and her husband and, looking back, saw it hadn't been a bad life. Not really.

chapter 25

Nicole parked in the ten-hour parking section of White Rock, before heading off to the Trident ticket office. Although only eight o'clock the sun felt warm on her face as she stood in the queue. She hadn't expected to see many people waiting at that time of the morning, but it looked like Herm was popular that day. Groups of parents, burdened with rucksacks and beach bags, shepherded young children clutching the ubiquitous buckets and spades. Mixed in the queue were several older couples and the occasional singleton like herself. *Mm, guess those lucky enough to have been out clubbing last night will be catching a later ferry.*

Clutching her ticket, she moved off with the others to wait by the steps for embarkation. Stepping aboard the gently bobbing boat, Nicole felt a thrill of excitement. In about twenty minutes she would be landing on Herm and, hopefully, into Ben's arms. Pulling on a cotton sweater as protection from the sea breeze, she climbed up to the top deck. The ferry had eaten up the passengers with room to spare and Nicole found herself a vantage point from which to mark their three mile journey.

She was glad of her sweater as the ferry steered its way past the harbour entrance and out to sea, into the embrace of a strong breeze. Gazing back towards St Peter Port Nicole had the traitorous thought that the waterfront was more attractive than that of St Helier. Boats large and small bobbed up and down on their moorings, forming a colourful display in front of the picturesque frontage of shops and restaurants. The harbour itself was guarded by the old, battered Castle Cornet, a relic from the thirteenth century according to her guide book. Nicole had been reading up on Guernsey, keen to know more about the island to which she was so strongly connected. Turning towards Herm, she saw its tiny neighbour, Jethou, like a small off-shoot to the right and, further out to sea, the larger island of Sark. A heat haze shrouded the islands giving them an air of mystery and separateness; the same air which prompted thousands of people to travel back year after year. Fortunately, not all at the same time.

Of all the islands, Herm captured her imagination the most. According to legend it had not only been the home of Neolithic man, monks, smugglers and a Prussian Prince (all true), but also of ghosts and fairies (not confirmed!). What could be more romantic, she thought, as the tiny harbour came into view. She identified the large white building off to the right as the appropriately named White House Hotel. Beyond the harbour to the left stretched a sandy beach scattered with rocks and guarded by boats drifting at anchor.

The harbour wall came ever closer. Nicole's eyes swept over the people queuing alongside a tractor and trailer, from which cases and bags were being unloaded. She tried to pick out Ben. Ah, there he was! Standing to one side, hand shading his eyes as he searched the ferry for her. A simultaneous wave of their hands made them both laugh.

'Morning. Have a good trip?' Ben welcomed her as she jumped onto the breakwater. This was followed by a quick kiss as they sidestepped the other passengers pushing past.

'Fine, thanks. And what a gorgeous day! Can't wait to start exploring.' Nicole replied, anticipation of the day ahead causing her pulse to race.

'There's loads of time. Thought we could start by having breakfast at The Mermaid,' he waved his arm towards a clutch of buildings off to the left. 'The others will be down later after their lie-in.' He took her hand and headed off past the Harbour Office. It appeared that other day trippers had the same idea about breakfast as a small group followed them past the shops and into the courtyard of The Mermaid. Ben found them a table before going off to order the food.

The sun slanted in through the neighbouring trees, highlighting tiny specks of midges and dust motes dancing in the air. The excited chatter of visitors continuing on their way past the pub died down leaving the courtyard in peace. Nicole closed her eyes, happy to be still for a moment.

'Don't tell me you've fallen asleep already! Doesn't bode well for the hectic day I've planned.' Ben grinned at her, lowering a tray onto the table. Nicole's eyes shot open.

'Just enjoying the atmosphere. Don't worry, I'll be up for anything after a refuel.'

Ben laid out the coffees, juice and toast and they tucked in.

'Seriously, I thought you might enjoy a mixture of relaxing on the beach and walking round the island. As it's only a mile and a half long that won't take much time, but there's lots to explore and, of course we'll need to stop for lunch. Can't let your blood sugar get too low, can we?'

'No, Doctor, we can't.' Nicole sent him a cheeky smile before adding, 'Where will we have lunch?'

'Nick suggested The Ship, which has a great seafood menu. Will be quieter there too as it gets busy here once the day trippers start piling in. I thought we could explore first to work up an appetite and then head off to the beach this afternoon. Sound ok to you?'

'Very okay, thanks.'

Ben reached out and touched her hand. 'If you enjoy yourself today, we could always come back on our own sometime.'

'Sounds good. I'm sure – '

'Here we are! Hope we're not interrupting anything?'

Nicole looked up to see a tall, lanky man grinning down at them, accompanied by what she deemed a loved-up couple holding hands.

'Jonathan! Let me introduce you to Nicole, the friend I was telling you about. Nicole, Jonathan. He's another saddo like me, a doctor so devoted to his patients that he doesn't have time to meet lovely ladies like you!'

Nicole laughed as she shook Jonathan's outstretched hand.

'And here's our happy couple, Jeanne and Nick. They were married in Herm last year and are now expecting Mauger junior.'

Jeanne, grinning broadly, slid onto the bench opposite, Nick joining her. After a flurry of greetings, Jonathan went in search of coffee. Nicole liked what she saw of Ben's friends. Jeanne's smile was warm, spreading to the bright blue eyes framed by long dark hair. Her bump was barely noticeable under a loose T-shirt. She guessed that Nick looked close to forty, his dark brown hair flecked with grey and the lines around his eyes crinkled as he smiled. His deeply-tanned face was that of a man who spent most of his time outdoors. As his arm closed protectively around Jeanne, Nicole felt a momentary pang of envy. Not because she fancied Nick, attractive as he was, but because Jeanne looked as happy and content as *she* wanted to be. Glancing towards Ben, she caught him looking at her with a speculative look and her stomach flipped. *Perhaps I just need to be patient...*

The little group settled quickly into animated conversation, sharing basic information as to their backgrounds and how they had become friends. Nicole was intrigued to learn that Jeanne had written a best-selling book based on her family's history and love of cooking, titled *Recipes for Love*.

'Wow! That's brilliant! I'd never have the patience and dedication to write a book. Have you written anything else since?'

'I've started writing a novel set during the Occupation but I'm not sure if I'll finish it before I get…distracted,' Jeanne laughed, patting her bump. 'Four months until our lives change forever.' Nick smiled and kissed her and again Nicole felt a pang. *Stop it, you stupid idiot, remember how people used to be jealous of you and Tom!* That did the trick and she focussed once more on her companions, managing a quick squeeze of Ben's hand which earned her an answering smile.

Fortified by the coffee they set off up the steep hill towards Le Manoir, roughly the centre of the island and where the Manor House and cottages were to be found. Nicole paused periodically to enjoy the view through the trees towards the harbour and over to Guernsey. She also needed to catch her breath, wishing she was more fit. The tennis in Spain had helped but she hadn't done much since. As they came around the last bend the lane levelled out and to the right was what appeared to be a fortified village, protected by a tall granite wall, and entered through a stone archway.

'Here we are, home sweet home.' Ben's arms encircled the village composed of cottages, a small church and what looked like a castle. He grinned, 'Actually our home's this cottage.' He pointed to one of a row facing out to sea.

'Great views,' Nicole said, standing with her back to the village and looking out across to Guernsey. A short journey by boat but a world away in atmosphere. Nicole appreciated how quiet it was, untroubled by the sounds of people or traffic. Not even cycles were allowed and the only vehicles were the tractors and quad bikes used by the staff.

After a tour, which included the tiny school for the islanders' children, they set off eastwards. They took their time, giving Nicole a chance to savour the beauty of the island; passing a sea of tents staked out in the campsite as they headed to the cliff path. A few minutes later, stopping to rest on a southerly cliff, Nicole had not only a clear view of Sark but could make out Jersey on the horizon.

'I can see why you love coming here. It's as if we're on another planet!' Nicole said, spinning round with pleasure. The men smiled but Nicole noticed Jeanne's face had clouded.

'What's the matter? Are you in pain?'

Jeanne shook her head. 'No, just an old, bad memory that's all. Nothing to worry about.' Nick hugged her close, a concerned look on his face.

Nicole was puzzled but felt she couldn't pry and let Nick and Jeanne take the lead on the path. Jonathan tagged behind them, leaving her and Ben to bring up the rear .

'What was that about?' she whispered to Ben.

'It's a long story, but her parents were killed when their boat was forced onto rocks on the way back to Guernsey from Herm. Jeanne, only sixteen, was injured and suffered amnesia. She didn't learn the truth of what happened until a few years ago and was left pretty scared of boats, as you can imagine. Anyway, thanks in part to Nick, Jeanne's made a full recovery. Having their wedding here was a way of celebrating that it was behind her.'

'Poor Jeanne! How awful for her! But at least she seems so happy with Nick and with the baby on the way…'

'Yep. They're a great couple. I guess she must be missing her mother, though. Women need their mothers when they have babies, don't they?'

'I suppose so. If I ever have a baby there'll be two mothers vying to be involved!' Nicole laughed.

'Oh, you do want children? As you hadn't any with your husband I assumed you didn't.'

Nicole noticed an odd expression on Ben's face.

'Yes, I do. But I've only recently realised that. I was too busy with my career before and Tom wasn't that keen.

I've…changed my mind about lots of things lately.' She shrugged. 'It's as if I'm finally growing up and seeing what's really important in life. Which is people, relationships. Not high-flying careers which can leave you isolated from family and friends. Whatever I end up doing, I'm not going to make that mistake again.'

Ben smiled warmly.

'Mm, sounds as if you've been doing a lot of soul-searching. I suppose your biggest decision is what to do about…Tom. And your job.'

She took a deep breath.

'I've decided to divorce Tom, though he doesn't know yet. We've grown apart. And if our marriage ends there's no way I can return to my job. Which is fine by me. I could do with a fresh start.'

'Ah, right.' Ben pulled her close and kissed her. A long, slow kiss that promised so much.

Settled under an umbrella in the garden of The Ship, the little group enjoyed a bottle of chilled Sauvignon Blanc while waiting for their food. Jeanne, sipping fruit juice, had recovered her composure and they were all laughing at one of Jonathan's jokes. Nicole had been surprised at his ability to amuse. Under the nerdy exterior of black-framed glasses and pale face lurked a natural entertainer. And, according to the others, a great doctor.

The walk along the steep cliff paths had produced a healthy appetite as Ben had predicted. As their order of freshly cooked mussels, sea bass and lobster arrived, the appetising smell and sight brought the conversation to an abrupt halt.

They rounded lunch off with much needed coffees, before setting off along the lower coast road, skirting The Mermaid Tavern. As they came abreast of the beach Nick pointed out his boat, a sleek cabin cruiser at anchor a few feet from shore.

'You'd be welcome to join us for a trip sometime, Nicole. We often come over for the day in the summer and another woman would even up the numbers a bit.' He grinned.

'Love to. Used to enjoy boating when I lived in Jersey.'

'Nick refurbished the boat himself and I can vouch for its comfort. No expense was spared on the boss's boat, eh?' Ben said, in reference to Nick's business as a boat-builder. 'I could do with his skills at my house but for some reason he's not keen to help!'

'Haha,' Nick replied with a grin, 'you know I was working flat out on both the cottage and the boat for months and needed to relax with my lovely wife.' As if to prove his point he wrapped his arm around Jeanne, giving her a resounding kiss.

After much exaggerated sniggering from the others, they settled to a steady walk, the two couples hand in hand, letting Jonathan lead the way.

'So, what's this about a cottage?' Nicole asked Jeanne, coming abreast as the lane widened.

'I inherited an old cottage from my grandmother and decided to renovate it before selling. But then things changed,' Jeanne glanced at Nick with a smile, 'and I stayed. My builders did all the heavy work but Nick offered to provide fitted cupboards and wardrobes which took him months in his spare time.' Another glance at a now grinning Nick. 'His offer was conditional on his being allowed to move in with me. I wasn't too sure at first but then he proposed!' She giggled.

'That's soo romantic! Where's your cottage?

'Perelle, on the west coast. Next time we have a barbecue you must come. We're famous for our barbecues, aren't we, Jonathan?'

'You sure are. I was present at the first one Jeanne held, before these two became an item. And there's been many since. They've become part of our social calendar and not to be missed.'

'Sounds good to me. My social calendar's pretty empty these days.'

Ben gave her a quick kiss before whispering, 'I'd be only too happy to fill it up for you.'

Nicole caught her breath. *What's made him so much more flirty? I thought he wanted to just stay friends? But that kiss! And now...*

By this time they were approaching the sandy common, covered in scrub grass and wild flowers. They had to watch their step, with rabbit holes ready to trap unwary ankles. Ben pointed out the landmarks of an obelisk to the north and Neolithic burial chambers to their left, known as Petit Monceau. Ben assured Nicole that he'd show her around more thoroughly another time. Fine by her, the sea and beach beckoned. And it meant he thought there would be another time.

The path wound round the edge of the common, bordered with ferns and spiky marram grass. Hardly a soul came into view before they stepped onto the dunes of Shell Bay. With most of the visitors stretched out near the little café on their right, the friends headed left along the beach before spying a large, open space. Flopping down on her towel with a contented sigh, Nicole asked Ben if he'd mind applying her suncream. With a grin, he squeezed the cream on her back and legs and slowly, sensuously, rubbed it in. Wonderful! It had been so long since she'd enjoyed a man's touch and she was drifting into a trance-like state when Ben gave her a light tap on her bottom, saying, 'My turn now!'

Nicole was happy to reciprocate as she rubbed in the cream as slowly as she could. The sight and touch of his smooth, muscled legs and back were producing a decidedly erotic response within her when Jonathan shouted, 'Hey, you two! Do we have to throw cold water over you?'

Looking up she saw the three of them looking on in amusement and had to laugh.

'No, we're fine, don't worry!'

It wasn't long before they were all comatose from the combination of hot sun and wine.

Later, they enjoyed a long refreshing swim in the clear, blue water, warmed by the jet stream. While they were towelling off, Ben checked his watch and told Nicole it was time to make their way to the Rosière Steps for the ferry. Thanks to the steep drop in the tides, the boat could only use the harbour at high tide and it was now low, meaning a longer walk to the boat. The others insisted on accompanying them, so bags were packed and after much pulling on of T-shirts and shorts they were ready.

They were crossing the common when it happened.

Nicole had twisted round to catch something Jeanne was saying and her foot caught in a rabbit hole. With a cry, she stumbled, jerking her ankle. All went black.

chapter 26

'Wha...what happened?'

As Nicole opened her eyes she found Ben staring down at her, his face filled with concern.

'It's okay, you fainted after you fell. Looks like you twisted your ankle, but I don't think it's serious.' He put his arms under her shoulders. 'Take a deep breath and I'll help you sit up.'

Sitting up she felt a lot better and registered the protective circle of her friends. She managed a wan smile. 'That was a bit dramatic! I don't normally fall at people's feet!'

Jonathan said 'Well, I think the patient's not on the danger list so we can relax, folks.' He turned his attention to Nicole's right ankle. Gently, he removed the strappy sandal and ran his fingers over her foot.

'How's that feel when I move it?'

Nicole, still supported by Ben, felt a stab of pain as Jonathan slowly rotated her ankle. 'It hurts. Shall I try and stand?'

Ben held on as, putting all her weight on her left foot, Nicole stood up. Holding her breath she shifted her balance so that both feet were flat on the ground. Pain flicked through her foot but she kept her balance.

'Okay, now try to walk. Don't worry, I'll catch you if needed,' Ben said, letting her go.

Nicole managed to hobble a few steps, gritting her teeth against the pain.

'Oomph! It hurts!'

Ben and Jonathan exchanged glances before Ben said, 'There's no way Nicole can go home on the ferry today. If we can get her back to the cottage would it be all right with everyone if she stayed here tonight and rest her ankle? We can use ice to bring down the swelling and I've got some anti-inflammatories that'll help.'

'That's fine by us,' replied Nick, having received an answering nod from his wife. Looking at Jonathan he went on, 'There's the sofa-bed if you don't mind moving out of the bedroom for Nicole and Ben.' Jonathan nodded. 'Good. I'll ring the office and see if they'll send the Gator to carry Nicole back to our cottage.'

Ben helped Nicole to sit down on a tussock of grass and dropped beside her. He gave her a hug. 'Sorry about this. Hope it's not going to spoil your weekend. If you rest your ankle for the rest of today you should be able to walk tomorrow.' He grinned. 'You know, not many people get to have two doctors on call for a twisted ankle!'

She murmured, 'Looks like I'll be able to check out your bedside manner later.'

He frowned. 'Mm, I think we'll keep it purely professional, Mrs Oxford. Wouldn't want to risk further injury, would we?'

Nicole felt confused. Was he serious?

The Gator deposited Nicole at the rented cottage and the driver helped her to sit outside while she waited for the others to arrive. Although her ankle throbbed she felt relaxed. It hadn't been pleasant, but the bottom line was she was in good hands. Very good hands! Hélène, on receiving a call from Nicole, expressed only mild concern once she learned that Ben and Jonathan were on the case. Nicole hadn't felt it necessary to explain the sleeping arrangements that night. She smiled. Even if nothing happened between them, it was a good feeling knowing they'd be sharing a room. She'd assured her mother that she'd be back in time for the family lunch the next day.

'I can hardly miss meeting my brother and sister, can I?' Nicole said before signing off.

It didn't take long for Jonathan to make up an ice pack for her ankle, securing it with a light bandage. It was to remain in place for twenty minutes and then again every few hours. A couple of ibuprofen completed the treatment. Nicole stretched out on the sofa, her foot raised on cushions while Jeanne made tea in the kitchen. The men, grabbing beers, disappeared outside to set up an impromptu barbecue.

'Here you are, strong sweet tea just as the doctor ordered.' Jeanne said as she put the mug down next to her.

'Doctors are bossy aren't they? I hate sweet tea! But, if I must…'

She grimaced at the first sip, but felt obliged to continue. It was meant to help with shock but, given a choice, she'd have asked for a brandy.

They chatted amiably as the men fired up the portable barbecue Nick had brought over on his boat. They hadn't planned to use it that night but to go down to The Mermaid for a Black Rock Grill. Nicole's enforced presence scuttled those plans but they'd assured her that their own barbecue would be as much fun. Fortunately, Nick and Jeanne had brought plenty of meat and fish with them and they'd picked up fresh bread from the local shop on the way back. It wasn't long before the appetising smell of barbecuing steak, sausages and prawns wafted through the open windows.

The evening drifted by, fuelled by good food and alcohol. And good company. Nicole had been helped outside, sitting with her foot up on a chair, while the others stood or perched on the low granite garden wall. Occasionally, the sound of music wafted up from the harbour village but it still felt as if they were in a world apart. The painkillers kicked in and, together with the ice packs, reduced the pain in Nicole's foot to a barely noticeable level. The couple of glasses of wine her "doctors" had allowed her to imbibe may have played a part. Not wanting to disturb their neighbours, they moved back indoors around ten o'clock and it wasn't much later when Nicole started yawning.

'C'mon you. Bed.' Ben supported her and, after goodnight kisses all round, she hobbled off to their bedroom feeling pleasantly woozy.

Ben left her to undress, saying he'd be back in a minute. It was only after she'd stripped off her T-shirt and shorts that Nicole felt unsure of herself. She covered herself up with the duvet on one of the twin beds. Hmm, what happens now? Was he really planning on maintaining the "professional" approach?

Ben knocked on the door before coming in to sit down on her bed. He reached out to stroke her hair.

'It's been quite a day, hasn't it? How are you feeling now?'

'Much better, thanks. Hardly any pain. I feel a bit of a fraud…'

'Don't be daft! You'd have been hard pushed to get back to Guernsey on that ankle. Anyway, you'd missed the last boat,' he grinned.

She reached out to touch his hand.

He shook his head. 'Get ye behind me, Satan! You need to sleep. I'll sit up a bit longer with the others.' He bent down and kissed her cheek, pulling away before Nicole could react.

Feeling disappointed, she turned over and, in no time, was fast asleep.

Her friends, forgoing a lie-in, escorted Nicole to the harbour on Sunday morning in time for the nine o'clock ferry. Ben was returning with her so that he could drive her car back to La Folie. Hélène had agreed to take him to White Rock to catch the midday ferry, allowing him to enjoy his last afternoon in Herm as planned.

Nicole was relieved to find her ankle almost pain-free and insisted that she could walk unaided. Ben maintained a gap of only a few inches between them to be sure.

After much kissing and hugging, she said goodbye to Jeanne, Nick and Jonathan, promising to see them again soon. They'd exchanged phone numbers and Jeanne was particularly insistent that Nicole popped down to Perelle soon, 'So we can have a girly chat without the men getting in our way.'

The return trip was so different to the one she'd made only the day before. Then, Nicole had been full of anticipation and excitement, wondering what Herm had in store for her. Now she knew. Not only was the island even more beautiful and beguiling than she'd expected – in spite of the rabbit holes – but she was pretty sure she'd found love. In the shape of the man who now stood on the deck beside her, holding her tight. Although nothing had actually *happened* last night, Nicole felt that something had changed between them. Although Ben was still sending out mixed messages she was sure he had feelings for her. Or nearly sure.

Nicole had been worried that she would have been booked for overstaying in the car park but was lucky. No ticket. She was able to relax on the drive home, wanting to enjoy the time on her own with Ben. Remembering the lingering kiss on the cliff, she shivered.

'You okay? Not cold are you?' Ben asked, glancing at her.

'No, I'm good, thanks.' She smiled at him.

He nodded. A few minutes passed and he cleared his throat.

'I'm sorry about what happened to you yesterday, your ankle. How about if I take you out to dinner tomorrow night? Make amends?' He grinned.

'Thanks, I'd like that.' She felt her stomach flip-flop. At last!

They drew up outside the house and Ben strode round to help her out.

'Hey, I can manage! I'm not an invalid, you know.'

Raising his eyebrows, he took hold of her elbow as she swung her legs out of the car. Grinning at him, she set off to the front door while Ben followed with her rucksack.

'Hello, I'm home!'

They headed to the kitchen and found Hélène and Eve finishing their breakfast.

'How are you? Ankle better?' Hélène asked, coming forward to give Nicole a hug.

'It's not bad, thanks. Just the odd twinge. But I did have free expert medical care!' Nicole turned and grinned at Ben. 'I've been used to the NHS and forget it's private health care over here. I presume I won't be billed?' She asked, her head tilted to one side.

'Oh, I think I can stand you a freebie. As long as you don't make a habit of it.' He smiled before sitting down next to Eve, asking how she was. Apparently better, she was happy to chat to Ben while Hélène made coffee for everyone. Eve demonstrated how well she managed her frame by walking outside, watched on either side by Ben and Nicole, who said, 'I could have done with a frame like that yesterday!'

Hélène told Nicole that Adrian had asked to come round and meet Eve after the family lunch.

'He has to earn my seal of approval if he wants to court my daughter,' Eve said, glaring at Hélène.

Her daughter's face dropped.

Eve snorted. 'I was joking! But I hope he behaves himself like a gentleman this time or he'll have me to contend with.'

'Grandmother! Don't be mean. This is a big day for us, meeting the family for the first time.' Nicole reached over and touched her grandmother's arm. She had the grace to look apologetic, mumbling 'sorry' to Hélène.

Ben cleared his throat and stood up. 'I think it's time I made tracks to the ferry, Hélène, if you're ready?'

'Of course. Won't be long, Mother.'

Nicole followed them out to the car, where Ben turned and kissed her. On the cheek. 'I'll pick you up at seven tomorrow,' he murmured in her ear, 'And careful with that ankle!'

'Yes, Doctor. See you later.' Nicole grinned.

★★★

Hélène was thoughtful as she drove home again. On an emotional level, anxiety and hope were vying for space. Anxiety about Karen's reaction to her and hope that at least Michael would accept her as his father's new partner. She saw this lunch as a test that she wanted – needed – to pass. Adrian hadn't said that he'd give her up if Karen insisted he did, but her fear of rejection was still close to the surface. Negotiating the many bends that led home, Hélène reflected on the recent upheaval in what had been, until then, a fairly boring life. The only excitement had been her love affair with Adrian and that had ended badly. She sighed. She'd lost both him and her child and been reconciled to being a childless spinster. Not a happy prospect, but realistic. Then Nicole had appeared, bringing love and hope with her. She smiled at the thought of her vibrant daughter who shared her eyes but was much more outgoing and confident than she'd ever be. The young woman who'd not only brought herself into her life, but had been instrumental in reuniting her with Adrian.

Come on, woman, get a grip! Stay calm and know that you're loved and it will be all right.

With that thought whirling around, Hélène pulled in to the drive and went to see if Nicole was ready to leave.

★★★

Nicole, dressed in cropped jeans, a red T-shirt and matching sneakers, slid into the passenger seat.

'You like nice, Hélène. Green suits you.'

Hélène, wearing a green stripy top and a white skirt, turned and smiled.

'Thank you. I love the bright summer colours, don't you? Helps you to feel more cheerful.'

'Guess we both need to feel good seeing as we're the potential "Spectres at the Feast".' Nicole saw Hélène turn pale and reached out to touch her arm. 'Hey, it'll be all right. They can't eat us, you know! And whatever they think of us is their problem. We'll still have each other.'

Hélène gave her a quick, grateful-looking smile.

'Thanks. That means a lot to me. I've been so worried that if his children really take against me that Adrian will…'

'No, I know what you were going to say, but he won't. He loves you, anyone can see that. And remember this lunch is going to be much harder for him. He's the one who betrayed their mother, in their eyes at least. Although he did stay with her and they must give him brownie points for that.' She took a deep breath. 'Whereas you…lost both of us. So don't feel bad on their behalf.'

Hélène glanced towards her with a whispered 'Thank you.'

Nicole stroked her arm again before looking ahead. If truth be told, she was feeling as nervous as Hélène, but was determined not to show it. Acting confident was something she was good at. Very good.

The car park at Crabby Jacks was filling up fast. Getting out of the car Hélène pointed out Adrian's car. Nicole linked arms and, smiling broadly, led her towards the entrance.

'Hélène! Nicole! Over here.' Adrian waved at them from an outside table in a quiet corner, set for six plus a high chair. Three pairs of eyes swivelled towards them as Nicole steered Hélène forwards.

Nicole swept a brief glance over the woman and two men staring at them. Karen, unsmiling, turned her head away, giving her attention to the little boy in a high chair. Mm, not a good start. Now which is…

'Let me introduce you all. Hélène and Nicole, this is my son Michael, son-in-law Dave, daughter Karen and my grandson Luke.' Adrian's arms waved towards the seated figures.

Michael, a younger version of Adrian, tall with thick brown hair, smiled and stood up to shake their hands. Dave, shorter with fair, cropped hair and wearing a serious expression, also stood to shake hands. Not bad so far, Nicole thought, turning towards Karen. She was met with barely disguised hostility, a look encompassing both herself and Hélène. Determined not to let it get to her, she reached out her hand, but Karen ignored it, turning back to Luke. Uh, huh. So that's how she's going to be. Looks like goodbye sister, Nicole felt a pang. She'd always wanted a sister…

There was an uneasy silence.

Adrian coughed and ushered the two women into seats opposite Michael and Dave, placing himself opposite Karen. Nicole saw Hélène's face drop and squeezed her arm. At least Adrian was sat on Hélène's other side for support, Nicole comforted herself.

Adrian asked what everyone wanted to drink and motioned a passing waiter to take the order. No-one seemed to want to begin a conversation so Nicole took a deep breath and plunged in.

'This must feel as weird for all of you as it does for me. I've never been the family skeleton in a cupboard before and, I admit, it's not a nice feeling.' She looked around the table, making eye contact with all but Karen, who still insisted on looking at her son.

Michael was the first to speak.

'It does feel weird, you're right. Until a few days ago I...we didn't know you existed. But it's not your fault, so don't feel bad.'

Dave looked as if he'd prefer to be anywhere but here, trying not to look at his wife.

Adrian spoke next. 'I want to make it clear to all of you,' he let his gaze settle on Karen for a moment before he went on, 'that I love Hélène and I... gave her up reluctantly many years ago.'

Hélène started and he gripped her hand. Luke seemed fascinated by the sight of his grandfather, smiling broadly at him. Adrian smiled back. He then continued, 'And I don't intend to lose her again. This time I want to give our...relationship a chance.'

Again it was Michael who spoke.

'Dad's right. I haven't seen him look so happy since...I can't remember. I always knew he and Mum weren't getting on and often wondered why he didn't leave her.'

Karen let out an audible gasp.

'How can you say such a thing?'

'Because it's true. She...she was pretty horrible to him at times but he hung in there and nursed her through that horrible cancer.' He looked from Adrian to Hélène. 'If he's found love again then I'm happy for him. What happened in the past is the past. We need to get over it.'

Hélène threw Michael a warm smile.

'Thank you, Michael. I appreciate your understanding.'

The focus shifted to Karen, who must have felt the gaze of several eyes upon her, for she lifted her head and mumbled 'I'm not as ready to forgive as my brother is. But I can hardly stand in Dad's way if he wants to take up with...with her again.' The look she gave Hélène was chilly.

Adrian looked less confident as he said, 'And there's Nicole, my...daughter. I'd like her to play a part in my future too.' Nicole smiled at him and his face cleared.

Before anyone could reply the drinks arrived and were handed around.

Dave, after a brief glance at his wife, looked at Hélène and said, 'I never met Carol so have no feelings about what happened in the past. But I do know how hard this is for Karen as she was very close to her mother.' He reached for his wife's hand before continuing, 'However, I agree with Michael that if Adrian's happy that's okay by me. And as Nicole is an innocent party then she should be accepted as such.'

'Thank you, Dave. That's very good of you,' Adrian said. He looked round the table before adding, 'Now, I think it's about time we looked at the menu and ordered some food. Agreed?'

The menus were picked up with what, to Nicole, seemed a collective sigh of relief. She felt the tension still palpable around the table and she admitted to herself that it wasn't panning out the way she'd hoped. Realistically, she couldn't have expected to be welcomed with open arms, but after all, these were her siblings. All were innocent parties as both Dave and Michael had pointed out. Karen was the stumbling block, for acceptance of both her and Hélène. She couldn't see that they could ever be one big happy family. But, as she sipped her wine, she asked herself if she actually needed that. She had two lots of parents and that should be enough for anyone, right? She sighed, not sure about that.

Glancing across at Michael she saw he was studying her intently.

'It was good of you to speak up on our behalf, Michael. Thanks. I'd like us to be friends if that's possible.'

169

'Sure, why not? I'm more relaxed about it than my sister. My *other* sister,' he grinned.

'Great! So, what sort of work do you do?'

'I'm an administrator for a Trust company. Bit boring but it pays well,' he took a sip of beer. 'What about you?'

Nicole told him about her television work and he plied her with questions, showing a keen interest in what she did. For a moment Nicole was able to forget why they were all there, enjoying the company of someone her own age.

The food arrived, providing a temporary break in the conversations. Looking around Nicole noticed that Hélène was chatting to Dave while Adrian and Karen fussed over Luke. As everyone started to eat Nicole stole a quick look at Karen. A big woman without the height to carry it off, she had scraped her hair back in an unflattering pony tail. *Mm, doesn't look as if she cares about how she looks. Is she that unhappy? She certainly looks uptight as she hasn't stopped frowning. Could just be because of us, I suppose.* Nicole looked over at Luke, a smiling little boy who possessed his father's fair hair and blue eyes, and whose face was now smeared with tomato sauce from his pasta. She would love to get to know him but realised it wouldn't happen yet.

Michael must have noticed her gazing at the others as he leaned forward, whispering, 'Families, eh?'

'I guess. Mine was very small, no siblings or cousins. Only elderly aunts and grandparents who died years ago. Quite boring, actually.'

Michael checked that the others were deep in conversation before continuing.

'Well, I'd settle for boring any day if it meant no rows or tears. I'm for the quiet life, me.'

'Don't you want to marry and have a family one day?'

He shook his head.

'I'm not that keen. Happy to be the bachelor boy who can please himself. I've got my own flat in Town and a good social life. What more could a chap want?' He spread his hands and grinned. 'What about you? I understand you're married but you've split up?'

Nicole swept her hand through her hair and sighed.

'Yes, it looks as if we'll be getting a divorce. But it hasn't put me off marriage. I'll just be more choosy next time.' As she tackled her steak, Nicole thought about Michael. He seemed nice enough, not very deep, but she could live with that. At least he didn't seem the type to make waves. Unlike Karen...

'Have you lined up a replacement yet?'

Nicole nearly choked on her steak. 'Certainly not! It's far too soon. Why do you ask?'

'Oh, I've got a couple of mates who'd love to be introduced to my gorgeous sister,' he grinned.

'No thanks. I'm happy to be single at the moment. But thank you for the offer.' She felt rattled. Michael had only been trying to help, but it hadn't felt right. Perhaps because she *did* have someone in mind, but couldn't admit it. Lost in thought, she continued to eat her steak in peace while Michael and Dave settled into a chat about what sounded like a local racing car event on the beach. Not her thing at all.

By the time desserts and coffees were ordered and, helped no doubt by the effect of the alcohol, everyone seemed a little more at ease. Dave and Michael changed places so that Dave could talk to Nicole.

'How are coping with meeting us? Not been easy, has it?' Dave asked her.

'No, it hasn't. Not surprising, I guess. I...I'm sorry that Karen feels the way she does. Is there anything I can do to help her accept me?'

'Not yet. She's best left to come round in her own time. However long it takes,' he shrugged. His face portrayed the look of a man who had learnt the hard way to let his wife make up her own mind.

171

They chatted long enough for Nicole to discover that underneath his seriousness there lurked a sense of humour. He was even happy to poke fun at his profession, acknowledging that lawyers were perceived to be a "necessary evil".

Adrian brought the meal to an end by announcing that he was off to settle the bill, his treat. The others protested, but he was adamant. 'I suggested that we all came here as I wanted my family to meet each other. So it's only right that I pay.' His eyes swept over the table, pausing as he came to Karen, cleaning Luke's face. 'I'd like to think that the ice has been broken and that we can meet again.'

Michael murmured, 'I don't see why not.'

Adrian smiled at him before adding, 'Hélène and I are going away shortly,' Karen's head swivelled round, her eyes wide in surprise. 'And perhaps we could have a meal together at my house when we return.'

Karen cried out, 'Going away? It's a bit soon, isn't it?'

Her father said gently, 'I've wasted too much time all ready, Karen. My new motto is to live in the present.' He walked off to the bar.

Hélène moved into Adrian's vacated chair and leaned across to Karen.

'I know this has been very hard for you, Karen. It's not been easy for me either,' she said earnestly. Taking a deep breath, she went on, 'What happened between your father and me over thirty-five years ago may not have been right morally, but we genuinely loved each other and that can never be wrong – '

'Of course it's wrong if someone's married! How dare you try to excuse yourself. What you did was horrible and a…a sin. You hurt my mother and I don't think I'll ever forgive either of you!' Karen burst out, red in the face.

Hélène blanched. 'I'm so very sorry for what happened to your mother and you quite rightly honour her memory. But I…I had to give up my child, who I loved from the moment I first saw her.' Reaching out for Nicole's hand, she went on, 'If you can't forgive me that's fine. But can't you at least acknowledge Nicole, your half-sister and, as your husband said, is innocent…'

Karen stood up, looking as if she were fighting some inner battle. Her mouth opened as if she were about to speak but nothing came out. Dave touched her arm but she shrugged it off and strode towards the building and straight into an emerging Adrian's arms.

chapter 27

They were drinking tea in the garden when the doorbell rang. Hélène returned with Adrian, bearing a huge bouquet of flowers.

'Mother, this is my…my friend Adrian.'

Adrian smiled at Eve as he handed her the flowers. 'I'm very pleased to meet you at last Mrs Ferbrache. I understand that you like pink roses.'

Eve nodded her thanks and asked Nicole to put them in water. Then she studied this man who had had such an impact on her daughter. *Hmm, not bad I suppose. At least he has some manners.*

'Good afternoon, Adrian. I may call you that, may I?' He nodded. 'Good, Well, I'm also pleased to meet you. Won't you sit down?'

Hélène poured tea for Adrian and Nicole returned, sliding into her chair.

Eve looked from her daughter to Adrian and noticed Hélène's eyes brighten as she handed him the cup. His answering look spoke equal volumes. So, they *are* in love, she thought, a small smile playing around her mouth. *I do hope they can sort out the problem with his daughter – his* other *daughter. From what Hélène said she behaved quite rudely at lunch. That will be for Adrian to sort out, but I don't want to see Hélène hurt again.*

Eve proceeded to grill Adrian on his background and, on hearing he was a Bourgaize, realised she had known his parents. They ran a grocery shop in St Peters after the war and she had been a customer. She had liked the couple, hard-working and always pleasant. Eve vaguely remembered their son helping out in the shop on Saturdays. Again, polite and hard-working. Adrian went up further in her estimation.

'I expect Hélène has told you about our lunch and that my daughter Karen wasn't, er, too happy,' Adrian said, frowning.

'Yes, she did mention it. What a pity.'

'Mm. We talked after everyone else had left and I'm hopeful that she'll come round. I'm afraid Karen can be pretty stubborn when she wants but her husband, Dave, thinks she just needs time to accept the situation.' He turned to Hélène, who was gripping her tea cup so hard it's a wonder it didn't break. 'Even if Karen refuses to be friends with you, it won't alter my feelings and I still want us to try and make our relationship work.'

Nicole, a silent observer until now, cried 'Bravo! After all, you've waited long enough.' She grinned at her parents.

Eve gave a silent prayer of thanks. Perhaps all would be well after all.

★★★

The next morning heralded the arrival of a carer for Eve who would get her ready for the day. Another one would arrive in the evening to help with the bedtime ritual. Their cleaner Liz had agreed to work longer hours to help out until Eve went into respite care the following weekend. A less-stressed looking Hélène sat in the kitchen with Nicole as they discussed arrangements for Hélène's holiday.

'I'm perfectly happy for you to stay here while I'm away, Nicole. You could always invite Ben around for a drink or even a meal,' Hélène shot her a sly look, 'Unless you'd rather return to Jersey?'

Nicole grinned. 'Thanks, you know I'd prefer to stay here. It'll mean I can pop in on Grandmother, make sure she's all right.'

'I'd appreciate that. I am worried about how she'll cope. You know, she's never even been in hospital so it'll be a shock to her system. Having to do what she's told,' Hélène sighed.

'I bet she'll run rings round the staff by the end of the first day, you'll see. But if she really does hate it she can come back and I'll manage with the help of the carers.'

Hélène frowned. 'I wouldn't want you to take on the burden, after all you've only just met us and...'

'And I'm family, remember? I've grown quite fond of her and she's much more interesting than my other grandmothers.' Nicole reached over and patted Hélène's arm. 'Don't worry, it'll be fine. You and Adrian go off and enjoy yourselves and I'm expecting you to come back as good as engaged.' She laughed.

Hélène turned pink. 'Oh, I don't think – '

'Well, *I* do! Now, tell me more about the places you plan to visit...'

Nicole spent time working in the garden that morning, it not being sunny enough for the beach. It gave her time to think. Spending time with Adrian and Hélène together on Sunday had brought home to her that these were *her* parents. Even though she already had Mary and Ian. The problem was she was becoming fond of her new family. The thought prompted a twinge of guilt. How could she love them without betraying Mary and Ian? They'd spent years bringing her up and yet Hélène and Adrian – and Eve – had sort of taken over, with very little effort. They'd missed all the sleepless nights, worry of illness and accident (like the broken leg when skiing). As she attacked more weeds the problem wouldn't go away. She was beginning to feel disloyal to Mary and Ian, and it sat like a lead balloon inside her. *But what can I do? I can't stop loving any of them. Does it have to be mutually exclusive? I see Hélène and Adrian more like an aunt and uncle, not Mum and*

Dad. Mm, perhaps that's the way to go, won't encroach on my feelings for my adoptive parents. They'll always be special to me...

She took special care getting ready that evening. It had been a long time, in fact a *very* long time since she'd gone out on a proper date. Not since she'd first met Tom... Pushing down that memory, she concentrated on what to wear. The choice was limited but she had packed the mini dress she'd worn out with the girls in Jersey, just in case of a social event. Not that it had seemed likely at the time. But it made her feel good. And sexy. So, the mini dress it was, together with wedge sandals and a glittery necklace and matching earrings. Studying herself in the mirror she couldn't resist a huge grin. *Yep, not bad, girl, not bad.* Her hair gleamed, her skin glowed from days in the sun and the red dress clung to her body in a way that had drawn many admiring glances in Jersey. A slick of lipstick and she was ready.

Downstairs Hélène and Eve were finishing their supper when Nicole walked in.

'Mm, you look lovely, Nicole. Ben doesn't stand a chance!' Hélène said.

'That dress looks a bit short to me. But you do look pretty, I must admit,' Eve sniffed, looking her up and down.

'Thank you both. Thought I'd better make an effort as you warned me that Da Nellos was pretty smart and I...' The doorbell rang and Nicole checked her watch – only 6.30 – thinking Ben must be keen, she headed for the front door. Wearing a welcoming smile she pulled it open crying, 'You're early...' and her smile froze.

'Tom! What the bloody hell are you doing here?'

'Not quite the welcome I'd hoped for, darling. And who's early? Presumably the someone you've dressed up for.' Tom looked nearly as angry as she felt, his eyes raking her body as if he were mentally stripping her.

She felt her face burn. With anger and humiliation.

'None of your business! Just say what's so important that you had to come all the way here to tell me. Then leave.'

Before Tom could reply Hélène appeared at Nicole's shoulder.

'I heard raised voices and wondered what was going on. Who are you, young man? And why are you upsetting my daughter?'

Tom took a deep breath before answering,

'I'm Tom Oxford, Nicole's *husband*. I didn't come here with the intention of upsetting her, but as she appears to be going out on a date *I'm* upset. I only wanted to talk to her face to face, to try and save our marriage.'

Hélène put her arm around Nicole's shoulder. 'Would it be better for him to come in so that you can talk things through? I'll listen out for your...friend.'

Nicole felt shattered. All her joy at the prospect of the evening ahead had evaporated, leaving her feeling on the verge of tears. Perhaps she could get it over with as quickly as possible and he'd leave. Quietly. With a wave of her arm she ushered Tom in, steering him towards the sitting room. Hélène gave her a quick thumbs up before disappearing to the kitchen.

Tom, apparently deciding that anger was not a good idea, turned on the charm as soon as they were alone.

'Darling! I'm sorry I was so angry but – '

'Shut up Tom! I don't want to hear any more. You had absolutely no right to come barging in on me like this. I thought you were going to write. If I'd known you'd planned to come here I'd never have given you the address!'

'How else could I see you? You've blanked my calls for weeks and I *needed* to see you. To explain how much I've changed. How much I love –'

'Stop right there! I have something to tell you.' She paced around the rug, trying to steady her thoughts. Finally, she looked him straight in the eyes and said, 'I want a divorce, Tom. No more pretend separation – '

'You've met someone else, haven't you?' Tom's face grew red with anger and he grabbed her arms.

'Tom! You're hurting me. Let go!' Nicole felt his fingers biting into her flesh, at the same time registering the sound of the doorbell. *Oh my God! I don't want Ben to witness this. So humiliating!*

'Well, have you?' His fingers dug deeper into her bare arms.

'Yes...yes I have but –'

'I knew it! That dress that leaves little to the imagination,' he snarled, 'I suppose you're sleeping with him, are you?'

'No!' Technically true, she thought, though if he hadn't turned up she'd hoped... 'My decision is nothing to do with...with the man I've met.' She wasn't sure if that *was* true but still... 'I've thought long and hard about us, Tom, and I know in my heart that it's over. I want a new life, perhaps here in Guernsey. I don't know. But I do know that I no longer want to be your wife. I'm sorry.'

Tom let her go and collapsed in a chair, his head in his hands. Sobbing.

Nicole rubbed her arms, horrified by the marks clearly etched on her skin. Painful.

Feeling desperately in need of some moral support she crept out and headed for the kitchen, assuming that Hélène would have sent Ben away. She was wrong. He strode towards her, reaching for her inflamed arms.

'Nicole! What's he done to you? Bastard!' He went as if to leave the room in search of Tom, but she stopped him saying, 'It's okay, Ben. He grabbed my arms too hard, that's all. He...he was upset. I've told him I want a divorce. I don't think you two should meet, it'll only make matters worse.'

Hélène said, 'I agree with Nicole. You both stay here and I'll go and talk to him. Persuade him to leave quietly, if I can.' As she headed for the door, she added, 'Nicole, there's some arnica in that drawer for your arms,' pointing to a drawer behind her. 'And there's brandy in the cupboard above.'

Nicole almost fell onto a chair, feeling stunned by the turn of events. The evening was ruined. Bloody Tom! Ben gently rubbed the arnica cream into her arms before pouring a glass of brandy.

'Here. Just what the doctor would have ordered,' he said, smiling grimly.

'Thanks.'

The liquid burned its way down her throat and into her empty stomach. She felt light-headed. Looking around, she clocked that her grandmother wasn't there. Thank goodness!

Ben seemed to read her thoughts. 'Your grandmother's in her room. Apparently Hélène took her there when she heard the noise at the front door. My poor girl! What a nasty surprise for you.' He stroked her hair.

'Yes, it was. And I was so looking forward to tonight.' She gazed up at him with eyes threatening to release tears. She grabbed a tissue to blow her nose.

'And me. Look, if you're up for it I can see if it's okay for us to be a bit late. Or we can postpone – '

Nicole shook her head.

'I'd still like to go tonight if we can but I'd need to cover my arms to avoid gossip,' she managed a wan smile.

Ben checked his watch. 'It's only just after 7. I'll ring them and see, but what about Tom?'

'Oh, he can go to hell! I'm hoping Hélène will sort him out.'

Ben grunted and took out his mobile. While he was talking to the restaurant Nicole heard the front door open and close and held her breath. Please God, let him have gone! Hélène walked in and gave her a hug.

'It's okay, he's on the way to the airport to catch the last flight to England. He promised me he'd not bother you again.'

Nicole let out a sigh of relief.

Ben came off the phone to say that he'd managed to change the table to 8 if she still wanted to go. She shot upstairs to repair her make-up and grab a shrug.

Ten minutes later they left for Town.

The restaurant buzzed with life and with the first sip of her Bellini Nicole felt marginally calmer. But images of Tom, angrier than she'd ever seen him before, kept floating into her mind, threatening to unbalance her. Ensconced in the bar while waiting for their table, she began to feel that it might have been a mistake to come…

'Better now?' Ben asked, squeezing her hand.

'A bit, thanks.' Not wanting him to see her as an hysteric, she made an effort to appear calmer than she felt. 'What a great place this is. I love the décor, so…so Italian!' She waved her arm, encompassing the exposed stone and unusual artwork. *Mm, perhaps if I keep drinking I'll cope.*

'Good. And the food's even better. Ready to order?'

The waiter went off with their order of antipasto, followed by scallops and Dover Sole, allowing them to sit and talk. Nicole explained what had happened with Tom in more detail, bringing a frown to Ben's face.

'Perhaps I should have come in but Hélène insisted…'

'No, it's all right. I guess we had to sort it out between us and with you present Tom might have lashed out at you too. And I've never had the slightest desire to have men fighting over me.' Nicole forced a smile, slipping her hand into his. 'Mind you, I've always liked the idea of a knight in shining armour coming to the rescue when needed. When there's a dragon or two about!'

Ben grinned.

'I don't think there's many of those around here, but I'll happily be your knight whenever M'lady needs one.'

Nicole hoped that the need wouldn't arise and that Tom had caught the plane as promised. She wasn't sure she believed he'd go quietly after his outburst. As she sipped her cocktail unwanted memories of the past forced her to review her marriage to Tom. The first time she'd found he'd been unfaithful, with that tart on reception. She didn't have two brain cells to rub together but she did have big boobs and Tom...Then there was that bimbo in Make-Up, always cooing around him before a show, saying how gorgeous he was...Aagh! Bloody man!

'Nicole? You okay?' Ben was gripping her hand.

'Sorry. Was...was somewhere else. I think it's... got to me. I'm not very good company, am I? And you were trying to make up for Saturday!'

'Hey, it's okay. Let's at least enjoy our meal. And remember Tom's probably half –way back to England now. He can't hurt you again.'

God, I do hope you're right.

chapter 28

Hélène looked up from the paper as Nicole walked into the kitchen for breakfast.

'Did you have a good evening?' she asked, getting up to put the kettle on.

'Okay, thanks. But I was still so upset about Tom it spoiled it a bit. But the food was great.'

'Are you seeing each other again?' Hélène asked as Nicole grabbed a mug.

'Yes. We're having a drink tonight and he's going to show me his place afterwards.' She had felt disappointed that he hadn't suggested it last night, but, to be fair to him, she *had* been distracted. Before Tom had turned up she'd hoped that the evening might have flowed into the night but...She sighed. She definitely had the hots for Ben but she still wasn't sure how he felt.

'Nicole? What's wrong?'

'Oh, nothing. I'm still on edge about Tom, worried he might still turn up on the doorstep and cause another scene. And Ben...I'm not sure what he feels about me.' She sat down with her coffee.

'Do you think it's likely that Tom will turn up? He seemed genuinely upset last night, keen to get home.'

'I don't know. I think I've lost the knack of knowing what men will do or think. If I ever had it.'

'Are you talking about Tom or Ben here? Or both?'

'Both, I guess. Ben and I seem to hit it off and want to spend time together. But,' she sighed, 'I think I'm keener than he is and then there's Tom...'

Hélène nodded.

'Hmm. But from where I'm sitting you make a great couple and I hope it works out for you. I've always liked Ben, he's a genuine man who clearly loves his job and his patients.' She laughed. 'Perhaps you'd better brush up on your baking, after all food is the way to a man's heart and Ben loves cake!'

'Oh dear! I'm not the world's best cook, but I'll give it a go.' She sipped her coffee. 'How's Grandmother this morning? Does she know what happened last night?'

'She's fine. The carer's getting her ready. I must say, it's been a big relief not having to do that anymore.' Hélène looked serious for a moment. 'I had to tell her what went on last night as she'd heard the shouting. But she was quite calm about it. Wasn't impressed that Tom had turned up like that and seems to think you're well rid of him.'

'Yes, I'd rather it hadn't happened like that but...' Nicole shrugged.

'How are your arms?'

Nicole pushed up the sleeves. 'See, they're much better, thanks. It was so hot wearing this in Da Nello's but I didn't want Ben to be accused of assault. Not great for a GP!'

They chatted for a few more minutes before the carer came in to say that Eve was now in her sitting-room.

'I'll go and sit with her,' Nicole said, getting up and leaving the room.

'Good morning. Wondered if you'd like some company.'

'Yes, I'd like that. Did you have a good evening?' Eve gave her a searching glance.

Nicole gave her a short description of the meal before suggesting that her grandmother might like to continue her story. She didn't want to think about her own problems at the moment.

Eve looked thoughtful, twisting her wedding ring around her finger. Appearing to come to a decision, she smiled and asked where they'd left off last time.

Now it was Nicole's turn to think.

'Oh! You told me about Philip...'

Eve bit her lips.

'So I did. But that was right at the end of the war. It was fortunate for all of us that we didn't have crystal balls and still had hope.' She gazed at Nicole. 'Anything's bearable as long as you have hope. Hope for a better future, an end to an awful war which claimed so many lives and uprooted families.' Pausing to take a sip of water, she continued, 'We kept praying each Christmas that it would be over by the next one and life would return to normal. We made such plans for the future!'

'Who did, you and Philip? Were you in love?' Nicole held her breath, worried that her grandmother would be upset.

'Yes, we were in love, but it was a secret. His parents wouldn't have approved, you see. They had a far more eligible young woman in mind for their eldest son than a mere Land Girl!' Eve's tone was bitter and for a moment Nicole wondered if she should call a halt to their chat. But Eve took a deep breath and smiled at her.

'We had an ally in the form of his grandmother, who lived in the Dower House. She stayed on there after the Hall was commandeered and I used to deliver her produce from the farm. We got on like a house on fire!' Eve chuckled. 'Turns out she wasn't exactly Top Drawer either. Her family owned a factory up North and although they were wealthy were considered only middle class.'

'So what happened? How did she meet Philip's grandfather?'

'She was sent to a boarding school where she became best friends with the sister of Edward, her later husband. One year she was invited to spend part of the summer with the family. Apparently it was love at first sight when they met and Edward never wavered in his desire to marry her when she was older. And Lady Helen told me they were extremely happy.'

'Lady Helen? Did you name my mother after her?'

Eve shifted in her chair.

'Yes, she was such a lovely old lady and I…became very close to her. I was like a granddaughter to her and she was on her own a lot so I'd pop round whenever I could.' Eve chuckled. 'She could tell such stories! Just imagine, after she'd married Edward, she was introduced to Queen Victoria! Her husband had loads of influential friends so she enjoyed quite a social whirl.' Eve paused for another sip. 'For someone with my background, her stories were mesmerising. So I happily kept her company.'

'Did Philip tell her he loved you?'

'Yes, she wasn't a snob like his parents. And she'd organise it that if I called in while he was visiting her, she'd say she was tired and leave us alone for a while.'

'That was kind of her. She must have been very fond of you both.'

'Philip was her favourite grandson. His younger brother, Richard, took after Sir Michael, an arrogant man.'

'What happened to Richard?'

'I've no idea. He was a Captain in the army in the Far East and hadn't returned before I left. He was the heir by then, of course…' Eve's face clouded over and Nicole reached out to take her hand.

'I'm sorry, it must be painful to rake up the memories.'

Eve shook her head.

'No, it's all right. It was so long ago and I've had a good life since.'

'Did you stay in touch with Lady Helen after you left?'

Eve looked surprised.

'Oh, I haven't told you, have I? The dear lady died a few months before the end of the war. Before Philip was killed.'

Nicole wondered about her grandmother's relationship with Philip. She'd got the impression that they would probably have married if he'd lived but hadn't wanted to probe too deeply. *If she wants to tell me, she will.* That didn't stop her speculating why her mother had been named after Lady Helen. *Could it be that...? No, surely not!* If her mind had not been taken up with where, if anywhere, the relationship with Ben was heading, together with the now ever-present spectre of Tom, she might have given it more thought. Added to which, Hélène and Adrian were going away that weekend and she was feeling decidedly unsettled.

Hélène had driven off to the shops and Eve had retired for a nap when it happened. Nicole was in the garden, tackling the ever-present weeds when she felt arms grab her from behind.

'Who...' she cried before she was spun round to find Tom, dishevelled and bleary-eyed, staring at her. Her heart quickened in fear.

'Tom! You're supposed to be in England. What –'

'I missed the plane and anyway, I wanted to talk to you, darling. You didn't let me –'

'I don't want to hear what you've got to say! Can't you understand that it's over between us?' Taking a deep breath, aware she had to diffuse the situation, she went on more calmly, 'I'm sorry, Tom. Really, really sorry. But I...I can't be married to you anymore.'

Letting her go, he pushed his hand through his unkempt hair. His eyes pleaded with her as he said, 'Why? I know I've not behaved properly in the past, but I can change. I love you, Nicole. If I lose you it'll be like losing part of me!'

Nicole dropped her eyes, unable to look at him.

'I…don't love you the way I used to. It's over, Tom. You just have to… accept it.' She stepped back, afraid of his reaction. But he just stood there, white and still. While she held her breath, he suddenly straightened up, saying, 'I see. You really mean that, don't you?'

'Yes, I do. Please go home, Tom. Let's sort this out in a…civilised way. So we can both move on.'

'You're in love with someone else, aren't you? The man you were seeing last night?' His look was accusing.

'I…I'm not sure. But that's not the point. I've stopped loving *you*, Tom. So please…'

It seemed to her that Tom was dredging up all his strength as they faced each other.

'All right. I'll go. You can have your…divorce.' His voice broke before he added, 'Goodbye, Nicole. And…good luck.' He quickly kissed her cheek before striding off towards the front of the house. As she stood still, feeling completely spent, she heard the welcome sound of a car starting up and being driven fast down the drive.

Slumping down on the grass, she wept.

chapter 29

It had taken a while for Nicole to compose herself after Tom had left and was still in tears when Hélène arrived home. After telling her all that had happened, Nicole felt as if she could finally let it go. That Tom now accepted the inevitable and that she could make her own plans for the future. She wasn't sure what they'd be yet, but at least she was free. Or would be soon.

Before leaving for her drink with Ben, Nicole, wanting reassurance, phoned the farmhouse. After a few rings, while her stomach tied itself in knots, it was answered.

'Hello, Tom Oxford speaking.'

Relief flowed through her as she put the phone down. He *had* gone home! Good, now she could focus on Ben and whether or not they could be a couple.

They were meeting in The Ship and Crown overlooking the harbour, and Nicole felt the familiar butterflies in her stomach as she walked in and saw him at a table by the window.

'Hi, how are feeling now?' he asked, kissing her cheek.

'Much better since I found out Tom's left,' she replied, going on to tell him what happened that morning. Ben looked shocked but she said she was fine and believed that Tom had finally agreed to a divorce.

Nicole asked him about his day and they drifted into a relaxed conversation. When their hands touched she felt the electricity shoot through her. *Oh, surely he must feel it too? It can't just be me?*

'Right, shall we make tracks? It's not far but I'll make sure you're still following me.'

She drove up St Julian's Avenue and into The Grange, turning right behind Ben's car near the top of the road. A few minutes later he pulled into the small drive of a white stuccoed end of terrace, leaving her room to park alongside. As he opened the front door Ben said, with a grin, 'Remember it's a work in progress, so please ignore the mess.'

He was right. Lovely proportions, original covings and woodwork abounded but so did bags of plaster, boxes of tiles and pots of paint. Normally happy to explore other people's houses, Nicole had other, more pressing things on her mind as Ben led the way to the kitchen. This at least looked user-friendly, though not quite finished.

'Drink?' Ben asked, reaching for a bottle of wine.

'Please.'

'Here you are. Let's go to the sitting-room, one of the few rooms that I have finished.'

'Oh, this is lovely, Ben! And you did this yourself?'

She gazed around at the spacious room, admiring what looked like the original wooden floor and fireplace, the walls painted a soft buttery cream. Two sides of the room possessed tall windows dressed with their original wooden shutters. An enormous old brown leather chesterfield took pride of place along another wall, complimented by an antique dark red rug.

'Yep. Apart from the electrics and plastering, I leave that to the professionals. Make yourself comfortable while I close the shutters.'

He joined her on the sofa, nestling up close. Lifting up her chin, he stroked her face before planting a light kiss on her lips.

'Is this okay? If you'd rather not – '

'No, it's fine, honestly.' More than fine, she thought, desire coursing through her body.

Ben took her glass, placing it on the nearby table before pulling her down on the sofa. His kisses became more urgent as Nicole felt her need for him quicken. She began undoing his shirt buttons as his hands cupped her breasts under her top. He pulled back, whispering, 'I think it's time for bed, don't you?'

Happy to agree, Nicole let Ben lead the way upstairs. From her quick view of it, before she fell on the ultra-modern bed, his bedroom looked mercifully finished. Ben closed the shutters before joining her, helping her to slip out of her clothes. Nicole undressed him with practised ease and they slid under the duvet. Hands explored bodies and her breath quickened as Ben's fingers brushed first her breasts and then her stomach before slowly caressing her inner thighs. Her own hands stroked his muscled torso as they kissed. Her emotions threatened to overwhelm her. She'd wanted this man since that first, electrifying look. Hoped it was love and not lust. Now she knew it was love and she couldn't wait to share herself with him.

Passion drove them on and Ben entered her gently as she laced her legs around him.

'Oh, Nicole! I've wanted to do this since we met. It's been so hard to wait…' Ben groaned as he covered her with kisses, thrusting deeper and deeper inside her. She didn't want it to end, feeling the delicious rise of her body's response engulfing her in a tide of exquisite pleasure. As she let out a final cry, Ben shuddered and pulled away. Reaching out he curled his arms around her, murmuring, 'My darling, darling Nicole.'

She kissed him, feeling euphoric. *He loves me, I think he loves me.* Her last thoughts before she drifted off, content.

Nicole woke the next morning feeling on top of the world. The memory of the previous night's love-making stirred her body and she reached out for Ben. To find an empty space. Frowning, she sat up quickly before spotting a note on his pillow "Sorry to leave you like this, Sleeping Beauty, but one of us has to go to work. Catch you later. Ben x"

Grinning, she showered and dressed before going downstairs to find the ingredients for breakfast laid out in the kitchen. As she ate she felt as if she'd never been happier. It had been so long since she'd felt so in love...

Over the next few days she saw Ben in the evenings, staying over a couple of times. He made her laugh and she felt the hurt of the past few months melt away. During the day she either went to the beach or continued licking the garden into shape. Hélène gave her a hand when she could and by Friday they declared themselves satisfied with their handiwork.

'I can't remember when the beds looked so gorgeous,' Hélène remarked, tossing down her trowel. 'My parents were struggling to cope years ago but couldn't afford help and I could barely manage my own garden. I feel guilty about not doing much since I moved in,' she sighed. 'I was so resentful about giving up my home that I didn't care about this garden. Which was mean and stupid of me.'

Nicole gave her a hug.

'Don't be so hard on yourself. It was a big deal coming back and not having any support, emotional or physical. That's now changed, so it'll be easier to enjoy it.'

Hélène smiled. 'How come you're so wise and I'm so stupid? Isn't it supposed to be the other way around?'

Laughing, Nicole said 'I don't know about wise! I've got a lot of things wrong over the years but I'm slowly learning. Now, I'll put away the gardening tools and how about we bring Grandmother out for a tour of inspection? Followed by a celebratory glass of wine, perhaps? I think the sun's over the yard arm by now.'

'Good idea. I'll open a bottle of white and we can sit on the terrace.'

Hélène brought out the wine while Nicole fetched her grandmother.

'Please have a little walk round the garden and tell us what you think.'

Eve used her frame to walk onto the terrace, smiling as she saw Hélène with the wine.

'What's the occasion? We don't usually have wine at this hour.'

'No we don't, but we thought we'd celebrate our work on the garden. Mainly Nicole's, I have to admit. So, if you'll allow us to escort you, Mother, and then we'll sit down with a glass.'

Eve went ahead while Nicole and Hélène kept pace behind. Eve stopped at intervals to gaze at the full blooms of the herbaceous borders so long neglected. Now a riot of colour, with oriental poppies jostling roses, delphiniums, lupins and hollyhocks ranked against the fragrant hedges of escallonia. As Eve turned round Nicole saw the tears in her eyes.

'Are you all right, Grandmother?'

Eve pulled a tissue from her pocket and blew her nose.

'I...I'm overwhelmed. You must have worked so hard! It's lovely, thank you both so much.'

Nicole and Hélène shared a quick grin before they turned back. Hélène made Eve comfortable on cushions before pouring the wine.

'Here's to La Folie and its amazing garden!'

They clinked glasses and sipped their wine.

'It's hot enough to eat supper out here tonight. Would you like that, Mother?'

Eve nodded.

'That would be most pleasant. A lovely memory to take with me when I go to the home tomorrow.'

Hélène's brow creased.

'You are all right about going – '

'Yes, of course I am. It's only for a week and then I can come back to my lovely garden. Something to look forward to.'

'And don't forget I'll be popping in every day to check up on you. Hélène's told me they have a beautiful garden so we can sit outside if it's fine.' Nicole had a sudden thought. 'Why don't I pick some flowers for you to take in with you tomorrow? Remind you of home.'

'Thank you, my dear. I'd like that. Now, my glass is empty. More wine, please Hélène!'

Saturday morning saw La Folie in a state of bustle unknown for years. Hélène rushed about, checking that nothing had been missed from her mother's case, while finishing off her own packing. Nicole helped where she could, assuring Hélène that anything missed from Eve's case could be easily remedied. Gazing at her mother, Nicole couldn't help thinking how much she had changed since their first meeting. Not only were her eyes brighter but her mouth seemed less pinched, even though she was stressing herself over the packing. Nicole really hoped that the holiday in France would be worth it. She'd caught a glimpse of Eve's face in an unguarded moment and seen the pain and doubt reflected there. Her grandmother was putting on a brave face, but it looked as if she wasn't as happy about the respite stay as she'd maintained. Probably doing it to repay Hélène for her sacrifices. Nicole popped outside to pick the biggest bunch of flowers she could without denuding the garden.

Adrian arrived to pick up Hélène and emotional farewells were exchanged.

'Bye, Mother. I do hope you enjoy your stay – '

'Yes, yes. I'll be fine. Get along now and have a good holiday. And Adrian, you look after my daughter, now.' Eve glared at Adrian as he bent down to give her a peck on the cheek.

'I will, promise. Is there anything you'd like us to bring back? Cheese, wine, chocolate…?'

'A new heart would be welcome! But failing that, I'm quite partial to a nice Brie. Now you'd better go, don't want you to miss the ferry, do we?'

Nicole hugged and kissed Hélène, whispering, 'Good luck.'

Hélène whispered, 'And you' before getting into the car. A quick hug for Nicole from Adrian and they were off.

A few minutes later the ambulance for Eve arrived and Nicole helped carry her case and the flowers.

'I'll pop in tomorrow afternoon. Give me a ring if you need anything.' Nicole kissed her grandmother before waving her off.

It felt strange walking into the empty house and for a moment Nicole felt as if she'd been abandoned. Shaking her head at the daft thought, she headed for the kitchen to make a much-needed coffee. Only ten o'clock, it felt as if she'd been up for hours.

As she sipped her drink on the terrace she smiled at the thought of the weekend ahead. Ben was coming round at lunch time and they'd head off to the beach for a picnic. The deal was he'd supply everything for the lunch and Nicole would cook supper that night at La Folie. A worrying thought as she'd not cooked properly for yonks, but Hélène had dug out some recipe books for inspiration. Flicking through them, Nicole decided that fish was a safe bet for the main course, preceded by a starter of Parma ham and figs. The dessert could only be strawberries and cream, she thought. Easy-peasy!

By the time Nicole had unpacked her grocery shopping it was nearly time for Ben to arrive. She dashed upstairs to change into T-shirt and shorts, grabbed her bathers, towel and sun cream and ran back down to hear Ben's car crunching on the gravel.

'Did they get away okay?' He asked, planting a kiss on her lips.

'Yep, so I'm Home Alone!'

He grinned. 'Not this weekend you aren't! I've packed my toothbrush,' he pointed to a rucksack on the back seat. 'Right, let's head for the beach.'

Ben headed up to the north-west of the island, the road winding round the coast. Nicole had driven on the same road on her island tour but now enjoyed the luxury of being able to focus on the scenery while he drove.

'Where are we headed?'

'Le Grand Havre, a sandy bay with a little harbour. It's quieter than some of the other beaches but has a kiosk in case we run out of food.'

As they passed Cobo and The Rockmount, she noted how busy it looked. Still, bound to be on a sunny Saturday afternoon. Less than ten minutes later Ben pulled off onto a gravel car park serving a stretch of golden sand, with boats bobbing in the distance.

Grabbing their things they walked across the beach, sheltered by low slung sand
dunes.

'Oh, this is lovely!' cried Nicole, gazing around at the mass of nearly empty sand, dotted with rocks near the water's edge.

'Isn't it? I come here to clear my head after a heavy week at work. Although normally I like the sound of children, sometimes it's nice to have some quiet.'

'Uh huh. So why is this not as popular? It's gorgeous!'

Ben grinned. 'The toilets are a bit of a hike round the next bay. You've been warned!'

Making a mental note to watch how much she drank, Nicole settled herself on her towel while Ben unpacked the picnic. Her mouth watered as he set out crab ciabatta sandwiches, tubs of olives, a bowl of mixed salad and the requisite cutlery and plates. Reaching into the cool-bag, he pulled out a bottle of white wine.

With a flourish, Ben produced a white tea towel, placed it over his arm and gave a short bow.

'Lunch is served, Madame.'

Nicole giggled. 'Idiot! But it looks wonderful, thank you. You did remember the bottle opener and glasses?'

Ben reached into a bag, producing the very same.

'Happy now?' he smiled, before opening the bottle and pouring two glasses.

'Santé!'

'Santé!' Nicole replied, as they touched glasses. You couldn't really clink plastic.

Stretched out on their towels, they helped themselves to the food.

'Mm, this crab's delicious. Did you make the sandwiches yourself?'

'With my own fair hands! Which, by the way, got pretty messed up in the process. A friend catches crab in pots and I bought a couple off him, but I'd forgotten what a performance it is to pick crab. You might need to watch for elusive bits of shell. They're a bugger to find once you've picked the meat.'

Nicole nodded, her mouth full of crab sandwich.

Once they'd eaten their fill, Ben reached into the cool-bag for a bowl of mixed fruit. A few handfuls later Nicole, succumbing to the combined effects of wine and sun, yawned and said she'd like a nap. After packing away the detritus, they stretched out on their towels and closed their eyes, the sound of waves gently hitting the shore providing a soothing lullaby.

Their lazy afternoon was rounded off by a lengthy swim, incorporating much splashing and chasing in the shallows. Laughing and invigorated, they raced to reclaim their towels and get dressed. Moments later they were on the way home.

As Nicole unlocked the front door she felt like a usurper. After all, this wasn't *her* house but for the next week she was in sole charge. And here she was with a man in tow! Albeit one who had full permission to be there. Shaking her head she pushed open the door saying, 'Welcome! To my not so 'umble abode.'

Ben grinned as he carried in his bags.

After they'd cleaned up the picnic items they headed out to the garden with glasses of chilled wine.

'Hey! The garden's looking great. Who's the gardener?'

Nicole explained how she'd wanted to surprise her grandmother before she went to the nursing home.

'Well, if you like gardening so much mine needs some work, as you probably noticed.'

Nicole recalled the garden so overgrown that you couldn't even sit outside. A good size, it had potential to be beautiful once the shrubs and trees were cut back. Tiered areas of paving and grass added interest. Or they would if you could get through the brambles and weeds.

'*Some* work! A bit of an understatement, don't you think? I *might* be prepared to give you a hand if you'd clear it first. I've always thought walled gardens were a bit magical, but yours needs a large dose of fairy dust to pave the way. If you'll excuse the pun!' She smiled.

'Haha! You could be right. Sitting out here, surrounded by beauty – and I'm not just referring to the garden – does make me want to have a beautiful garden.' He sighed. 'It's the old problem, lack of time. I'm still struggling with the inside, let alone the outside. And I don't possess one green finger.'

Nicole, who hadn't missed the compliment, reached over and kissed him.

'If I do stay here a while, I might lend you my not-very-green-fingers, but you'd need to get a professional in first for the heavy clearing. This garden,' she waved her arm, 'only needed light digging, weeding and pruning. Yours needs a man with a digger and a machete!'

'Garden apart, do you think you'd like to stay here? As in get a job and somewhere to live?' Ben put his arm around her shoulders. She liked the feeling and cuddled into him. She was *so* in love with this man. But was he in love with her?

'Mm, I've thought about it, of course. Particularly since I've no pressing reason to go back to England, or even Jersey. I feel I'm in a Catch-22 situation.' She trailed her fingers down his arm. 'If I wanted to spend more time with you, then I'll need to stay and get a job. A big commitment. It depends on how *you* feel about me. You've seemed a bit reluctant to get...serious. And I've got my own issues after Tom. So...what *do* you feel about me?'

Ben cupped her face in his hands before kissing her lips.

'You're right, I didn't want to rush into anything. But I knew you were special from the first time I saw you.' He stroked her face, letting his fingers brush her lips. She felt her heart pumping away so fast surely he was bound to hear. 'I think I might be falling in love with you, but we both need time to see where it leads us. Would you be willing to take the risk and stay here? Without any promises?'

What had she got to lose? There wasn't anything waiting for her elsewhere, she might as well stay here – and hope.

'Yes, I'm willing.'

chapter 30

Nicole woke up the next morning and stretched. Her hand hit something soft and warm and she smiled. A big, full-of-wonder smile. Turning on her side she gazed at the recumbent form of Ben beside her. His hair spiked up from his head on the pillow, his mouth curled up in a smile. Mm, wonder what he's dreaming of? She continued to take in his face, resisting the urge to stroke it. He needed his sleep, she reasoned, particularly after such a night. Their lovemaking had reached an even higher pitch, Ben tender but insistent and she, well, "brazen hussy" came to mind. Perhaps Hélène was right, and food was the way to a man's heart. Ben had complimented her on the supper which, she admitted modestly to herself, had been delicious. They'd ended the meal by feeding each other strawberries dipped in cream. Messy but *so* erotic! The memory stirred her body in response, and she was considering waking Ben for a repeat performance when he stirred.

Opening his eyes he turned towards her, pulling her close.

'Morning, darling. Sleep well?'

'Mm, yes. Like the proverbial log. Though how logs can sleep…'

Ben's kiss silenced her and within moments all thoughts of logs vanished.

An hour later they sat in the garden enjoying breakfast. Nicole felt as if she'd burst with happiness. Their fingers constantly sought each other's, making it hazardous to drink steaming mugs of coffee.

She giggled. 'Perhaps we should focus on our breakfast or we'll be here all day.

'Okay. If we must.' He gave an exaggerated sigh before continuing, 'What shall we do for lunch? I'm happy to take you out somewhere.'

'Honestly, you men! Always thinking about your stomachs! Don't forget, Doctor, that we're visiting my grandmother this afternoon.'

'Us men need to keep our strength up, particularly if we have demanding girlfriends like you!' He grinned before kissing her cheek. 'Okay, let's have a scratch lunch with yesterday's leftovers. We can go out for dinner tonight instead.'

'Sounds good. So, how about a walk on the cliff this morning?'

The private nursing home looked welcoming as they swept through into the drive. The abundance of flower beds helped to create the appearance of a large, family home. The front door stood wide open, leading onto a tiled entrance hall furnished with polished tables topped with vases of flowers. Although Ben had assured her that the home was one of the best, Nicole had been concerned at what she'd find. So far, so good.

He held her hand as he guided her down the hall to a large, but homely, sitting room. Nicole searched for her grandmother, spotting her in a chair by the French windows. She grinned. Nothing changes! Before they could move, a nurse approached them, crying, 'Doctor Tostevin! How nice to see you. Are you here to see Mrs Ferbrache?'

'Yes, but not as her doctor, just a friendly visit. This is her granddaughter, Nicole Oxford. She'll be visiting every day while Mrs Ferbrache is here.'

'Of course. Nice to meet you. Your grandmother's told me all about you. She's settling in very well and has already made a friend or two.' The nurse smiled warmly at Nicole before bustling off to welcome more visitors.

'Hello, Grandmother. How are you?' Nicole bent to kiss her cheek.

Eve looked up and smiled.

'I'm well, thank you. Can we go out into the garden?'

Ben helped her with the frame and they found seats on the lawn, nestled under a spreading oak tree.

'Ah, that's better. The staff aren't keen on my coming out on my own in case I fall. I told them I'm perfectly capable of walking a few yards but they didn't listen.' Eve grumbled. Ben and Nicole exchanged glances.

'Are they looking after you all right, Mrs Ferbrache? Any problems and I'd be happy to talk to Matron.'

'Oh, no. Everyone's been very good to me. It's not like being at home, of course, but I can't complain.'

Reassured that all was well with his patient, Ben left the women to chat while he went in search of tea.

'You and the doctor seem to be getting on well, my dear.' Eve scrutinised her granddaughter. 'You in love with him?'

Nicole gasped. Nothing gets past this old lady!

'I…think so. I've decided to stay in Guernsey and look for a job and see what happens between us.' She looked her grandmother in the eye. 'Do you approve?'

Eve chuckled.

'Wouldn't matter if I didn't! But, as it happens, I do. I'd like to see both you and your mother settled before I…'

'Grandmother! Don't talk like that. You'll be with us for a few years yet. I promise.'

Eve looked as if she were about to say something, but changed her mind. Ben arrived with tea and cake and the conversation shifted to what Eve had been doing since her arrival.

Before they left, Eve showed them her room. On the ground floor, it had a large window onto the garden and

Nicole thought it looked very comfortable, if a tad small compared to what her grandmother was used to at home.

Nicole's sat lost in thought as they drove away. She didn't like the idea that her grandmother might not have long to live.

'Ben, is Grandmother very ill? She spoke to me as if she was.'

He remained quiet a moment, as if pondering how much to tell her.

'She has a dicky heart and is refusing to have the operation that could give her a few more years. Both your mother and I have tried to persuade her but...'

'I see.' She felt her throat tighten. 'How...how long has she got?'

Ben looked at her, his eyes full of sympathy.

'About a year, perhaps less. I'm sorry.'

Nicole nodded, feeling tears threaten. Ben squeezed her hand before concentrating on his driving. She searched out a tissue from her bag and blew her nose.

'She's been telling me about the time she spent in England during the war and how she fell in love with an airman. I think she's holding something back and I'm wondering if she doesn't want me to know until after she's...she's gone.'

'Hmm. If she does have a secret then it's up to her whether or not to share it. You don't think she's told Hélène?'

Nicole shook her head.

'No. Hélène's been surprised that Grandmother talks to me about the war. And I haven't repeated anything she told me as I wasn't sure if I should, or if Hélène would be interested. They weren't all that close, as you may have gathered. But I think that's changing. I hope so.'

Despite her concerns about her grandmother, Nicole enjoyed the rest of the day with Ben. After dinner they returned to La Folie for a nightcap. Ben didn't stay the night, having an early start on Monday, but he promised to cook her a meal the following night. He also agreed to engage a heavy-duty gardener at his house, Santa Rosa, to prepare the way for Nicole's "finishing touches", as he put it, grinning.

The next day Nicole sat on the terrace drinking coffee while browsing the Situations Vacant pages of The Guernsey Evening Press. The preponderance of vacancies were in the finance sector, of which she knew nothing. Her experience in the world of media was extensive, but she knew opportunities on the island would be scarce. A memory stirred in her brain, prompting her to dig out the phone book from under a pile of newspapers in the kitchen. Finding the number she made a call. Pleased with the outcome she thought, guiltily, that she hadn't phoned her parents for over a week. *I mustn't forget how important I am to them and how much they mean to me. Which they do, in spite of my "new" family...*

'Hi, Mum. How are you?'

'Oh, Nicole! We're both fine, thanks. It's so good to hear from you, how are things?'

'Well...' Nicole told her mother about Tom turning up unannounced but not about his outburst. And that she wanted a divorce. She went on to tell her about Ben and that she was planning to get a job and stay in Guernsey.

'My! Things are happening so quickly! Are you sure it's not a rebound thing? I don't want you getting hurt, darling.' Her mother sounded concerned.

'No, don't worry Mum. And I'm sure you'll both love Ben. Perhaps you could come over to meet him and...and Hélène soon. You could combine a visit with a trip to Jersey, couldn't you?'

Her mother was silent for a moment and Nicole heard muffled whispering and guessed she was conferring with her father.

'Your father and I think that's a wonderful idea. We were planning to come to Jersey later in August when it gets too hot here. But where will you be living? Not with Ben, surely?'

'Oh, no, it's much too soon for that! Hélène is happy for me to stay here until I get a job and then I'll rent somewhere until my divorce settlement comes through. I might then be able to buy something.'

Her mother sounded relieved. 'That seems very wise. And have you met Adrian's family yet?'

Nicole told her mother about Karen, Michael and Luke, leaving out Karen's reaction. Her father came on the line and they chatted for a few moments before they said their goodbyes, promising to meet soon.

One more call to Susie and she could relax.

'Hi, it's me! I've sooo much to tell you!'

After lunch Nicole popped in to see her grandmother who, although clearly pleased to see her, didn't want to talk much. Nicole felt she looked tired so didn't stay long. She fitted in a quick swim at Vazon before returning home to change for the evening.

Ben cooked a simple spaghetti bolognese with a side salad. After they'd chatted about their day, he gave her a quizzical look.

'Something you're not telling me? Only when I asked what sort of job you were looking for, you went a bit vague. Is there a problem?' He stroked her hair as they cuddled on the sofa.

'No, not exactly. It's just that there's not much call for high profile TV journalists in Guernsey. I think I'll have to lower my sights a bit,' she sighed.

'Uh huh. Are you having second thoughts about staying here?'

Nicole quickly reassured him.

'Oh, not at all.' She gave him a lingering kiss. 'I want to be here with you, for sure. But I'm having to reassess my career and I guess it's unsettling. I've put out some feelers so we'll see what happens.'

'Right.' He dropped a kiss on her head as he got up to refill their glasses. 'By the way, I've arranged for a gardener to come and have a look tomorrow and all being well, he can start later this week. So you might have a job of sorts soon!'

She laughed.

'But not a paying one! Unless...'

He wrapped his arms around her. 'I'm afraid I only pay in kind...'

The following morning Nicole studied her reflection in the bedroom mirror. She'd chosen a knee-length linen skirt, matched with a silky T-shirt and a toning linen jacket. Smart but not over the top. Glancing at her watch she saw it was time to leave. Climbing into the car, Nicole was struck by the thought that she ought to look at buying a car. If all went well today she'd make it her priority.

As she drove towards St Peter Port Nicole pondered on life's synchronicities. An old colleague from Bristol had moved to Guernsey a few years previously to work for Channel Television. Knowing it was a long shot, she'd phoned her yesterday to see if there might be a slot coming up for an experienced TV reporter. Cheryl had suggested she pop in for a chat as there might be something in the pipeline and could she email her CV to the boss.

Half an hour later she pulled into the Channel Television car park on Bulwer Avenue. Nervous butterflies danced around her stomach as she approached the front door. She hadn't had a job interview for years...

'Cheryl! It's great to see you and you're…you're – '

'Pregnant!' Cheryl, a bubbly blonde, patted her bump as she laughed at Nicole's expression. 'That's why I was so pleased you phoned. I'm off on maternity leave in a couple of months and we're having problems finding a replacement. No-one will move to the island just for a temporary job, and you can't blame them, can you? And there aren't many experienced reporters on the island. Though for the right person, there might be something long-term.' Cheryl gazed at Nicole. 'You didn't say what brings you here. I thought you were pretty settled with Tom at Bristol. Is he moving over too?'

Nicole explained about the split and that she'd discovered she had family in Guernsey and wanted to settle there. She didn't feel it appropriate to mention Ben.

'Oh, Nicole, I'm so sorry about Tom! I thought you two were the perfect couple. Still, *c'est la vie!* And, being selfish, I'm so glad you're here.' She lifted her phone, 'Tea or coffee?'

'Tea, please.'

Cheryl ordered the tea and sat on a chair next to Nicole.

'I thought it best if we had a chat before you met the boss. After all, if you're not happy with the position then you needn't waste your time. Or his. Right, I'm covering the news and on-screen reporting…'

Nicole listened as Cheryl described the job. It wasn't quite what she was used to, in fact she should be able to do it standing on her head, but didn't say that. Cheryl went on to say that officially she'd only be away on maternity leave, but she might not return.

'Please don't tell anyone, will you?' Nicole shook her head. 'Good. Only my husband's applying for a job in London and if he gets it then we're off.' Cheryl leaned forward as much as her bump allowed, whispering, 'I've not told my boss in case it doesn't happen. If it did, would you be interested in taking over on a permanent basis?'

Nicole smiled broadly. 'You bet! But I've got to impress your boss first.'

Cheryl waved her hand. 'Oh, that won't be a problem! You're perfect for the job. In fact, you're more than qualified for it.' She frowned. 'Are you sure you'd be happy here? It's not like Bristol…'

'No, it's not. But that's fine. I'll have more time to spend with my family and…friends.'

Cheryl was proved right. The interview with the boss, a Mr James, had been more of a chat than a searching interrogation. Her CV must have made an impression and, it seemed, Cheryl had sung her praises. She had a job! Or at least she would have in a couple of months. In the meantime she could spend time with her extended family. And although the salary was much lower than what she'd earned at Bristol, she'd manage. Nicole celebrated by treating herself to lunch in Town before heading off to visit her grandmother.

She found her a little brighter and Eve couldn't hide her delight when Nicole told her about the job.

'I'll be able to say that my granddaughter's on television,' she said, conveniently ignoring the fact that Nicole had been on English television for years. Nicole just smiled, happy that her grandmother felt proud of her.

'Oh, by the way, I had a call from Hélène this morning. They're having a wonderful time, but eating far too much!' Nicole grinned. 'She said she'll need to go on a diet when they get back. She sounded very happy.'

'I'm pleased for her. And this Adrian, your father, seems a decent chap after all.' Eve, twisting her wedding ring, pursed her lips.

'Yes, he's very nice. It's such a pity they didn't…'

'I know. They should have been a couple years ago. But they are now, so that's all that matters.'

As she opened the front door Nicole noticed several envelopes on the floor. Giving them a cursory glance, she was surprised to see one addressed to herself. Her heart sank as she recognised Tom's handwriting. What on earth did he want now? Dumping the other letters on the kitchen worktop, she made a cup of tea and walked out to the terrace. Taking a deep breath, she opened the envelope.

chapter 31

There were two letters. One handwritten by Tom and the other in a typed envelope. She read his first:

Dear Nicole

I'm sorry for my behaviour on both occasions last week. I was so desperate to see you, having convinced myself that maybe you'd had second thoughts and we could get back together. I realise now that it was all in my own mind and that you were right to be angry with me. That first time I called, the shock of realising you'd met someone caused something to snap. I'm sorry for hurting you and frightening you the next day. I hadn't slept and had had too much to drink. But that's no excuse for behaving badly.

Now I've had time to think I see that we need to start the divorce proceedings asap. Perhaps you could quote 'Unreasonable Behaviour' rather than adultery? Might be less embarrassing for us both, but it's up to you. I've already talked to a solicitor (letter enclosed) and would like to buy your share of the house. It'll mean a quicker settlement for you rather than waiting for it to sell. I want to be fair, darling. The solicitor's arranging independent valuations and, of course, feel free to request your own. Everything will be split down the middle and if you email me a list of what furniture & stuff you want from the house, I'll get back to you. Hopefully we can come to an agreement.

Your own solicitor can get in touch with mine to sort out the finer details.

I just want to finish by saying how sorry I am that our marriage is over and I really, really wish I could go back in time and not do what I did. But I can't. Perhaps one day we could at least be friends but for the moment it's better if we don't meet.

All my love

Tomxx

Nicole reached for a tissue as her eyes filled with tears. *Oh Tom! You're a bloody idiot.* For a moment her mind filled with images from the past – their past – laughing, happy faces as they danced their first dance in a grotty nightclub; proud smiles as Tom stepped up to collect his first TV award; their joy when they found the farmhouse, ripe for renovation and perfect for a family home…

It took a few minutes for her to calm down enough to read the solicitor's letter. A confirmation of what Tom had written, but stated in legalese. Tossing it to one side, Nicole returned to the kitchen and poured a glass of wine. A large one. As she sat on the terrace sipping her drink, her thoughts turned to the present. Until now she hadn't actually considered the reality of what a divorce would mean, but now she knew. Spelt out in black and white. A split down the middle of what they'd worked so hard for. It was only fair as she'd put in just as much as Tom, bumping up the deposit with some of her inheritance. His desire to buy her share was a relief; she might be glad of an early settlement to buy her own place in Guernsey. It would be okay. Painful, but okay. She swirled the wine in the glass. And now she had Ben. Gorgeous Ben. If they could make it work. *We have to! It has to be right this time.*

Putting down her glass she went to fetch her laptop. She needed a solicitor.

The next few days sped by. Nicole emailed Tom, thanking him for his offer of the buy-out and informing him of her solicitor's details. She said she'd email soon with her list.

The formal offer of the job at Channel Television arrived and Nicole went car hunting. Ben, delighted that she'd not only lined up work so quickly but had also begun divorce proceedings, insisted that he come with her to check out the cars. Normally she'd bristle at the sexist implication that she didn't know what lay under the bonnet, but actually he was right. She only knew that she liked her cars fast and sexy. Although with an island top speed of 35mph perhaps "fast" might be redundant. Smiling at the thought, she browsed the list of sports cars on offer.

It was love at first sight. A bright yellow Mazda MX5. Only a year old and low mileage.

Nicole's face split into a huge grin.

'It's perfect!' She cried, running her hands along the bodywork.

'Uh huh,' Ben muttered, lifting up the bonnet. The salesman hovered close by, suggesting Nicole take it for a run. With the wind streaming through her hair she manoeuvred the lanes with ease, arriving back at the garage beaming from ear to ear.

Ben gave the car his approval and Nicole happily completed the paperwork to become the proud owner of what became known as her "little ray of sunshine".

On Friday Nicole drove off to the nursing home for the last time. Eve would be returning home the next day to coincide with Hélène's return. Surprised not to find her in the sitting room, Nicole asked a nurse where her she was.

'Mrs Ferbrache's been a bit off-colour today and she's in her room. But I'm sure she'll be happy to see you.'

Nicole knocked on the door, receiving a faint 'Come in' she found her grandmother lying in bed.

'What's the matter? The nurse said you were off colour, whatever that means.' Nicole scrutinised the old lady's face. She did look pale and drawn.

'Oh, I'm just a bit tired, that's all. Be right as rain when I'm back home.'

'Hmm. Have they asked Ben to check you out? You might need some medication.'

Eve shook her head.

'There's no need to bother the doctor. He was only round a couple of days ago and seemed pleased with me.' Eve scowled at Nicole. 'Promise me you won't bother him. I'll be fine.'

'Okay. But if you're not any better tomorrow I think he should take a look at you. Agreed?' Sighing, Eve agreed.

Nicole stayed long enough to have a cup of tea with her and then left her to rest. On the way out she spotted one of the senior nurses.

'I'm a bit worried about my grandmother. She tends to play down how she's feeling, not wanting a fuss. Do you think she's okay?'

The nurse steered her into an empty room.

'Mrs Ferbrache is quite poorly, as you know. She has good days and bad days. Today's a bad day but there's nothing to worry about. If there was, rest assured, I'd call the doctor.' She patted Nicole's arm. 'It's been a bit of an upheaval for her, coming here after the routine of her own home. Perfectly natural, of course. And she's really looked forward to your visits, helped her to feel more at home.' The nurse added briskly, 'Unless there's a change for the worse we'll be sending her home tomorrow as arranged. I'm afraid I have to go now, so if that's all?'

Nicole nodded and continued out to her car. Even the sight of her "ray of sunshine" not lifting her mood.

Ben arrived to spend their last evening together at La Folie. Nicole had suggested she cook, but he'd offered to bring an Indian takeaway and the aroma of lamb curry preceded him to the kitchen.

'Let's eat outside. There's beer in the fridge if you could grab a couple of bottles, please,' Nicole said as she loaded a tray.

'What have you been up to today?' Ben asked after taking a gulp of beer.

'I visited Grandmother this afternoon and found her in bed. "Off colour" the nurse called it.' Nicole frowned.

'Sorry to hear that. But I'm sure I would have been called if they were worried.' He stroked the back of her hand. 'She's an old lady. There's not much anyone can do about that,' he murmured. 'But I'll check her out when she comes home tomorrow to be sure.'

'Thanks.' She smiled at him

'My pleasure! And, changing the subject, you'll be pleased to know that the gardener started today and I can now see what the garden really looks like!' Ben grinned. 'According to Jim, at some point it's been properly planned and the bones are still evident. I'd love your take on what we can do to bring it back to life.'

'*We?* So you'll be helping, will you?' Nicole said, with a tilt of her head.

'Well, if I have any time and energy after finishing off the kitchen, dining-room, bedrooms, study…' He counted off his fingers.

'Point taken!' she laughed.

'I'll go home once your family's back in the morning, so would you like to come round later? Have a look round the garden and stay for supper? I'll cook.'

'Now that's an offer a girl can't refuse!'

Nicole and Ben tidied up the kitchen the next morning after he'd had stowed his bag in the car.

The ambulance pulled up at ten thirty and Eve's wheelchair was pushed to the front door.

Nicole, hoping to see her grandmother looking brighter, caught her breath as she saw her grey face. Ben, standing by her, squeezed her hand before helping to wheel Eve indoors.

'How are you feeling today?' Nicole asked, planting a kiss on her cheek.

'Tired. I think I'd like to rest for a bit. Those ambulances shake my bones about.' Eve grimaced. She must have seen Nicole's worried frown because she went on, 'But it's lovely to be home, my dear,' patting her arm. Looking at Ben she said, 'I've quite a welcoming committee, haven't I? Has she,' nodding her head at Nicole, 'been telling tales about me?'

Ben's face gave nothing away. 'I'm here as a friend of the family, to welcome you and Hélène back. But as I *am* here shall I give that heart of yours the once over? My bag's in the car.'

'Harrumph. If you must,' Eve said.

Ben wheeled her to her bedroom, telling Nicole he'd manage.

Feeling in need of something to occupy herself, Nicole wiped down the kitchen surfaces again before putting the kettle on.

Ben appeared, his face serious.

'So? How is she?'

'Her heart's struggling a bit so I've given her something to help her sleep. I've left her dressed in bed and she's quite comfortable.' He put his arms around her. 'I'm afraid it's not looking too good. Unless she has the operation…'

Nicole choked on a sob.

'How…how long?'

Ben shook his head.

'I really can't say. But it's likely to be weeks rather than months. I'm so, so sorry.'

Nicole clung to him as tears trickled down her cheeks. The image of her grandmother's grey face filled her mind. *It's not fair! I've only just met her, getting to know and love her…*

Ben lifted her chin and kissed the tears.

'Hey, come on. You can't let her see you're upset. And Hélène will be home any minute. She'll have to know, of course, but perhaps not today.'

Nicole nodded and wiped her face. Taking a deep breath she asked Ben if he'd like a coffee. Nodding a yes, she filled two mugs and they went outside.

By the time Nicole heard the sound of a car crunching on the gravel, she'd had a chance to compose herself. She didn't want to spoil Hélène's return.

'Hi! You look wonderful! So brown and...and glowing!' Nicole cried as she embraced a transformed Hélène. She really did glow, there was no other word for it. Her eyes shone and her mouth seemed somehow fuller, younger.

Hélène laughed.

'I *feel* wonderful. We've had a great time, haven't we?' she turned to a beaming Adrian, his arm linked through hers. He looked equally brown and radiant.

'Yes, we have. It was just what we needed, I feel rejuvenated,' he grinned.

He carried in Hélène's case and Nicole suggested they head for the terrace.

'Is Mother home?'

'Yes, but she's sleeping. She said the ambulance shook her up.'

'Right, well I'll pop in later. How did she get on in the home? Did she settle in all right?'

'She was fine. And I saw her every day.'

Hélène smiled her relief.

'Thank you, Nicole. I'm not sure if we'd have gone if you hadn't been here.' She turned to Adrian with a tilt of her head. He nodded.

'We...we've got something to tell you. Adrian asked me to marry him and I said yes!' She held out her left hand, the diamond catching the sunlight. 'We're engaged!'

chapter 32

'Oh my God! That's fantastic!' Nicole threw her arms round Hélène before hugging Adrian. Ben kissed Hélène before shaking hands with her beaming fiancé.

'I didn't want to risk losing her a second time,' he told Ben. 'Life's too short.'

Nicole felt a lump in her throat. So true!

'Let's open a bottle of wine to celebrate. There's some cava in the fridge, not exactly champagne, but…' Nicole said, going off to the kitchen.

On her return Ben opened the wine and Nicole said, 'I'd like to propose a toast to the happy couple, Hélène and Adrian!'

They clinked glasses before sipping the pink bubbly.

Hélène linked her arm through Adrian's, saying 'We'd meant to tell you and Mother together, but I couldn't wait. And the ring's a bit of a giveaway!' she laughed, gazing at her solitaire.

'I'm sure Grandmother will be thrilled, she's very tired but should be awake at lunchtime.' Nicole looked at Ben who gave a small nod.

The talk turned to the holiday in France and Adrian described in detail the chateaux and vineyards they'd visited. Safely stacked in the car's boot were cases of the wines they'd particularly enjoyed. He disappeared to bring in a case, together with a whole Brie and boxes of chocolates.

Hélène handed a large box of chocolate liqueurs to Nicole, saying, 'It's not much, but I'd like to thank you for keeping an eye on Mother while we were away. And here's a few bottles of wine for you and Ben to enjoy.'

Nicole's heart sank. Knowing that her grandmother was gravely ill, it didn't seem right to accept the gifts. But there was no choice, she couldn't bear for Hélène to know the truth yet.

Muttering a quick thank you, Nicole was relieved when Ben said that he had to be off and she went with him to the car. He stowed the wine and turned to hug her.

'I know how you feel, I saw it in your face. Telling her in a couple of days isn't going to make much difference.' He stroked her hair. Nicole held on tight, glad of his support. How would she manage without him at this time?

'Do you still feel like coming round later?'

'Yes, of course. The carer's back this evening so Hélène will have help. And perhaps Adrian will stay over now that they're practically married!' She grinned.

After sharing a passionate kiss, Nicole promised to be round later.

As Hélène and Nicole prepared a salad for lunch, Nicole asked how Adrian had proposed.

Her mother smiled dreamily at the memory.

'It was so romantic! We had arrived at this fabulous chateaux hotel in Le Loire a couple of hours before dinner. I was having a quick shower when I heard a knock on the door. Adrian answered and when I came out there was a bottle of champagne on ice and two flutes on a tray. I was just about to say there must have been a mistake when he kneeled down and said, "My darling Hélène, will you marry me?" What could I say but yes? So he popped the cork and we got sloshed on champagne. We only just made it to the restaurant in time!' She giggled.

Nicole put her arm round her mother.

'That's so cool! I hadn't thought of Adrian as the romantic type.'

'Neither had I!'

Just then the man in question popped his head round the kitchen door.

'Table's set on the terrace, ladies. Do you need anything else carrying out?'

The women exchanged grins before Hélène replied that the salad was ready. She went off to check on Eve while Nicole and Adrian carried the food outside. Nicole shifted restlessly in her chair before Hélène returned with the news that Eve was awake. Nicole breathed a sigh of relief.

'How is she?'

'Exhausted. She doesn't want to eat yet so I'll take her something later. But she wasn't too tired to notice my ring!' Hélène gazed at it before looking at Adrian. 'Mother is very happy for us and wants to know if we've set a date yet. I told her we needed to confer with the family, but we expect it'll be within the next few months.'

Nicole gripped her hands under the table. Please, please let them make it soon!

Later that afternoon Nicole pulled up outside Santa Rosa. After the trauma of hearing about her grandmother, and then the admittedly, happier news from her parents, she felt badly in need of a diversion. Planning Ben's garden might prove to be just what she wanted.

After she told a relieved Ben that Eve was awake and seemed okay, he led her outside.

'What do you think?'

Thinking it looked like a war zone she remained silent. As she gazed at the heaps of shorn-off tree branches, massacred hedging, clumps of weeds and dead plants, Nicole wondered if she'd bitten off more than she could chew.

As if reading her mind, Ben said, 'I know it looks awful now, but when all the rubbish is taken away, it'll look a lot better. But if it's too much for you, I could ask Jim to come back.'

She nodded, heading off to explore, side-stepping piles of detritus. On closer inspection, Nicole acknowledged that there was cause for optimism. A circular design of pretty terracotta tiles created an ideal space for dining, with room for the ubiquitous barbecue. The area must have been hidden under layers of brambles, now pushed to one side. Old granite walls had been exposed, previously obscured under the neighbours' encroaching hedges. Rampant ivy had been cut back and the herbaceous borders weeded and cleared of dead planting. A few lonely flowers created splashes of colour in the wasteland. The clearance made the garden look wider and longer.

'Well, there's not many flowers left, are there? And even I know that it's not the right time to plant. We'll need to wait until autumn.' Pointing to an attractive arch formed of overhanging trees she added, 'That's a great focal point to work from. Your garden's got potential but you won't see much improvement this year.' She flung her arm out. 'I could clear the moss and weeds from the tiled areas which will give you space for a table and chairs. All you need for a cold beer on a hot day!' she grinned.

'Sounds good to me! There's no rush with the rest. I definitely don't want you wearing yourself out.' He pulled her close, kissing her gently on the lips.

'Don't worry, I won't. Have to save my energy for more important things,' Nicole murmured, with a saucy wink.

Laughing, they returned to the house and while Ben applied himself to preparing dinner, Nicole sketched out ideas for the garden. When her own garden had been landscaped, she'd noted how the designer had started with rough drawings and notes of plantings. Although it was early days, perhaps, just perhaps, one day she might be sharing this garden. Better get it right!

'How's Grandmother today?' Nicole asked Hélène, finding her in the kitchen the next morning.

'Not good. She seems very listless today. I don't know whether or not to bother Ben.' Her face creased with concern, she looked up and Nicole saw that yesterday's glow had dimmed.

Not knowing what to say, she put the kettle on. She'd left Ben finishing a hearty breakfast and knew he wouldn't mind coming round, but what could he do? Or say?

'Tell you what, shall I ring him and see what he says?'

Hélène's face cleared.

'Would you? I'd feel happier.'

Nicole went outside to make the call. As she'd suspected, Ben said there was little he could do and if he came round he'd need to tell Hélène the truth. The alternative was to give it another day and see if Eve rallied. They agreed on the latter and Nicole returned to the kitchen.

Crossing her fingers behind her back, Nicole said that Ben wasn't surprised at Eve's tiredness and not to worry, he'd pop in on Monday to look at her. In the meantime, if Eve worsened, she was to ring him.

Hélène looked relieved.

'Thanks. It's such a worry, having an ageing parent. You never know...' She shook her head.

Nicole, feeling decidedly guilty, gave her a hug. Trying to lighten the mood, she joked, 'And you've only got one parent to worry about – I've got three!'

Hélène managed a smile.

'You'll have your work cut out then! But let's hope not for many years.'

Finishing her coffee, Nicole asked if she could look in on her grandmother. Hélène said yes, but not to stay long.

'Good morning, Grandmother, how are you?'

Eve, propped up on pillows, turned lacklustre eyes towards Nicole.

'Tired, my dear. So tired. Odd, as I slept deeply yesterday. I think that doctor friend of yours gave me

221

something that knocked me out.' Eve grimaced. 'Perhaps he can give me something to wake me up next time!'

Nicole clasped the old lady's hand. It felt weightless, the skin like paper. Her heart hammered in her breast with the knowledge that Eve's days were numbered and wondered if she herself knew.

As their eyes met, Nicole saw that she did.

'The doctor didn't need to tell me, my dear. I knew, and have done for a few weeks now. I think people do you know, when…when it's their time. But am I right in thinking my daughter hasn't been told?'

Nicole, her eyes blurred, shook her head.

'No, we…we didn't want to spoil the happiness of the engagement.'

Eve nodded.

'I'm glad. I've never seen her so happy. She radiates joy. And it's what I wanted for her…' Tears ran down Eve's cheeks.

Nicole handed her a tissue before wiping her own tears.

'We think she should be told, Grandmother. They're talking of getting married in a few months and – '

'I may not be around.' Eve blew her nose. Releasing a sigh, she continued, 'I want to be there so you're right, Hélène will need to know.'

Nicole twisted the tissue in her hand.

'Ben's planning to come round tomorrow and will talk to her.' More twisting. 'And Adrian's telling his children about the engagement today and hopefully they'll be okay about it and a date can be set.'

Eve lay back on the pillows, her face pinched.

'Look, I'd better go now, I hadn't meant to stay so long and I've tired you. I'm sorry.'

'I'm glad we had this…chat, my dear. Cleared the air. Tell your mother I want to sleep now, there's a good girl.'

Nicole kissed her cheek and left.

***

Adrian knew he shouldn't feel nervous but he did. It was almost worse than preparing to propose to Hélène. And that had been nerve wracking enough. As his mind slipped back to their time in France, he smiled. It was as if all the long years apart hadn't existed. As if they'd picked up where they'd left off more than thirty-five years ago. Only this time it was better, they were free to go about as a couple, without fear of censure. And in France they were taken for a long-married couple, so at ease were they together, Hélène even laughing at his jokes. It had been fun finding out what they shared, including a love of exploring old chateaux. Hélène told him of her own trips she'd made to France over the years. And she proved to have a much better sense of direction than him, getting them back on the right track a few times. In all senses of the word, he thought. She was good for him and he couldn't wait to make her his wife. And the passion they'd shared so long ago was still there…

'Dad! We're here!'

At the sound of Michael's voice, Adrian shook himself and went to the front door.

'Hi, Dad. You look well. Did you have a good holiday?'

'Yes, thanks. Very good. Come in, all of you. Hello, Luke! Granddad's got something for you,' he ruffled Luke's hair.

Karen, holding Luke's hand, followed Dave and Michael into the sitting room. She kissed his cheek before sitting in the armchair that had been her mother's.

Adrian handed a large, oddly shaped package to Luke, who began ripping off the paper, a look of glee on his face. Everyone watched with indulgent smiles.

'A boat! Ganddad give Luke a boat!' Luke smiled broadly as he pulled the paper away from what was actually a ship, furnished with tall sails, rigging and miniature crew. The Jolly Roger flew at the mast head. 'It's a pirate ship, darling,' Karen said, 'and what do you say to Granddad?'

'Tank oo, Ganddad.' He gave Adrian a big kiss.

Karen smiled at her father.

'That's a lovely present, Dad, thank you. He'll love playing with it. So, the holiday went well?' She leant back in her chair.

'Yes, it did. You know how I love France, particularly the food and the wine!' he laughed, patting his stomach. 'And I've gifts for you grown-ups as well. Wine and cheese, hope you like them.' He handed round the presents.

'Great, Dad, thanks. I always appreciate adding to the ol' cellar!' Michael grinned.

Karen looked puzzled. 'It's lovely of you, Dad, but you don't normally buy us stuff when you go away. What's so special this time?'

Adrian knew it was time.

Taking a deep breath, he looked at the three faces staring at him and said, 'I…I wanted to share with you the good time I…we had in France. And I asked Hélène to marry me and she said yes.'

There was a stunned silence.

Michael was the first to react, jumping up and throwing his arms round his father,

'Congratulations, Dad! That's great news, I hope you'll be very happy.'

'Yes, congratulations, Adrian, please accept my best wishes,' Dave said formally, joining Michael at his side.

Adrian looked at his daughter's white face. Please, Karen, please allow me this happiness…

After what seemed hours but was only seconds, Karen stood up and walked towards him.

'I can't deny that I'm not thrilled at your news, Dad, but I can see that…that Hélène makes you happy, so I wish you well.' She pecked his cheek before walking out through the French windows and disappearing into the garden hut that had been her refuge as a child.

But not before Adrian saw the tears running down her cheeks.

chapter 33

Nicole set off for a walk on Monday morning, in need of a mental and emotional clear-out. As she strode along the cliff path towards Pleinmont she reviewed the events of the past few days. On the plus side was the engagement of Adrian and Hélène, something that had pleased everyone. Or nearly everyone. Hélène had heard from Adrian that Karen wasn't exactly ecstatic and no-one knew if she'd come to the wedding. Another plus was her relationship with Ben. Just thinking about it brought her out in goose bumps. As much as she'd love to live with him, it wasn't possible until her divorce came through. She didn't want any chance of him being cited for adultery. Much better to wait. Though hard.

As she picked some wild flowers, the minuses popped up. The number one being her grandmother's health. It felt like a black cloud hanging over her and she couldn't shake it off. At the moment Hélène didn't know, but Ben would be round that afternoon and then...She sighed. Hélène's bubble of joy would be burst. The other minus was her divorce and that she really needed to return to the UK soon. Not only did she need to sort out her belongings and arrange for their transportation to Guernsey, but she wanted to meet with her solicitor. She wanted to be free as soon as possible and, all going smoothly, that could be as soon as three months. Afraid that Tom would change his mind, she wanted it done and dusted before he had time to reconsider.

Unthinkingly tearing the petals apart, Nicole worried about being away with Eve so ill. If only she knew nothing would happen while she was in the UK! Nicole stopped for a moment to stare out to sea, focusing on the outline of Jersey emerging from the early morning sea mist. It was where her life had begun, although created here in Guernsey. And now her biological parents were shortly to be married. Both their lives and her own were being irrevocably changed. For the better, admittedly, but not without pain. She thought of her adoptive parents and how difficult it must be to share her with Hélène and Adrian. She'd be living in the same island and they could see her as much as they wanted, while her "proper" parents were a thousand miles away. Oh my God! Perhaps her parents could be here for the wedding!

Wondering if her walk had cleared her thoughts or caused more confusion, Nicole turned back. Lots to organise.

Ben arrived mid-afternoon and Hélène took him in to see the still bedridden Eve.

Nicole boiled the kettle and set chocolate cake on the trolley. It seemed important that the normal routine was followed. Hélène joined her, worry etched into her forehead.

'Thank you, Nicole. We'll have it outside, I think. I'll take Mother's in when Ben's finished examining her.'

Ten minutes later they heard a door open and shut and Nicole made the tea while Hélène led Ben outside. As Nicole pushed the trolley onto the terrace she heard Hélène asking Ben about Eve.

Ben and Nicole exchanged glances before he turned towards Hélène, reaching for her hand.

'There's no easy way to say this, I'm afraid. But your mother is worse than we thought. Her heart is weakening and, I'm sorry, there's nothing we can do.'

Hélène's hand flew to her mouth.

'Oh, no! But what about the operation?'

Ben shook his head.

'It's too late. Even if she agreed to it, which I doubt, we couldn't risk it. Her heart's too weak.'

Nicole poured the tea while Hélène sat stunned.

'How…how long has she got?' she whispered.

'A matter of weeks. I can make her comfortable and she won't be in any pain.'

Nicole put her arms around Hélène, who finally let go the tears. Ben, tactfully, grabbed his cup and walked away down the garden.

'I'm so, so sorry.'

Hélène's tears slowed and she wiped her face. Looking at Nicole with reddened eyes, she said, 'You already knew, didn't you?'

'Only since Saturday, when Grandmother came home. We didn't want to spoil…'

'That was kind of you. It must have been hard not saying anything.' She reached for her tea, sipping quickly.

'It's a shock, we thought she'd got so much longer…' Hélène managed a small smile. 'We must get the wedding arranged as soon as we can.'

'Yes, she would like that, she's so happy for you.' Nicole picked up her cup. 'Grandmother knows she hasn't long. She…she told me she'd known for a while. And I think she's ready.'

Her mother nodded, still dabbing at her eyes.

'Mother's always been strong. I've never known her to be afraid of anything. Oh! Her tea! I completely forgot.'

'Don't worry, I'll take it. You relax a minute.'

While Nicole went off, Hélène sat nursing her drink, awash with emotion. Somehow she'd always assumed that her mother would go on forever. Even with a weakened heart she seemed invincible. God knew they'd had their differences, but these past few weeks she'd felt closer to her mother than she ever had. Ever since Nicole had erupted into their lives, demolishing the wall of resentment that lay between them. Hélène sent up a small prayer of thanks for her daughter. She would be a great comfort when…when the inevitable happened. And her beloved Adrian, of course. Oh, they had to be married soon!

Nicole returned, giving Ben the signal to re-join them.

'Feeling calmer?' Ben asked Hélène.

'Yes, thank you. Mm, Ben, is Mother going to be bed-bound now? Or could she be pushed in a wheelchair?'

'I think she'll spend more time in bed, for sure. But there's no reason why she couldn't sit in a wheelchair occasionally. She'd need lifting in and out, that's all.'

Hélène nodded. Then she looked at Nicole and Ben's enquiring faces.

'I was thinking of the wedding. I desperately want her to be there with us, so if she can be in a wheelchair that'd be perfect.'

'Have you thought of where you'd get married?' Nicole asked.

'I'd like it to be at Torteval Church and then come back here for the reception. And the church has a wheelchair ramp. We weren't planning on anything grand anyway, so if we have to…to be quick then we can still do that.' Hélène topped up her tea.

'I'd better be going, I've more patients to see, Hélène. I'll call in tomorrow afternoon.'

Hélène thanked Ben and Nicole walked him to his car.

As he kissed her, she said, 'I need to go to England for a couple of days to see my solicitor and pack my stuff in the house. Should I go soon?'

'There's no imminent danger, but if you go this week that might be better. Then you needn't worry so much. I can give her drugs to boost her heart but they only work short term. And the wedding should take place within the month, to be on the safe side.' He stroked her hair and lifted up her chin. 'Will you need to see Tom? I'm worried how he would react.'

'No, I don't think so. I'll arrange to visit the house when he's at work. And he made it clear he didn't want us to meet.' She sighed. 'I'll make an appointment with my solicitor and book my flights. Oh, I'll miss you!'

'And I you. How about I take you out for dinner tomorrow night? And you can stay over, if you're good,' he grinned at her.

'Oh, I'll be good!'

★★★

Hélène phoned Adrian with the news and he came straight round. Nicole disappeared to her room to give them space. They sat out on the terrace discussing what to do.

'I've been in to see Mother and told her that I know. She seems calm and accepting, so that's something.' She stroked her engagement ring. 'Mother's made it clear she wants to be at our wedding, even if it means arriving on a stretcher!' She couldn't resist a smile at the image of her mother being wheeled into Saint Philippe's on a gurney. 'Not sure the vicar would be impressed, so we'll aim for a wheelchair. Do you mind very much having the wedding soon, Adrian?'

He wrapped his arms round her.

'I'd be very happy to make you my wife tomorrow if it were possible. We'll need a licence so I'll talk to the vicar today. It's not as if we'd planned to invite people from off the island, so it'll be fine. Everyone's already here.'

Hélène had a thought. Nicole's adoptive parents! Would they want to come to her wedding? She knew they were planning a visit in August so...

'What about Mary and Ian Le Clerq? Should we ask them?'

'Of course! The more the merrier! And we owe them a debt of gratitude for how they've taken care of our – their – daughter.' He stroked her face. 'Are you worried about what they'll think about you? For giving her up for adoption?'

Hélène had thought of little else since she knew their visit was imminent. Would they judge her or accept that she had made the decision with the best of intentions, even though her heart was breaking?

She nodded.

'Well, I think you've nothing to worry about. From what Nicole's told me, they sound very nice, and very grateful. Thanks to your sacrifice they had the child they yearned for so, in my book, they owe you. But they could be critical of me, the adulterous husband,' he frowned.

'You're more than making up for that now. So don't worry!' Hélène patted his arm. 'Seems both of us are a bit scared of the Le Clerqs. It's like being back at school!'

They both laughed, the hovering black cloud receding a little. After spending a few minutes discussing who needed to do what, Adrian left to see the vicar.

The next morning Nicole fixed an appointment with her solicitor for that Thursday and booked her flights. Leaving on Wednesday mid-morning, she would return early Friday evening. She felt this gave her plenty of time to sort and pack her personal possessions. She'd emailed Tom the short list of furniture she wanted and he'd agreed to her selection. She didn't want much, preferring a fresh start, devoid of memories. Hélène was pressing her to stay at La Folie until after her divorce.

'After we're married Adrian and I will live here while Mother's still...with us.' Hélène bit her lips. 'Then we'll move to his house. I'll put this place on the market but I can't think there'll be people queuing up to buy. You could stay here while you see how it goes with Ben, you'll have your own space when you want it. Although I imagine you'll spend more time at his house,' she said, raising her eyebrows.

Nicole's cheeks warmed.

'That's kind of you, Hélène. I had planned to rent somewhere so I'd be happy to pay the running costs...'

Hélène shook her head.

'No, I wouldn't hear of it. And Adrian agrees with me, it's the least we can do to provide a roof over your head until your life settles down. The only downside is that you'll have a bit of a trek to work every day. So, bearing that in mind, the sooner you and Ben get together properly, the better. It'd be much quicker from Town to Bulwer Avenue!'

'Amen to that!' Nicole giggled.

Nicole was to store her possessions at La Folie, making it easier for her to hang on to items of sentimental value and the odd bits of furniture. She'd surprised herself by how much she did want, but over the years she'd amassed an eclectic collection of items; prints and water-colours; mementos from foreign holidays, including beautiful Murano glass and Mediterranean pottery; a small library and a couple of pieces of furniture. And the clothes! She'd had to look stylish, reflected in her extensive wardrobe.

Thinking about her clothes reminded her that she needed something suitable for her imminent role of Matron of Honour. Hélène, admitting that it was a not entirely appropriate title for a soon-to-be divorcee, acting for her own never-been-married mother, but she could hardly be a bridesmaid, could she? Smiling at the thought, Nicole remembered that she'd bought a striking deep green silk dress just before the bust-up with Tom and it was still hanging, unworn, in her wardrobe. Perfect!

The date was set for Saturday 25th August, slightly over three weeks away. The vicar, admitting that they were not exactly overrun with weddings, had agreed on a one o'clock service and approved the requisite Common Licence, avoiding the need for Banns. Nicole crossed her fingers that her grandmother would live to play the part of Mother of the Bride.

chapter 34

As her plane approached Bristol airport Nicole craned her neck, searching the landscape beneath for her marital home. She knew where to look as it had always given her a buzz to spot it about the time the landing gear dropped down. There it was! The sun reflected off the red tiled roof and she could just make out the pond surrounded by shrubs. In a flash it was gone. She sighed. It was going to be hard to say goodbye, in spite of the promise of what might be in her new life. It helped that Tom couldn't waylay her, something she'd dreaded. As luck would have it he was away, sunning himself on some foreign beach and probably, she guessed, not alone. The thought didn't upset her the way it would have done only weeks ago. No matter what happened between her and Ben, she was cured of Tom.

Picking up her hire car she set off towards Bath. It was a treat to drive on wide, fast roads after the restrictions of Guernsey and she enjoyed the familiar roads leading home. Or what had been home for the past seven years.

Nicole pulled into the circular drive, parking in her usual spot next to the central island covered in rocks, heathers and alpine plants. Getting out, she looked around her. Nothing had changed. What she could see of the garden looked well-groomed so at least the gardener was still coming in. She'd half expected to see a wilderness. Taking a deep breath she headed to the front door, the original battered oak salvaged during the renovation. As she stepped into the hall, Nicole retrieved the mail on the mat and walked through to the kitchen. Her pride and joy. She sighed in relief as her eyes swept over the immaculate worktops and shiny Aga. Tom had obviously kept the cleaner, too. She put the kettle on the Aga before putting away the few supplies she'd bought for her stay.

Without warning, she was hit by the memory of that last time when she and Tom were in the kitchen, and she'd asked him to leave. The marriage was over. Nicole slumped onto a chair. Threads of ghost-like memories wove through her mind and she had no choice but to let them. The past needed to be exorcised, so sitting with her eyes closed she focused hard on a technique she recalled from an interview with a psychotherapist. She visualised the memories, and the emotions they evoked, pouring into a big bin liner and throwing it away over a cliff. After a few moments she opened her eyes, feeling calmer.

Cradling her coffee, she made her way through to the sitting room. Again, it looked immaculate. So much so that she began to wonder if Tom still lived here. Pulling out her list, she checked off items as she studied the room. The sunny yellow walls were covered in pictures and photos, some of which were on her "approved" list. Tom had indicated that she could add the odd item she might have forgotten to put on it. She briefly imagined his reaction if she hired a van and cleared the house completely. Not likely to be a happy bunny!

She finished her coffee and began her tour of the house, list in hand. The dining room held nothing she wanted except a deep blue Lalique bowl in pride of place on the oak dining table. Her study held most of her favourite *objets d'art* together with her collection of books and her PC. The cream leather chair, chosen for its comfort as well as good looks, was already on her list, together with the antique partners desk. She scribbled a couple of additions before going upstairs.

Pausing on the threshold of the master bedroom, Nicole breathed deeply and pushed open the door. Neatness reigned but her heart hammered loudly in her chest as she scanned the room. Trying not to think about the nights she'd spent entwined in Tom's arms, she quickly checked that all her clothes and accessories were still waiting for her in the walk-in wardrobe. Her jewellery had its own fitted drawer and she pulled it out slowly. All there. Most of it had been gifts from Tom, layered with bitter-sweet memories. Her fingers trailed over the most expensive piece, a stunning Cartier necklace of pink gold orchids studded with diamonds. Her favourite. A present for their fifth anniversary, Tom had later bought the matching earrings for her birthday that year. Biting her lips she wondered if she could wear them again. *Of course you can! Grow up, girl, it was given and received with love. And it will set off the green silk dress perfectly.* She closed the drawer and looked along the rails of clothes waiting to be rescued and worn again. Sliding the green silk out of the protective polythene, she held it against her and gazed at her reflection in the mirror. Yes, it would be perfect for the wedding. She'd just need to find something for her hair. A matching silk flower, perhaps? Realising that this wasn't the time to plan her outfit, Nicole checked the other three bedrooms before returning downstairs. As she made a sandwich for lunch, the doorbell rang.

'Mrs Oxford? I've been asked to drop off these boxes to you. I believe you're having them collected on Friday afternoon with some furniture for delivery to Guernsey.'

The removal man pointed to a stack of folded boxes and cardboard hanging wardrobes. And a big roll of bubble-wrap and sealing tape.

'Thank you. That's right, if you could call back at three o'clock on Friday, please.'

'No problem. I'll carry them in for you.'

After stacking them in the dining room he left and Nicole returned to the kitchen to eat her lunch before starting on the packing.

It was late when she finally called it a day and crawled upstairs to bed. In one of the guest rooms. She'd never slept in it so it held no memories, except that Tom had been banished there when she'd discovered his wayward behaviour. As she snuggled under the duvet she fell asleep quickly. But not peacefully. Images filled her mind. Tom was chasing her around the garden in the middle of the night while she ran away in panic. As he was about to catch up with her she fell headlong into the pond and woke up gasping for breath. Switching on the light she felt relieved to see there was no-one there but went over to the window to check outside. Moonlight cast an eerie glow over the trees and shrubs and turned the pond silver. Craning her neck, she couldn't see anyone out there. It was only a bad dream. Taking deep breaths to calm herself, Nicole pulled the covers over her and after a restless half hour, fell asleep.

Waking the next morning Nicole's remembered bits of the dream and shuddered. *I'm too uptight, I'd better take something tonight to knock me out. The sooner I get out of here the better.* She was also pretty fed up of packing boxes, particularly with books. It made her smile to think that the appointment with her solicitor would provide a welcome respite. She'd been tempted to pop into the TV station but decided against it. There'd be questions she didn't feel ready to answer yet. If she had to return for some reason, maybe…The compromise was having lunch with a friend with whom she'd worked years ago. Not close, but good company.

Her appointment was at eleven o'clock and at ten forty-five Nicole pulled into the NCP car park in Prince Street. From here it was five minutes' walk to the solicitor's office. An elegant woman, slightly older than herself, shook hands before wasting no time in getting down to business. For this Nicole was glad, she wanted to answer the questions, sign the forms and leave.

An hour later, feeling relieved of a burden, Nicole emerged from the office and stood facing the river. Her next destination lay on the opposite bank of the historic harbourside. A few minutes later she had walked round behind the ferry landing and arrived outside The Watershed. A popular cultural centre showcasing various visual arts, it had long been a favourite of hers. It also ran a great café/bar.

Penny, hair sticking out in all directions and wearing clashing colours of red and orange, ran up to her, panting.

'Sorry I'm late, I lost track of time,' she puffed.

'You're fine. And it's so lovely to see you again.'

They hugged and headed inside to the lofty open-plan café.

Penny had worked with Nicole at the radio station and was always good for a laugh. A bit ditzy, as evidenced by her late arrival and appearance, she made a refreshing change from the aggressively-ambitious colleagues Nicole had been used to in television. It wasn't long before Penny had Nicole laughing at her latest mishap at work. A studio technician, Penny had accidentally left a live microphone switched on when a presenter, thinking he was off air, had blurted out what he really thought about his producer.

Nicole, remembering the people involved, thought it was hilarious. The producer, apparently, didn't.

Penny sighed.

'I'm not actually sure if I still have a job, but how was I to know the idiot would sound off like that? God, I could do with a drink!'

'Me too! Shall we order the fish and chips and bottles of lager? I always loved that combo.'

A calmer Penny waved goodbye to Nicole after their catch-up lunch. Nicole smiled broadly as she reclaimed her steps to the car park. Penny had proved a bright relief to the solicitor and the relentless packing. Now it was back to the grindstone!

After a, thankfully, undisturbed night, Nicole packed a few more boxes before taking a break in the garden. Alert to her new role as garden planner for Ben, she studied her own with more attention than usual. She didn't know the names of many of the plants but she appreciated the beauty of partnering certain colours for the greatest effect. Green setting off red, yellow next to blue. She made notes as she walked, planning to ask Hélène for help with the names of plants. Sitting on the bench by the pond, she closed her eyes for a moment. It occurred to her that until recently, she'd never spent much time actually *sitting* in a garden, drinking in the peace while serenaded by birdsong. Gardens had been to look at, or to socialise in, not to relax in and enjoy as an escape from a busy world. Nicole felt pleased that Ben had a garden that could provide a space to chill out in. Once it no longer looked like no-man's-land! Her own life had been lived at full tilt and little time had been spent at home except to eat and sleep. It would be different from now on, she vowed. Time to smell the roses!

Opening her eyes, she sat for a moment mesmerised by the goldfish swimming in the pond, in and out of the rushes and the lily pads. Adding "pond with fish" to her notes she stood up with a groan. *Oh, my back! Thank goodness I've nearly finished that dratted packing.* Rubbing her aching muscles she returned to the house to finish the last couple of boxes.

A large removal van turned up at three o'clock and the driver and his mate quickly loaded up the boxes and furniture. Nicole signed the forms and watched as her possessions were driven away. Luckily a Bath family were moving to Guernsey that weekend and her small load had been added to theirs; she would be reunited with her boxes on Monday.

It wasn't easy making a last tour of the house. Memories continued to jump out at her when she least expected, threatening to overwhelm her. It was horrid to say goodbye to the place she'd loved but she also felt relief that she had accomplished what she'd set out to do. She wouldn't need to return. Biting her lips, she locked the front door, dropping the key through the letterbox. Then, without a backward glance, she drove off.

chapter 35

Nicole was pleased to hear that Eve was a little stronger, even getting out of bed a couple of times while she'd been away.

'You can look in on her if you like, the carer's made her ready for bed but she's awake. I'm sure she'd love to see you,' Hélène smiled.

Leaving her case in the hall, Nicole headed for Eve's bedroom.

'Nicole! I'm glad you're back. Come and tell me how it went,' Eve patted the bed beside her and Nicole sat down. Her grandmother's face had regained some colour and her eyes looked brighter. She smiled with relief before regaling Eve with details of her trip.

Eve relaxed against the pillows.

'Well, that all sounds good, my dear. You can relax a bit now and help your mother prepare for her wedding.' She chuckled. 'You know, I never expected to see my daughter marry, certainly not at this age! She looked set for spinsterhood. And I understand you're to be the Matron of Honour! Something else I couldn't have dreamed of.'

Nicole grinned.

'It's weird, isn't it? But a nice weird. And I've brought my dress back with me so I do hope Hélène approves.'

'She'd approve if you wore a bin liner! She's so excited about the whole thing and, do you know, we've chosen what I should wear. Look, it's over there,' pointing to the back of the door.

Nicole admired the pale blue dress and jacket, saying how much it would suit her.

'I've only worn it once and no-one will remember it. Hélène's going to buy me a hat to match so I'll look very smart.'

A few minutes later Nicole left her to sleep. She found her mother in the kitchen preparing her a supper of chicken salad.

'Thanks, Hélène, but I could have…'

'No problem, just sit down and eat. Then we can bring each other up to date.'

They chatted over a glass of white wine. Hélène had wasted no time in booking a caterer for the wedding and posting out invitations.

'I wasn't sure what to do about your parents' invite. Would it be better if I emailed them? A letter could take ages.'

'Good idea, I'll give you the address.' She wrote it down for Hélène before asking, 'Have you bought your outfit yet? I know you'd seen something in Town.'

'No, I wanted you to go with me. I'd trust your judgment more than mine. I've hardly ever bought anything smart and you always look so stylish.'

Nicole felt touched.

'I'm flattered! And I'd love to go with you. What about tomorrow morning? I want to buy some accessories for my own outfit. Would you like to see it? I brought it back with me in case there was a delay with the removal men.'

She fetched her case and held up the dress, shaking out the creases.

'Oh, it's lovely! And the colour really emphasises your eyes.' She grinned, 'I'll need to buy something with a real wow factor to compete!'

Nicole's face dropped.

'I'm sorry, I didn't…'

Hélène gave her a hug.

'Don't be silly! I'm very proud of my gorgeous daughter! You could upstage me dressed in a track suit, so don't worry. Just help me choose something stylish and I'll be happy.'

On Saturday morning mother and daughter set off for Town while the carer stayed with Eve. Hélène felt a tingle of excitement at the thought of buying her wedding outfit. Although hardly a *young* bride at the age of sixty- two, inside she *felt* young. Adrian had rekindled the youthful side of her which had almost withered away; instead of the dried-up embittered woman she knew she'd become, she felt alive and loved. The passionate sex felt wonderful and had been unexpected. She'd assumed they'd both be past it, but how wrong could you be! She felt her face burn at the memory and risked a quick glance at Nicole to see if she'd noticed. Fortunately, as the driver, her eyes were fixed firmly on the road.

After parking on the Crown Pier they headed to Le Pollet and the boutique Hélène had in mind. She went over to the racks of suits and pulled out the cream brocade she'd chosen.

'What do you think?'

'W-e-e-l-l, it's okay, but I'm sure we could find something with a bit more 'oomph'. Let me look.'

Hélène was happy to let Nicole choose. She'd had second thoughts herself after seeing the suit again; although beautifully made, it did look a little bland.

Nicole moved over to the racks of cocktail dresses.

'How about this?' She held out a dark blue lace v-necked sheath with short sleeves.

She fingered it. 'It's gorgeous! But do you really think this would suit me?'

'Definitely. You've got a good figure and you'll look very glam. Go and try it on and see.'

Hélène went into the changing room feeling the dress was a mistake. She came out smiling.

'Wow! You look absolutely fantastic! Turn around.'

Hélène hardly recognised herself. The dress gave her an hour-glass figure and seemed to make her look two inches taller.

She beamed at Nicole.

'I love it! Thanks for pointing it out, I'd never have considered it myself. I actually *feel* like a bride in this.'

Nicole hugged her.

'Good, 'cos that's what you are. Now let's find something for your hair and then it's time for shoes.'

The nearby Creasey's department store provided the perfect finishing touch. A pretty pearl studded short veil topped with intricate folds of cream ribbon. Hélène felt close to tears as she studied her reflection. The veil cleverly softened the lines around her eyes, taking years off her face. Nicole was proving to be the ideal "personal shopper" she needed.

Her daughter also found the perfect match for her own dress, a twin diamante headband attached to a pale green satin rose. Remembering she needed a hat for her mother too, Hélène continued looking and found a wide-brimmed navy boater decorated with organza flowers and band. Delighted with their choices, they made for Hélène's favourite shoe shop, Celaro. The girls were only too happy to help, congratulating her on her marriage. Hélène finally decided on a pair of high heeled navy sling-backs with a detachable silver bow. Nicole chose a pair of silver satin sandals with diamante caged straps and high heels. Happy but tired, they decamped to nearby Christie's for a celebratory lunch.

The next couple of weeks flew by. Nicole's belongings arrived promptly on Monday and she unpacked her summer clothes and accessories. She hoped that by the time winter arrived she'd be living with Ben. If not, then she'd rent some place near the television studio. During the week a letter from her solicitor arrived, confirming that she'd submitted the necessary documents to the court in request of the divorce. Nicole had nothing more to do but wait.

Mary and Ian phoned to say that they'd be delighted to attend Hélène's wedding, arriving in Jersey on 11th August before flying over to Guernsey on the 21st . Hélène had invited them to stay at La Folie but they declined, preferring to book into Old Government House Hotel in Town. As Mary explained to Nicole, 'There'll be so much going on for you all and we don't want to get in the way. But it was very sweet of Hélène to offer. And there is her mother to consider…'

Nicole agreed it was the better arrangement and was looking forward to seeing them. She and Ben had spent as much time together as possible over the weeks and she'd made a start on the garden. The patio area was now clear and Ben had purchased a weather-proof modern table and chairs. At least there was somewhere to sit and have a drink after the hard work of weeding, she consoled herself.

Eve's health remained stable and she ventured out of her room several times. She'd been unhappy to need "that dratted wheelchair" as she called it, but wasn't strong enough for her frame. Nicole wheeled her out to the terrace for afternoon tea the Saturday before the wedding. Hélène was out with Adrian.

August was proving to be a hot dry month and the garden needed constant watering. Nicole positioned Eve under the parasol and poured the tea.

'Not too hot, Grandmother? I can take you back inside if you like.'

Eve shook her head.

'I'm fine. It's lovely to be outside again. Oh, I've missed my garden! I can smell the roses from here!' she sniffed appreciatively.

'We're keeping an eye on the cream ones for use in our bouquets. It's such a clever idea of Hélène's to use our own, isn't it? It would be a shame to buy flowers when we have

245

so many!' Nicole waved her arm towards the lush, vibrant borders.

'Yes, and the *Jardin de Bagatelle* is a particularly lovely rose, I've always admired its strong perfume. They'll look beautiful with your dresses. My corsage is to be made of a rose and baby's breath. Oh, I'm so looking forward to it! You don't get much excitement at my age and I plan to make the most of it.' She chuckled.

Nicole smiled, but inwardly she felt like crying. How much longer would her grandmother have to enjoy her family? Eve put on a brave face, acting as if time was of no consequence. But it was. Drugs were helping for the moment, but for how long? The proverbial elephant was in the room but, by tacit agreement, no-one mentioned its presence.

The following afternoon Ben called to collect Nicole for a barbecue at Nick and Jeanne's. After checking that Eve was all right, he helped Nicole load up their contribution from the kitchen: wine, beer and salads. Ben started the engine and drove off, heading towards the coast and Perelle.

'I'm so looking forward to seeing everyone again. It seems ages since Herm when I promised to stay in touch. But so much has happened since...'

'They'll understand, I'm sure. And now you're definitely staying here you can make more friends, network a bit.' Ben grinned at her, 'You'll soon be that new face on the TV and be recognised everywhere.'

She groaned.

'Being recognised can have its disadvantages, you know. Means you have to be nice to everyone, even if they're the pits.'

He laughed, patting her arm.

They arrived at Le Petit Chêne to find the drive jammed with cars, the overspill parked up the lane. After finding a spot, they carried their supplies round to the back as directed.

'Hi, you two. It's good to see you again,' Jeanne greeted them as they deposited the food and drink.

'You're positively blooming, Jeanne!' Nicole cried, her arms stretching round Jeanne and The Bump. Ben leaned in for a kiss.

Jeanne grinned.

'Yep. I'm six months now and, boy, can I tell! Junior's a lively one all right. Kicking when I'm sleeping but quiet when I'm awake!'

Nicole grinned in sympathy. Then she had a quick look at her surroundings.

'Wow! What a beautiful garden! I love the pergola! And you've even got an orchard.' Nicole gazed around wide eyed.

'My grandmother was the genius behind it, actually. I just added the patio and pergola and replaced the over-the-hill planting.'

Before Nicole could get stuck into a conversation on gardens, Nick waved them over to the barbecue, introducing them to a girl who'd been chatting to Jonathan.

'Nicole, Ben meet my little sis, Colette, the best chef in Guernsey!'

Colette, a petite brunette with deep blue eyes like Nick's, laughed.

'A slight exaggeration, bruv, but thanks. I opened my own restaurant at Easter thanks to Nick's generosity,' she said, giving him a hug.

'That's great. Where is it? I'd love to check it out,' Nicole said.

'At The Bridge in St Sampsons, near the harbour. It's only small, but it's a start. One day I'd like to open a restaurant in Town but that'll need mega bucks so...' she shrugged.

Other guests came up and Nicole was introduced to them, trying desperately to remember everyone's names.

Drinks were poured and the conversations became animated, with bursts of laughter floating up in the air. With most of the guests in their thirties like her, Nicole felt very much at home, happy to be meeting so many new people. During a lull in conversation she noticed a more mature couple chatting to Jeanne. Glancing up, Jeanne waved her over.

'Come and meet someone who knows your parents, Peter Ogier and his wife, Molly.'

For a moment Nicole felt confused. How could these people know her parents? Then the penny dropped. But still…was it now public knowledge about her birth?

Peter must have seen the puzzlement on her face.

'I worked with Hélène and Adrian years ago and later on Adrian was the headmaster at my school. He retired a year before I did. We've been invited to their wedding.' He kissed her cheek. 'I recognised you from Adrian's description. We're both so happy for them, aren't we, Molly?' Peter, a big bear of a man, smiled broadly at her.

'I'm pleased to meet you both, you're the first of their friends I've met.'

Molly, a cuddly looking woman, gave her a hug.

'It's like something out of a Mills & Boon, isn't it? Boy meets girl, boy loses girl, boy finds girl. And I understand if you hadn't popped up out of the blue, they might still be apart. That would be such a pity!'

Nicole and the Ogiers chatted for a few minutes before Ben came up, putting his arm around her waist. Nicole introduced everyone before they were called to help themselves to food.

The barbecue went on until after nine o'clock, at which point people started to drift away. Nicole and Ben said their goodbyes to the hosts with Nicole promising Jeanne she'd be in touch soon.

'Had a good time?' Ben asked as they walked arm in arm towards the car.

'Great. You do realise we'll have to reciprocate once the garden's decent, don't you?' She sighed, 'I'm so jealous of their gorgeous garden, but it has given me a few ideas for yours.'

'I don't think anyone will mind coming round now it's more user-friendly. At least there's now no risk of being stung by nettles or caught up in brambles.'

'True.' Nicole snuggled up closer as they reached the car. 'Are you taking me back to my place or...?'

'My place is fine. I'll run you home in the morning.' He gave her a lingering kiss.

'Mm, lovely.'

Nicole paced up and down the inter-island arrivals area at the airport on Tuesday morning, her parents due any moment. So much had happened since she'd seen them! Only weeks ago, but it felt like a lifetime. Becoming so much enmeshed in her "other" family's lives, it had felt hard at times to remember her original family. They were only two people compared with the seven surrounding Hélène. Not wanting them to feel pushed out, Nicole planned to spend as much time with them as possible. Starting with taking them to their hotel for a catch up before throwing them to the wolves at La Folie, so to speak. Grinning at the image of Eve and Hélène as wolves with bared fangs, Nicole glanced up to see her parents wheeling their cases towards her.

'Mum! Dad! Great to see you both!'

Caught up in a group hug it was a moment before her parents could reply.

'It's lovely to see you again, darling. And looking so well! Living here seems to be agreeing with you,' her mother replied, surveying her.

'I agree with your mother, Nicole. You do look well.'

Nicole grinned at them.

'Right, let's get going shall we? Once you've collected your hire car you can follow me into Town.'

Half an hour later Nicole drove down Ann's Place, guiding her parents to the OGH, before going on to park her car. Returning to the hotel she settled in a chair in the Centenary Bar, waiting for her parents to finish checking in to their room. When they arrived the waiter took the order for coffee.

'Not quite the same as having a coffee in a bar on the arenal, is it?' Nicole grinned.

'No, but this is a gorgeous hotel and it looks like we're in for some pampering. Your father booked us a beautiful sea-view room with a balcony. I've been spoilt!'

Ian fidgeted in his chair.

'You deserve spoiling, after putting up with me all these years!' he said, patting her arm.

Nicole laughed.

'Is this some sort of second honeymoon, Dad? Should I leave you two to get on with it and catch you later?'

Her mother blushed and fiddled with her cup while her father grinned and said, 'Haha!'

Mary, in an apparent effort to change the subject, began asking questions about Hélène and Adrian. Nicole then had to go into detail about Eve before Ben became the subject of choice.

Ian remained quiet, taking it all in as if he was still an Advocate listening to testimony. Finally, in an obvious move to halt the interrogation, he suggested they transfer to The Olive Grove, the garden dining terrace, for lunch. Nicole threw him a grateful look as she stood up.

'What a lovely view!' exclaimed Mary as they stepped outside. Castle Cornet and the open sea were clearly visible as they drank in the panorama laid out before them.

During lunch Nicole managed to keep the focus on her parents and what they'd been up to in Spain. It seemed to boil down mainly to golf, tennis and Mary's amateur dramatic group. Their lives sounded rather less eventful than her own over the past weeks, she thought, smiling inwardly. Still, at their age did they need drama other than the amateur kind? Probably not, she decided.

'So, what's the plan for today? Are we meeting Hélène?' Ian asked.

'Yes, we thought it would be nice if you came round for afternoon tea to meet both her and her mother. Adrian will call in a bit later so it's not too overwhelming meeting everyone at once.' She cleared her throat. 'And Ben's offered to take the three of us out to dinner tonight. If it's easier for you, we could eat here as he says The Brasserie's food is very good. But if you'd rather we went somewhere else, that's fine.'

Mary and Ian looked at each other and smiled.

'It sounds as if you've thought of everything, darling. I'm looking forward to meeting everyone and do tell Ben that we'd be happy to be his guests here tonight.'

'Good. So would you prefer to follow me to Torteval in your car, Dad?'

'Yes, I know how confusing the roads are from the time your mother and I visited some years ago. I'd better make sure there's a map in the car or we'll end up lost again,' he chuckled.

'Well, I don't know about you, dear, but I want to go upstairs and unpack.' Mary checked her watch. 'What time shall we need to leave, Nicole?'

'Say in an hour? I can nip to the shops while you're unpacking and I'll see you later.'

★★★

At three thirty Hélène heard the arrival of cars in the drive. Swinging open the front door, she plastered a smile on her face to hide the rising panic within. Oh, God, please let this go well, for Nicole's sake, if not for mine.

'Hi, Hélène, please let me introduce you to Mary and Ian Le Clerq, my…parents.'

chapter 36

Hélène took a deep breath, fingernails digging into her palm. Releasing the door she reached out to shake hands with Mary and Ian, who looked like perfectly ordinary people and not the ogres she'd created in her head.

'Hélène, it's lovely to meet you at last! Ian and I have been quite excited these past weeks. And you're getting married! How wonderful!' Mary gushed, looking flustered as they shook hands.

As Ian grabbed her hand in a firm clasp, Hélène took in his air of authority. A man used to being in control. She felt unsure of herself as he said, 'Pleased to meet you, Hélène, and congratulations on your forthcoming marriage.'

Nicole, perhaps sensing the tension in the moment, suggested they all went through to the terrace and she'd make the tea.

Hélène went to protest, but Nicole pushed her into leading her parents down the hall.

'Go on, there's nothing to worry about, they owe you, remember,' she whispered in her ear, giving her arm a quick squeeze.

'Why, your house is enormous, Hélène! Nicole warned us it was big but still…' Ian swept his arm around the hall as he surveyed the staircase and various corridors.

'Yes, it's a bit of an anachronism these days, isn't it? A Victorian, gothic folly built by a man with more money than sense!' she laughed nervously. 'You probably noticed the twin circular towers at the front?' Mary and Ian nodded.

'Well, the architect was apparently inspired by the round tower of Torteval Church, only built in 1818. It has the tallest steeple on the island and houses a fifteenth century French bell. It's a lovely little church and I…always wanted to get married there.' She knew she was babbling from nervousness, but couldn't help herself. In spite of Nicole's reassurance, she felt awkward with these people. Her daughter's parents.

Mary and Ian nodded and they continued out to the terrace.

As they exclaimed over the garden and view Hélène tried to relax. Nicole wheeled out the tea trolley, saying she'd go and fetch her grandmother. She returned a few moments later pushing Eve's wheelchair.

'Here we are. Grandmother, I'd like you to meet my parents, Mary and Ian. Mum, Dad, this is Eve.'

They all shook hands before settling themselves around the table.

The conversation was stilted as Nicole poured the tea and passed round cake. General comments on the weather and the house were tossed around but Hélène still felt ill at ease. She glanced over at Mary and thought she looked equally as uncomfortable, despite her opening words. *It's not easy to acknowledge each other. We both have such a vested interest in Nicole that it was bound to happen. I'm jealous of her! She had all the joy of those early years and is responsible for the way she's turned out. I only supplied my womb!*

Eve and Ian drifted into a conversation about the Occupation and evacuation of the islanders. Born in 1939, Ian was sent to England with his mother in 1940 and he and Eve compared notes on their experiences. Being so young, his memories were hazy and very different to Eve's but they still had something in common. Hélène saw that Nicole was leaning towards them, listening, apparently fascinated.

This left Mary and Hélène apart.

'You must have found it very…strange meeting Nicole after all this time,' Mary began, barely looking up from her tea.

'Yes, it was. I'd given up hope of her wanting to…to find me. So it was wonderful that she did.'

Mary looked up. 'It was quite…upsetting for me, us. We wondered if she felt we hadn't… loved her enough.' She was chewing her lips and Hélène noticed the over-bright eyes.

'Oh, not at all! She's told me what great parents you were, are.' Hélène leaned forward. 'She loves you both very much, believe me.'

Mary reached for a tissue and blew her nose.

'But she's planning to stay here, be near you. You'll see her all the time!'

'She isn't staying because of *me*! It's Ben she wants to spend time with. We've…become close, yes, but you're still her mother. I…I can't compete with what you've done over the years. I envy you that. And I know I can never make up for those years. But I do love her, as any mother would love her child.' She felt the tears pricking at her eyes and Mary handed her a clean tissue from her bag. 'Thanks,' she muttered.

Mary put her hand on her arm.

'I think we both have to accept that Nicole has two… mothers now and we'll have to share her. It won't be easy but we…we must try.'

Hélène nodded, feeling as if she and Mary had reached some kind of understanding. Acceptance.

She'd hardly drawn breath when the doorbell announced Adrian's arrival and she left to let him in.

Adrian gave her a long hug before pulling back and whispering, 'Are you all right? You've been crying! Are they being horrible to you?'

She managed a weak smile.

'They can't hear you, they're on the terrace. And no, they're being okay. Mary's obviously upset about me being part of Nicole's life now, but I think it can be worked out. I haven't spoken much to Ian as Mother took him over. Come on, before they wonder what we're doing.'

'Mary, Ian, I'd like you to meet my... fiancé, Adrian Bourgaize.' She couldn't bring herself to introduce him as Nicole's father.

After the requisite handshakes, Adrian joined them at the table and Nicole went off to make more tea.

Hélène held her breath, praying that Adrian wouldn't meet with the judgment he feared. She sensed an initial wariness from Ian, who, she thought, might be feeling at a disadvantage meeting the man who had fathered the child he couldn't.

The two men seemed to eye each other up, the way men do when they are in competition for a woman. Only this time not for a lover, but a daughter. But Adrian had not spent years as a headmaster for nothing and she watched, fascinated, as he turned on his easy charm. The charm that had worked on her. Twice.

Sitting back in her chair she listened as Adrian focused the conversation on Mary and Ian, encouraging them to talk about their life in retirement. Once golf was mentioned as a mutual interest, the three of them became like best buddies. Eve reached over and whispered to Hélène, 'I think it's going very well, don't you? You can stop your worrying now, my girl, and look forward to Saturday,' she smiled slyly.

'You knew I was worried about us meeting them?'

'Of course! But I always knew it would be all right. Nicole's such a lovely girl that her parents had to be nice too,' Eve said, patting her arm.

Nicole returned with a fresh teapot and the little tea party continued while Hélène slowly relaxed.

Ben collected Nicole that evening, eager to know how the meeting of her parents had gone. Or the Clash of the Titans as he so wickedly referred to it.

'Well, there certainly wasn't any battle, not even of the egos. I admit I'd been worried on Mum's behalf, as she could have seen herself usurped by Hélène. I sensed some tension initially, but by the end of the afternoon they were all getting on like a house on fire. So, a result!' she grinned at him. 'More like "The Famous Five" than "Clash of the Titans", with golfing anecdotes taking centre stage rather than feuds between the gods of the universe!'

Ben laughed.

'Good! So now it's my turn to be inspected. Hope I'm not found wanting!'

'Just be on your best behaviour and you'll be fine. They're becoming quite mellow in their old age; Dad could be quite scary when he was in full Advocate flow. I was always glad I never ended up on the witness stand in front of him.'

'Oh, thanks a lot! That's really boosted my confidence. Not,' he said, glancing towards her while he steered the car onto the main road.

She leaned over to give him a quick kiss.

'Seriously, I'm so pleased that The Parents have hit it off. Could have been very awkward at the wedding if they hadn't. And Hélène is *so* excited, I think she's finding it hard to believe it's really happening. After all these years.'

'It's a big deal for her, so it's to be expected. Is everything under control with the preparations?'

'Yep. The cleaner's been working overtime, smartening up the dining room and sitting room. Everywhere you go the smell of furniture polish mingles with the perfume of cut flowers scattered about the house. It's as if the old place is finally waking up and putting on new clothes.' Her face dropped. 'It's such a bitter-sweet time for everyone, though.

Underneath we're worried about Grandmother and how long she'll be with us.'

Ben reached out and gripped her hand.

'Hey, don't get maudlin! She's determined to make it for the wedding and she will. After that, no-one can say, but at least there's something great to celebrate and Eve would be the first to admit she's had a good innings. And she's as excited about the wedding as Hélène is.'

'True. Okay, let's focus on the good stuff for now. And your imminent cross-examination by my father!' She grinned at him.

'Great!'

Fifteen minutes later Ben parked the car near the OGH and walked hand in hand with Nicole into the hotel. Her parents awaited them in the Centenary Bar and Nicole, squeezing Ben's hand, walked over to their table.

'Mum, Dad, I'd like you to meet Ben. Ben, my parents Mary and Ian Le Clerq.'

'How do you do, Mr Le Clerq,' Ben said, shaking hands.

'Please, call me Ian. I'm very well, thank you, Ben. Glad to meet you. Nicole's told us a lot about you, hasn't she, Mary?' Ian turned to his wife who smiled up at Ben from her chair.

Ben leaned down and kissed Mary's cheek.

'Nice to meet you, Ben,' she said, adding 'and please call me Mary.'

Ian summoned a waiter to take the order for drinks and to bring menus for The Brasserie. He then asked Ben a little about himself, and it wasn't long before the two men became involved in a conversation about their professional experiences. Nicole and Mary sat back with their G and Ts as they listened. Nicole was pleased that her father didn't bombard Ben with questions but let Ben chat about his work. Once the menus arrived their attention turned to their choice of food. The order duly given, the conversation turned back to Ben.

'So, Ben, do you see yourself staying here for good? So many young people seem to find the islands a bit claustrophobic.' Ian asked.

'I can't see myself leaving, though I know what you mean by being claustrophobic!' Ben grinned. 'As long as I can get away and stretch my wings occasionally I'm happy. I took a gap year before uni and spent it touring Australia and New Zealand. Absolutely brilliant! But I felt a bit overwhelmed by the vastness of Australia and couldn't imagine living there. I'm much more at home in a place like Guernsey where I can be anywhere within thirty minutes or so. And I'd hate to be far from the sea.' He turned to face Nicole, 'I do wonder how you'll settle here after the buzz of Bristol. We're a bit of a backwater in comparison.'

'Don't forget I grew up in Jersey so I'm used to "backwaters",' Nicole laughed. 'I admit I enjoyed living on the mainland but I've enjoyed the slower pace of life here. It suits me, I don't want to be striving to prove something all the time.' She touched Ben's hand before adding softly, 'And they do say home is where the heart is, so I'm very happy to live here.'

Mary cleared her throat.

'Well said, darling. Your father and I were happy to stay in Jersey until he retired and we've no regrets about it. The islands are lovely places to bring up children, so much safer than the mainland.' Mary blushed. 'Oh, I wasn't implying that you two…'

'It's all right, Mum! If Ben and I do get together then we'd like to have children. But there's the small matter of my divorce first!'

The waiter arrived to tell them that their table was ready and they moved down from the bar into the restaurant. He escorted them to a table by the window of the conservatory, offering a view of the garden and out towards the harbour.

Ben had ordered a bottle of champagne and they raised their glasses for a toast, crying 'Santé'. Waiters served the local sea food they had ordered and the serious business of eating began.

The combination of good food and wine contributed in making the evening slip by pleasantly. By the end of the meal it looked to Nicole that her parents had taken Ben under their wing as a prospective son-in-law. Once the existing one was unhooked, of course.

'What do you plan to do while you're here, Ian?' Ben asked as they sipped their coffees.

'We thought we'd pop over to Sark for a day tomorrow as we haven't been there since Nicole was a girl. Might hire cycles so we can explore as far as Little Sark and treat ourselves to lunch at La Sablonnerie. Then, weather permitting, we'll have a day in Herm on Thursday or Friday. It still gives us plenty of time to retrace our steps in Guernsey before we leave on Sunday.'

'You'll need to rest when you return to Spain, Dad!'

'That's the beauty of being retired, my dear. We can do as much or as little as we want. It's now too hot for anything physical like golf or tennis, so we'll just take it easy and read. Your mother's filling up a case with paperbacks while we're here to keep us going till winter!' Ian chuckled.

Mary replied, 'Well, it's lovely to wonder round bookshops full of English books for a change. We do have one bookshop in Javea but the choice is quite limited. And your father's right, it's too hot to do much at this time of year. I think we'll make it an annual event to come back in the summer, spending time in both islands. It'll mean we see more of you, darling. And, it goes without saying, you're both welcome to visit us whenever you like.'

'Thanks, Mum. We'll be over as soon as summer's over,' Nicole laughed, glancing at Ben.

'From what Nicole's told me, you live in a great place, Mary. I don't know Spain very well, as I only ever drove around France.'

The conversation turned to a comparison of the merits of France versus Spain before Ben suggested that he and Nicole should leave. After an exchange of goodnights, Ben and Nicole walked back to the car.

'So, what did you think of my parents? I think they liked you.'

'I thought they were great. Your father's Old School with a soft centre and your mother's very motherly. And I'm looking forward to a free holiday in Spain,' he grinned.

'Hey! Cheeky!' She punched his arm. 'When they visit next year would it be all right if they stayed with us? I don't like to think of them needing an hotel when we have room.'

'Fine by me. As long as you can give me a hand finishing off the guest bedroom, bathroom…'

'Okay, point taken. But the money from my divorce should be more than enough to cover the cost of employing professionals and I'd like to contribute to the house, if you have no objection.'

Ben turned towards her.

'That's generous of you, Nicole. I'll think about it. In the meantime let's get home and you can offer me a rather different kind of contribution,' he said, squeezing her thigh.

'Oooh, Doctor! You are naughty!' she giggled.

chapter 37

The next few days passed in a haze of final preparations for the wedding. Nicole helped the cleaner, Liz, to go through the house thoroughly, so that even the rooms not being used still had a clean and tidy. With the weather forecast to remain fine for Saturday, Hélène decided to use the garden, hiring chairs and tables with parasols. As a backup the house was more than large enough to cater for the forty invited guests.

Eve conserved her strength by resting as much as possible. But she liked to keep her finger on the pulse and would ask Hélène and Nicole to keep her updated on the progress of the preparations, offering advice as she deemed appropriate. One of her good ideas was to ask the ladies from the Western WI, of which she had been a member, to arrange flowers from the garden in the church. Two ladies turned up to cut flowers chosen by Hélène, bearing them off to St Philippe's to fill the altar vases.

Nicole only saw Ben when he came round to check on Eve. His visits were not medically essential as Eve seemed stable, but they reassured the family. It was agreed that he would move in at the weekend while Hélène and Adrian spent a couple of nights in Jersey. They didn't want a longer honeymoon while worried about Eve. The carers would come in as usual and at no time would Eve be on her own. Nicole kept her company when she could and, although still intrigued about Eve's experiences during the war, hadn't pursued her questioning.

Adrian came round to mow the lawn and tidy the hedges on Thursday and Nicole noticed that he looked distracted as he talked to Hélène in the garden. When she returned to the kitchen Nicole asked her if there was anything the matter.

Hélène frowned.

'He still hasn't heard from Karen about whether or not she's coming to the wedding. He'll be devastated if she doesn't but she's not answering his calls.' She sighed, 'I'd hate to be the cause of a family split but what can I do?'

'Has Michael spoken to her? He is coming, isn't he?'

'Yes, he's coming but I don't know if he's talked to Karen. I'll have a word with Adrian later. Oh dear, families!'

Nicole gave her a hug.

'Karen's just making a point and I'm sure she'll be there. Either way, it's *your* day so don't let anything spoil it for you. Go and sit down and I'll make you a cup of tea.'

By Friday there'd still been no word from Karen but Michael had promised to have a word with her. It was a question of wait and see.

Saturday dawned warm and clear and as soon as the carers arrived for Eve, Nicole and Hélène drove off to the hairdressers in St Peter Port. Then it was on to the beauticians for a manicure and pedicure. They were home by eleven and Hélène went to check that Eve was properly attired in her dress and jacket while Nicole went into the kitchen to make coffee. Hélène wheeled Eve outside and Nicole remarked how well the blue suited her.

'Thank you, my dear. I can't wait to see you both in your glory later. And I like that new hairstyle, Hélène, it suits you.'

Hélène smiled, patting her flicked-out hair, a more youthful style than normal. 'Thanks. Nicole talked me into something different and I'm glad she did.'

The women chatted over their coffee, an air of barely suppressed excitement flowing like an electric current between them. Hélène's fingers tapped on the table as if she were pacing out a particularly fast tune. The heady perfume of roses hung in the air, mixing with the aroma of their fresh coffee. Nicole felt as if time was suspended, the hiatus before the real purpose of the day could begin. It didn't last, the peace being shattered by the doorbell, announcing the arrival of the caterers.

Hélène and Nicole went to direct operations and moments later the flowers also arrived. The level of excitement went up a notch as the bouquets were admired. Hélène's flowers, tightly packed cream roses and yellow freesias encased in glossy green leaves, were hand tied with a blue satin ribbon to match her dress. Nicole's slightly smaller bouquet of roses and leaves was tied with a green ribbon.

'They're gorgeous, Hélène! Your florist friend's done a great job,' Nicole said, breathing in the fragrance. She looked at her watch before adding, 'It's time to get changed. I'll bring Grandmother inside and fix her corsage before I go.'

Once she was dressed, Nicole went along to Hélène's room to see if she needed a hand.

As Hélène opened the door there were mutual cries of admiration.

'You look stunning, Hélène! Adrian will be bowled over!'

Hélène's face glowed with pleasure.

'Thanks, I hope so! And you make a gorgeous Matron of Honour!'

Nicole helped with her mother's headdress before they went downstairs to join Eve in her sitting room.

As they walked in Eve looked up and, although she smiled, tears began to run down her face.

'Are you all right, Mother?' Hélène rushed over to her chair.

'Yes, dear, I'm just overcome at the sight of you both. My beautiful girls! Let me have a closer look.' Eve wiped her eyes as Nicole gave her a hug.

After reassuring herself Eve was fine Hélène went to check on the caterers.

Ben arrived shortly after to escort Eve to the church in a hired limousine. As he set eyes on Nicole, his face lit up and he let out an appreciative whistle. She dropped a mock curtsy and they shared a quick kiss before he wheeled Eve outside and lifted her into the car. Once the wheelchair was in the boot they left, waving at Nicole on the front step. Hélène stayed discreetly out of sight in the kitchen and Nicole joined her to collect her bouquet. The arrival of their own car was announced by the crunch of tyres on the gravel and mother and daughter, holding their flowers tightly, were greeted by the uniformed chauffeur bowing them into the car.

The white Rolls purred down the drive and Hélène reached out for Nicole's hand.

'I'm not dreaming, am I? I am sitting in a Rolls Royce on the way to my wedding, aren't I?'

Nicole giggled.

'It's no dream, it's for real. Now, just enjoy it. This is *your* day remember. It'll be wonderful!'

★★★

The church bells rang out as the Rolls approached, the joyful sound seeming to echo around them. With weddings being rare occasions at St Philippe's, a few heads popped out of windows to watch the car pull up. Ben, hovering in the porch, signalled their arrival to the vicar. As Hélène and Nicole stood at the door, the organ burst into life with the resounding sound of Wagner's Bridal March. Hélène had asked Nicole to walk by her side down the aisle, only moving away as they reached the altar.

Hélène's heart hammered as she stepped towards the man she loved, barely registering the congregation standing in welcome. The sun poured through the stained glass window behind the altar, splashing rainbows of colour across the white plastered walls. She smiled her joy as Adrian turned around. Glancing quickly at the pew behind him, she was relieved to see Karen, Luke in her arms, standing between Dave and Michael. As Hélène reached Adrian's side their eyes locked and a feeling of calm spread through her whole being. At last, she was marrying the man she loved!

'Dearly beloved…'

Cheers rang out in the garden of La Folie as the guests toasted the bride and groom, glasses of champagne held high. The caterers had spread the tables and chairs on the terrace and lawn, leaving the guests to sit where they wished. Neither Hélène nor Adrian wanted speeches, conscious of the feelings of his children. Hélène had wanted a little "pomp" as she called it in the church, but now informality reigned. Michael had sneaked in an iPod and speakers, setting it up on the terrace so that soon music was wafting across the garden. Nicole cornered him, asking which songs he'd chosen.

'60s music mainly, being the most age-appropriate,' he grinned. 'And I've chosen a great track for the first dance,' he added, tapping his nose.

'Can't wait to hear it!' Nicole looked across at Karen, sitting at a table with her husband and son. She wore a long face and Dave seemed to be trying to cheer her up.

'What did you say to convince Karen to come?'

Michael shuffled his feet.

'I just asked her to think about how it would look to everyone if she didn't. Guernsey's a small island and people love to gossip. And Dad's always been popular, everyone got on with him more than Mum. She...she didn't have many friends, you know, and although I loved her, I can see why he fell for Hélène.' He hesitated before continuing, 'Karen's not as angry about the affair itself as about the fact that you're Dad's daughter too. She's jealous, Nicole. Jealous of *you.*'

'Oh! I see. Well, let's hope in time she'll see there's nothing to be jealous of, Michael. None of us can change the past and I for one am very happy with the way it's turned out between them,' she nodded towards the newlyweds.

'Me too, Sis!'

Nicole grinned at him before joining Eve, holding court as the "mother of the bride".

'Enjoying yourself, Grandmother?'

'Yes dear, it's such fun isn't it? Everyone's been so kind and someone, I'm not sure who, even brought me a lovely selection from the buffet. Have you eaten yet?'

'No, I'll go in a minute. I just wanted to make sure you were okay.'

'Off you go, before there's nothing left!' Eve chuckled.

On her way back from the dining room Nicole caught up with her parents, who'd been chatting to Peter and Molly Ogier. Mary seemed a little emotional as she kissed her.

'Wasn't it a lovely service? And I thought you both looked beautiful. We'll chat later when everyone's gone.'

Joining Ben at a table near the bride and groom, Nicole was finally able to relax. It had been a busy and poignant few hours and, judging by the laughing faces of Hélène and Adrian, with a happy outcome. She sighed, would she have a happy ending? Glancing at Ben through lowered lashes, she caught him looking at her intently.

He leant over, whispering, 'Happy? I was very proud of you as you walked down the aisle, darling. I think you're the most beautiful woman I've ever seen.'

Nicole's heart beat faster.

'Of course I'm happy. And thank you, kind sir!' She said lightly.

They carried on eating, only breaking off to chat to the other couple on the table. At a signal from the caterer, the wedding cake was brought out, prompting an outbreak of cheers and clapping. Hélène had chosen a simple iced sponge decorated with tiny iced roses encircling their entwined initials.

Once the cake had been ceremoniously cut, Michael called out 'First dance!' as he fiddled with the iPod. Adrian pulled a laughing Hélène to her feet as the sound of The Ronettes singing "Be My Baby" rang out from the speakers. Nicole grinned at Michael. A good choice!

After the bridal pair had completed a circle on the lawn, other couples got to their feet. Ben grabbed Nicole's hand and whirled her into a fast waltz. As she spun round she noticed that Dave had managed to persuade Karen to dance. Thank goodness! Karen even managed a smile. Nicole settled happily into Ben's arms.

By five o'clock the celebrations were drawing to a close. Hélène and Adrian went upstairs to change as the caterers started the clear-up. Some of the guests had already left while a stalwart few remained to cheer the bride and groom on their way. Nicole pushed Eve's wheelchair into the hall for the send-off. As the taxi arrived, the remaining guests laughingly threw confetti over the newly-weds. Hélène turned her back to the group and threw her bouquet high in the air. Instinctively, Nicole rushed forward and caught it. As Hélène turned round she smiled and, giving her a hug, whispered, 'You next!'

chapter 38

Eve was so exhausted by the wedding celebrations that she retired to her bed as soon as the happy couple and remaining guests departed. Once the carers had made her comfortable Ben popped in to see her.

'How is she?' Nicole asked as he returned to the terrace where they'd been enjoying a quiet drink.

'Not too good, I'm afraid. I think she was operating on overdrive today and it's caught up with her. She might be better after a couple of days rest, but I can't guarantee it.' He stroked her hair as she slumped into his arms.

A shiver ran through Nicole as she imagined the worst.

'Will...will she live till Hélène gets back?'

'I hope so. You know I'll do my best, but...' He shrugged.

All the happiness and laughter of the day suddenly dissipated, as if a strong wind had swirled around the house, blowing the joy over the cliff. *It's not fair! Grandmother must hold on for Hélène, she must!* Ben continued to hold her tight as she willed Eve to live. At least for a few more days...

Early on Sunday morning Nicole, holding her breath, tiptoed into Eve's bedroom. As she gazed at her grandmother's recumbent form she searched for signs of breathing. The slight, ragged rise and fall of Eve's chest reassured her that all was well. For the moment. She was about to leave when Eve's eyes opened.

'Morning, Grandmother. How do you feel?'

Eve's voice came out in a whisper.

'Very…tired, my dear. I…overdid it yesterday, but it… was worth it. What a… wonderful day!'

Nicole helped her to drink some water and Eve sank back on the pillow.

'Thank you. I'll stay…bed today… rest.'

'Would you like anything to eat or a cup of tea?'

Eve shook her head, closing her eyes. Her face was grey in the muted light of the bedroom and Nicole's heart clenched. She was reminded of when she visited her other grandmother for what proved to be the last time. Her face had borne the same ashen tinge.

Ben took one look at Nicole's face and hugged her.

'She's still alive but I can see it can't be long. She's refused anything to eat and wants to sleep.'

'I'll check her now.'

Nicole, on autopilot, filled the kettle and put the bread in the toaster. As she set the table Ben returned.

'I've given her an injection to stabilise her heart. She's asleep now and I'll look in later.' He sat down and sipped his coffee.

'Should I get in touch with Hélène?' Nicole asked, feeling her shoulders tighten.

He shook his head. 'They're back at lunchtime tomorrow and I think we've got a few days yet. It would be a shame to spoil their weekend unless it's…urgent.' Reaching out to grab her hand, he added, 'Don't worry, I'll be keeping an eye on her.'

Nicole, buttering her toast, could only hope he was right.

Mary and Ian arrived later that morning to say goodbye and were shocked to hear about Eve. Nicole hadn't told them how little time Eve had left, not wanting anyone to know before the wedding.

269

The mood was subdued as they sat outside drinking coffee in the sunshine, making a painful contrast to the joyful atmosphere of the previous day.

The conversation turned to the subject of a visit to Spain.

'Much as I'd love us to come over soon, Mum, it might be a while. As I start my new job next month I'll have to clear any holiday with my boss.'

'Of course. How about joining us for Christmas? It'll be a lot warmer than here!'

'Love to, if we can get away.'

After a few more minutes of desultory conversation, Ian announced it was time for them to leave for the airport. Nicole and Ben accompanied them to the front door and hugs and handshakes were exchanged.

'Ring me when you get home!' Nicole cried as her parents strapped themselves into the hire car.

'Will do.' Mary waved as Ian started the engine and drove off.

Nicole peeped in on Eve on the way to the kitchen. She was relieved to see that her colour looked a little better and she was sound asleep. Relaxing her shoulders, she set off to prepare lunch.

Ben disappeared to work the next morning, but not before he'd arranged for a nurse to come and sit with Eve. He told Nicole that it would be prudent to have someone with Eve at all times now and she said she'd sit with her until the nurse arrived. As she settled into the chair by her bedside her grandmother stirred and opened her eyes.

'Hello, Grandmother. Can I get you anything?'

'Water…please. My throat's…so dry.'

Nicole poured a glass of water from the jug on the bedside table and helped Eve to take a few sips.

'Thank…you. Is…Hélène back?' Eve croaked.

'Not yet, another few hours. Is there something you need?'

Eve beckoned Nicole to lean closer and spoke so quietly that she strained to hear.

'Hélène has...right to know...the truth. My diaries...all there...father...in the attic...tower. You must...find them. Tell her. I...I can't...not strong. Too late...years ago.' Eve gripped Nicole's hand. 'Promise me...you'll do it.'

Nicole, not sure what she was promising, nodded, anxious to ease Eve's distress.

'Thank...you. You...good girl. Want to...sleep now.' Eve closed her eyes, letting go of Nicole's hand.

Her mind whirled with questions. What was the "truth" Eve referred to? And what had it to do with Hélène? She'd already had her suspicions and it looked like she might have been right...If she was, then Hélène wouldn't be the only one to be affected. Not liking the thought, she knew she simply *had* to find the diaries; as soon as the nurse arrived she would head for the attic. At least she knew where to look...

The attic seemed even dustier than last time, the sun's rays highlighting the dust motes disturbed by her arrival. Nearly overpowered by the heat she pushed open the windows, breathing in a welcome blast of fresh air. Nicole turned towards the higgledy-piggledy pile of boxes, cases and chests, letting out a groan. Where to start? Where would secret diaries be hidden from prying eyes? Well, not amongst family photos or childhood mementoes, she thought, as she shifted aside such stuff. No, it was likely to be connected with Eve's time in England so she needed to look for an old case or chest from that period.

It was an hour before Nicole found anything promising. An old, battered cardboard case so small that it had fitted into a tea chest, and further buried under a pile of old books. Dragging it out she read Eve's maiden name written

271

in faded white ink on the top "Eve Bisson". Taking a deep breath she opened the lid and found, wrapped up in a moth-eaten man's jersey, Eve's wartime diaries.

Nicole barely had time to put the diaries in her bedroom drawer when she heard the crunch of a car's tyres on the gravel. Quickly wiping her dirty hands, she dashed downstairs to welcome Hélène and Adrian home.

After an exchange of hugs and kisses, Hélène asked after Eve.

Nicole, with a quick glance at Adrian, admitted she was gravely ill. Hélène, with a gasp, darted off to her mother's room. Nicole filled Adrian in with the details before they followed Hélène down the hall.

The nurse, a matronly woman with a kind face, came out to say that Eve had woken when Hélène arrived and perhaps they should leave them alone for a while. Nicole suggested a cup of tea was in order and Adrian followed her into the kitchen.

'Did you have a good time in Jersey?' Nicole asked, filling the kettle.

'Yes, thanks. We explored a bit around the coast but spent most of our time at L'Horizon. It's such a comfortable hotel that we were happy to chill out and do nothing.' He slumped onto a chair. 'It's such a shame about Eve. Hélène did her best not to worry. But it was always there, in the background. What's Ben said about...?'

Nicole bit her lip.

'A few days at the most. There's nothing more anyone can do except keep her comfortable. We think that she kept going for the wedding and now her heart's finally giving up,' she sighed.

They sat in silence for a few moments, cradling their mugs of tea. Nicole was wondering what she'd find in the diaries when the chance came to read them. She had a feeling it would only cause Hélène more pain.

The door opened and her mother came in, collapsing onto the chair next to Adrian. He put his arms around her while Nicole poured a mug of tea and set it beside her.

'She looks so ill! It's hard to believe that only two days ago she seemed so much better!' Hélène sipped her tea, tears moistening her eyes. Nicole explained about the need for someone to be with Eve at all times and that's why Ben had organised nurses.

Hélène nodded.

'I'll sit with her at night and grab some sleep when I can.' She looked at Adrian, 'Sorry to desert you so soon but I have to…'

'Of course. I can take a shift too and perhaps Nicole…?'

'I'd be happy to help. That way we can all get some sleep and we'll only need a nurse during the day.' She stood up, 'Now, what would you both like for lunch? I can offer you cheese salad or a sandwich. Any preference?'

The day ticked slowly by. Eve slept most of the time, only waking for short periods and asking for a drink of water, no food. Hélène and Nicole took it in turns to relieve the nurse for a few minutes at a time and Adrian volunteered to do a supermarket shop, driving off with a hastily scribbled list from his wife.

Ben called in and had a chat with Hélène before checking on Eve.

Nicole was hovering nearby as he came out of her bedroom. Telling him she needed to talk, he followed her into the dining-room. She recounted what her grandmother had said that morning, adding that she'd already retrieved the diaries from the attic.

'I'll start reading the diaries tonight when I'm sitting with Grandmother. In one way I'd like to know the full story as I've already heard so much that's intrigued me,' she finished, with a sigh.

'Let's hope that Hélène finds the truth equally intriguing,' Ben replied, dryly.

Nicole settled down in the armchair in Eve's bedroom. It had been moved away from the bed and near a table lamp to enable reading without disturbing Eve. Hélène had left at ten o'clock and Nicole's watch would finish at four in the morning when Adrian would take over until the nurse arrived. It helped that none of them had to go to work in the morning and Nicole, once a seasoned clubber, was used to late nights.

Nicole retrieved the diaries from the large brown envelope she'd brought with her and now began examining them more closely. The faded blue, dog-eared exercise books were filled with neat lines of writing under daily date headings, beginning June 1940 and finishing in May 1945. After sorting them into chronological order, Nicole began to read.

chapter 39

The first few entries confirmed what Eve had already told Nicole about the evacuation to England. What was also clear was Eve's instant attraction to Philip: "I stood rooted to the ground as this Young God smiled at me. He even knew my name!"

Flicking through the pages Nicole read vivid descriptions of Home Farm – "The farmhouse is an old granite building in a lot better state than my parents' farm. It's a long, low building with the dairy at one end, next to the pens for the chickens. I was told we have to lock 'em in at night to keep them safe from the foxes, something we don't have to worry about back home. During the day the hens are allowed to roam everywhere and our job is to search their favourite laying spots for eggs. The other girls said one of 'em always lays right on top of the hay bales, meaning a bit of a climb for us. Pesky bird!...The cows are enormous! Big red South Devon cows they are, so different to our gentle Guernseys. But I'm told they're good milkers."

Nicole was intrigued when, further along, she found descriptions of Moreton Hall, the family home. It certainly sounded grand – "I've not seen anything like it before! It's bigger and grander than Saumarez Manor and they told me it's Elizabethan. It does look very old, for sure. Made of stone, with tall chimneys sticking up into the sky and dozens of little leaded windows watching everywhere you go. I went there when us Land Girls were introduced to Sir Michael and Lady Andrews. They were that snobbish that they made us stand in the hall while we gave them our names. We were then packed off to the kitchen for a cup of tea with the cook. Of course, they only lived in The Wing, the main part was for wounded soldiers. But it would have been nice to see something of the house. I did see the enormous black oak staircase and loads of beams."

The diaries went on to describe the daily life on the farm, making Nicole feel thankful for her much easier lot in life. "The milking barn ...freezing, with a draught through the large open doorway...had to check for signs of rats...and in the hay barn...set special traps. Our bedroom...so cold that we've slept in our clothes, huddled under our coats and bedspreads...so tired...up at five."

Eve also recorded how she became friends with Lady Helen, Philip's paternal grandmother, while delivering food from the farm to the Dower House. "By rights I shouldn't have seen Lady Helen as I was directed to go straight to the kitchen. But as I was headed there, she came out from the garden and asked me who I was. We got chatting and she seemed to like hearing about Guernsey and asked me to call in again. So I will."

Philip became a prominent part of Eve's daily musings and Nicole read of her growing feelings for him. Initially it seemed that Eve thought Philip was merely flirting with her and couldn't be serious. The social gap was too great. "When he looks at me with that big smile, I feel all gooey inside, like I'm the only one he has eyes for. But I know that can't be true, as Mrs Combe told me his parents hope Philip will marry a Miss Leyton from a nearby estate. So I know he can't love me. Not like I love him."

Nicole felt Eve's pain from all those years ago. A young woman, only eighteen, and in a strange country and in love with a man supposedly out of reach. But it seems Philip was a good man and loved her in spite of his parents. Eve's joy shone through as she realised her love was reciprocated. "When he kissed me tonight after the dance, he whispered, 'I love you and I want to marry you'. Marry me! He said he

276

wanted to marry me. I nearly fainted in shock. I'd never dreamed…although I'd hoped…He said we'd have to wait a while…the war…But I'm happy to wait. I only need to know we'll be married one day. For now, we have to keep it a secret…his parents…but he's telling his grandmother."

Taking a break from reading, Nicole stood up and stretched before checking on her grandmother. Eve slept peacefully, her breathing still slow but less laboured. Nicole returned to her chair and unscrewed the top of the Thermos flask holding much needed hot chocolate. As she sipped the thick, reviving drink, Nicole found her mind filling with images brought to life by her grandmother's words. It felt so real and as she gazed at the recumbent form before her, it seemed as if her grandmother's life was flashing before her eyes, a bit like that of the proverbial drowning man. Although, in reality, only a very small part of Eve's life, Nicole knew it was the most significant.

As Nicole read on towards the end, she discovered what Eve had meant by the "truth". And her heart sank.

After being relieved by Adrian promptly at four o'clock, Nicole crawled upstairs to bed. Weighed down by more than physical tiredness, she fell asleep instantly, not waking until late morning.

Walking into the kitchen Nicole made herself a coffee and took it outside, hoping the fresh air would help to revive her. She let the sun's rays play on her body and began to feel the tension of the night ease. The caffeine hit also played its part and she was just about to return to the kitchen for some toast when Hélène appeared.

'Morning. Did you manage to get much sleep?'

'Yes, thanks. Just coming round now. How's Grandmother?'

Hélène bit her lip. 'No change. The nurse is with her now and I'll relieve her at lunchtime. Hope you didn't get too bored last night, did you have a good book to read?'

If you only knew! Nicole thought, muttering that she had.

After finishing her toast Nicole told Hélène she was going out for a walk.

With a shock, Nicole realised she'd not left the house since the wedding four days ago and struck out along the cliff path in pursuit of serious exercise. The fresh breeze carried the salty air from the sea below, soon clearing the cobwebs. She shifted into a light jog. Squabbling seagulls wheeled and shrieked over her head but otherwise it was as if she was alone; just her and the sea shimmering below. Her thoughts careered around her brain as she reviewed what she'd learnt. Letting out a heartfelt sigh, she returned home, trying to prepare herself for what lay ahead.

Ben arrived that afternoon and, after checking on Eve, told the waiting family that he could find no change.

Hélène poured him a cup of tea as they sat on the terrace lost in their own thoughts.

'My mother's not in a coma is she? Only she hasn't woken for hours now.'

'Not quite, no. Her body's slowly shutting down. Sleep is natural at this stage but she may still wake up and want to talk before becoming unconscious again.' He gripped Hélène's hand. 'Your mother's very peaceful and she's in no pain. But please call me at any time if you're worried.'

Nicole walked with Ben to his car and told him she'd read the diaries. She shared what she'd learned and they both agreed that it would be better to wait before telling Hélène.

After another night of shared vigil Nicole was glad to creep back into her bed. Eve had remained unconscious but her breathing had changed. Shallow, quick breaths were followed by spaces of no breathing, leaving Nicole on edge during the long, weary hours. Even the latest PD James novel failed to grab her attention.

She was aroused from a deep sleep by the nurse shaking her arm.

'Nicole, wake up! Your grandmother's come round and wants to see you.'

Dragging on jeans and a T-shirt, Nicole followed her downstairs to Eve's bedroom. The nurse stayed outside as Nicole hurried over to join a white-faced Hélène at Eve's side.

'I'm here, Grandmother.'

Hélène moved away to give her room and Nicole reached for Eve's white hand. It felt icy cold. Eve's eyes flicked open and for a moment Nicole thought she saw a slight spark.

'Did you...find the...diaries?' Nicole strained to hear Eve's hoarse voice.

'Yes, and I've...I've read them. It's all right, Grandmother, I know what to do. Don't worry.' Nicole's eyes filled with tears as Eve released a soft sigh, a smile hovering around her mouth.

'Thank you...my dear. Be happy...won't you? Love is...important. God Bless.'

Eve closed her eyes and, as Hélène reached for her other hand, let out her last breath and lay still.

chapter 40

The death of a loved one leaves shock and hurt in its wake. Even when it's been expected. Hélène, after the initial outburst of grief, felt as if she was in a dream, a horrible dream, where she was expected to say and do things without really understanding what was happening. Part of her knew that her mother was dead, but another part couldn't, wouldn't, accept it, wanting to carry on as if nothing had happened. It wasn't until Adrian, thrusting a glass of brandy into her hands, saying, 'Drink this, it'll help,' that she realised that the dream was reality. That her mother – the infuriating woman who'd never been a hands-on mother, and who'd she resented so much for asking *her*, Hélène, to give up her home, her freedom – was indeed dead. Her mother, who if she was honest, she'd almost wished dead at times so that she could be free. Her mother, who over the past weeks had mellowed and been so proud of her on her wedding day…

The fiery liquid burned her throat and brought warmth to her cold limbs. Oh, she felt so cold! She heard a voice say 'in shock' and assumed they meant her. Her teeth chattered as she took another sip of brandy and slowly the warmth spread and her mind cleared. Looking up she saw Ben hovering nearby, his face creased with concern.

'The nurse rang me and I've seen the…your mother. Her heart just gave out. I'm so sorry. Do you need anything?'

She shook her head.

'No, thank you. I'll be all right once…once it sinks in. You think you're prepared but…'

'I know. It's still a shock. Look, I'll fill in the forms and Adrian's said he'll organise the…funeral directors, so there's nothing you need to do for the moment. Why don't you lie down for a bit?' His voice was gentle.

She agreed and Adrian helped her to their room. After he'd left her lying on the bed she felt something nagging at her brain. Some memory. Something to do with Nicole. What was it? Perhaps it would come back. Sighing, she closed her eyes and drifted into an uneasy sleep.

With the formalities completed and Eve's body driven away, Ben returned to his practice, promising Nicole that he'd call round that evening. She felt numb, shocked by how quickly the end had come for her grandmother. But at the same time she was relieved that she hadn't suffered a lingering, painful death.

In the kitchen Adrian made coffee for them both before disappearing to make the necessary phone calls to the family's advocate and the vicar.

Back in the kitchen he told Nicole that the vicar would be round later to have a chat with Hélène about the funeral. Bags under his eyes vouched for his lack of sleep and his face wore a puzzled look.

'What's the matter?'

'It's a bit odd. Advocate Lowe said that Eve called him in when she was in the nursing home and changed her will.' With a shrug he continued, 'He'll call round tomorrow to read it to Hélène so we'll find out then what's been altered.'

'I'm sure it'll be fine. Grandmother probably added a bequest to St Philippe's or something. I'm sure it's nothing to worry about.'

Nicole and Adrian joined Hélène when the vicar arrived at teatime. The sombre discussion of hymns and prayers in stark contrast to the joyful occasion of only a few days previously, when Hélène was choosing the wedding music.

Eve had informed Hélène of her wishes with regard to the service, choosing her favourite hymns and insisting she didn't want lengthy eulogies or prayers.

The vicar, in his sixties, had known Eve for years and smiled as Hélène relayed her instructions.

'Your mother always knew her own mind, Hélène. And she always liked to be prepared, didn't like surprises, unless they were nice ones like an unexpected granddaughter,' his eyes twinkled at Nicole. She felt herself flush.

The mood in the sitting room seemed to lighten and even Hélène managed a smile.

After arranging the funeral for the following Tuesday at ten o'clock, the vicar left to visit a sick parishioner. Adrian offered to cook supper that evening, suggesting that Hélène and Nicole go for a walk. Relieved to get out of the house, they set off towards the cliff path.

Linking her arm through Nicole's, Hélène stopped for a moment and gazed out to sea. The women took deep breaths of the ozone-laden air as they watched a sailing yacht tacking towards Baie de la Forge. They stood in silence as if mesmerised by the boat cutting through the waves. Hélène saw its passage as symbolic, wondering if her mother's soul was now pursuing its own homeward journey. A comforting thought in spite of her pain.

'I'm so glad you and Mother had time to get to know one another. It was clear to me how much she enjoyed your stay these past weeks. I…I think she died content.'

Nicole squeezed her arm.

'I'm sure she did. Her face looked so peaceful, almost happy. She was ready to go after seeing you married, she was so proud of you.'

'Mm, I guess so. We…we became quite close at the end. I just wish…' Hélène sighed.

'Hey! No regrets now. The important thing is that you *did* get closer. Hang onto that thought and let go how it might have been. That road only leads to pain.'

Hélène turned to her daughter and smiled.

'You're being the wise one again. By the way, what did Mother want to say to you this morning? She seemed very keen to ask you something.'

Nicole shuffled her feet and looked away.

'Oh, it wasn't important. Shall we go back? Ben said he'd call in after surgery.'

Hélène sensed that Nicole was hiding something but decided to leave it. She had enough to worry about.

They found Ben and Adrian in the kitchen, nursing bottles of lager. Ben kissed Nicole before asking Hélène how she was feeling.

'A bit better, thanks. Our walk did me good.' She sniffed appreciatively. 'Mm, something smells good!'

'An alcohol-laden beef stroganoff. It's nearly ready, I've just got to make the salad. Care to join us, Ben?' Adrian asked.

'Love to, thanks.'

While Adrian and Hélène finished preparing the meal Nicole and Ben set the table on the terrace, complete with a bottle of Rioja to satisfy the tacit, unspoken need for a dose of alcohol after the day's trauma.

Glasses were raised in memory of Eve, the women's eyes glistened and the men looked sombre. Then Adrian served up the stroganoff and they tucked in. Later, Hélène, slightly squiffy and glad of it, suggested that Ben stay the night rather than drive home. After a quick glance at Nicole, he accepted, saying he'd leave early in the morning. By ten o'clock they were all yawning and made their respective ways to bed. Hélène, leaning heavily on her husband, still hoped she was dreaming and that when she woke up all would be well, her mother still alive. If only...

★★★

Advocate Lowe arrived the next morning and, to her surprise, asked that Nicole be present for the reading of the will. Hélène, pale but composed, led the way into the dining room and the Advocate removed various papers from his briefcase before sitting opposite the two women.

He cleared his throat.

'As you are probably aware, Hélène, your mother wrote a will leaving everything to you as sole beneficiary. However,' another cough, 'she recently altered her will to include her granddaughter, Nicole, as a beneficiary.'

Nicole saw her own surprise mirrored on Hélène's face.

The Advocate continued.

'Mrs Ferbrache leaves the value of the house and contents, when sold, to be split evenly between you both. She assumed that you wouldn't want to live here, Hélène, but if you did then you could have a life interest in the house and...'

Hélène shook her head.

'No, I don't want to live here and I'm very happy for Nicole to share the proceeds. It's only right. She'd inherit everything from me one day anyway.' She gripped a stunned Nicole's hand. She'd thought perhaps a little memento, something to remember her by...but not half a house!

The Advocate adjusted his glasses.

'Good. I think that's what your mother hoped you'd say. Now, although there's not a lot of money it should more than cover the funeral costs. And there is one further bequest to Nicole. A ring, which I have here.' He lifted out a small velvet box from his briefcase and handed it to Nicole.

She knew before she opened it what she would find. A dazzling diamond and emerald engagement ring. Given to Eve by Philip only weeks before he was killed.

Advocate Lowe left soon afterwards, in a hurry to get to a session in court. Adrian, who'd been waiting in the kitchen, said that he'd bring them coffee shortly if they'd like to sit outside.

Hélène, who'd made no comment about the ring, now turned to Nicole asking, 'Is there something you know that I don't? I've never seen that ring before and I'm certain Mother never wore it. But you didn't look surprised when you opened the box.'

Nicole recalled what she'd read in Eve's diaries.

1st March 1945 *"So excited! Philip...meet him in London...next week...on leave. Stay...family's town house...parents...here...Hall...local...'do'. Oh...hardly contain myself. Be the first time...night together...sure we'll...do 'it'. We've come so close...he's always held back...disturbed...no...privacy. Taking...me...dinner... somewhere posh...my green velvet skirt. So happy...not since Lady Helen died...so sad...miss her."*
10th March 1945 *"We're engaged! He proposed...diamond and...emerald...ring...his...grandmother...left...him... jewellery...money...Philip gave it all to me...in case...but he'll be home soon...all know war...over. We...made love...wonderful! I love him so much...can't wait...marry."*

And then...
21st April 1945 *"Telegram...Sir Michael...Philip killed...think I'm pregnant..."*

Nicole felt relieved when Adrian arrived with the coffee. They were all going to need it.

'Yes, I do know something...'

chapter 41

Hélène felt numb. Her father was not her father? The man she'd loved and who had loved her so dearly. At least it explained why she didn't look like him, she thought, reeling from this extra blow. Questions began to surface in her mind.

'So, did my father…I mean Reg, know my mother was pregnant when he married her?'

'Yes, he did. Grandmother continued to write a diary after she returned to Guernsey and she says she told him she was newly widowed, which was almost true, and pregnant. Apparently Reg had always loved Eve and was happy to marry her anyway. They…married quite quickly, before you were born. It was such a common story during the war that no-one would have questioned it. And…um,' Nicole paused, 'your mother was very wealthy.'

'Wealthy! But how…' Hélène nearly choked on her coffee. How could a poor Land Girl end up wealthy?

'It seems that Philip's grandmother, who died a few months before, left him some money and a set of jewellery, including the engagement ring he gave Grandmother. She wanted him to pass the jewellery to his wife, knowing he planned to propose to Eve, and the money was to help them set up home together. Lady Helen was very fond of Philip and she and Eve had become close.'

'Lady Helen? So that's why…' her mind struggled to take in this new side to her mother. She'd lived a life that she, her daughter, had known nothing about. If Philip had lived she would have been a lady, with a grand house and possibly a title. And would never have returned to Guernsey.

'So, how did Mother have the money and jewels? They weren't married.'

'No, but Philip was about to return to duty and knew he'd be risking his life again. So he gave everything to Eve as he wanted her to have some security if he didn't return. They…they planned to marry on his next leave but…'

Hélène nodded. Philip sounded such a lovely man and he must have died not knowing he was to become a father. How sad! She looked up and caught Adrian looking at her so tenderly that a sob escaped from her as he folded her in his arms.

For a moment she lay still in that safe place, feeling loved and protected. Sorrow for her mother and the love and life she'd so tragically lost filled her heart, washing away the initial hurt that she'd been lied to all her life. It dawned on her that Reg must have colluded in the lie, wanting the world to know that she was *his* daughter. She knew that her parents had later lost a baby boy and could only imagine what this had meant to Reg.

Hélène gently pulled back from Adrian and faced Nicole.

'So would I be right in assuming that the money and jewels paid for La Folie?'

Nicole nodded.

'Yes. Apparently Grandmother sold most of the jewellery in England before she returned in May, after the Liberation. She kept the engagement ring and I think she'd planned to give it to you one day, on your own engagement perhaps, but you surprised her.' Nicole picked up the box. 'I think you should have it, it was your grandmother's.'

Hélène smiled and pushed it back to Nicole.

'No, Mother left it to you for a reason. It can be *your* engagement ring; remember Lady Helen was your great-grandmother. And I hope it won't be long before you wear

287

it.' She patted her daughter's hand, happy that her mother had been so generous towards Nicole. After all, she was a descendant of her mother's beloved Philip. A thought struck her.

'Did my mother find out what happened to the Andrews family?'

'She didn't keep in touch, not even telling them about her pregnancy. I think she felt they would have disowned her, but we'll never know. There was a younger brother, Richard, who would have inherited the estate, but he was away fighting in the Far East at the end of the war.' Nicole shrugged. 'He may have been killed, Eve didn't stay to find out. She wanted to get back here, away from the memories.'

Adrian looked thoughtful.

'So, it's possible that you and Hélène are the only living descendants.'

'Yes, but not legal heirs! I don't think we stand to inherit a large country estate, even assuming it hasn't been converted into flats or something equally horrific.'

For a moment they sat in silence, thoughts of an alternative past – and future – playing through their minds.

'Would you like to read the diaries for yourself, Hélène? I'd be happy to fetch them.'

'Please. I'd like to learn more about Mother. I feel as if I hardly knew her at all.' Hélène sighed.

Nicole returned a few minutes later and, as she was handing the books to Hélène, she dropped one. Picking it up, she realised that it was the last diary with only a few entries at the front and the fall had dislodged a piece of paper stuck in the back. Turning it over she saw it was a photo and she handed it to Hélène.

'I think this may be your…your father. And my…grandfather.'

Hélène gazed at the picture of a young, handsome man in RAF uniform, with his arm around a young woman, sitting at a table in a club or restaurant. They were raising champagne glasses as if in a toast and smiling broadly at the camera. Clearly visible on the woman's left hand was a large engagement ring. The same as the one now on the table in front of her. Hélène gasped.

'It's their engagement photo! Oh, they look so happy. And Philip...my father looks lovely.' She passed it to Nicole.

'I hadn't seen this in the back. Mm, isn't he a dish? I can see why Grandmother fell for him. And she's very pretty, they make such a great couple.' She looked up at Hélène, adding 'I can see who you take after now. The shape of the eyes, the head...'

Adrian peered over their shoulders.

'Yes. It's something you both share. Pity we can't see the colour of his eyes.'

'I do wish Mother was still alive. There's so much I'd like to ask her, I wish she'd told me the truth years ago.' Hélène felt the pain of her loss welling up and tears leaked through her eyes. Adrian suggested that she go and lie down and lifted her up, guiding her upstairs. The shocks of the past two days were proving too much to bear.

Nicole left a message with Ben to ask if she could see him that evening and, if possible, stay the night. The emotional rollercoaster that had floored Hélène was affecting her too, leaving her in need of some moral support. With Adrian there for her mother, she felt able to disappear for a while. Ben replied that he'd be happy to see her and suggested she drive round about six. Relieved, she spent a quiet afternoon in the garden, a book offering her some much needed escapism. After a quick change and packing an overnight bag, she said her goodbyes before driving off to Town.

Nicole almost threw herself into Ben's waiting arms and he had to hold on tight to keep them both from falling.

'Hey! Have you missed me that much?' he joked.

Reluctant to let go, she pulled back enough to say, 'Of course. It's been all of twenty- four hours! Please kiss me.'

Only too happy to oblige Ben kissed her with a passion equal to her own and she felt her body respond. 'Let's go upstairs,' she whispered, not wanting to wait any longer. They ran up to the bedroom, pulling their clothes off with abandon. By the time they fell on the bed there wasn't a stitch on either of them, allowing Nicole to feel the heat of Ben's skin against her own. He kissed her breasts, her back arching towards him and his fingers trailed slowly down her stomach towards her thighs. She gasped, 'Please, now!' Ben thrust into her, slowly at first, then faster until they could hold back no more, their bodies shuddering with release.

'Mmm, that was sooo good! I really needed that.' She rolled towards him, flinging her arm over his chest.

Ben held her tight, stroking her hair off her face.

'I'm glad I could oblige,' he murmured. 'So, what's been happening to bring out the sex-fiend in you?'

She grinned. 'Hardly that! But so much *has* happened today...'

As they lay entwined in each other's arms, Nicole filled him in with the events of the day, from the reading of the will to the spilling of the truth regarding Hélène's real father.

Ben lay so quietly that she thought he must have fallen asleep. She nudged him.

'I am awake, I'm just coming to terms with it. And the fact that as you're now quite a wealthy young woman, I could be seen as a gold-digger. Or whatever it is men are called if they date wealthy women.'

She giggled.

'Gigolo? You'd make a very good one, based on my, er, experience.' She sat up, propping herself on one arm while stroking his chest with the other. 'Seriously, though, who said anything about being wealthy? Half a house and a ring wouldn't be worth that much, surely?'

'Depends on the house. Your grandmother once mentioned that they'd had La Folie rated as Open Market back in the days when there was a choice, realising what a prime spot it was for wealthy incomers. With very few cliff top houses in Guernsey there's a premium on anything that comes on the market. I'd guess you're talking about four million for the house as it is now although – '

'Four million! But…but that would mean about two million for me,' she cried, shocked.

'Yep. Sure would. Worth a hell of a lot more if it's modernised, but that's up to whoever buys it. A lot of wealthy people like moving here for tax reasons, just like Jersey. But we don't insist they have a huge income like you crapauds do.' He ducked as Nicole aimed a mock blow at his chin.

'Well, if you're right I can't accept. It's too much and should go to Hélène,' she said, biting her lips.

'Don't be silly, from what you said Hélène was very happy for you to inherit your half. I'm sure she's well aware of the house's potential value and she's not short of a bob or two, is she? Adrian's quite comfortable and they'll have more than enough to see them through retirement. And it might take ages to sell so you don't have to panic now.'

Nicole didn't know what to think. So much had happened. And there was the ring…

'Oh, I must show you the ring, it's beautiful.' Reaching into her bag, she pulled out the little box and opened it.

'Hey! That's some ring. No wonder your grandmother hung onto it. Try it on,' he said, slipping it on her ring finger.

She looked at the ring sparkling on her finger and had to agree, it was gorgeous. A beautifully cut emerald, surrounded by diamonds in a traditional gold setting. It was clearly old and of the highest quality. For a moment she thought of her grandmother and how she must have felt when Philip presented it to her. A wave of sadness washed over her and she quickly pulled the ring off and replaced it in the box.

'You know, one of the saddest things is that Philip was my grandfather so part of me comes from him and his family, not the Ferbraches. There could be a whole other family out there that I'm connected to. And I'll never meet.' She looked up at him. 'And as he and Grandmother weren't married it's almost like history repeating itself; Hélène and Adrian weren't married either.'

'Mmm, you're right. But you'd not met Reg, so you're no worse off. Not really. And for all we know, the Andrews family may have died out. It happens. And you still found your parents, didn't you? That's the main thing.'

'I guess.'

Stroking her face, Ben said, 'Shall we go out for dinner? I think you need cheering up.'

She smiled her thanks before heading to the shower.

The next few days leading up to the funeral passed quickly. There was little for anyone to do since the funeral directors organised everything. Hélène and Adrian decided to stay on at La Folie until after the funeral and would then move to his house as originally planned. Nicole wasn't sure she really wanted to live on her own in the house, but felt she didn't have much choice. Advocate Lowe instructed various estate agents to value the house for probate and eventual sale. Ben was proved right – the valuation came in at around 4million. Nicole tried to refuse her share, but Hélène wouldn't hear of it.

'As a family we owe it to you, Nicole. Your parents brought you up at some cost, so I got off lightly. Call it pay-back time.'

Nicole couldn't argue with that and accepted that, once the house was sold, she'd be secure for life. It didn't affect her decision to work, she was looking forward to her new job next month, but it meant that if, one day, she wanted children, then she'd be able to take time out. She couldn't see herself ever being a full-time mother like Mary, but it felt good to know she could be at home during the child's early years.

Ben continued to be a loving support and she stayed over several times before the funeral. The benefit was two-fold; time for her and Ben to be together and for Hélène and Adrian to start settling into married life.

Tuesday dawned a little cooler than of late, though still sunny. Hélène, hating black, chose a navy suit she'd hardly worn, buying a matching hat with a short veil. She knew her mother would approve, she'd never liked black either.

Nicole came downstairs wearing a knee-length purple dress and black shoes. Hélène endorsed her choice; elegant and unfussy, she thought. They shared a quick breakfast with Adrian in the kitchen and they'd barely cleared away when the cortege arrived.

As she stood on the doorstep, Hélène felt tears threaten at the sight of her mother's coffin in the hearse. Her simple wreath of white and pink roses from their garden adorned the casket, together with Nicole's wreath, a small heart of red roses. Hélène had visited her mother in the Chapel of Rest but couldn't relate the wax-like figure dressed in the blue suit she wore for the wedding with the feisty, sharp-tongued woman she'd known all her life. Feeling strongly that her mother's spirit had winged its way days earlier, all that was left was to pay respect to the shell, the body, as it was laid to rest with that of her husband, Reg.

Hélène gripped Adrian's hand as the three of them were ushered into the mourner's limousine and the last journey began. An old phrase played in her mind: "Oh, what a tangled web we weave, when first we practise to deceive!" *Oh, Mother, if only we could put back the clock...*

chapter 42

The small group of mourners mingled in the garden, bearing glasses of sherry and plates of nibbles. Voices were hushed amongst the dark-clad men and women of a certain age. Nicole felt herself to be the oddity, a mere youngster among those who'd known her grandmother for years. Ben, mobbed by such a group, lifted his head and flashed her a quick smile. Her heart lifted at the thought that he was there for her, keeping her strong during this awful time. The funeral had brought home to her the finality of her grandmother's death. The lowering of the coffin into the freshly dug grave brooked no going back. With a sigh, she turned to look at Hélène, pale against the navy dress and veil, clinging onto a stalwart Adrian.

Gazing at her natural parents, she felt as if she'd known them forever and not just a few months. So different to Mary and Ian, but she loved all four of them. She considered herself truly blessed to have four wonderful parents when most people have to settle for two, at best. Lost in her reverie she didn't notice Molly and Peter approach, offering their condolences.

'We're both so sorry for your loss, Nicole. You'd only just got to know her, too. But hopefully you'll have good memories of your time together,' Molly said, lightly touching Nicole's arm.

They chatted for a few moments before Nicole was called to be introduced to another old friend of Eve's. Within an hour the mourners began to drift away, leaving the little family in peace with their thoughts and memories.

A few days later Hélène and Adrian were ready to move to his home in St Peters. Hélène had given in her notice at school, finishing at half-term. She'd been allowed compassionate leave for a week and this gave her and Nicole time to sort out a few things. They checked the items in the attic and sorted what was to be kept and what was either to be given or thrown away. They had both kept mementoes of Eve and Hélène held onto things belonging to Reg. Neither Hélène nor Nicole cared for the dark, heavy furniture in the house and agreed it could all be sold. As they sorted through Eve's clothes and personal possessions Hélène insisted Nicole keep a couple of pretty small vases as keepsakes. The clothes were going off to the charity shops. An unhappy but necessary task, they were both relieved when, finally, the last bin bag was filled. Adrian ferried car loads of Hélène's things to St Peters.

'Are you sure you'll be all right on your own? You'd be welcome to stay with us for as long…'

'I'll be fine, don't worry. Most of the time I'll be at Ben's working on the garden and with a bit of luck he'll be offering to feed me as payment in lieu.'

They hugged before Hélène moved off to the car, giving Adrian a chance to say goodbye.

'Don't forget we're expecting you and Ben round for dinner on Sunday and you know you're welcome to call round any time. And any problems with the house, just give me a shout.' He threw his arms around her and kissed her cheek. Nicole felt a twinge of uncertainty about being in the vast house on her own, she would miss them both. But they were newly married and she didn't want to play gooseberry. So, forcing a smile, she waved them off before turning back into the house.

A week later a letter from Nicole's solicitor arrived. The decree nisi had been granted and in six weeks she would be single again. Letting out a cheer, she sent a text to Ben at work, saying she'd like to take him out to dinner that night. His answering text, 'Great, thanks xx', arrived moments later and, smiling, she rang to book a table at Le Nautique in Town. Then it was time to spend a few hours in Ben's garden, a job she found surprisingly rewarding.

Later, as she leaned on the fork, Nicole surveyed the progress she'd made in such a short time. Where there had been bare, stony earth there were now pockets of colourful shrubs and plants luxuriating in freshly applied compost. She had splashed out on mature shrubs such as acacia, daphne, berberis and ceanothus, set amongst bamboo, fig, olive and palm trees to give the garden instant impact. Large containers of geraniums, lavender, petunias and dianthus dotted around the terrace created the desired Mediterranean look. Guernsey's mild climate encouraged more adventurous planting than that seen anywhere but the far south in England, and Nicole was copying ideas from her parents' Spanish garden.

After a quick shower she changed into a short strappy dress and her silver sandals, ready for the planned night out. Ben arrived home at six, wanting to know if they were celebrating something.

'You haven't got a buyer for the house already, have you?' he asked, giving her a hug.

'Nooo, although the agent says there's a lot of interest.' Cupping his face in her hands, she planted a lingering kiss on his lips before adding, 'but we're celebrating my decree nisi!'

Ben whistled.

'That's great! So you're virtually a free woman again. Definitely cause for celebration. How about you join me upstairs while I, um, change?' His wandering hands leaving her in no doubt as to his meaning, Nicole laughed and hurried up the stairs close on his heels.

Their table was the best in the restaurant; enjoying an uninterrupted view over the Victoria Marina towards

Herm, Sark and beyond. Ben looked suitably impressed as they took their seats. Nicole, on a high, ordered a bottle of Veuve Clicquot as an aperitif and smiled at Ben.

'This is my treat remember, and I can afford it. The solicitor's letter said that Tom has agreed to pay me the £300,000 for my share of the house. I'll receive it when the decree absolute comes through in six weeks.'

Ben cocked his head on one side, saying 'You know, I could get used to this high life. The thought of being a gigolo is beginning to appeal to me. I might even give up work...'

She reached across the table, playfully slapping his hand.

'No way, José! I'm not keeping anyone and you know you love your job. Just think of all those devastated patients if you dropped out. No, we'll both work to keep boredom at bay. Although if I were to get pregnant...' She had a sudden vision of herself holding a newborn baby and her heart flipped.

Ben must have sensed her distraction because he said, 'Look, I think we've a lot to talk about, but can we order the food first because I'm starving!'

Laughing, Nicole agreed and they read through the menus, both choosing the chef's hors d'oeuvres to start, followed by grilled lobster.

As the waiter disappeared with their order, Ben held her hand and appeared to be coming to a decision.

'I've been thinking. Now you have your decree there's no reason why you can't move in with me. I can hardly be cited at this stage and who's to know if Tom's not already shacked up with someone? So, how about it?'

Nicole smiled broadly. It was what she hoped he'd say, but it still felt good to hear it.

'Yes, that's a great idea. I won't have so far to travel to work for one thing.' She grinned mischievously.

'Mm, is that the best you can come up with?' His eyes locked onto hers and she didn't hesitate.

'Apart from the fact that I love you and can't wait to be with you. Will that do?'

Ben's smile matched her own.

'That'll do nicely. Santé!'

epilogue

Three months later, Nicole arrived home one Friday at Santa Rosa, tired after a busy week at work. With Christmas just around the corner, there had been numerous events to be covered for her news programme. At least it was the weekend and she could relax, with two whole days to enjoy chilling out with Ben. The thought brought a smile to her face as she skipped upstairs to shower and change.

She was chopping vegetables for their supper when Ben's key turned in the lock. Calling out, 'I'm in the kitchen,' she poured a glass of wine ready for him.

'Hi, darling. How was your day?' Ben asked, planting a kiss on her proffered cheek.

'Fine. Did you hear what happened at White Rock today?' Nicole filled him in with the latest news while Ben, loosening his tie, sat on a bar stool and sipped his wine.

They had slipped effortlessly into a relaxed, easy relationship, as if they'd known each other years instead of months. Nicole still couldn't believe her luck in being with someone whom she loved to bits, and who made it clear how much he loved her in return. She'd never felt happier and, judging by Ben's Cheshire Cat smile these past months, he was also pretty happy. Her decree absolute had come through in October and her bank account now looked incredibly healthy. Any regrets she might have had about the end of her marriage to Tom never came into being. She knew that, whatever happened between her and Ben, Tom was history. And the icing on the cake was the imminent sale of La Folie, at the asking price of four million pounds. The only fly in the ointment was Ben's continued refusal to let Nicole use her money on the house.

'So, what's for dinner tonight? I'm hungry!' Ben smiled, his head on one side.

'Well, would Sir be happy with the finest rump steak, accompanied with mushrooms, being chopped as we speak, tomatoes and potatoes dauphinoise, already in the oven?'

He grinned. 'You know, you're turning into quite a good cook. You just needed a good teacher.' She threw a tea towel at him. Ben *had* been teaching her, but she'd always known how to cook, just hadn't had much time in her previous life. Taking on board Hélène's advice, she'd even started baking, much to Ben's surprise and delight.

Later that evening they sat curled up on the sofa, replete after the delicious meal. Nicole mentioned that she planned to visit Jeanne over the weekend.

'How is she? And the baby?'

'They're both fine. Jeanne's very tired, but sounded so happy on the phone. She says she just wants to curl up with baby Harry on the sofa all day. Nick's gone back to work but became a dab hand at nappy changing and feeding while he was at home. By the sound of it, Jeanne misses his help. I might offer to take Harry out for a walk to give her a break; would you like to come?'

'Okay, if I've finished painting that bedroom door.' He twisted his body so that he faced her. 'Um, there's something I'd like to ask you. In fact I've been thinking about it for a while.'

'Oh? Sounds ominous!' She looked at his serious looking face.

He moved quickly and, before she could register what was happening, knelt down on one knee and grabbed her hand.

'Would you do me the indescribable honour of becoming my wife, my darling, darling Nicole?'

She giggled. 'Oh! Of course I will! Although the honour's...' She was silenced by a long, lingering kiss.

'Good. That's a relief! Can I get up now?' Ben grinned as he threw himself back on the sofa. 'I know it's the family tradition to use the ring Eve left you, but if you prefer I could buy you a new one.'

'The family ring would be perfect. I'll fetch it, hang on.'

She returned moments later and handed Ben the velvet box. He took out the ring and slowly slipped it onto her ring finger. The emerald and diamonds glittered under the lights. Nicole's heart hammered in her chest, as if it would burst with happiness. Flinging her arms around Ben she ensured that he knew exactly how happy she was.

The next morning, after a round of phone calls to all the parents – two sets for her and one for him – the newly engaged couple sat down to breakfast with huge grins on their faces. Nicole had got on well with Ben's parents from the first moment they met, just after moving in with him, and Ben now passed on their congratulations.

'We've been invited round for dinner tomorrow, if that's okay with you? Mum's also keen to know if we've set the date, but I told her we haven't discussed it yet.'

'Hélène and Mum asked me too. There's no hurry, I've only been divorced a month! But I've always liked the idea of a spring wedding, my last was in winter and everyone was freezing.' Nicole nibbled on her toast, picturing herself in a slinky strapless bridal grown. 'Will we be able to marry in church as I'm divorced?'

Ben, putting down his coffee, said, 'I think some of the clergy here are okay with it. I'll check. Would you mind if it was a register office wedding?'

Nicole shook her head.

'No, anywhere would be fine with me, as long as we're married.' She reached for his hand. 'There is one condition, though.'

'Oh? And what's that?'

'I want you to let me hire professionals to finish the house. So that you don't have to spend precious free time on DIY. And so that, if and when we start a family, we'll have a nursery all ready for our mini Tostevin. Agreed?' Nicole tilted her head, smiling broadly.

Ben sighed an exaggerated sigh.

'All right. Agreed.'

Lightning Source UK Ltd.
Milton Keynes UK
UKOW05f2333151113

221198UK00005B/254/P